Tudor

Rose

To Chuck & Judy
Best Wishes
Sue Allan

A Novel By

Sue Allan

domtom publishing ltd

ISBN 978-1-906070-09-0

First published 2009 by domtom publishing ltd

Acknowledgements

The author would like to acknowledge:
her collaborator and researcher,
Roger Thomas Vorhauer together with
Russell Hocking for his contribution to editing.

Printed and bound in the UK by
DPS Partnership Ltd
www.dpsltd.net

This book is dedicated to David.

This novel is based upon the amazing true life events of a uniquely courageous woman born in the reign of King Henry VIII of England. Her name was Rose Locke.

Introduction

We Lockes were rich. Very rich. We were also an age-old family that could trace its noble lineage back beyond pre-Norman times. And yet we were also by now that most modern and dangerous of families. We were Protestant English at a time when it was still dangerously illegal to be so. But we held firmly to hope.

In the long and dark English night, John Wycliffe[1] came forth as streaming light to our hard pressed world. He demanded that the Truth, the written word of God, for so long shaded by the servants of Rome, be set free amongst the shadows to then reach, touch and free the souls of good English Christians, too long chained like starved prisoners in the half-light. Every person, he demanded, should have the right to read the Bible in English!

But in 1526, after more than one-hundred-and-forty years, we English were still waiting...

---

[1] English theologian and revivalist who translated the Bible into English. He lived from 1329-84.

Prologue

Gainsborough Hall, 1610.

I am growing tired; not of life but of living. As I write, I am in my eighty-fifth year and living within a failing body that was never meant to live as long as it has. And yet though it now constantly ails me, I cannot but marvel that both it and I have survived for so long and through so much together. Even so, I look forward to that hour when my gracious Lord and Saviour shall call me forth. Often, especially in the restless hours of this twilight, I look back with gratitude, and as someone who has been humbled, upon all the Lord's most merciful deliverances that He hath given me and my loved ones.

Recently, I read something of my father's life – set down in Holmshed's[2] Chronicles. Having done so, I realise that I have locked within my head so much more of what others have long since forgotten or taken with them to their graves.

And so I believe that it will serve well for my descendants and other readers for me to now set down in writing an account of my life. This includes the exploits of the family Locke, my family, and of the struggles that we true Protestants have weathered under the unrighteous dominion of others – of all that has been brought to rage and war against our faith and conscience. I write that this account might then ever endure to bear true witness to those trials, so that my children and children's children shall know of the hard-won victories that have preceded them into this life, and so be better equipped themselves to then defend and maintain these for following generations.

---

2   Rose writes '*Holmshed's*' but modern writers quote 'Holinshed'.

Chapter One

London, 1526.

Through the shroud of smoke from ten thousand Christmastide fires, the weak moon let forth light from on high. It glimmered upon the pure white feathers of snow drifting silently to earth as if in a vain effort to redeem this defiled and filthy city. As it did so, by the equally subdued light of four-and-twenty flickering candles, I quietly slipped out from my exhausted mother's body and into the safe hands of her equally weary midwife.

The date was the twenty-seventh day of December, in the year of our Lord, fifteen-hundred-and-twenty-six; the seventeenth year of the reign of our most dread and Catholic sovereign, King Henry VIII.

'It's a little girl, my lady,' the midwife sighed with some deep note of disappointment.

Then, as she held me aloft by my tiny ankles and slapped me firmly across my buttocks, to get me breathing, my mother said that I let out such a rush of lusty yell that it all but drowned out the cry of the watchman in the street below as he called out the hour and that all was well.

Once pinked up, my ever faithful nursemaid, Maggie, then took charge of me. Gently she bathed me in a shimmering hammered-copper bowl of soothing warm water set before the still glowing embers of the fire. After that, she swaddled me in fine white linen. And then, as she had me nestled lovingly in her arms, hurried me outside the bed chamber to present me to my waiting father.

''Tis a daughter, sir!' she exclaimed, smiling triumphantly. 'Such a pretty little thing too, with a mouth like a rosebud.'

I am certain he met me with genuine welcome and joy. For I was not the tortuously awaited son and heir to his fortune, because he had already come and been followed by spares. Instead, I was but one of

3

nineteen children that this man beyond his time would eventually seed into this life. Those who survived, he would cherish and lavish boundless time and love upon. And he would see all his offspring educated with equal measure at a time when education for a woman was viewed equally as being either commendable or damnable, depending upon the disposition of the woman's future husband.

I was born by far luckier than the numberless others who entered into the world that day, and who by fate were condemned to a limited lifetime of hunger and poverty. Instead, mine was destined to be a life of privilege, for which I remain ever mindful.

My father, William Locke, was outwardly the very essence of a loyal Tudor subject. He was an unimaginably wealthy London merchant and a notable member of The Worshipful Mercer's Company of London[3]. We lived at Cheapside; close to the Mercers Hall and Chapel, in a fine mansion amply befitting our high station in life. After all, not only were we Lockes rich, but we were an age-old family able to trace our noble lineage back beyond such pre-Norman worthies as the Earl Leofric of Mercia and his famous lady, Godiva. And yet we were also, by now, that most modern and dangerous of families – we were Protestant English at a time when it was still dangerously illegal to be so. More than this, we were Bible smugglers[4].

Mercers, like my father, became the conduit for our particular style of evangelical Protestantism to enter England. In my time, many another young mercer apprenticed into the Low Countries trade became converted to it whilst staying at the English house in Antwerp. There, they could be baptized into a new way of thinking with the latest ideas upon religion.

---

3   Livery Companies, or Guilds, as they were also known, began in medieval times as 'fraternities' or 'misteries' (from the Latin for occupation) to protect the interests of particular trades and the practitioners of those trades.
4   Martin Luther had also asked for the Bible in German and argued for common reformation of the Church. German princedoms that supported him were ordered to return to the Catholic Church in 1529. They PROTESTED. Thus, during that century, many European Protestant churches began to break away from Rome.

Before I was born, even Thomas Cromwell[5] had likewise been well versed in this 'heresy' when he was still a very young man working for merchant adventurers, though I scarce say he was never brave enough to admit so to the King.

Thus, through brave mercer families, like us Lockes, Master Tyndale's latest books could be had fresh from his press, having been smuggled into England by being hidden amongst the bales of fine cloths and silks we brought into London by the shipload.

I can clearly recall my mother from those days. She had come to the truth of the Gospels by way of some English translations smuggled into the country for her by my father's factor on the continent. Mother often called my two sisters and me into her chamber to read aloud to us from out of those very books. Yet this she did in the strictest of privacy, for fear of 'outsiders' finding out. For then such translations were condemned as 'heretical' by both the Pope and our King.

For more than ten years, a Mercer named Mister Packington had been involved in smuggling Protestant writings into the land from abroad. My mother and father knew him well.

Early one November morning[6], at about four of the clock, Mister Packington left his lodgings at the sign of 'The Leg' in Soaper's Lane. As usual, he was going to mass, but on a day when dawn was breaking upon one of the mistiest and foggiest that any alive in London could remember.

A gang of labourers, already at their work, witnessed Packington turn the corner and walk on into Cheapside. The Mercer was not heading towards the nearest parish church of Saint Pancras. Instead, he was making his way to the Mercer's own chapel, close to the Great Conduit. Packington paused momentarily as he reached just opposite Ironmonger's Lane, before he began to walk across the eerily empty thoroughfare. He never made it to the other side.

---

5   Thomas Cromwell – English lawyer who under Henry VIII rose to become statesman and devised the legislation that would make the English Church independent of Rome.
6   November 13th 1936 – five near contemporary accounts of this murder exist – the first gun crime documented in London.

The labourers in Soaper's Lane heard the gun shot as it echoed down the empty street. Throwing down their tools, they immediately ran to see what had happened. They found Mister Packington lying dead upon the bloody cobbles with his chest blown apart. There was no assailant in sight. And none was ever brought to justice for this cold blooded murder.

Very few in The City laboured under the illusion that this had been some random crime of violence. My father, for one, was certain that his friend had been assassinated on orders of the clergy, because of his reformist views.

'You must listen to me, children,' Mother urged. I can still recall the look of terror etched upon her face and the tremor in her voice as she drew my sister, Alice, and me close to her. 'You must promise never to tell anyone that I have a copy of the Gospels or that I have read them to you. Do you understand? You must tell no one. Someone may even try to trick you, or ask you to make an oath upon the Bible. But you must never tell them anything. For if you do, the Bishop will have me taken away and burned to death!'

So we swore that we never would breathe a word about her secret.

I was not told who had killed this man, or indeed if anyone knew who had done so. The hatred for those like us ran deep, especially amongst the Papists. To them we Protestants were the same as the Jews, or the Muslims or atheists. For they considered every living person outside the fold of their Holy Roman Father as a heretic, and therefore someone who could justly be consigned to hell.

Thus, throughout my lifetime, the Company of Mercers has been a channel for this tide of movement towards the reformation of our Church. This was carried out covertly at first. But then, in later times, we stood in defiant openness – to be loathed by both Anglicans and die-hard Catholics alike. Yet we did so willingly, knowing that God had called upon us to be new disciples and to guide the faithful back to the true ways of His early Church, as Christ had intended it to be.

As far as the rest of Europe might suppose, at the time of my birth I was entering into the very 'model' of a Christian kingdom, where our most sovereign and Catholic King Henry was held up by the Pope to be a shining example of all that a Christian prince should be. Henry was intelligent and, in his youth, considered quite athletic. He spoke French, Latin and Spanish, and was so religious that he heard mass three times a day, even whilst hunting – a pastime of which he was passionately fond. Henry Tudor was also an accomplished musician and composer, as well as being a good and faithful husband to our beloved Queen, Katherine of Aragon, and being a loving father to their only surviving child – the young Princess Mary.

Yet it was for the writing of a book, attacking Martin Luther and defending the Roman Catholic Church, that lavished upon Henry the greatest praise of all, and for which the Pope bestowed upon him the accolade of 'Defender of the Faith'. This was a title that he would prize highly and hand down to all four successive monarchs under whom I have tried to serve God faithfully through my long life.

But in executing his new position of 'Defender of The Faith', Henry saw fit to blacken England's fair earth – with the burning of a number of early Protestant 'heretics' who had been raised in this country.

No sooner had I reached my first birthday than this pretty English illusion began to be exposed to the world for that which it was; an ugly and deceitful sham set to cover the dark truth beneath. Even as I was born, this once blessed realm of England was about to be rent apart for two simple reasons.

Firstly, King Henry's wife had failed to provide a son to continue the only recently created Tudor dynasty. And as Katherine was already nearing forty years of age, it seemed increasingly unlikely that she ever would produce an heir. Coupled with this iniquity, the much younger King was by now certain that this failure was by no means down to his personal prowess. For to disprove any blot upon his masculinity, he had already embarked upon a string of adulterous affairs that resulted in the birth of several boy bastards. Even though Henry could legitimise any of these at the stroke of a quill, such action would not end all of the problems at hand, because the situation had become too complicated.

As the last blush of Katherine's youthful good looks faded into middle age, the ever lustful King Henry was hopelessly smitten by love for one of Katherine's young ladies-in-waiting. Her name was Anne Boleyn. But having seen her sister defiled, used and abused by the King, before then being cast off completely, she steadfastly refused to submit to Henry's increasingly carnal desire of her. Anne would not do so until she lay legally upon the royal marriage bed. To achieve that end, Henry would need to have Queen Katherine ousted. So lust – impure and simple – ultimately set Henry upon a path that would change the course of England's history and faith.

In order to free himself of his first wife so that he might marry his new love, Anne Boleyn, Henry set upon the only real option open to him – to have his marriage to Katherine annulled. As he appealed to the Pope, Henry claimed that the marriage was cursed because, according to the book of Leviticus in the Bible, the union was 'unclean' on the grounds of Katherine previously being the wife of the King's late elder brother, Prince Arthur.

However, for the marriage between Henry and Katherine to have gone ahead in the first place, the Pope had issued a special dispensation, and so it was logical that this could not later be deemed to have been effected against the Church's laws. Therefore the Pope refused to grant either annulment or divorce.

So Henry was left in the unenviable position of seeking another seemingly legal way around the problem. It was then that, quite suddenly and astonishingly, Henry's stance towards certain Protestant attitudes seeping in from the continent softened. He realised that these new ideas might hold the answer to his problem!

I remember well my father later telling me about this time, as he whiled away the slow days and weeks leading to his death, and as I waited for the birth of my first son, William.

While still young enough to do so, Father used to go beyond the sea for Anne Boleyn. The Queen-in-waiting had engaged him to bring her parchments of the Gospels, Epistles and Psalms, all written in English and French instead of Papist Latin. And all of this so soon after the time when such an open request for them from one so highly placed in Henry's court would have been unthinkable.

Amongst many of the Lutheran papers that came into my father's possession, was one that proved beyond all dispute that the 'Donation of Constantine' – the single document under which the Pope claimed sovereignty over all emperors, kings, and princes – was nothing more than a much later forgery. The implications of this deception were not wasted on Anne Boleyn, King Henry, or his advisers. Armed with this knowledge, Henry felt it was within his rights to reject Roman control altogether and to instead place himself at the head of the Church of England.

By that time, Henry had already met a then little known cleric named Thomas Cranmer, temporarily decamped from Cambridge in the wake of a visitation of the plague. He was a man in whom my father set as high hopes for the furtherance of our own Protestant cause as he did upon our zealous Boleyn.

Cranmer was a man more than willing to advocate on Henry's behalf in his Great Matter[7], and so the King had sent him to the Protestant princes of Germany to learn more about Lutheran doctrine. When the Calvinists and Lutherans were officially approached upon the subject, their opinion that 'the marriage was sinful but repentance must blot out past sins and that the King's marriage must not be dissolved.' Henry was so angered by this response that the relationship

---

7   Henry's sought after divorce.

between them and the King immediately soured.

However, Cranmer became so immersed in the new religion that by the time he had to return to England, he too did as the Lutheran clergy had done – in taking a wife! However, when Henry then raised him up to become the next Archbishop of Canterbury, Cranmer was forced to keep his marriage a closely guarded secret in the still firmly celibate Protestant Church of England. They say that he was then forced for a very long time afterwards to smuggle his wife from place to place as she accompanied him when he moved. She lay concealed in a large oak chest that he claimed necessary for his great quantity of vestments and books.

Naturally, when the King's Great Matter was then again set before his own bishops in England to judge, Henry was eventually granted the much sought after legal annulment from his first wife.

Nevertheless, Queen Katherine steadfastly refused to bow to unrelenting pressure piled upon her by the King to publicly acknowledge the same, even when Henry forcibly removed the Princess Mary from the care of her mother and forbade the two to be allowed to meet again. And when Henry ordered her to hand back certain royal jewels, so that he might give them to Anne Boleyn, Katherine bravely retorted, 'I will not give them up to a person who is the scandal of both Christendom and a disgrace to you.'

In Katherine's eyes and those of the wider Catholic Church, she was still, had always been, and ever would be, King Henry's lawfully wedded wife in the sight of God. And since no mere men could put the marriage asunder, Anne Boleyn was therefore naught but a whore.

Chapter Two

As a girl just turned ten, I was coming of an age when I was fully beginning to take in all that was going on about me. Until then I had been fit only to take lessons from my tutors or to be found about the nooks and crannies of our house, where I would be playing with my doll or be in the company of our loyal nurse maid. Never had I questioned the comings or going of members of my family, or the arrival of my many and ever growing number of siblings, or even sometimes their sudden absence forever, or of my own mother's seemingly constant condition of pregnancy, or to question it.

As for matters pertaining to our sovereign, they too were becoming more and more curious to me; especially those relating to our situation of being a land with 'two queens'.

I have found recently, whilst reading a printed copy of Holmshed's Chronicle with my protégé, Dorothy, a story about my late father. And so being his daughter, I have thought to enlighten my children and descendants a little more upon that and other related matters as I remember them.

In the twenty-fifth year of our sovereign King Henry's reign, fifteen-thirty-four, on hearing of the fate of the Lady Katherine Dowager, Pope Clement VII issued a Bull proclaiming a curse upon our King Henry and this entire realm. It was set up at Dunkirk in Flanders – the nearest point that his agents dare post it to England.

Upon witnessing the King's rightful rage, one London mercer, Mister William Locke, took it upon himself to immediately go to Dunkirk and to tear the wretched thing down and to then bring the offending article home and cast it low at His Majesty's feet. For this act of great daring, King Henry gave my father one-hundred pounds a year and made him a gentleman of his Privy Chamber. He was also made the King's Mercer, and His Majesty vouchsafed to dine at our house.

Moreover, my father was knighted and so became Sir William Locke.

However, despite this display of unquestioning love and loyalty on my father's part for his sovereign lord, not always would there be sweetness and light from the King to my father. For Henry proved a most difficult man to whom one could be bound, and those who are bound together are oftimes destined to suffer together. Those two men, for a while made close by fate and friendship, would soon share in such bitterness and darkness that would slowly turn my father's love for his King into loathing.

*   *   *

Henry's appearance at our country lodge one day was most unexpected. So much so that I had no time to withdraw from my father's side as the King suddenly burst in upon us. So I quickly hid behind him.

As His Majesty stood before me – he was dressed in the finest pale blue suit of clothes with intricate feather detailing all picked out in silver threads – to mine eyes the King looked like a giant, standing well above my father's goodly stature. I remember well His Majesty's complexion being most fair, and thinking how well it set off his bright auburn hair – which he had combed straight and cut short beneath his great plumed cap.

Once suitably greeted by my father, His Majesty slipped off his riding gauntlets to pass a few moments with trivial pleasantries. These were exchanged easily enough until, as I perceived in the King's sudden change of tone, the most vexing of questions arose.

'Still no sign of a child, Sire?' said my father, as he enquired after the Queen.

'No!' The King snapped. 'Yet I have oftimes reminded the Queen that it has now been over a year since the death of our infant son, and of her duty to conceive for me another! It is alright for you Will!' The King's smile hinted of a sneer. 'You cannot step about your household for tripping over sons!

'To tell you the truth,' Henry continued, as he leaned in towards my father and confided in little above a whisper, 'I am glad to be away from her and Hampton Court just now. For the Queen goes about hissing and snarling at me like some she-cat straight from the alley. I swear she shall drive me away altogether before much longer!'

It was only then that the King espied me in the fold of my father's clothes.

'God's teeth!' Henry exclaimed. 'What do we have here? A spy?'

Although terrified, I immediately stepped forward and threw myself into a low curtsey, as I had so often practised with my mother. I was too afraid to look up into his eyes. My older brother, Matthew, had teased me once – saying that if the King came to our house, little girls like me should never meet his eyes with mine, for the King's glare could turn such a small person straight to ashes.

'May I present my daughter, Your Majesty? This is Rose.'

The King reached down with his great hand and lifted up my chin. To my relief, as I did so, my brother's warnings were proved false. Instead, I found the King to be smiling broadly at me, and with such twinkling eyes that I could not look away from them.

'Good morning my Lady Rose,' he said, bowing graciously. 'I am honoured to meet such a fine young gentlewoman.'

I stifled a would-be giggle and politely dipped in slight curtsey again, while still trapped fast in his gaze.'

'Such delightful manners!' The King beamed. 'But tell me child, can you answer me a riddle?'

I did not know if I could do so, and smiled nervously at this unexpected proposition.

Without further ado, the King launched into his question.

'Tell me, my Lady Rose,' he continued, 'what is it that a child owes to both her father and her sovereign

King?'

As quick as a heartbeat I replied.

'Obedience, Your Majesty!'

With that the King's eyes widened and, holding fast his belly, he threw his head back in an almighty roar of laughter.

Although startled, I nonetheless managed to keep my poise.

'Well answered, my young lady!' he exclaimed. 'God's teeth, William, but you have schooled the child well!'

Then the King leaned down once more towards me and, gently caressing my pale cheek and looking me in the eyes, made a comment with what I perceived in my innocence to be with all sincerity. 'Had I not already a wife I would marry you in an instance. One day, Lady Rose, you shall be a fine asset to any future husband.' Then he glanced at my father before warning, 'But be certain, Will, to choose one for her who has a wit about him. For this daughter of yours would be wasted upon a dullard!'

With that, His Majesty quickly produced a small leather pouch. Then he loosened the drawstring, carefully tipping something delicate out into the palm of his hand. It was a small string of something milky and glistening.

'Here, my lady,' he said, proffering me the jewels. 'Pearls for a perfect young lady of great wisdom beyond her mere years.'

'Your Majesty...' instead of grasping at the lure as a young girl might, I instead hesitated and looked towards my father's face for guidance.

'It's alright, Rose,' he said. You may accept the King's most generous gift.'

Then Henry smiled a most pleasing smile when, again, I politely curtsied as he handed me the string.

'Again, Will, I praise you for your young daughter's fine upbringing... but then I should expect no less from a child of yours.'

After that, the King slated his thirst with a large

goblet of wine before quickly making his farewell once more.

'Was that the King's voice I could hear, Will?' asked my mother, as she came down from her chamber where she had been attending to the baby.

'Yes it was, Kate,' Father replied, 'but he is gone now and on his way back to Cheam.'

'Was the Queen out riding with him?'

'No, she was not,' Father replied cryptically, for I was still present and he would not dare for me to understand his true meaning. 'And I very much fear that our sovereign might have his foot already in the stirrup of a certain Winchester brood mare and riding her hard...' To which my mother seemed somewhat alarmed.

It was impossible, at that time, for me to understand that the 'Winchester brood mare' of which he was speaking was a certain young woman who had already in the recent past been 'boarded' upon us, on occasion, at the personal request of the King himself. Neither could I have fully comprehended, as a child, how much of a risk my father and certain friends of his had already taken in backing the King over his split with Rome. They had only done so with ardent hope for radical reform of the now Protestant English Church. To consider that Henry might now be casting aside Anne Boleyn in favour of a Papist sympathiser must surely have made my parents blood feel as thought it were freezing in their veins. This, after all the risks and sacrifice taken on my father's part for 'the cause'! In the run-up to and execution of the King's 'Great Matter', and his divorce from Queen Katherine, it must have struck him cold to learn that Henry had since engaged upon an affair with this other woman. And what a dangerous woman she might turn out to be!

As for the pearls? I have oft wondered why the King had them about his person that day. Were they perhaps a love token for a yet unseen mistress? Or perhaps a trinket for a princess? For one thing I know with certainty, they were never intended for me. Then, my being naught but an innocent child, at first I proudly wore the gift that King Henry had given me that day. But my pride eventually waned as I grew towards my womanhood and began to appreciate the circumstances under which the gift was given. And although I could not bring myself to part with them, neither could I bring myself to wear them any longer. For to me they were to become naught but a pretty string of beads handed down to me by a monster.

Chapter Three

I was soon to realise that the year of fifteen–hundred-and-thirty-six was to be one indeed of wicked 'happenings' at court. It was also the year in which I began to understand with chilling clarity that any childhood illusions I might have had about honour and kingship were to be horribly shattered. And I realised as well that those who are sometimes set above us mere subjects, even though they are anointed to do so in the name of God, would have been more suited as disciples of the devil himself.

Hardly had January begun than news shook London that the Lady Dowager Katherine was all of a sudden dead. There was even rumour abroad that she had been poisoned. Afterwards, when her body was opened, her heart was found to have completely turned black and misshapen.

Queen Katherine, older than her former husband Henry, had been fifty years of age at her death, and although so humiliatingly put aside by him in favour of the new Queen, Anne, she had never lost the love and respect of the common people of London. These very same people now hated the upstart Boleyn with such intensity that they hissed and booed her when e'er she dared to be led along the streets of the city. And far beyond London, many could not resign themselves to the break from Rome. In quiet corners up and down the land there was whisper of would be rebellion and of bringing the Princess Mary to the English crown instead.

In the privacy of my own home, I overheard much from my own parents' intimate conversations discussing such matters as the business of the King. Much was said openly by my parents in the confines of their private chambers in the certain knowledge that it would seep no further. Discretion was a lesson instilled early on in us Locke offspring.

In addition, I was able to glean much more as I began to listen in intently on exchanges between my much older step-siblings, or at the gossip slipping between the household servants when they thought that I was immersed in my play, or who assumed that I was ' too innocent' to understand. Perhaps up to a point they were right. I was a still a child and oblivious to the wicked depths to which some adults will stoop to fulfil their lust for power and position, or even just for flesh. I knew nothing of how the good and the innocent might be blackened by evil lies – so that these people might the more easily be set aside in the pursuit of carnal knowledge of the otherwise forbidden lover. Kings and queens alike may in turn break each one of God's commandments whilst on this damnable earth, yet even they must one day bow before Him and give account for that they have done with their lives.

'It is sad to hear of her passing,' my mother said of the old Queen, 'for she always carried herself with great dignity, I thought.'

'I could never find fault with the lady myself on her queen-ship,' my father replied, 'other than for her misfortune in being unable to produce the King a male heir. And of course for being born a stubborn Papist!'

Undoubtedly, failure to produce a male child on demand seemed to be the most heinous sin that a wife could inflict upon any man, especially the wife of a king. It was this notion above all else that I found so outrageous once I had grown to womanhood. Does a queen have some magical power invested upon her that allows her to choose for herself the gender of a child she conceives off her sire? Likewise, whether or not she should be barren or no? If so, then why hath it not pleased God to invest this power in the man himself instead of with his hapless dame?

'And yet this poor woman's 'misfortune' proved to be God's instrument in leading our King and this realm into Protestantism,' Mother noted. 'Should we not at least be thankful to her for that?'

In a simplistic way my mother was right. Had it not been for the Queen's ill fated misconceptions in trying to produce a male heir, then closeted Protestants, like my father, might never have dared to show their true colours in matters of religion when the King's Great Matter had come about and he sought to obtain an annulment of his marriage. Especially as King Henry had in the past burnt many a Protestant earlier on in his reign as 'heretics'.

'It is a blessed relief, Father added, 'for now the focus on the Catholic elements in the country is gone. Perhaps with her wizened corpse, the King could bury at last any remnants of guilt he might have felt about discarding the lady for Boleyn.'

'And does the King reproach himself for causing the Lady Katherine so much anguish in her final days?' Mother asked.

'I think perhaps that in private he does,' Father replied. 'For, after all, they were married for a very long time. But at court today he was dressed all in saffron and gold, as was Queen Anne. Then again, you know how loathe the King has always been to see mourning clothes worn in his presence...'

I never saw Anne Boleyn close up, but my mother had when the Queen called upon my father at our house in Bow. Her visit was compelled by a matter of some great urgency.

'She is, I suppose, pretty,' Mother conceded when I once asked about her, 'but not especially so. Her skin is rather olive-coloured and her hair thick and dark. In fact, she is much as you might expect a Spaniard to be, and yet the late Lady Katherine, in all, was fairer in complexion and hair by far... And yet,' she added curiously, 'the one feature that most marks out Queen Boleyn in my mind are her eyes. Close up, the Queen has large, dark, brooding eyes that I once noticed flash as dark as jet when some trifling thing had made her just a little displeased.'

I had seen Queen Anne myself but it was from a distance and when I was only six years old. I can still remember the excitement. My little sister and I had been dressed in red velvet dresses by Maggie. Then we stood on the balcony of our house at Cheapside beside my pregnant mother, looking down as Queen Anne's coronation procession passed by far below. Maggie held on to my hand tightly while Mother cuddled Alice in her arms and explained what was going on to us. It goes without saying that my father was not home with us that day, because he was at the time much involved in the royal ceremonies and in the lengthy preparations leading up to them.

Father, with the Lord Mayor of London, the aldermen, and representatives of all the guilds of the City of London, had on the Thursday, May the twenty-ninth, fifteen-hundred-and-thirty-three, made their way by barge to Greenwich to officially receive the already pregnant Lady Ann. From there they brought Boleyn along the Thames to be received in a freshly renovated suite of rooms in the Tower of London.

As she had landed there, Father later told me how His Majesty had tenderly taken a hold of Boleyn's slender gloved hand and lovingly guiding her slight frame safely down to earth. Boldly she then stood at his side before the cheering leap of lords looking on as, in those moments, a shatteringly loud volley of shot rang out from the Tower of London, and then to echo all about the city. Almost simultaneously, more guns were fired from Limehouse, to be joined by countless others from ships lying at anchor all along the Thames. Later, some people said that they had heard those reports as far away as Merton, Richmond, and beyond.

On the Saturday, my father was amongst those who rode out with Boleyn from the Tower in the company of lords, knights and gentlemen, all attired in their richest garments. Anne herself had ridden through London in a chariot richly adorned with cloth of silver, and with a matching canopy held above her by the four scarlet-gowned Lords of the Ports. Her swift chariot was followed closely by four others, all fully occupied by ladies, while other noblewomen rode side-saddle behind them dressed in gowns of bright crimson velvet.

As Anne neared the city, she was greeted with

the sight of the Lord Mayor and his Alderman, standing in Cheapside. There, my father's fellow merchants, all dressed in their finest livery, had poured out from the Mercers Hall, to proudly line the street. Then, in perfect order, they had been joined by the men of every other guild of London.

When the Lady Anne came to a stop before them, the recorder made a goodly speech after which the Lord Mayor stepped forward and presented her with a golden, cloth purse containing a thousand marks of angel nobles[8] by way of a gift from the whole of the city.

After that, my father and the lords had conveyed Lady Anne to the Palace of Westminster, where she was to spend her last night as an ordinary subject of the realm. For the following day, was to be her coronation.

In the morning, Lady Anne had set off in procession from Westminster and through the streets of London beneath a canopy of cloth of gold. She was dressed in a crimson velvet kirtle[9] beneath a rich purple robe trimmed with ermine. Her long train had been carried by the aging Duchess of Norfolk and supported in the middle by her Chamberlain, Lord Burgh.

Upon her head, Anne had worn a delicate cap of glistening pearls topped off with a dazzling jewel encrusted gold coronet. How it sparkled as the sunlight played upon it! Heralding the entourage, the Duke of Suffolk walked purposefully ahead, carrying the gleaming royal crown that was carefully borne upon a purple velvet cushion. Behind the Duke, two earls stepped briskly, side by side, each carrying a queenly sceptre of gold. Following these noblemen came ten ladies, all dressed in scarlet robes trimmed with ermine, and each with a gleaming gold coronet perched high upon her head. And then following them came all Anne's maids, also dressed in scarlet gowns but, more befitting for their status, trimmed with Baltic fur.

In most solemn procession behind this group, and no doubt with much trepidation, came all of the

---

8   Gold coins.

9   A woman's long dress or skirt.

monks of Westminster, dressed in copes[10] of gold. Accompanying them were thirteen abbots, all wearing upon their heads their tall, ceremonial mitres. Closely after them came all of the King's chapel, again in rich copes, with four bishops and two archbishops dressed in richly decorated robes and mitres. They were accompanied by all the Lords of Parliament, also resplendent in elaborate finery.

Once inside St Peter's Abbey, Father described to us how Lady Anne was placed upon her royal seat, raised high upon a platform before the holy alter. There she was duly anointed by the Archbishops of York and Canterbury and thereby crowned Queen of England.

After the coronation mass was over, Queen Anne was then taken outside under her canopy. She smiled jubilantly as she wore her crown and gripped the two gold sceptres. From there she was paraded back to Westminster Hall where, under its great hammer-beamed roof, the most extravagant feasting my father had ever witnesses soon followed.

Yet this coronation was not by any means well received by everyone in the capital that day. Father was uncertain whether or not the Queen Anne, as she passed through the streets, had heard various insults spasmodically shouted out from the crowd. These included shouts of 'whore' and 'concubine', abuse clearly audible to him, along with a great deal of mocking laughter. Many of my father's Catholic contemporaries, noble knights or lords of the city, though dressed for the part, were not cheering and showed little genuine enthusiasm for the day. And judging by the faces of the many Papist gentlemen, a mournful dirge would have seemed more befitting than a triumphant chorus of fanfare. This was clearly noticed by the Queen.

'How liked you the look of the city?' King Henry was heard to ask of his 'entirely beloved Anne'.

'Sir,' she replied to him curtly,' I liked the city well enough – but I saw a great many caps on heads, and heard but few tongues of congratulation.'

After almost three difficult years passed by,

10   A long cloak-like ecclesiastical vestment.

undoubtedly Queen Anne must have rejoiced greatly, and perhaps even crowed a little, on hearing of the demise of the King's ex-wife Katherine. Yet even now, and unknown to Queen Anne, the crooked wheel of deceit that had earlier spun in her favour was about to freewheel out of her control. Queen Katherine, for all intents, had been officially reported to have died an entirely natural death. However, her main tormentor in this life was fated soon to suffer an altogether unnatural one.

*   *   *

Anne must have thought she was safe, for she was pregnant again, and this time she was certain that she was carrying another boy-child. Any misgiving his Majesty or the people might have against this current marriage would pale away once she was delivered of a healthy son. As the mother of the future King, her position as Queen would be unshakable.

However, even then as her belly had begun to swell with Henry's new planting of seed, the often sullen and sharp-tongued Anne could have little realised that she had already slipped far short of Henry's favour.

On the very day of Queen Katherine's funeral, I overheard my parents hotly discussing some 'incident' that had occurred at the palace earlier. It involved Queen Anne and her maid of honour, the Mistress Jayne Seymour. I tried to hear more about it, but on noticing my presence my father suddenly paused and changed the subject. Something had to be very wrong. And whatever it was, I could see how deeply it worried my mother.

Shortly afterwards, an official royal circular announced that the King had taken a tumble from his horse and been rendered unconscious. Although he quickly recovered, the shock of the news had made Queen Anne so distressed that she had pitched prematurely into labour. On January the twenty-seventh she gave birth to a stillborn child. A boy.

However, I was to learn much later that this had not been the truth at all. In fact Queen Anne had apparently stumbled in upon her husband to find the King seated upon a chair with Jayne Seymour astride his lap in what one may only describe as a moment of great intimacy.

Anne fell into a fit of hysteria, running along the corridor, screaming and swearing about the 'harlot Jayne' in terms no doubt reminiscent of those cried out in anguish by Queen Katherine. As a result, the Queen suffered a miscarriage. From that moment onwards, she must surely have known full well that her own days as Queen were numbered.

Yet how was the King to get rid of a wife for whom he had risked civil war and alienated a great deal of the population? He had already discarded a long suffering and faithful Queen of many years in favour of someone many of his subjects regarded as a faithless concubine. And so it was this latent hatred of Queen Anne that the King seized upon to discredit her. He did so utterly and ruthlessly. It was a cowardly act by a hatchling tyrant who, having already been shown once that he might act against either man or God unhindered, in order to fulfil his own wicked needs, might thereafter feel at liberty to go further in committing even greater outrages. Yet even more cowardly, one might be forgiven for saying, were those who stood by and let this tyranny reign on unchecked. And that surely amongst those, I must number my own father. Yet who would a tyrant, set on such a selfish course as this, listen to if he was capable of such cruelty even to his wives? And had he not already had executed men who had once considered themselves to be amongst his closest friends? If those he claimed to have loved were expendable, then so equally perhaps were any others about him.

Thomas Cranmer, who had helped to anoint Anne, would soon try to intercede on behalf of the Queen. 'If it be true that which is openly reported of the Queen's Grace...' he wrote to the King, 'I am in such perplexity that my mind is clean amazed; for I never had better opinion in a woman than I had in her; which maketh me think that she should not be culpable... Next to your Grace, I was most bound to her of all creatures living... I wish and pray for her that she may declare herself inculpable and innocent... I loved her not a little for the love which I judged her to bear towards God and His Gospel...'

But even his pleadings fell upon deaf ears. For on the second of May, Queen Ann was arrested at Greenwich and informed of the charges being made against her; that she had not only committed adultery with several men, but also engaged in incest with her brother. Yet far worse than this, she was also accused of plotting against her husband. All highly punishable by death by burning.

Boleyn was taken by barge to the Tower of London, ironically along the same path by which she had travelled in preparation for her coronation.

At first the manner in which Queen Anne was to be disposed of appeared to be no measure short of despicable. Many believed that the charges made against her were trumped up, and that the whole process or her arraignment, and of those arrested with her were 'questionable' to say the least.

Yet it was not only the fate of the Queen now hanging precariously in the balance. There was the tiny Princess Elizabeth's future at stake, too. To ultimately execute the Queen would still leave her little daughter in line to the throne ahead of any female heiress that a future Queen might bear.

So my father found it most curious to discover that, shortly before her planned execution, Anne's marriage to the King was to be dissolved and declared invalid, and thus at a stoke bastardising the young Princess Elizabeth. The fact that, in law, Anne could now longer have technically committed adultery if she was now deemed never to have been married to the king in the first place seemed to escape the notice of the judiciary. Yet so were so many other things that made little sense at that time, or simply remained unproven.

However, my father later told of something that he, being a gentleman of His Majesty's privy chamber, had witnessed. It happened on the very night that Anne Boleyn was taken to the Tower Of London. The King's beloved bastard, but acknowledged son, Henry Fitzroy, the Duke of Richmond, came to his father's chamber to wish him 'goodnight' and to ask his father's blessing, just as he did every night when residing under the same roof as the King. Only on this particular night, Richmond was somewhat taken aback to find Henry sitting silent by the fire in his great chair, staring aimlessly off into the flickering flames of some other world. My father said that as the young man approached, the King suddenly broke down into tears. Sobbing, Henry had grasped a hold of the lad and started kissing his outstretched hand, saying how both he and his sister, the Lady Mary should thank God that they had escaped from falling victim to a most dreadful fate planned for them by 'that accursed whore'. For Henry then went on to claim that Queen Anne had been determined to poison them, and him too, so that she and her own could inherit the throne.

Father told me that at the time he was convinced that this scene he had witnessed unfolding was no less than utterly genuine, especially on the part of the young man who had tried then so tenderly to ease his father's distress while crying so many tears of his own. Yet in times to come, my father would also look back and not wonder if it might have equally been a carefully staged piece of play-acting on the part of the King. All a deliberate show, on his part, in order to gild his stance against the now doomed Anne...

Chapter Four

My father had always said that Jayne Seymour was naught but a French-finished coquette. True, she was demure and far less obvious than the bold Boleyn had been in stalking the King for his attention, yet for all that my father for a long time before had considered her a scheming man-trap waiting to be sprung.

It happened during a visit alone to the Seymour's family home of Wolfhall, in Wiltshire. Knowing full well that the royal marriage was under strain, Seymour's scheming family deliberately baited this particular snare and lulled the disheartened Henry into accepting this succubus[11] into his bed. Where Anne had thrown tantrums and given the King vinegar, the Seymours had coached the outwardly modest Jayne to quietly offer him honey instead. Well known to be a sympathiser of ex-Queen Katherine, my father was certain that Jayne had been an all too willing participant in the subsequent downfall of Queen Anne. Moreover, in doing so Jayne must have had no doubt in her mind at all that by embarking on such a course of action it would end things badly for Boleyn. For how could the King justify another divorce in the eyes of his subjects and other kings?

And like a cuckoo in the nest easing out the natural fledgling to its doom, Jayne knowingly set about causing the disinheritance of Anne's innocent daughter, the tiny Princess Elizabeth, in preference to her own future Seymour offspring. Yes, what a sweet creature this new love of His Majesty's must have been – to have skulked off home to her parents, to oversee the preparations for her own marriage to the King while Anne was drawing her last breaths on Tower Green as she awaited the swordsman – who would behead her.

As was so often the case, on that day[12] my father was attending Henry in his capacity as a gentleman of the privy chamber. Dressed as if for hunting and yet with his mind seemingly not set upon the chase at all,

---

11   Succubus – a female demon supposed to descend upon and have intercourse with a man while he sleeps.
12   May 19th.

the King stood beneath a large oak tree on a hillside overlooking London as if waiting for a something to happen. As the sun began to claw its way through the early blanket mist and up high in the bright, mid-morning sky, the sickening boom of a distant gun being fired from the Tower of London took the shine away from the day. Suddenly, it was as if every bird, far and near, across the wide valley had taken to sky in a shock of flight. Many among that royal hunting party dare not look in the King's direction for the shame of it all. Yet my father did.

He saw how it brought a great gaping grin of satisfaction to King Henry's face. For the gun's report had been the pre-arranged signal to mark the moment Anne Boleyn's head was struck from her neck. In glaring delight, Henry immediately mounted his horse and rode off at break neck speed with my father and the King's huntsmen in hot pursuit.

They all ended their ride at Wolfhall, where my father felt sickened to realise that he, and sundry members of the Privy Council, would be called upon the following day to witness the wedding of King Henry and Jayne Seymour.

'Had I been forewarned,' as my father many years later spoke of his great disgust, 'I would have feigned sickness or even death to have avoided it!'

Yet he could not, dare not, be seen to hold any objection to the new match. For he knew that a slighted Jayne could so easily do to him what she had done for the hapless Queen Anne. His fears were fuelled when it seemed that every Seymour wolf-pup that ever was whelped was now being showered with riches and wealth and taking over every great or lucrative position at court.

More worrying was the fact that, with both Queen Katherine and Boleyn dead, an unimpeded pathway had been cleared, making it possible for the King to be gently shepherded back towards a reunion with Rome. All Seymour had to do was to provide the King with a long awaited legitimate male heir to have it in her power to bend Henry toward that will. And if she succeeded in that, then each and every unrepentant English Protestant 'heretic' would be in danger of losing his or her life.

After the wedding ceremony, the King and his new wife went to Winchester for a few days' 'privacy' together before returning to the capital. Then, on the twenty-ninth day of May, King Henry held a great court where he publicly introduced Jayne as his new Queen. And then, one month later, the proud King set about presenting his new wife to the public at large. He took her to Mercer's Hall, where she surveyed the annual ceremony of the Setting of the City Watch from on high, at one of the great windows.

A few days after this ceremony, Parliament was summoned to 'declare the heir apparent, and to repeal the act in favour of the succession of Anne Boleyn's issue'. In short, both Lady Mary and Lady Elizabeth were now barred from the line of succession. Henceforth it would be Queen Jayne's future children, whether they be male or female, who would legally inherit the Crown of England, and the Seymours would undoubtedly be the power behind the throne.

Katherine and the hated Boleyn were now gone and the crowds in London, at least, seemed to adore Queen Jayne. The stage now seemed set for the King and his subjects to be reconciled at last. Old grievances had been buried... Yet in fact old grievances would not lie quietly in graves. Instead, they festered until like a great carbuncle – the puss came busting forth.

In the north of the realm, centred around York and troublesome Lincolnshire, a rebellion threatened to break out from a multitude still at anguish with their enforced break from Rome and the great wrong that so many thought done to their late Catholic queen. There were those at Henry's court who even feared some great harm might befall the King and that rebels might have his daughter, Lady Mary, brought to the throne in stead. Yet Henry managed to crush the revolt, just as he crushed anything that dared raise its head to stand in his way.

As for the King's beloved Henry Fitzroy – he had died of consumption on the eighteenth of June at St. James' Palace, just as an act had been progressing through Parliament to enable the King to name him as the heir to his throne.

So Queen Jayne now had everything that once Queen Anne had so reckless enjoyed and believed to be indisputably hers; all that apart from the lavish coronation, that Jayne believed she now deserved and which should, by rights, surpass the one made for Boleyn. Yet, as fate would have it, that summer there was a dreadful outbreak of plague in London and so plans for the coronation had to be postponed.

With no great regret, my father immediately took leave of both the newly-weds and the city to see, for once, to the immediate care of his own family. He moved us out to the safety of the country, seven miles south of the Thames to our peaceful retreat at Merton where, until the end of the autumn, we passed the most idyllic of times as something we so rarely were – together as a simple family.

*   *   *

Cheapside is packed in from east to west with one grand timber-framed mercer's premises after another. Many of these have three or even four private floors overhanging from above, complete with tall brick chimneys and great shimmering expanses of expensive, leaded-glass lights[13] looking out onto the wide thoroughfare beyond. Some, like my father's, even had balconies on which to stand out upon. Thus, from up on high, my family has witnessed many a great spectacle unfold.

Cheapside is where almost all the London mercers live and trade, as well as the city's wealthy goldsmiths. Day in, day out, Cheapside is crowded with the most well heeled people swarming about like brightly coloured, silk-clad bees drawn to the lure of all manner

---

13 Windows.

of luxury goods on offer in our ample shops below. At one time, my father owned over a dozen properties in this one great street, with mayhap a dozen more in the surrounding parishes, as well as our great house in Bow Lane.

I shall soon write much in praise of Merton, so one might suppose that I hated living in the city. In truth, that is mostly the case, yet I do have some of my fondest childhood memories fixed in London, and these can never be removed. For me, London then was the unpleasant day to day reality of life in a dirty, crowded city, while Merton was like some magical escape into an altogether cleaner, alternative world. Yet, even that appeal of Merton diminished for me in a short while, and then sadly began to slip away from my affection for many years. Though now, as I write and think of it once more, I feel a smile ease across my face.

So, I suppose you might ask, what was London like in that far distant time of my childhood of more than seventy years ago? Today I hear the good citizens of that place wail that the streets in London are plagued by young men with knives; dispossessed youths with no work to employ them. And so, in idleness, they fall into the foul hands of all manner of vice. In pleasuring their habits they turn to robbery and violence – making it unwise to walk in the city streets as the shadow of night begins to creep over them. Yet even in my childhood London was a place of violence. And it still is so and most likely always shall be. Much of my own growing up at Cheapside was coloured by my brother Matthew's gleeful retelling of terrible deeds carried out there, and some of those but a stone flick from our own front door.

Opposite Honey Lane, stands the infamous Cheapside Standard[14] and water fountain. This is where, as painted in our minds by Matthew's telling, many a gruesome punishment was metered out across the years. My brother's detailed accounts included hands being stricken from arms and heads from shoulders. In the third year of King Edward's reign, for example, he told us how two fishmongers were beheaded there,

---

14   A large, tall water cistern.

for aiding a riot. And then there was another tale of a rich merchant named Richard Lions, who had his head stuck of by the rebel Watt Tyler.

In the middle of the east end of Cheapside, at its junction with Poultry, stands the Great Conduit, while at the west end is the Little Conduit facing Foster Lane and Old Change. The larger of the two brings in water to the city from the infamous Tyburn through underground pipes made of lead. Here I often saw giggling serving girls idly chatting away with man-servants and apprentice boys, while they waited in turn to engage the services of the strong backed, iron-armed water carriers to supply their masters' houses for the day.

Not far from this, in an open spot facing Wood Street, stands Cheapside Cross. It is just one of many such crosses raised up by the first King Edward to mark the spot where the coffin of his beloved wife, Eleanor, was rested on its way from her death place in Lincoln to her burial place at nearby Saint Peter's Abbey. In the almost three hundred years it has stood here, it has since been rebuilt, embellished and re-gilded several times. I used to think how good and kind the poor beggars must be not to climb up and rob it of its jewels. Only later would I learn that the studded gems were but moulds of lead, painted and with flecks of gilt to catch the sunlight and create the illusion.

As a small child I was, and I imagine like generations of people passing by before me, filled with awe at the sight of this cross. I witnessed many stop and marvel at its grace and beauty. It had been exquisitely fashioned with three octangular compartments, each supported by eight slender columns. I remember there being in the first niche the standing figure of some long dead Pope or another; and around the base of the second were four apostles, complete with a nimbus around each of their heads. Above those sat an effigy of the virgin Mary, with the infant Jesus dandling gently on her knee and supported by her arms. She reminded so much of my mother.

In the highest niche of all were four standing figures of some people unknown to me, but above that I clearly remember the crowning glory of a beautiful cross surmounted by a most graceful dove. It was always the dove that drew my eyes, as I looked up thinking it might at any moment fly off above the rooftops of London.

I sometimes saw priests stop there, before they passed by and continued on their way, muttering a prayer to the by then almost faceless Mary. Once, when I was still very young and walking out with my mother, I saw a young girl stop there, curtsey and cross herself before the virgin. So, thinking I would please my mother, I quickly stepped forward too and did likewise, thinking it fitting to copy the other child's actions. That was until my mother tugged hard at my hand to hurry me away. When we reached home and were in the privacy of our chambers, she told me that I must never do that again.

'Tis but Papist idolatry,' Mother explained. 'And we are no Papists! The only time that I shall bow before Christ is when I stand in His presence to give account of my life on earth, and then I will gladly humble myself down to the ground before Him.'

From that day forth, I had to pass by Cheapside Cross quickly without seeming to take any notice of it at all. And yet still a part of me could not shut out the sheer beauty of the thing, as hard as I might try to do so. Besides, I believe it served me well as a reminder that death spares neither king nor subject.

With the shouting and hustle and bustle generated by the sheer volume of people, always crowing into Cheapside, little wonder that the sounds I remember most of all was the evening quietude and the great bells ringing out from the newly repaired steeple of the Romanesque Church of Saint Mary the Virgin at Bow.

The church stands back from the street at Cheapside by about forty feet, with its churchyard bounded by both it, Bow, and Goose Lanes. Though the church itself is but a mean and low building, my ancestor, John Lok, is buried beneath a great arched tomb in a chapel dedicated to Saint Thomas on the south side. To the north side of the church is a great stone building which cuts out a deal of light from reaching into the gloomy interior of Saint Mary's. From there on high, past kings and nobles have watched jousting or witnessed many a city spectacle passing through from West Cheap.

My father told me of a tale from the King's own lips. When the then young Henry had only just come to the throne, on the mid-summer night of Saint John' Eve[15], the King went there dressed in the livery of a yeoman of the guard, complete with halberd resting upon his shoulder. There he stood witnessing the ceremony of the Setting of the City Watch. Afterwards, he quietly went on his way again with none having recognised him as their sovereign King. But on the following Saint Peter's night[16], King Henry came there again, but this time dressed in all his regal splendour and with Queen Katherine upon his arm so they might behold the spectacle together.

Saint Mary the Virgin at Bow also has a bloody story attached to it. Matthew told me once that a long, long time ago, a goldsmith was murdered there while seeking sanctuary after a drunken brawl in a tavern went too far. The goldsmith had run away and hid himself up in the steeple. But as he later lay sleeping, his pursuers crept in and slew him. After that, his killers then convincingly posed his body so that his murder might be mistaken for a suicide.

With self-killing being not only a felon but also believed to be a most heinous crime against God, the goldsmith was tried posthumously by the coroner's jury. He was duly found guilty, even though his poor widow did plead with the judge that her good Christian man would never have done such a thing to himself. None the less, she was left penniless as everything her dead husband owned was then seized and immediately forfeited to the Crown. Even the debts owed to him were swiftly gathered in.

---

15   June 23rd
16   June 28th

So Matthew then went on to describe how the dead man was buried with all of the customary indignities. For his 'sin' against God, the goldsmith was denied a Christian burial and instead made subject of the most macabre and profane ceremony. The night after the inquest, the parish officials, aided by the church wardens and others, but with no priest to say prayers, carried the corpse to the nearest crossroads, dug a pit there, and then flung the man's naked corpse into it. Then they drove a wooden stake through the goldsmith's chest, to pin him to his grave, before they hastily shovelled dirt on top of him. Thus, they believed, he might never find eternal peace, nor any who came to mourn him.

But it later came about that there was also a boy sheltering in the church that night, who had seen everything that had befallen the goldsmith, but had hidden himself from sight in fear of also being murdered. Later, he told the magistrate about what he had witnessed, which led to the murderers, including a woman, being arrested and eventually executed.

For a time after that, the Church of Saint Mary was interdicted[17] and its windows and doors became choked shut and overgrown by brambles until, after some while, it was reinstated.

'Some people', Matthew told us, 'have seen the ghost of that slaughtered goldsmith a-wandering about the street at night, as he seeks small children to eat.'

However, no matter how grisly or frightening my brother's tale was then, it could not detract from my love of that comforting peal of Saint Mary's wonderful bells that can be heard all about that part of the City.

When I was a young girl, as the go-to-bed bells rang out at nine of the clock, I can still remember the rhyme that my mother recited to us children, just as I would one day recite it to children of my own.

---

17   Roman Catholic ecclesiastical censure whereby an offending person or district is excluded from participation in most sacraments and from Christian burial.

'Clarke of the Bow bell, with the yellow locks,
For thy late ringing, thy head shall have knocks'
Then to this the clerk replies-
'Children of Cheap, hold you all still,
For you shall have Bow bell rung at your will.'

Yet the most favourite of all my childhood memories relates to London and my mother and younger siblings, and to our beautiful garden there. The walled garden was at Grubb Street, and apart from us children, it was our father's only real indulgence. For its upkeep cost him dear, according to his accounts, and yet it turned in no profit that one could see. Yet to him the balance was in our family's wellbeing while confined to London. It was our escape from the horse and dog fouled streets beyond; from the open running sewers, and from the foul stench of all living humanity cleaved so closely together in this heaving city.

It was our own private piece of paradise; but a short walk from the Lock at Cheapside and yet as far away as our beloved Merton. Here we could come and be amongst grass and trees; with clipped box hedges enclosing the sweet-scented roses and grey leaved lavender or the spill of physics[18] that had the power to ease both our senses and our ills.

We could walk with Mother in the confines of the small garden courtyard at the back of our Bow house, but here at Grubb Street she could sit and enjoy watching us at play, exercising our limbs instead of just our minds. This was where we younger Lockes could cast off our heady books and run like children amongst the bushes, instead of being the slow pacing little paragons of virtue demanded by the grandeur of our house and high status. Here we might idly brush against Rosemary or mint, and then, once back at our studies, the honest perfume would linger on. It would remind us of the moth that Michael failed to catch, or of the shiny black stag beetle that he had caught, or of the game of tag that Alice and I had played while Maggie shouted out for us to 'have a care'. For she had 'enough

---

18   Plants cultivated for their medicinal purposes.

sewing already to last her a month of Thursdays' without having to darn any new holes from our clothes being recklessly snagged on a thorn bush.

Come autumn, in its small orchard the gardener's boy would climb up the tree and toss down rosy red apples to us so that we could fill Maggie's willow basket with them. Those were the best tasting apples I have ever eaten!

*   *   *

That winter of thirty-six was the hardest I can remember in all my childhood. As I scratched patterns in the icy leads of our great house at Bow Lane, the city beyond looked transformed into a glistening spread of white roof tops, with the grey smoke of chimney pots labouring to curl itself upwards into the brilliant skies above.

Wrapped in furs and muffs to brave the cold, Father took us to promenade beside the river. The Thames was frozen solid from north bank to south bank and had caught many vessels fast in its icy grasp. We saw sailors slipping down ropes from their ships and watched bemused as they then strolled towards the shore. People everywhere were spilling out onto the river to traverse it on foot, or even with carts, instead of squeezing across by its only bridge. Rosy-cheeked children, with naught but rags bound about their feet and thin coats upon their backs to save them from some chill, slipped and slid in play upon the ice. They squealed with delight while their dirty mongrel dogs yapped excitedly; all with great plumes of white breath panting out into the cold still air. Then someone stopped to bid good day to my father and told him how King Henry and Queen Jayne had earlier ridden by and across the ice all the way towards Greenwich. I remember thinking then how sweet London could be without the foul stink from this great open sewer that would compel those of us who could to flee to the country when summer returned.

Chapter Five

I had always known that my father had been married before, but I had never fully understood the implications of that. I had known that this first wife, Alice, had died after begetting my older half-brothers and sisters by him. I had not known Alice and so consequently had not been affected by either her life or her death. And because I saw with my own eyes the happiness he shared with my own mother, I assumed that he had not been affected by her death either. I simply accepted that Alice had lived and then died, and so didn't ask any questions. Neither did I fully comprehend until a certain point that, for almost each one of the siblings and half siblings that I loved and cherished, another had died, forgotten or unknown by me along the way. Nor had I understood how tenuous and feeble is the grasp that we each have upon this life.

Be we born king or pauper, and from the day of our births we all dangle above that same yawing chasm, never knowing when it will be our turn to drop. Yet drop, we all do. Mayhaps it is for the best that we do no know or the clinging may become all the more terrifying and the dread of the impending fall unbearable.

I shall never forget the year fifteen-hundred-and-thirty-seven. I have just cause for it to be seared into my soul until the end of my days. And so too would the King. It was early in that year that my younger sister, also named Alice, died after an all too sudden illness. My mother was so distraught, so beside herself with grief, that I could hear her at night, crying in the darkness. Alice had always been my favourite sister. She had been the most adorable blush-cheeked, bright-eyed child I was ever to see in my life. I used to love brushing out her curls and playing with our dolls together, or running through the field by St Mary's Church to pick the bright red poppies that grew amongst the tall meadow grasses. She had only been coming on to nine years of age.

As for the previous autumn's rebellion, by late spring there was no longer any open resistance to the

King in the North. With the introduction of martial law, all rebellion had been terrified into submission. Along highway and byway, in trees and from gibbets, hung the blackened fruit of their subjugation and none dare voice aloud any hint of sympathy for those rotting corpses suspended by ropes and chains.

Many women, however, ventured out under cover of darkness to reclaim their dead loved ones, in order to bury them as good Christians, in consecrated ground. With their children they dug graves by themselves and made makeshift the rites, for no priest dare to step forward to help for fear of reprisal from the State. Thus any feeling, other than for disgust at such blatant revolt against the King was successfully repressed, although a justice of sort was painfully seen to be had.

For their part in the previous October's rebellion, on March the sixth, the Abbot of Kirkstead and thirty four others had been arraigned at Lincoln before a special commission. Of course, they were all found guilty and executed the next day. On the twenty-sixth day, and this time in London, a Doctor Mackerell, prior of Barlings, and Kendall, the vicar of Louth, along with ten companions were swiftly condemned to death at the Guildhall and then slowly dispatched at Tyburn. And among others from the north were the Lords Darcy and Hussey who were condemned and taken to the Tower.

Meanwhile, within nine months of the first outbreak of rebellion that started in Lincolnshire, and with the official announcement of the Queen's pregnancy at last reaching these outposts, the King had amply regained his authority. However, Henry still had to fulfil a promise he had made – that he would visit the North to discuss any remaining grievances on the part of those lords there. This he was now successfully able to put off by way of excuse – 'owing to the Queen's condition'. And as for the promise he had made at the same time to the rebels, that he would have Parliament meet to consider these same matters, no more came of it.

Again, that summer was to prove extremely

unhealthy for tarrying in The City. Once more plague had reappeared in London, and by July even a servant of Cromwell's had fallen ill with it. So high was the anxiety that the King might contract the plague that, from thence forward, even his closest Minister was forbidden to meet with Henry anywhere other than in the open air of the hunting field, and even then he was neither to touch the body of the King nor to pass any note nor anything else into his sovereign's hand.

The King and his household withdrew from London to the relative safety of Hampton Court Palace, in fear for not only himself but also for Queen Jayne, too, as she was by now more than five months pregnant and nothing was to be allowed to threaten her safety. At last, a male heir to the throne of England might be soon brought into this realm! And Queen Jayne herself was convinced that the child now swelling her womb was a son: and Henry was firmly convinced of that also.

Yet anxiety followed even at Hampton Court, where one of the gentlemen in attendance on the Queen received word that one of his servants at home had suddenly fallen ill. He was immediately dismissed and sent packing to his house in Hackney, until such time as whether he could be proved infected himself or nay.

Luckily, my father had already moved our family, though much earlier than usual, to our house at Merton. He had hoped that the change of air and the peacefulness of that place might ease my mother's delicate spirits. More especially so as she was now also equally advanced as the Queen with child.

Father sorely wanted to spend more time with Mother that summer, but as he was amongst the favoured few who were deemed 'safe' from the taint of London, he was kept even closer to King Henry than usual. Although not always so close, for in the August the King sent him across the sea; outwardly as his royal mercer on mundane matters of business. But, covertly, he was to gather information to send back to Cromwell about how the conflict was going betwixt France and Flanders. Much my father found out for himself, but he also acted as a secret go-between, bringing back intelligence from King Henry's own sister.

Father also wrote to my mother from Antwerp, explaining that when the Burgundians were on the eve of winning Thérouenne, to everyone's astonishment, a ten-month truce was suddenly called and accepted. He explained that there was general discontent with the truce amongst the community there and that no-one knew anymore other than it was to last ten months. People were astonished, because they were convinced that the town would have easily fallen and that the Emperor could never expect to have such an advantage again. In a post script he said that he 'was wont to write to the King, but there is nothing worth reporting. Mister Governor is not yet come to the mart[19] from the Lady Regent[20]...' After that he professed his love for my mother and said that he was soon to hurry back home to her with gifts and trinkets for her and the children.

When Michaelmas[21] came and passed, I knew that we should already be back at Cheapside, but the sweating sickness in the city was not yet abated. So, instead, Mother decided it safer to go into seclusion at Merton, in anticipation of the birth of her next child. Besides, our nursemaid suggested to my father that it might also be less distressing to wait until after the birth before returning to the house where Alice had so recently died. That way Mother would have the baby to keep her busy and to occupy her thoughts. Father agreed. However, he would still have to find some way of attending to both his family and the King's business, yet also avoid contact with sickness. So he decided conduct matters from a rented house near Kingston, where he could receive messengers more easy from both home and King. When my mother's time was near, word could be sent to him there and he would swiftly ride back.

And so Mother, my young siblings, and I stayed on in Merton to enjoy the glorious fall in all its beauty, kicking through the carpet of golden leaves and picking

---

19 Mart – a market place or such.
20 King Henry VIII's sister.
21 Michaelmas – a church festival celebrated on September 9th in honour of the archangel Michael. Ne of the four quarter days in England, Wales and Ireland

up horse chestnuts along nearby lanes and revelling in our extra freedom before we would have to eventually return to the dirty confines of the city of London.

All was well... until Friday October the twelfth, when around noon time my mother went into her labour. At first she was convinced that it was nought more than indigestion for it was too soon for the baby to come, and the gripes were neither harsh nor near together. So she made little fuss and instead took to her bed thinking that if she rested, then all would be well by the evening. But within a few hours her waters had broken – a certain sign that the baby was coming.

Outside it had begun to rain in torrents as a gale suddenly swept up, whipping through the willows beyond the garden wall with a fury, sending long slender branches flailing madly through the air. Nonetheless, a rider was urgently dispatched to Kingston, to take word to my father and summon him home.

Later that night, Mother cried out so loudly that it awoke me and the rest of the household.
Stumbling from my room and still half intoxicated by sleep, I found Maggie already up and coming along the upstairs hall way.

'What is it, Maggie?' I asked.

'Ne're you mind, Lady Rose,' she said, turning me about and back towards the direction of my room. ''Tis nothing but your mother kicking up a great deal off fuss over this baby that's a-coming. But do not be afeared. The midwife is in with her now and she knows just what to do.'
With that I was hurried back to my bed and firmly told that I best stay there and go back to sleep.
But I could not settle down like the little ones already had. My mother's screams increased into a harrowing crescendo – then suddenly halted abruptly.

Heedless of Maggie's instruction, I crept from my room once more and up to my mother's bed chamber. Peeping through the crack-opened door, I saw my mother slumped back upon a huge bank of pillows. Her pale, cream nightdress was dragged up above her waist and her legs were splayed apart and from between them a pool of scarlet was steadily creeping out across the crisp white bed sheets.

I watched as Maggie hurriedly bundled vast quantities of blood-soaked rags out from between my mother's thighs and into a large wicker basket by one side of the bed, just as something limp and blue was being lifted forth by the midwife standing at the other. Gently, she dangled the thing down from the clutch of one of her bloodied hands and then swung it, gently, through an arc, twice, thrice. Then the 'something' suddenly whimpered weakly, like a mewing kitten, into life.

'There! That's done it, thank God!' the old woman sighed. 'At least the poor mite is breathing now, but best fetch the minister, quickly, so that he might at least be baptized!'

In my terrible curiosity, I must have leaned a little too close against the door, for it of a sudden creaked in loud warning. Then I saw the look of horror etched across both Maggie's and the midwife's faces as they turned in unison and realised that I was standing there.

'Shoo! Shoo now!' Maggie said. 'Back to your room Lady Rose! Go!'
I knew from the hollow look on her face that something was terribly wrong.

'No!' I heard my mother protest breathily, and scarce above a hoarse whisper she pleaded: 'Let Rose stay if she wishes.' With that, her eyes closed and she slipped away into sleep. And from then I stayed by her bedside, praying through her slumber. Nothing, nothing on God's earth could have then torn away from my mother's side. I was determined to watch over her until my father returned, as I knew he must do so very soon.

But unknown to us, my father at first could not be found by our messenger. As a gentleman of the King's Privy Chamber, Father, along with countless others bound close to the King, had been summoned from Kingston to attend Henry at Hampton Court Palace. Queen Jayne was also in labour and had been since the day before.

Some while later, my mother awoke and did so relieve me by her smiling countenance. On hearing her mistress stir, Maggie quickly fetched some Rosa Solis [22] in a dish and put up to mother's lips but she could not suffer to even sip a mouthful.

'Mother,' I asked, for I was confused as to how she could be so content after the tortures I had earlier witness her valiantly braving, 'Why are you smiling so?'

'Oh Rose,' she rasped, 'you would be smiling too if only you had seen what I have seen.'

'What have you seen, Mother?' I could tell that she was desperate to tell me.

'I have seen God the Father...and Jesus at his right, stretching forth his hands to receive me.'

With that, Maggie fetched the baby to set him in his Mother's arms, but she was too weak to lift them to receive him. Then, with a long, low sigh, my mother closed her eyes once more and in comfort went forth from this life.

When my father eventually made it back to Merton the following day, in keen anticipation of seeing his wife and new baby, he broke down on hearing of my mother's death. He did not even get to see their tiny son in life, for he too died earlier that morning. At first Father could not speak for the tears that filled his eyes and mouth. No comfort could I or the others give him – for he did so bitterly reproach himself for not being at Mother's side in her hour of departing. Yet when Maggie afterwards told me to come forward and relate to my father those last moments of my mother's life, his countenance eased greatly. For he then knew for certain that from her death-bed testament my mother had been truly received now into the care of our Loving Father and His eternal Kingdom, and some of his bitter tears became instead those of rejoicing.

---

22 *Rosa Solis* or *Rosolio* is a cordial, distilled from the insectivorous bog plant, sundew, probably originating in Renaissance Turin. It often included hot provocative spices like cubebs, grains of paradise and galingale.

Later, we children were gently ushered into my mother's chamber, where my father stood in silence, still red-eyed, beside the great red-curtained bed. On it, beneath crisp fresh sheets, bravely turned down over her favourite dark green counterpane, lay my mother. Her fine and sleek chestnut hair, un-coifed and lovingly brushed by her maidservant, Maggie, was fanned out across the pillows and falling gently about her face as I had never seen it do in life. Her soft brown eyes were now closed against this fallen world, and on her wax-like countenance was the most peaceful of smiles. She looked stunningly beautiful; she was like a bride laid out by her kinswomen and awaiting the arrival of her groom.

Then, my eyes travelled down to her awkwardly posed arm. In its crook, wrapped in fine linen, lay the tiniest baby I had ever seen. His wrinkled grey face peeped unseeingly out from the folds of white along with a shock of dark hair clotted against his forehead. How I hated him! For to me, he was the undoing of all our lives.

My father beckoned us to draw near. And so, like quiet mice, we quickly skirted past the bed to slip beside him at its head. Then, one by one, we were encouraged to kiss my mother farewell. My turn came, and as I leaned down and my lips touched her paled cheeks, I was taken aback by the coldness of her face; and by her smell. She did not smell like my mother anymore. Instead, she smelt of May[23] flowers.

---

23   May – a common name for the flowers of the hawthorn tree. They are considered unlucky if brought indoors.

Chapter Six

My mother's simple burial should have taken place on the Monday, but even in death the King's needs took precedence over those who were but his mere subjects – no matter how grave or pressing they might be.

The official christening of the new prince was to be held on the Monday and Henry had ordered that all the privy gentleman who had attended the birth be compelled to be at Hampton Court for the ceremony as well.

How dreadful it must have been for Father to return to that place, still ecstatic with rejoicing over the birth of the King's newborn son, when Father had just stepped away from the deathbed of his cherished wife. To have to then walk in upon all of that delirious happiness when, had he the choice, he would have hidden himself away to grieve in private.

So then, having been informed of my father's most recent and crushing loss, how had the King rewarded or simply acknowledged his many years of loyal service and unfaltering friendship?

On seeing my father, Henry turned upon him in a typical hiss of venomous tongue and rebuked him soundly.

'God's teeth, Will!' he hissed. 'Why do you show yourself here in my presence wearing black? Can you not show some consideration for your sovereign when you know how much I abhor such mourning weeds? Go take them off! I shall not suffer your presence here until you do!'

The joyous stupor into which the King had been cast at the deliverance of this long desired heir seemed to have robbed him of any notion of consideration for the plight of others; or it was the consequence of him having had them bound there so closely when he should have set them free to attend to their own obligations. For while the King had kept my father at Hampton Court, he had deprived my mother of his comfort in her dying.

Neither had the King given any real consideration to the newly delivered Queen. Her labour had not been without mortal danger either. Indeed, the Queen's ladies and the royal physician, being greatly alarmed by the baby's long and difficult transition, had at one point sent word to His Majesty to pose the cruellest of questions... Would he wish for his wife or the infant to be saved?

Equally cruel then came the King's response, though not to be repeated within poor labouring Jayne's hearing.

'The child by all means, for other wives could easily be found!'

Unlike my mother, Queen Jayne survived the tortuous birth of her son and briefly rested, slowly began to recover from her ordeal. However, regal etiquette dictated that the child be officially christened and that the Queen, ill or nay, was to play her part in the ceremonies.

Thus, on the Monday, the Queen was taken from her lying in, dressed, and placed upon a heavily decorated litter. It was embellished on its back with the crown and arms of England wrought in threads of gold. There she reclined, propped up on four great cushions of crimson damask decorated with gold work and wrapped in a mantle of soft red velvet, trimmed with ermine. The rest of her body huddled beneath a counterpane of scarlet cloth, again trimmed and lined with the regal fur.

Once readied, to a fanfare of trumpets and attended by her ladies, Queen Jayne was joined by a clamorous throng from the court who then begin the procession from her bedchamber to the palace chapel. There, by torchlight the baptismal ceremony began with the young prince being presented at the font by his half sister, the Lady Mary. Throughout the rambling rites, the visibly beaming King remained firmly seated at his Queen's side. All with eyes could see that, although wrapped up against the numbing chill, Her Majesty looked cold and not at all well.

In all, the ceremonies did not conclude until well after midnight. Even thereafter came much boisterous hustle and bustle, instigated by the King himself in the poor woman's bedchamber. So the Queen's ladies found much delay and difficulty in returning the exhausted Jayne back to her bed.

Although, day by day, the sweating sickness was still casting a diminishing a shadow across the city of London, all was merriment amongst the court and throughout the realm at the birth of the Prince Edward[24]. All was rejoicing, apart from my family at Merton.

Father returned home to us the following morning for the burial of my mother and her baby, together in St Mary's Church. Immediately afterwards, my father had our servants prepare to make shift back to our house in the London before the worst of the frost and wet had time to break down the roads once more.

Yet within days, the previously happy mood of the rest of the country would suddenly change to a sombre tone. The Queen, who had already been so very weak from her labour, had taken to her sick bed within hours of the christening. Then quickly she became so desperately ill that she was swiftly administered all the last rites of the old religion. She lingered unchanged in this state for a full week more; even to rally so much on the following Wednesday that my father received a note from King Henry, apologising for not meeting with him at Kingston as he had commanded that day. This was because the King had chosen to tarry instead at Hampton Court due to Queen 'having been so poorly the night before'. However, the King had added that with Queen Jayne having improved somewhat, the physicians were confident that so long as she survived that night, God willing, she was over the worst and that Henry fully intended to meet with my father the following day.

By the evening, however, my father received a hurried note written by the hand of his good friend, Thomas Cromwell, saying that his presence was

24   The Prince was so named in honour of the fact that as he was born on the eve of St. Edward's Day.

urgently desired at Hampton Court; that there was little prospect of the Queen living for more than a few more hours, that is if she had not already died in the time it had taken to deliver the letter. Queen Jayne died shortly after midnight.

My father much later confided in me, that it had been Henry's reaction to the Queen's death that he had found so extraordinary. By then, my father had been close to the King for a long time and yet had never seen him display any great emotion. Yes, he had watched Henry laugh heartily until tears had run down his ruddy cheeks when sharing some lewd joke with his fellows, or great charge of excitement overtake him completely while out on a good day's hunting. For certain, Father had too many times seen the King's rage suddenly explode, when he would then thunder abuse at all and sundry. Yet, never had the King fallen heavy upon Father's shoulder before, and then sob, like a helpless child, as Henry had that night.

Was it regret for having enforced the royal etiquette that had dictated the sick Queen's presence for so long in that icy chapel for the christening? Henry, as King, could have so easily commanded there be an exception. Or was it guilt about, when during the labour, he too quickly opted for the child's life over the Queen's, and then adding callously that he could easily find another wife? Or perhaps his weeping was nought but the salty tears of self pity. As my father said, 'With Henry it was impossible to tell'.

In any event, the King appeared to withdraw into himself. After leaving the funeral arrangements to be made by members of his council, Henry almost immediately left Hampton Court for Windsor, refusing to speak to anyone other than for my father about the matter. For who else could fully understand the King's 'agonies' felt upon losing his wife as keenly as this trusty friend who had so recently lost his? Yet as my father increasingly found Henry's self-pitying wallow forced upon himself, it began to rub and wear my father's previous regard for his King like tinsel on a coat.

Moreover, despite Henry's well-cited protestations over the wearing of black or anything else that reminded him of death, he immediately wore widower weeds, and continued to flaunt them throughout Christmastide and far beyond Candlemas[25]. He wore his grief upon his sleeve, and woe betide any man or woman stooped in his presence who did not do likewise!

For almost two weeks the Queen's corpse had lain at Hampton Court. First to start the preparations of the body was the wax-chandler, who started in upon her the next morning, when her body barely cold. With much searing the Queen's entrails were removed, embalmed with precious spices and then bound in cloth before being given over to the plumber who soldered them into a specially fashioned lead chest. Then they were interred in the chapel.

On the Friday, the Queen's body was removed to a 'chamber of presence', where those privileged to do so, came to pay their last respects. It was placed beneath a hearse[26] with twenty one long slender candles set about it, made with wax from Wolfhall bees. There, ladies and gentlewomen of the court, dressed all in unadorned gowns of plain mourning black and with simple white kerchiefs covering their heads and shoulders, knelt beside the Queen's corpse throughout mass in the morning, and then afterwards throughout the Dirige[27].

A watch was kept over the body throughout that night, and every other, until the following Wednesday, the last day of October and the vigil of All Saints[28]. This date caused great angst amongst the many superstitious-steeped and still Papists-at-heart courtiers. Great strives were taken to ensure that every custom and ritual should be strictly observed and that the night's vigil be meticulously undertaken, lest any evil come to the Queen Jayne's newly departed spirit at this, the most dangerous of times.

On that morning the great chamber and the chapel, along with all of the galleries leading up to

25   Candlemas (Feb 2, 1537-8).
26   Hearse – a frame-like structure over a coffin or tomb on which epitaphs may be hung or candles placed.
27   Dirige – the office for the dead (that is sung), adopted from Psalms 5:9.
28   Halloween.

it, were hung with richly decorated black drapes. In the afternoon, the same were lined with the Queen's household of men and servants, standing in double file and each holding an unlit torch. Then the Queen's almoner, the Bishop of Carlisle, assisted by the Bishop of Chichester and the deans of the chapel, came into the chamber of presence. There they carried out the prescribed ceremonies: burning incense and casting both the room and body with holy water. When that was done, the great crucifix that had stood at the head of the Queen was carried out by one of the bishops, then came the other followed on by the rest of the priests. And then after them followed a stream of deathly silent nobles. Last to emerge from the room was the corpse, carefully carried shoulder high to join the procession making slow progress along the now torch-lit way to chapel. Once there, it was gently placed under yet another hearse, this time hung with banners bearing the royal ancestry.

That night, and every night thereafter, a night time vigil was kept, and every day countless Popish masses were heard, and with more Dirges sung, until Sunday. That was the twelfth day of November. On that bitterly cold and overcast morning, Queen Jayne's funeral procession finally set off from Hampton Court to make the journey to St. Georges Chapel at Windsor Castle – the place chosen by King Henry for her last resting place on Earth.

On a carriage pulled by six matched black horses, and beneath a rich pall of black velvet, Queen Jayne began this, her last journey, to meet with her husband. Her embalmed body was covered over by such a well-made effigy that many who saw it gasped at its likeness. It was dressed in the dead Queen's robes of state and crowned with real hair flowing down to its shoulders. The right hand grasped a queenly sceptre of gold, and its slender fingers were adorned with rings of glistening precious stones, and about its neck hung jewelled ornaments. When the light breeze driven up by the motion of the carriage stirred hems of the skirts, one could see clearly that even the shoes and hose beneath were made of golden cloth.

Close behind the corpse, riding upon a black velvet-trapped horse, snorting loudly in the cold air, came the small and slight figure of the official Chief Mourner – the young Lady Mary.

'It must have been a poignant sight for those still loyal to the late Queen Katherine,' my father commented, as he later recounted these events in detail. 'And for those who had known how hard Queen Jayne had lately tried to reunite the Lady Mary with her estranged father. One dead queen's daughter dutifully following behind another dead queen must surely have made Papists' hearts skip to the hope that it might prick sore enough at the King's conscience to have him restore Lady Mary to a place in the line of succession.'

Following the Lady Mary came an endless flow of black-clad mourners – streaming along the road, like a great black river of grief, all the way to Windsor. The common people, with raggedy children clutched at their sides, braved the cold and turned out from their hovels by the thousand to witness their dead Queen pass by. Row upon row they stood, and with such a public outpouring of sorrow as was never seen before in the memory of the living.

And so, Father told me, after this sickening show of unequalled pomp and ceremony, Queen Jayne was laid to rest at Saint George's Chapel in King Henry's already prepared tomb. She would hold for always the honour of being the only wife deemed worthy to lie, unto eternity, at Henry's side. And all this after only a mere eighteen months of marriage! Unlike her predecessor, Anne, whose mutilated corpse after execution had been hastily bundled into an arrow box and buried without ceremony in the grounds of the Tower of London. Jayne's burial was also very unlike that of the former Queen Katherine who, after twenty or more years of unadulterated duty to her husband, had been discarded in life and then in death laid at the side of Henry's dead brother, once more as if her marriage to

Henry had never been.

In all, during the length of the Queen's official mourning, more than twelve-hundred masses of the old religion were said for her soul in the City of London alone. Even so, as Father told me bitterly, there was nevertheless some complaint that, although the Lord Mayor and his aldermen had been lately at St Paul's to give thanks for the birth of Prince Edward, they had not also included a solemn dirge and had mass said at the Cathedral. The Lord Mayor and his aldermen should have been commanded to pray and to make offerings for the Queen's soul in the old way, was the grumble. For my father and some of his fellow Protestant aldermen, that would have proved a step too far. But for now, atleast, the threat of a return to Catholicism was dead.

Father added: 'Had Queen Jayne not died when she had, shrouded in Henry's guilt and enshrined in his own self-made myth of undying love, then maybe in time he would have discarded her, too, in search of greener grass. Yet the danger was always equal in that she might have instead commanded such a debt of his gratitude to have sought its repayment with a return to Rome.'

Then there was the King's 'beloved' bastard son Henry Fitzroy who, only the year before, had been considered worthy enough of legitimisation in preparation for him being officially named as the next King of England. And yet when this youth unexpectedly died, the King did not even attend his ceremony. Instead the lad's corpse had been slung onto a cart, covered over with straw and carried anonymously to his grave, with only two paid mourners to accompany his corpse there. It was this unevenness in the King's giving of 'affection', that my father confided about with me in his later years, that had made him grow to abhor his sovereign. And so from that time forth he began trying to distance himself from the contamination of that loathsome man.

It was a mournful winter that my brothers and sisters and I passed in London that year. Christmas came and went, as we children remained subdued and utterly bereft at the loss of our most beautiful and tender mother. No longer did the long gallery ring with our laughter, and beside the leaded lights, overlooking the dead brown stands of once vibrant flowers in the courtyard, the huddle of wooden settles remained vacant. For it was here that our mother used to read to us on dreary, grey afternoons. 'Twas as if her death had squeezed out every ounce of joy from within our shattered hearts and that time could never heal them.

Come the following break of spring into bold summer, and with the hedgerows clothed in showers of pure white May, we returned to my beloved Merton, where the fresh fields all about lay green in resurrection. Suddenly, I realised how lonely they would now feel without my sister Alice.

It was I who was first to jump down from our carriage and go running into our house, half- hoping, I suppose, and yet fully knowing it impossible, that I might find my mother inside waiting to embrace me once more. Instead, Maggie stopped me at the door and, on catching me by the arm, gently took up my right hand to her lips and kissed it. I pretended not to see her tears, as she did likewise when seeing mine, as we then slowly entered together.

My only solace over the ensuing months was to slip into the nearby church of Saint Mary the Virgin and to immerse myself in solitary quietude. Beneath huge oak beams and watched over by mute painted walls and even muter saintly statues, I silently recalled the many happy social events that I had attended in that long narrow nave with my family[29]. Such happy times had become very distant and shrouded by my idle tears.

There, I would let myself wander deep beneath my web of thoughts, only to suddenly surface and find myself much perplexed as to why it was that I could smell the sickly sweet scent of ill-luck May inside that church. Then mine eyes would search all about to find ne're a blossom in sight. Then, I would hold my pretty nose-gay[30] up close to my face to try to blot it out. Thankfully, in my childhood ignorance, I had not then

---

29   At this time it was common for the nave of the church to be used for secular events.

30   Nose-gay – a small bunch of flowers.

yet learnt to associate the odour that permeated the air with that of my mother's decomposing flesh imperfectly sealed somewhere beneath my feet. [31]

31   'Ill-luck May' – Botanists have since discovered that the chemical trimethylamine present in hawthorn blossom is also one of the first chemicals formed in decaying human or animal tissue. In the past, corpses would have been kept in the house for several days prior to burial, so Tudor people would have been very familiar with the smell of death. Hence hawthorn or 'May' blossom was unwelcome indoors because of this strong association.

Chapter Seven

Having mercer sons of age now to help him, Father all but stopped going across the sea himself, and instead turned his attention towards further expanding his family enterprise. His principle retail outlet in the city was in Cheapside and known to all as 'The Lock', marked outside by a large wooden sign depicting a silver coloured padlock upon a field of purple. There, all of London's nobility and gentry came to buy the necessary fineries from far across the sea. From finely spun cloth of gold, soft velvets, silks, to close woven linens for shirts fit for a king – all to be found beneath our roof. Fancy glass trimming beads for hats and kirtles, ostrich and peacock feathers, mother-of pearl, silk threads and hose, or fine Italian kid leather gloves – 'if not to be purchased at The Lock, then not be had in all of London'. My father took great pride in those words. And when it came to His Majesty, my father never failed to live up to those words or the King's expectation. When Queen Jayne was pregnant and all she desired to eat were quails eggs, out of season here in England, then my father sourced them especially from France himself. That is why he bore the coveted appointment of King's Mercer, just as his father had served Henry's father and my brothers and husband would serve his heirs.

After Mother's death, Father greatly extended The Lock by obtaining neighbouring premises, and so greatly increased both the size of his shops and holdings in general. He then had dwelling houses at The Lock; one in Bow Lane and another at the Bell in Cheapside, in which my older half-brother Thomas lived for a while with his wife, Mary, and dozen more close by.

*   *   *

At the time, I could not imagine that Father felt my mother's loss more keenly than we, her children. Therefore I could not understand why he could not come more often to us at Merton, so that he could help us grieve for her. For a good while after mother died, Father busied himself away from us, and I admit freely that at the time I resented him for that. Yet now I do not. For I believe that had been his way of coping with her death.

Father was in his late forties by then and must surely have hoped that after loosing his first wife, Alice, young, and having then shared fifteen happy years of marriage with my mother, that they, at least, might be allowed to grow old together. Yet now he was suddenly alone again, and still with a clutch of young children to rear. So he did what any dutiful father would do; he procured another mother for us.

I admit now, with shame, that I did not do my Christian duty towards that dear lady well. I was young and I was still grieving, yet this was no excuse for my wicked behaviour. Instead of welcoming her into our family with love, I met her with a steadfast and sullen resistance. Instead of allowing her outstretched arms to envelope me in hers, I vehemently wrestled my way free from her and fought against her every attempt to show me love. How dare she? How dare this stranger step into my dead mother's shoes and creep into my father's bed, as if my mother had never been? How dare she dandle my young sister, Elizabeth, upon her knee to steal away that child's innocent giggles and smiles and to make them into her own? No. I was determined to hate Mother Eleanor with every substance of my being.

I never stood near or sat beside her by choice, nor would I speak unless spoken to, share my books or silk-sew with her, or do anything that I had previously done in joy with my mother. All I did towards Mother Eleanor was the minimum that my duty towards my father commanded, and no more.

At Merton, when in the church on the Sabbath, I would sit at our family pew and fix my eye upon Mother Eleanor. Then, when I knew that I had drawn her attention, I would quickly cast my gaze upon the spot where my real mother lay buried beneath, then back to Mother Eleanor, as if to warn her that she might only be a temporary fixture in our lives.

And all that Mother Eleanor did in return was to try to love me and do her duty by her husband. I never took the time then to consider Mother Eleanor's part at all. How hard it must have been for her to have come to us young motherless children as an outsider, and at a time when our grief was still raw like an open wound. How closed in about us her life must have become as she tried to shoulder this great burden suddenly thrust upon her through this hastily arranged new marriage. And what of her grief for her own past life now taken from her? I was too wrapped up in my own selfishness to stop and contemplate how much my actions must have hurt her in those three years or so before she too died.

*   *   *

King Henry changed his religious views like pretty partners at a court dance. When His Majesty needed support for his Great Matter, it suited him to boldly reach out towards the Continental Lutherans and take their lead through the tricky steps ahead. With that mastered, and having then cast off his partner, Anne Boleyn, in favour of Jayne, it then suited Henry better to tiptoe about the conservative opinions at home instead. And woe betide any man suddenly found out of time with the King or who had, by some unhappy chance, stepped upon his toes.

'As in most aspects,' my father noted, 'at any given time one never truly knew where King Henry stood with the Protestant Church or it with him. Even up until his dying breath, we could never truly be certain as to what faith he would confess to at the very last.'

It had been sad for my father to realize that Protestantism for His Majesty was nought but a convenience, where as for we Lockes and our kind, it is, has always been, and always shall be, our one true hope in everything.

About a year after Queen Jayne died, a leading continental reformer, Philippe Melanchthon, personally wrote to King Henry. Here was a man who His Majesty had let it be known he much admired. However, much to his annoyance, Melanchthon's letters were highly critical of the King's continuing stance on supporting celibacy for the clergy. At the time, Henry had no inkling at all that his own Archbishop Thomas Cranmer had already married abroad, and had, since his return to England, kept a secret wife and children firmly hidden from public knowledge.

We Lockes knew full well that if King Henry's stance then seemed to be cooling towards Continental Protestants, Thomas Cromwell's certainly was not.

'Even if the King turned away from Protestantism,' Cromwell boldly told my Father, 'yet I would not. And even if the King did turn, and all of his people too, I would fight in this field in mine own person, with my sword in my hand against him and all others.'

These were strong sentiments indeed! So strong that an enemy overhearing might be tempted to construe them as treason.

After a Lutheran delegation arrived in London to build on Melanchthon's overtures, Cromwell wrote a letter to the King saying that he fully supported closer ties. Henry was not best pleased.

To every one's surprise, the King then suddenly decided to call Parliament. It was the first time he had done so in almost three years. Cromwell was by that time ill and so could not attend, but Archbishop Cranmer did.

A committee was drawn up and given the task of looking at the then current English Church doctrine with a mind perhaps to reform. But with such a wide remit and so little warning in which to make a thorough revision, little was achieved quickly. On noting this, the Duke of Norfolk instead steered the lords towards examining just six questions of doctrine, which became known as the Six Articles. All were affirmed – including the need for celibacy amongst the clergy. Cranmer must have feared deeply then that Norfolk had discovered his secret and that soon he might be made to face the ultimate penalty for his heretic Lutheran ways.

As this Act of Parliament inched ever closer to becoming Law, Archbishop Cranmer frantically smuggled his wife and children back out of the country and to the relative safety of the continent, before they were uncovered by his enemies. When the Act passed in the June, amongst those opposed to it was another bishop named Latimer, who then resigned in protest.

Yet by the September, Henry had become so equally ill-pleased with both the Act and its public supporters that Archbishop Cranmer and Thomas Cromwell thankfully found themselves back in His Majesty's favour once more. So much so, that Henry then asked the Archbishop to compose a new preface for his Great Bible. The first publication of this, King Henry's English translation, was overseen by Cromwell. And when the first Bibles were produced and chained in St Paul's Cathedral for all to read, Londoners queued all day just to do so.

From that time forth, Cranmer recognised Henry's authority in all things, and it served him well to stay alive. As For Cromwell, he was more than best pleased when the King agreed to his suggestion of marriage to Anne of Cleves, the sister of a Protestant German Prince. It quickly went ahead on the strength of Cromwell's own personal good reports of the prospective bride and a grossly over flattering miniature [32] of her by Holbein. At last, Cromwell could visualize the religious ties with our Lutheran continental allies being strengthened for good, and so the future for us Protestant faithful in England would be made safe.

My father had once asked Thomas Cromwell what it was like to be King Henry's chief advisor and closest confidant.

'Will,' he replied, 'it is like being trapped in a wood with a great aging bear that ails and festers with the foulest of humours. While he lies beneath a tree deep in slumber, one may tiptoe around him in complete safety. But if he should unexpectedly awake bad tempered, then one runs the risk of a mauling. And I, for one, do readily admit now that with the dawning

---

32   A small painting.

of each new day, my most sincere wish is to make my escape from the wood.'

The marriage to Anne of Cleaves was a disaster. King Henry could not find one thing about the woman that he liked. Not only that, but Cromwell's enemies, above all the Duke of Norfolk, then turned in upon him and pressed King Henry for his arrest.

On the tenth day of June, fifteen-hundred-and-forty, Cromwell was attending a routine meeting of the Privy Council. Suddenly, as if sensing what was about to befall him, Cromwell rose from his seat, took off his cap and threw it down upon the table, before bringing his fist down beside it in rage. The Duke of Norfolk and his cronies then stepped forward and, grabbing at Cromwell, yanked off his chain of office and tore off his robe of State, before manhandling him out of the chamber. He, all the while, vehemently protested his innocence of any wrong-doing.

Shortly after his arrest, Cromwell's house was subject to a search and correspondence allegedly found betwixt Cromwell and the continental Lutherans; letters so inflammatory that the King swore that he would see to it that the name of Thomas Cromwell's would be erased forever!

Cromwell was imprisoned in The Tower, but made subject of an Act of Attainer[33], which assured that Cromwell would be kept alive until the King could be divorced from Anne. He wrote two letters from his cell to King Henry, pleading his innocence to Norfolk's trumped-up charges and assuring His Majesty that he was a good and loyal servant, and a faithful Christian who had done him no ill. Henry ignored them. It was then that Father was told about Henry's new interest in another of Norfolk's nieces, and realised then that Cromwell was doomed – along with our hopes for early reform. And no matter how Cromwell pleaded his innocence, the King was not ready to hear a word of accusation against the Duke.

---

33   A parliamentary tool which dispensed with justice in favour of speed.

After a little bargaining, His Majesty came to some mutually acceptable arrangement with Anne of Cleves, whereby their marriage was annulled and she would receive a most favourable settlement – including the honour and privilege of being officially considered henceforth as 'the King's sister'.

Then, on the very same day of his marriage to Catherine Howard, King Henry had Cromwell executed – privately, on Tower Green, away from public scrutiny. My Father heard tell that Henry had been quite deliberate in his personal choice of executioner; a youth of very little, if any, previous experience.

Despite this most dreadful turn-about in His Majesty's favour towards him, Cromwell went with great dignity to the scaffold. He made a short speech proclaiming his innocence, then laid his head passively upon the block in expectation of a swift dispatch. But to my father's horror, the falling axe dealt but a glancing yet most injurious blow to the back of Cromwell's head. It sliced off some scalp and skull – exposing the brains beneath. Cromwell cried out in agony, and his whole body twitched in spasm. Many groaned aloud, choosing then to look away from this sickening butchery, while others openly gloated at the wretched man's suffering. Then, with his body all of a shake, yet his hands still clenched about the base of the block, and with a great deal of blood flowing, the axe-man struck again. With the second and deeper cut, Cromwell slid from his knees onto the scaffold floor, but with his head still not severed. The butcher boy, by now himself visibly trembling, stood astride the prostrate body and, at the third attempt, severed the head. To add insult to the agonies of his death, the King then commanded that Cromwell's head be boiled before being set upon a spike at Traitor's Gate, and positioned facing away from the City of London.

How Norfolk and his cronies rejoiced! They drank and feasted that night in open triumph, rejoicing that Cromwell had not escaped the fate they had all conspired for him to suffer, and yet with some lamenting of the fact that they had not been able to dispose of him some seven years before.

It is true that many clergy in the Church had not liked him, for indeed they did not like any zealous Protestant in their midst, including Archbishop Cranmer. And yet others, like my father and our family and friends, deeply lamented his passing; for here was a man who had never favoured any kind of Popery. Nor could he abide the sniffing pride of some of our prelates[34], which undoubtedly, amongst other things, had lead to his tragic and untimely demise.

While continuing to serve His Majesty as diligently as ever, my father did, however, begin to distance himself from the ebb and flow of the favourites at court, and from the ever vying Howards and Seymours. As a purveyor of the finest goods that money could buy, and by virtue of being His Majesty's Royal Mercer, Father kept in favour throughout the rise and fall of these others. He had, however, been deeply disheartened at the demise of Anne Boleyn and the positive effect that she might have been able to bring to bear upon the King by way of matters of Church reform. If only she had given him a son! As for her uncle, Henry Howard, Duke of Norfolk – who had so easily given Anne up for execution, not the least because of her growing Evangelical Protestant leanings in the latter years of her life, and for having clashed with the Papist ones of his own – my father detested him. Norfolk seemed to have a knack for side-stepping the taint of those he himself had set up to fall. He had even managed to survive Henry's wrath after the King found out the true extent of the miserly funeral Norfolk had arranged for Henry Fitzroy.

Then there had been this fifth marriage, again engineered by scheming Norfolk. Not content in already having procured several of his female relatives as concubines for Henry, Norfolk had then deliberately put forward his fresh-faced, teen-aged niece, Catherine Howard, as a sweet, young virgin for the King's perusal. How bitterly I recall my father's utter dismay, on having

---

34   Higher clergy.

witnessed King Henry so readily snap to that wicked bait, and to so easily dispatch his dear friend Thomas Cromwell.

'And that is why I now choose not to get involved in the politics of court!' my Father exclaimed. 'For I am far less now likely to fall from grace as merely His Majesty's Mercer. After all, whoever heard of a mercer losing his head for the sake of a piece of miss-matched silk?'

* * *

Within eight short months of Thomas Cromwell's execution, King Henry came to regret it deeply. In his own bloated sense of slight and anger, he had allowed events to charge ahead far too speedily, and without taking proper time to tease out the truth from amongst Norfolk's and his fellow plotters' tangled web of lies.

Henry raged at his remaining ministers, accusing them of bringing about malicious charges that had led to the downfall of the most faithful and loving servant that the King had ever had. His remorse was too late now to do any good for Cromwell, but it did serve to focus His Majesty's guilt over this dreadful matter onto trying to make some amends – by turning his support towards a now wary Thomas Cranmer. In return, the Archbishop tentatively tried his best by offering His Majesty what spiritual comfort he may.

Though often seen as out upon a limb, for the rest of Henry's reign, Thomas Cranmer was able to stand firm in the face of many plots and intrigues set against him. These were orchestrated by both conservative Protestants and Catholic sympathisers alike. In his customary manner, conspirators amongst his own clergy were immediately rebuked, yet in true Christian fashion the Archbishop would then forgive them and continue to call upon their services.

Meanwhile, quietly he maintained his efforts to reform the Church, and under his care and stewardship the first vernacular service was published. The Archbishop remained ever loyal to the King, and the

King in return, came to trust in Cranmer implicitly.

In matters of religion, my father had no doubt at all that the Church in England was in dire need of reform – along the line of thinking laid down first by Martin Luther and then taken up by John Calvin. But he was also wise enough to know that this could never be realised while King Henry was still alive. As much change as the Archbishop of Canterbury achieved under Henry, it was never quite enough for us zealous thinkers. And yet we recognised that Cranmer dare not push much further; because Lutherans and their like, in the main, were still considered heretics, even under English law. It was not yet time for a true reformation, and Cranmer must have conceded this, and so decided that patience would have to prevail for the time being.

Chapter Eight

Far from being chaste and pure, Catherine Howard had already had several lovers, and she possessed a veraciously lustful nature. Yet somehow she had managed to keep up the pretence of her youthful innocence long enough for the King to become absolutely besotted with her and then to marry her. It was only a year later before Henry found out about her true disposition.

While the couple were staying at Pontefract, during their summer progress, an unsuspecting Henry had occasion to send his servants to the Queen's bed chamber only to find the doors locked against them and Her Majesty steadfast in her refusal to open them up.

It was shortly after Their Majesties return to the capital that Queen Catherine stood trial for adultery, and soon after was executed. So many Howards were implicated in that trial that it was said that the Tower had run out of rooms to imprison them all. And yet Norfolk still managed to keep his head even in the wake this latest scandal. His continued survival seemed so unjust that the news of it moved my exasperated father to declare in dismay, 'I do swear that even if that man were set afire in hell he would not burn!' Then he looked straight into my eyes with a sudden calm before adding solemnly and sincerely, 'Yet, I do also firmly believe that God does not allow men who do such lowly acts and then to ultimately prosper by them!'

* * *

'She shall not marry any man for her head is always too busily buried in a book!' my ever loving brother Thomas had warned my would-be suitor. 'She shall die an old maid, of that I am certain!'

'Twas a hard sentiment for me to hear said by a loved one, but one that I must be the first to admit was then true. I so loved my books and my studies that I had come to consider any man other than my father and dear brothers as little more than an unwelcome distraction from them. Thankfully, Mister Anthony Hickman would not be so easily dissuaded.

Though he practically lived at my brother's side, and the two were often at our Cheapside house together, I scarcely ever paid Anthony an upward glance; so I never did see his lingering looks towards me. Not, that is, until Thomas shamed me by those blunt remarks.

The Hickmans were also a prominent family amongst the Company of Mercers and equally as staunch in their evangelical Protestant faith as we Lockes were. Therefore, such a match might easily have been expected by my brother. But not by me!

While many other mercers dressed themselves like vibrant peacocks, Mister Hickman, like us, preferred not to over adorn his person with ostentatious shows of the trappings of wealth. To the contrary, Anthony was a modest and quiet man but with an unshakable strength of character, and he was tall, thin, slender-faced and well above ten years older than I was. His eyes were like the sea; blue-grey and yet never stormy. No matter how hard-pressed he might be by others, Anthony's temperament was always calm – no matter the humour of those cast about him. That, above all, made me love him.

So it came about, after what others might have considered a tortuously long and drawn out attempt at courtship on Anthony's ever patient part, that he eventually somehow persuaded me to take note of him and furthermore agree to be his wife.

We were married on the twenty-eighth day of November, fifteen-hundred-and-forty-three at Saint Mary's Church in Bow, close to both our London homes. I was one month shy of my eighteenth birthday.

Before we even wed, Anthony was worth more than one thousand pounds[35], as my father's auditor confirmed on inspection of his accounts. It was not done on any account of suspicion that my father might have had upon his honesty. On the contrary, my father knew Anthony Hickman extremely well and held him in

---

35   At this time £20 would translate into around £9,000 in modern currency rates at the point of writing.

high esteem. And my brother, Thomas, even more so, because they were merchant adventurers in partnership together and as close in friendship as any natural born brothers might hope to be. No, Anthony Hickman did not have to subject his business dealing and his wealth to so close a scrutiny, but he wanted to all the same; for he was a man of integrity who needed to prove to my father that here was a man both honest and worthy of his daughter's hand.

Yet for all of this I could sense my father, at first, holding back a pace. For as I believe, he thought me worthy of a man of title, which my dearest Anthony lacked. To me this was but a trifle, yet something which others might have held against Anthony by way of him being an unequal match in status for noble William Locke's daughter. Nonetheless, my father, with gentle persuasion, soon gave his permission.

With God's great blessings, our joint Locke and Hickman family enterprise flourished and my husband and brother grew increasingly wealthy and famed for their trading exploits. Why, Mister Richard Hakluyt has even written of it in the second printed volume of his 'English Voyages' which my brother, Michael, helped to edit.

Anthony and Thomas owned many ships of their own, and I remember one in particular with pride and great fondness. They had this especially built and completely financed by themselves, and in honour of my sister-in-law, Mary, and of me, they named her the 'Mary Rose'. 'Twas such a very fine ship indeed and one that would take part in many a daring voyage.

*   *   *

Now let me tell you a little about the history of my family's and the country's trade during these times. When my father was born, the New World had not even been discovered. However, being an island race, we English had traded extensively with Europe since as far back as the beginning of England itself. Content with that, we further explored very little.

Meanwhile, in the time of King Henry's father, the Portuguese, after decades of creeping ever southward along the coast of Africa, had suddenly forged their way eastwards around the Cape of Good Hope – with the ambition of reaching the East Indies and Cathay. Like-minded for expansion of trade routes, Columbus led the Spaniards westwards in the hope of finding another root to the same ends.

But what about us English? Stirred by the excitement of this geographical renaissance, some of our merchants seemed eager to take on a similar enterprise. So led by Venetian John Cabot, an English band of explorers began to search for a 'North-West Passage' to Cathay – which resulted in Cabot reaching north of the New World. But, incredibly, when he had, no one even bothered to chronicle the details of his voyages – which therefore slipped from minds for many years.

At first King Henry VIII was keen also for such exploration, but in fifteen-hundred-and-twenty-one, when he suggested that our London mercers should finance a national effort, they strongly resisted. Our merchants argued: why should we – who already had enough trading partners through the Habsburg[36] Alliance willing to take our goods – throw away money into scouring the world for new trade routes? Besides, Henry was bound by politics, because he was then still married to Katherine of Aragon. An aggrieved Spain might retaliate by impeding our existing and lucrative European business. Therefore when His Majesty's interest for further exploration waned, so did that in the rest of the realm. For an entire generation, England let slip these opportunities.

Until then, our English economy had mainly rested upon our exports of wool and cloth with our principle markets being the German princedoms, Spain, and the Netherlanders. Thus based upon permanent mutual interests, King Henry's father had made sound and enduring commercial treaties with both Spain and

---

36   The Habsburgs were the dominant ruling house of Europe, who at one time held influence over Spain, Austria, the Low Countries, and parts of Italy and Germany amongst others.

the Netherlands. Later, when the King of Spain also became Emperor of the Netherlands and overlord of the Germans too, the dynamics of this arrangement seriously altered. However, so long as we stayed in favour with Spain, then our lucrative mercers' markets were safe.

Soon the vast amount of New World wealth beginning to pour into Spanish hands started to affect the trade of all European countries, not least England. So that by the time King Henry split with Rome, English relations with the Habsburg states were already cooling – resulting in costs rising and old contracts coming to an end.

Catholic Spain supported the Pope and hated what the Roman Catholics considered King Henry's heresy. Of a sudden, any of our traders who found themselves in Spanish territory were treated as hostiles and subject to persecution by the Inquisition. Though relationships were patched up for a time, it spelled out a warning of much yet to come.

Coupled with this, there was a real fear that England would have to go to war to fight for her newly acquired independence from Rome. Rumour spread about London that Spain and France had already discussed the possibility of invading the country and forcibly restoring it to Papal rule.

King Henry was able to buy off the Spanish Emperor, but as a result of continued worries, His Majesty spent what seemed to be a ruinous sum of money on strengthening his navy and the general defence of the realm. But that navy served him well, for in the year that Anthony and I married an invasion by the French was foiled. However, this brief state of war brought King Henry to the brink of bankruptcy and reduced him to debasing the coinage.

When English privateers began to raid ships of the now neutral Spanish and Lowlander flags in search of French enemy goods, the Emperor retaliated immediately. In fifteen - hundred - and - forty - five, he arrested all of our merchants in Spain and the

Netherlands and prohibited us mercers from trading for more than a year. When this situation ended, many of our merchants had lost property and many a good City trader faced ruin, whilst our Catholic Hanse[37] competitors were firmly advantaged.

Yet to men of vision, like my brothers, John, Michael, Thomas, and my husband Anthony, even this, the bleakest of prospects offered hope. While the future of our trade with Europe looked to be in decline, on the horizon they beckoned brightly. Russia, Africa and Asia; all were calling, and were about to be answered by our English adventurers...

*   *   *

Over the coming years, we Lockes and Hickmans would be made to suffer for our Protestant faith in many ways and upon many levels. At times this would be through open persecution by the monarch and at others by covert censure, through private letters of State or discussions held behind the closed doors of power. Yet, by the route I am about tell, is the most heinous torment of all; to make an innocent youth suffer unto death by the use of the simple word 'no'.

I had heard so many tales emanating from court to understand fully the evils that lust can do. Yet I know now through bitter experience all about the equal cruelty that 'romantic love' may also inflict.

My dear, sweet brother, Edmund, was so gentle a young fellow as ever a person might hope to meet. He was kind and honest and his heart and mind pure and faithful. Yet he died of his love for another.

I shall not name the object of his affection, for although now long dead, I know that she hath issue still living. And besides, she had no choice in the rejection of my brother Edmund's suit. No, for that and his death I lay the blame firmly at the door of her father.

She was the daughter of Sir Bryan Tuke, first secretary to Cardinal Wolsey, then Foreign Secretary to

---

37   Hanse -The Hanseatic League- an alliance of trading cities that maintained a monopoly along the coast of Northern Europe.

King Henry, treasurer to the King's Chamber and Clerk to the Signet and sometimes Ambassador to France. He was a man of power and considered very learned amongst his peers and highly commended for his great eloquence of both tongue and pen. And yet for all his fine words dripping from his quill, he had no heart at all.

Mayhap if his beloved wife, Dame Grissel, had still been alive then, she might have been able to talk her husband around to the match between her daughter and my brother. For I understand that she was much swayed towards our family's stance on religion and her husband much influenced by her opinion. However, she died about a year after my mother, and in the wake of her particular loss a great bitterness had eaten into Sir Bryan's soul.

I feel that I should explain here that many at court, and even more so throughout the country as whole, did not share my father's fervour for the Protestant faith. Over the preceding centuries, many a fine upstanding Catholic Englishman had founded chantries or endowed churches and other such holy houses with gifts of land or money, yet all the while hating the clergy themselves. Most hated of all were those foreign members of the clergy, especially any who held high influence in our English Church and had been foisted upon it by appointment from Rome.

Therefore there were many at King Henry's court who, although conservative in their doctrine, wanted to see reform in the jurisdiction of the Church by Rome and had therefore supported Henry in his Act of Supremacy. Many even helped him in the dissolution of the monasteries and in confiscating property, and yet curiously had never considered themselves to be set upon the road to Protestantism.

When Edmund first went to my father in the spring of fifteen-hundred-and-forty-five and told him that he and Sir Bryan's daughter had fallen in love, Father willingly agreed to act to broker a marriage between the two. But the girl's father would not hear of it. Instead, Sir Bryan flatly told my father that he would never allow any daughter or son of his to marry a Locke. Our wealth and position counted for nothing, for in his opinion it was far outweighed by the deficit of our radical Protestantism.

'You and those like you are the root of all the ill of this country', he had told my father bluntly. 'I would rather sell my daughter's soul to the devil than have her marry a Locke!'

Alerted now to the feelings of love between his daughter and my brother Edmund, Sir Bryan took active steps to impede the young couple from meeting again, or for my brother even to catch a glimpse of the daughter.

But even after this abrupt and cruel deprivation of his first and only true love, Edmund refused to give up hope that, one day, Sir Bryan might relent and give his blessing to their union. Then, when news suddenly came that his beloved was to be married to another man, Edmund took to his bed.

Day by day, week by week, we his family could do nothing to ease his heartbreak except to watch as he waned into but a shadow of his former self as he pined away for the love of this girl.

My father blamed himself. Clearly, Edmund was being punished for that which Sir Bryan perceived to be my father's own personal 'sin' and not for any of his 'innocent' son.

When Edmund subsequently died, I do not think that Father ever came to terms with his most needless death. He had lost many children in childhood, and that is hard enough for any parent to bear. Yet how much greater must the anguish be while, after watching a son grow to manhood, only then to watch him being struck down and broken by another man's hatred? And then to stand utterly helpless as that son wills himself into the grave, when instead he might have so soon married to raise a family of his own.

In the October of that very same year, Sir Bryan Tuke also died. Scant consolation for us Lockes still grieving for our own tragic loss. [38]

Chapter Nine

Although the King had rent away so violently and with much bitterness from Rome, my father feared that deep within Henry still beat a Catholic heart. His Church was now Protestant and he was at its head, but Henry was set in his manner of belief and would hear no more of radical change. My father knew that, for this to come about, the old King must first pass out of this world, and so Father was also resigned to the fact that in all probability he would most likely not live to see it happen.

'What do I care if, like Moses, I am destined to stand on the threshold of the Promised Land but be denied to cross over? So long as my children may enter in, then my struggle to get them there is reward enough.'

Not long afterwards, King Henry married for a sixth and last time – to a lady several times married and widowed. Katherine Parr had not accepted His Majesty's proposal in the hope of great gain by way of either wealth or position. Instead she had agreed to be his wife because she was a good Protestant woman who believed that in doing so she was obeying God's will. Perhaps she believed that she, a Christian mother figure, had been brought to such a position in order to nurture the young heir to the throne, Prince Edward. Whatever the motivation of Their Majesties, my father said that Henry had at last appeared to have found much comfort in this marriage during his final years.

*   *   *

On the sixth day of January, fifteen-hundred-and-forty-seven, my first child, Mary, was baptised at Saint Olave Church close to our home at Cheapside. As day by day this precious new life cradled in my arms grew from strength to strength, elsewhere King Henry's was slowly ebbing away. Despite Queen Katherine's diligent care, he had by then been in poor health for quite some time.

As a gentleman of the Privy Chamber, it had been one of my father's last duties to his sovereign to be amongst those few chosen to wait upon His Majesty in those last drawn out hours of his agony.

For eight days Henry had been confined to bed, slouched upon a great pile of feather bolsters and cushions. He was by that time so weak that he could not even raise his hand to lift a cup to his lips; nor to use the commode for his own relief. Instead, he lay upon a draw sheet with a swathe of linen about his loins like a large, obese, incontinent infant. The stench in the room was overpowering; not merely of stale urine and faeces, which on its own, as part of the sick-room and of the natural process of dying, would have been both tolerable and accepted. No, this stench was of rotting flesh and puss – as the multitude of abbesses upon His Majesty's legs and thighs burst forth to leak their putrid contents out into an already rank humour.

At one point during the day before he died, Father said that previously sleeping Henry's eyes suddenly opened and, with a start, His Majesty frantically began calling out for Thomas Cromwell to come to his aid. When the King was gently told that Cromwell had been dead these past six years, he seemed much grieved – as if he had not known, or struck again by remorse – and a tear trickled down his cheek.

Shortly after, Henry refused all attempts to part his lips for the letting by of a little broth on a spoon. His once piercing eyes began to grow increasingly glassy and dimmed as, at last, the will to linger on began to give him up in favour of what might have seemed for him to be the beckoning comfort of death. Or was it deepening despair – as he approached judgement by the eternal King of kings? Whatever Henry's thoughts, from that time forth all who were present knew it was but a question of hours until he was dead.

Faithful Cranmer sat at the bedside and held King Henry's hand during his final moments. Instead of administering the Papist last rites, the Archbishop gave His Majesty a reformed statement of faith, thus making certain that the King died, for all to witness, as a true Protestant.

From the day of Henry's death, Thomas Cranmer never shaved again. Instead, he grew a flowing white beard as both a sign of his mourning for the late King and as an outward token of his own break with the past and the Church of old. With the death of King Henry the time had come for the long awaited birth of change.

My family were among the few entrusted with the knowledge of the gravity of the King's final illness and his subsequent death. It had been thought best to keep it hushed until a few, last straggling loose ends could be tidied away so as not to hinder the incoming King Edward and the regent that Henry had chosen to watch over his son. Among these wayward threads that should have been cut had been the Duke of Norfolk. In accordance with King Henry's wishes, he had already been scheduled to be put to death the day after the King died. But, against Henry's wishes, he was consigned to life imprisonment in the Tower instead.

The King's funeral was as magnificent as one might have expected for a monarch of his standing, and once again my father played a prominent role when the Gentlemen of the Privy Chamber became Henry's guard of honour.

His Majesty's oversized coffin was drawn upon a chariot covered with palls of deep, blue velvet and cloth of gold. Atop of this, a life sized waxen effigy of the King lay recumbent; bejewelled, crowned and dressed in red crimson trimmed with ermine. In effigy, the King retained every last drop of menace in death as he had done in life.

From London to Windsor, along the route of funeral procession the roads were swept clean in readiness for his passing, and in some cases, even widened.

My Father recounted the most gruesome of all his anecdotes: 'With the daylight drawing short, the King's coffin was rested at Syon. During the night it burst open with the nauseas gases given off by His

Majesty's unusually swift decomposition. When the royal guards returned at day-break, they had to fight off the stray dogs scavenging at the royal remains.'

I winced at the awful image conjured up in my mind's eye.

'Remember,' Father warned, 'even a man bedecked in gold and jewels and such splendour, goes to his grave with nothing... unless he is what our Lord termed as "born again", having accepted with his heart the undeserved love and forgiveness offered to us by the crucified Lord Jesus Christ. In the Bible such a person is referred to as a "saint" – that is a sinner saved by grace.'

Two days after Henry died, Cranmer sat amongst the executors of King Henry's last will and testament. In it, Edward Seymour had been named by the late King as Lord Protector and regent of the new boy King. To many it must have seemed only fitting that Seymour had been elevated to this most trusted position; for surely as the boys own uncle, he would see to it that he served only the very best interests of his own dead sister's son?

There was also some fear in my family that he might try to persuade the country back towards Catholicism. But to our relief, and to the distaste of the then majority in the country, under Seymour's lead, King Edward's government became truly Protestant. We reformers, who were once hidden away in the shadows, were now destined to become a part of the establishment. At last, my generation with its zeal for change and the energy to exert upon that end came into its own. With the new King and his Lord Protector, we could at last start to reshape the Church towards a 'purer', more Bible-based, form of Christianity that Christ could now recognise.

We asked not for the impossible or, to our minds, for anything unreasonable or radical. Instead we wanted to forgo such as the signing of the cross over babies brought forward for baptism and other superfluous rituals that could not be found in the Bible, like the habit of bowing at the mention of Jesus' name or the use of a ring in the marriage service – all of which we considered Popery. Nor could we tolerate the pressure exerted upon ministers to wear the hated cap and surplus that set apart the shepherd from his flock. For our Lord Jesus had established a new order under a new covenant – by which we are all called to love one another as He has loved us, within the context of the Scripture-based 'royal priesthood' of every believer ministry. We also desired a sermon to be said whenever communion was administered; for we believed that preaching was the bedrock of our ministry. We asked only for the Old and New Testaments to be read in Churches, and not the highly questionable Apocryphal books – that the Roman Catholic Church had inserted between the two – of which many were still used by the Papists. Above all else, we asked for the Sabbath or the 'Lord's Day' to be kept holy.

As a result of a royal visitation of the provinces that summer, every parish visited was instructed upon the new and simplified style of service and, to that end, ordered to obtain the book Homilies, partly written by Cranmer himself. At last, in England, the Church began to be reformed in earnest. Praise God that my father had outlived King Henry to see the realm opening to bright new possibilities. For from this he was to take his greatest comfort in the final stages of his life.

Meanwhile, on the Continent, our fellow Protestants were once again facing the cruel hand of persecution by the Papist Spanish. Archbishop Cranmer sent out word to their leaders that England was both willing and able to shelter them. He even promised positions in English universities so that they might, in return, instruct a whole new generation of English preachers and help to assist in the on-going reformation of our Anglican Church's liturgy and doctrine. And so it was that for a few years at least, England became the major safe haven for persecuted Protestants. It was the chance at last for our leading English reformers to meet face to face with their European counterparts after, in some cases, more than a decade of correspondence.

Just before Christmas in fifteen-hundred-and-forty-eight, Archbishop Cranmer publicly abandoned the doctrine of Real Presence – by announcing that he believed that the Eucharistic presence was one in spirit only. 'Beads, pardons, pilgrimages, and such other like Popery,' Cranmer declared, were 'as weeds, but the roots of the weeds were transubstantiation, the Real Presence, and the sacrificial nature of the mass.' At first I could not understand why Father and so many like-minded people would find even such sagacious words so defining, but then he explained them to me.

'The Lord Jesus used the images of bread and wine to show his followers that his ripped flesh and shed blood were given, as it is written, "for you", that is us,' he said. 'This means that our Lord's self-sacrifice bore the judgement that was upon all mankind. And so by instructing his followers to re-enact the taking of bread and wine "in remembrance of me" as recorded in Luke 22:19, He was establishing the Eucharist, the Breaking of Bread, the Lord's Supper, the Mass, whatever we elect to call it, as a regular reminder of God's greatest deliverance.

'So our friend Cranmer is confirming the facts,' Father continued. 'He is reminding us that the Eucharist is nothing more than a re-enactment. God's presence is not found within the bread and wine, which remain simply bread and wine and nothing more. Yet these serve as a vivid reminder of two facts: firstly, that forgiveness is given to those who choose to receive it; and secondly, this "forgiveness of sin" under the new covenant was given once and for all at the most awesome cost. It was paid for by the body and blood of God Himself, and not simply by the token sacrifice of animals presented under the old covenant of the Old Testament.'

Father always had his own special ability to make difficult concepts easy for others to understand. Little did I realise that his teaching and nurture of my young and impressionable mind would be woven into a tapestry of events that would impact the lives of men and women who eventually changed the course of history.

After Christmas, the publication of the Prayer Book was backed by Parliament and the Act of Uniformity. Then, the most far reaching change to directly affect our Protestant clergy was announced; the legalisation of clerical marriage. At long last Archbishop Cranmer could officially recognise his wife and family!

In the summer of the following year, the use of the new Prayer Book was made compulsory. It triggered a wave of protest and rebellion in the West Country that travelled around the realm like a storm surge. The rebels demanded the return to the use of Latin for masses and that communion bread be given only to the laity. They also wanted prayers for souls in purgatory to be reinstated; a place between heaven and hell that is not even mentioned in the Bible and so no longer acknowledged as existing by the new Church. Also for the Six Articles to be restored and for the dissolved abbeys to be rebuilt.

Archbishop Cranmer commandeered St Paul's Cathedral and we Protestants went, en masse, to support him as he preached vehemently in defence of the reformed Church and denounced the rebellion as wickedness. The effect of the rebellion brought trouble to Lord Regent Edward Seymour. The Privy Council split and the majority fell behind John Dudley, the first Duke of Northumberland. Seymour was at sent to The Tower, yet despite the religiously conservative supporters of Northumberland, our reformers were somehow able to maintain control of the Government and continue our good works. By the following spring, Seymour was released and returned to the Privy Council. Cranmer was able to transfer his former chaplain, Nicholas Ridley, to London for support, and then incumbent conservative clergy were quietly uprooted and disbursed away from causing him harm.

Yet for all his goods works, many of us zealous Protestants were somewhat disappointed in Archbishop Bishop Cranmer. The Prayer Book, though by his own admission but a starting point for further revision, was still to our mind not 'purified' enough in its intentions. And then there was Cranmer's continued stubbornness when it came to the question of one item that we still found most offensive to our way of thinking and yet which he insisted upon upholding; the issue of vestments.

When John Hooper, a zealous Protestant preacher much admired by us, was selected by the Privy Council for the post of Bishop of Gloucester, matters swiftly came to a head. Hooper said quite boldly that he would accept the bishopric only on the condition that he would not be required to wear the customary richly adorned attire of a bishop. Hooper was just one among many Reformist clergy, backed up by Continental reformers, who was unhappy with the new Prayer Book and who objected particularly to superfluous acts of ceremony and, non-biblical 'Papist' vestments. Cranmer believed that this would be seen as a step too far and too soon ever to be accepted by the Conservative elements amongst his Church. He had thus far trod amongst these brethren carefully in order to keep reigned in. The Archbishop knew too well that if his program of reforms was to be maintained, then he could not afford to have his authority openly challenged in this way. One hint of infighting amongst the Reformers could be seized upon by his opponents and exploited to their own ends. So Cranmer had no choice other than to remove Hooper from circulation – by sending him to prison to cool his heels for a while. For the better good, Hooper gave in, was duly consecrated and preached before King Edward complete with his full vestments. Hooper's zealous forwardness, however, would not be forgotten. For there were those on hand already marking out this man for some not too distant attention.

However, dissent from amongst his own reformers and from without by the conservatives were not the only obstacle with which Cranmer now had to contend. The change of Regent for young King Edward was to prove to be one for ill: not only for the realm but also the good of our cause...

*   *   *

He was ever the constant in our, his children's, lives. He was the star by which we all guided our ships, the friendly harbour to which we, not withstanding how long or far we had journeyed, could weary come home to and safely drop anchor. Some said that my father was a difficult man and strict with his children. I prefer to say that he was firm with us. For does not the proverb say that to spare the rod is to spoil the child? And at least in my Father's case, the rod was only ever metaphorical, as it is in the Bible when understood in context. For the shepherds of the Holy Land only used their pastoral rods to gently prod and guide the flock in their care. Never would they actually beat their sheep.

I am grateful that for the greater part of the spring and summer of fifteen-forty-nine I was able to stay close to my father in London. As I was pregnant again, I chose to spend my seclusion at his house in Bow under the watchful care of his forth wife, Elizabeth, whom I fondly came to call 'Mother Bessie.'

Father had been unwell during the greater part of the proceeding winter and so had already relinquished much of the day-to-day running of his London business to the more able members of our extended family. Anthony was away several times across the sea, and so I was able to spend many an hour with my father and listen to him as he reminisced about the past and spoke hopefully about the future. Much of what he shared with me, I have been able to set down in these memoirs, whilst other things, those of a more personal nature, I have kept to mine own counsel.

Being with my father made my pregnancy all the much easier to bear, for he gave me such words of kind encouragement and support, as I imagine he must have given my own mother so many years before. It was then that I began to see Father in a completely new light.

He may have seemed hardly ever to have been at home throughout my childhood, yet from those little intimate moments that he started to related to me, I suddenly began to realise how deeply he had been involved in our rearing, and how close he had been to both my mother and his earlier wife. He told me poignant tales about the dead siblings I had never known, and of course about Alice and my mother. It was not, I sensed, as if he was in some way trying to unburden himself, but rather that he recognised that the time had come for him to open his heart about all things to me – as not only a daughter but as a woman and his special confidant. Maybe he knew even then that his life was running fast towards its close.

Father was beside himself with joy when I eventually gave birth to a son in mid June, and named him William in his honour. For truth, he already had so many other grandchildren, yet nonetheless took such delight in this my firstborn son. He accompanied Anthony and me when we took the baby for baptism.

To the north of Cheapside market, in Ironmonger Lane, dozens of metal workers clatter away, both by day and by night, in a mass of little workshops cramped into it and leading off into a maze of tiny alleyways . Abutting the Lane, and almost lost amongst the din, is the Norman church of Saint Olave in Old Jewry. It is but a short step away from where Anthony and I once lived. At that time the minister was a true Protestant much in the same manner as we were, and so this is where we brought our precious child to be received into God's Church with my proud Father looking on.

He had so much to endure during the final months of his life. Even a fool could see that he was in great discomfort, and yet he made no complaint and neither did he lose his grace nor his dignity in the face of it, and his intense interest in the lives of his children and how we fared did not wane either.

'You are my daughter Rose,' he said, when he became increasingly ill the spring before his death. 'Level-headed Rose,' he smiled, 'You are so much like me and in so many ways. So much so than even any of my sons. You are made of strong stuff, My Rose. Strong stuff indeed!'

I had always believed that my brothers had meant so much more to him than I did. For what was I other than a dutiful daughter without even the power to carry on the Locke name? So my father's words stayed with me, and still stay, deep in my heart like a treasure.

Then without warning, he suddenly went straight to the heart of the matter preying upon his lips.

'No tears now when I tell you this... but I know that I am dying. My doctors tell me so and this I must accept. No tears Rose,' he said, gently taking my hand. 'Nor do I want you to cry and fret about my bedside when I am at my last. And after... after I am dead, Rose, I will have need of someone to stand in my stead. Someone to see to it that I am buried as I desire, without fuss or pomp. And no mourning gowns... 'tis but money wasted that might be put to better use by the poor. After... your brothers and sisters will have need of your strength, Rose... especially your step-mother and little Elizabeth... for she is still so very young...'

'Do the others...' But he did not let me finish my question.

'No...I have not told them yet, Rose...' he continued falteringly, with eyes lowered. But on raising them once more to meet with mine he added, 'But I will... and soon.'

I held on fast to my emotion. I had been dreading hearing him say this and yet, if I am honest, I had long suspected his decline, though he had bravely striven to keep it from us. In a strange way, it was a relief to now have this out in the open between us.

'I understand,' I replied resolutely. 'No fuss, Father... I promise.'

'Good. Then we have an understanding?'

I nodded that we had and he placed his hand gently upon my head and, smiling, patted it, as he used to do so when I was young and my mother was alive.

'I am not afraid to die, Rose. I have your Mother

to thank for that. When I came home to hear that she had died after enduring such agonies, I felt very angry at God for taking her away, and angry at myself for not being there. I felt cheated, for she had struggled so bravely to do His bidding and yet He had let it end like that. But then, when the servants, and then you, told me that your mother had seen Christ beckoning her to come to Him, then I knew... I knew that we have nothing to fear from death anymore because He will be waiting to take us to Himself and, as it is written, "wipe away every tear" at the end. And besides,' he sighed, 'I have been blessed by more years than most, and within that span I have lived enough for a hundred lifetimes. I have travelled to places that some can only dream of, and I have lain down at night never knowing hunger or fearing poverty. Yet, above everything else, I have known that the Lord is ever with me. I have in God's written word the assurance that, when I die, I shall join with Him and with all those I have loved and have passed before me. Tell me, Rose, what have I now to fear of death?'

Father had intended to return to Merton that summer, to see the house there and to visit a while with Thomas and Mary and his grandchildren, but when the time came, he was far too frail and in too much pain to endure the carriage ride. So instead he stayed in the City and endured the stifling heat and stink of that summer closeted away in his house near The Lock.

When I returned in August to go once more into seclusion, I knew that he soon must die, and with each passing day his end inched nearer. And yet when he did die, still I found myself unprepared. It was on the twenty-forth day of August in the fourth year of our sovereign King Edward's reign. After enduring the most stifling of nights at his house in Bow Lane, when none in the City could sleep for the heat, around mid-morning Father had retired to his bed once more and nodded off to sleep. When Maggie went to wake him to take him a little something to eat, she found him already dead and at his peace. Without death-bed farewells or sad laments, he had quietly departed from this world just as he had desired. He had out-lived three of his wives and most of his twenty children, and he had lived to see a large scattering of grandchildren in whose delightfulness he had revelled, especially my son and his namesake, William.

Three days later, as he had stipulated in his last will and testimony, he was buried in the Mercer's Chapel beside his parents and his first wife. Being a Christian in deed as well as word, he left a large sum of money to charity and with no small irony, a goodly amount towards the upkeep of the inmates at The Fleet and four other prisons in London. He also left alms to the poor of Merton, Wimbledon, Tooting and Tottenham and money to other needy people.

To my five surviving brothers, Thomas, Matthew, John, Henry and Michael, he left all of his London houses and The Lock, which hoped they would continue in partnership together and to trade in his name as a family concern. And to Thomas he also left his lands at Merton and Wimbledon, with the exception of a small farm for which he left for my youngest brothers Michael and Henry. He also made provision for the future marriage of my youngest sister, Elizabeth, and the care and upkeep of his fourth wife and widow, Mother Bessie.

In December, I gave birth to another son, Henry. Within a year, Mother Bessie had followed my father to the presence of our Lord, leaving me, at the age of just twenty-five, the unwilling matriarch of our remaining family.

William Locke was dead, but in us, his progeny, his spirit lived on. And we made it our avowed intent to make certain that England had not heard the last of the name of Locke.

Chapter Ten

The year following my father's death brought an unwelcome shift in the delicate balance of power at court. Archbishop's Cranmer's influence began to wane as did the one-time Regent, Seymour's. In the October, Seymour was arrested once more on charges of treason. These were subsequently dropped but he was instead hastily found guilty of a felony and quickly executed.

Soon afterwards, the rift between Cranmer and Northumberland began to open, not least in the light of the increasing amount of ecclesiastical property being misappropriated by the Regent for his own use. None the less, the Archbishop continued relentlessly with his program of church reforms, and concentrated upon the long over due revision of the canon law. However, when it was completed and presented to be passed into law by an Act of Parliament, Northumberland effectively killed it. Cranmer then completed his work upon a revised version of the Book of Prayer, but again was so hampered by Northumberland's last-minute interventions that it was almost not printed in time for its compulsory use under the new Act of Uniformity passed that year. The next spring, and with Cranmer's draft of 'Forty-Two-Articles' now almost ready for publication, at last the arduous battle to complete the reform of our Church was almost done. We had won.

In his lifetime, Thomas Cromwell had successfully brought about the dissolution of the great and very wealthy religious houses of England. Had he not, then the Pope would have maintained a meddling hand upon our people as we moved towards reform.

Almost a quarter of all monastic wealth had come from 'spiritual income', whereby these religious houses had appropriated parish tithes by holding the advowson of a benefice. In return the monastery was legally obligated to care for parishioners either by endowing a vicar or supplying a stipendiary priest. It was these advowsons that King Edward's regents began to sell off.

At Merton, the Abbey had been dissolved and much of the fabric of the buildings stripped away and sold off to be used in constructing new houses. On the fourteenth of March, fifteen-hundred-and-fifty-three, in the name of King Edward, his regent sold the advowson of St Mary's Church to my brother Thomas and his wife Mary, and thereby granted the rectory of Merton to them and their heirs forever. At last, the Locke family became benefactors of our own Church, which meant that we had it within our will to appoint whichever clergy Thomas and Mary saw fit to serve at St Mary's. More than that, Thomas would act as its lay rector and his wife, Mary, as an able and at times fiery lay preacher.

All now seemed fit for us to complete God's work with our own hands and to carry out His will for our Church. I cannot here tell you in mere words how joyously happy my family and friends were at that time. Those of my father's generation, who had heard and then heeded God's word, had dedicated their lives to fulfilling the reformation of the Church gone astray. We, the next generation, had faithfully taken up the challenges that they had first faced and now seen them through. Yet how were we to know that, instead of growing closer to a heaven on earth, we were living in nought but a fool's paradise?

I had suffered a miscarriage a year or so after Anthony and I first married. I was young and so full of hope for this new life growing within me, just as those about me were as we neared the spiritual quickening of our Protestant Church in England.

I knew, of course, that when I married, pregnancy would surly follow. And though Maggie spoke often to prepare me for that event, I never truly knew what it would be like till I had experienced it for myself. At first I felt somewhat ill, and then sick to my stomach as the changes I felt came too quick and too soon for my liking. And yet there was nothing that I could do now that seed had been planted. Then, when the sickness passed, day by day, I could feel the stirring within me grow stronger and my whole demeanour began to change. I became accepting of my situation, knowing that I was now wholly committed to seeing it through its' natural course.

How I had planned for the future of that child! How I would love it and cherish its' coming into being! Yet it was not to come to term. One day in the fifth month I could not feel it make shift any more. Three days later I was suddenly taken by such a gripe that I thought I was about to die. Maggie took me to bed and ne'er left my side until the tiny half-formed creature was still-born. I was beside myself with grief.

'But I wanted it so much,' I wailed to Maggie as she took the tiny body away.

'Aye, I know, but mayhap you wanted it too much and afore you were truly ready,' she said. 'It was but half-made, my lady. It was not meant to be. Not now. That is all. This was not meant be – not this time.' Then she tried to gently reassure me. 'But soon. You mark my words, my Lady Rose. Next time, when the time is right then all will be well...'

Not this time. And as with that baby, our but half-reformed Church was about to be lost.

When Anthony came home all of a rush to tell me the dread news of the King that day, I could not help but bust into tears. That poor boy was dead at only sixteen years of age. Yet there was worse. Anthony said that that an undertaker often used by the Mercers had told him with considerable conviction, that the King's nightly spitting up of blood – evident upon His Majesty's bedclothes – were not from consumption, as the Duke of Northumberland would have it. They were indeed a sure sign of a slow and prolonged poisoning. But when pressed upon the matter of how he came about this knowledge, the undertaker would not be drawn further, only saying that for his own protection and the protection of others, Anthony should forget what he had already said. But he added, 'I hope the bastards who had done it will rot in hell!'

Not long after that, word came demanding that Anthony go straight away to attend upon the Duke of

Northumberland. He lost no time in doing so, yet leaving us both to fear that something very grave was about to befall us all. As my husband walked from our house, I had such a sickness come into my stomach, with the thought that my children and I might never see him again.

But to my utter relief, Anthony did return, though not until after some hours had passed. What he had to report was disturbing. Apparently, as far back as the preceding June, King Edward had made his will after being informed by Northumberland that he was dying of consumption. In the will, Edward had been persuaded to name his young cousin, the Lady Jayne Grey as his heir, expressly in contravention of the third Act of Succession.

Archbishop Cranmer, being much perplexed by this radical change to the order of succession, had tried to speak with Edward alone to make certain in his own mind that the young King was not acting under any duress. But he was refused a private audience, and so instead had to ask the King this question in the presence of his councillors. Edward replied with his own lips that he supported all he had written in his will. On hearing this, Cranmer could do no other than to verify and uphold this, His Majesty's dying wishes.

Meanwhile, the law continued to regard both Mary and Elizabeth as bastards. Henry VIII's own last will declared that, should none of his heirs leave heirs of their own, the crown of England should then pass to the descendants of his sister, Mary Tudor, Queen of France. The same will also expressly excluded the descendants of his older sister, Margaret, from succession – for fear of the Crown of England falling into the hands of the Scots, and so also preventing any person 'foreign born' from likewise succeeding to it.

'Lady Jayne is a descendant of Henry's favoured sister and cousin to the late King,' Anthony explained. 'And more importantly, she is Protestant.'

'Protestant or not, Anthony,' I ventured, 'how can we be certain that this succession is God's true will? Is not Lady Jayne also newly married to Northumberland's son and therefore naught but the Lord Protector's puppet?' I was not convinced that this was as it should be.

'That may be so,' Anthony continued, 'but none the less, Edward's signature was upon the documents, and by royal decree Archbishop Cranmer had already convened the Convocation to recognise the new succession.'

Cranmer? I thought to myself. If the Archbishop supported the new succession then I had every faith in him that it must be right. Yet it still beggared a nagging question, why had Northumberland summoned my husband? And many other questions made my head swim.

'And what did Northumberland want of you?' I asked.

'Powder,' Anthony replied slowly. 'He wanted me to go about the mercers urgently to arrange a supply of gunpowder, and a good quantity of it, to be sent immediately to the Tower.'

'But why? What does he want with gun powder?'

'It looks as if he is drawing together an army. As I was leaving, I saw guns of every size and description beginning to be stock-piled in the Tower. And that is not all. The Constable of the Tower has been dismissed, and in his place the Lord Admiral has instead been sworn in.'

The next day, all of the head officers and the royal guards were made to swear an oath of allegiance to Lady Jayne as if she were already the Queen of England. Then, on the day after that, preparations were made to swiftly see that presumption become fact. At around five or six o'clock in the evening, accompanied by a great rally of gunshot echoing up and down the City, the trembling fifteen-year-old Lady Jayne was received into the Tower of London with a great company of supporting lords and ladies. And then the Crown Jewels were delivered to the increasingly wary Jayne.

I watched from my window as, with trumpets

blowing, two heralds made their way up Cheapside and stopped at the Standard. There they proclaimed that the expected heir, Lady Mary, was unlawfully begotten and so in consequence Lady Jayne was now come to crown as Queen of England. It caused near riot. Especially after one young man immediately jumped up and declared that this was an evil act, because Lady Mary was the rightful heir to her father King Henry's throne, and not this upstart of Northumberland's. The next morning that same young man was put in a pillory by the Cheapside Standard and his ears were cut off for having dared to speak out. And there were other wicked reprisals, including mutilations and drownings meted out to other transgressors.

When news spilled out from the City of London of what was afoot, feeling on all sides began to rise to fever pitch. Soon reports came flooding across London of riots breaking out all over the country, especially in the provinces and the very heartland of those who had supported the uprisings of King Henry's time. Everywhere feelings began to rise to fever pitch.

In a game of chess, to protect the White Queen one must make strives to annihilate the Black. So it was with Northumberland's most dangerous game of chance. To make certain that Queen Jayne's succession succeeded, Northumberland now desperately needed to capture Lady Mary before she could gather enough support to overthrow Queen Jayne.

On the twelfth night of July, Anthony reported that three cartloads of weaponry had been received into the Tower, including guns, cannons, bills, pikes and powder – everything needed to supply a great number of men rumoured to be gathering close to Cambridge. Two days later, Northumberland and a great many knights and lords, gunners and guards left London to meet with this make-shift army for the sole purpose of going after the Lady Mary and to destroy her.

The threat of a bloody civil war terrified us and every one else within the City. So much so, that in the wake of Northumberland's hurried departure, fear itself began to reign supreme. Yet there was even greater fear amongst my family and friends than that of civil war. It was the fear of Northumberland's defeat, for if Northumberland failed and Lady Mary succeeded in overturning Queen Jayne, then the days of us English Protestants were numbered.

Then dread news came that the royal fleet had mutinied against Northumberland and instead openly declared their allegiance for the Lady Mary. Northumberland was never a popular man whilst in London, and so with his being far removed and unable to threaten the Privy Council, it could act on its own accord. In fear of their own lives, some members, including Winchester, swiftly deserted the new Queen and called instead for the arrest of Northumberland in 'Queen Mary's' name.

It was afterwards recalled that when Queen Jayne was informed that she had lost her throne, she let out a deep sigh of relief and quite naively asked her mother if she might now go home. Instead, when Lady Mary marched unopposed into London to claim her father's crown, Jayne was detained at her cousin's pleasure in the Tower. Northumberland, Jayne's father, the Duke of Suffolk, and the other ring leaders, were all quickly rounded up and imprisoned. And so Jayne's nine-day reign as Queen of England came to an end. She would never know the joys of another summer, or take pleasure in all that any other such like young woman should enjoy.

Meanwhile, as these events unfolded, King Edward's corpse still lay ripening and yet to received a funeral. And so on the eighth day of August, Queen Mary allowed her brother's burial to take place, and in accordance with the rites and procedure of Edward's chosen Protestant faith. The ceremonies were led by the still at liberty Archbishop Cranmer, even though he could by then have easily fled the country to safety. Yet, known by us to be a man of great honour, Cranmer would not desert this, his last duty to the young King.

Not long afterwards, one by one, our reformed

Protestant bishops and clergy were removed from their living as clerics, while those who had past proven themselves to be conservative were allowed to remain in situe. Our most zealous and outspoken Bishop Hooper had been quickly seized and imprisoned before he could speak out in public.

False rumours were then deliberately put abroad that Archbishop Cranmer had authorised the use of the old Latin mass in Canterbury Cathedral. Cranmer struck back immediately – by denouncing the lie in public, adding that 'all the doctrine and religion, by our said sovereign lord King Edward VI is more pure according to God's word than any that hath been used in England these thousand years.'

Mary's new Government naturally took Cranmer's outburst as sedition, and for such he was swiftly sent to Tower of London to keep good company with, amongst others, Hugh Latimer and Nicholas Ridley.

Our dreams and our visions of a Protestant England lay waste like my miscarried child. All we would have left to show for its being would be a blooded bundle of tattered rags. Ready for burning...

Chapter Eleven

I am now compelled to tell you how my good husband and I survived the reign of 'Bloody' Mary, for I have often thought about this turbulent period of my life with great wonder. I never cease to be amazed by the love and mercy God hath shown me in His deliverance of us from the evil of others. As with a lee in the storm, I sheltered in His love while the tempest raged all about – cruelly dashing others upon the rocks of persecution. Yet, by faith – that is believing what God has told us in his written word, the Bible – I have always held true to my trust in Him, no matter how hard the consequence of doing so threatened us otherwise.

Soon after Mary ascended the throne, as I spent my daily 'quiet time' alone with my Lord Jesus in prayer and Bible reading, a passage suddenly struck me, as happens from time to time. 'Mightier than the thunder of the great waters, mightier than the breakers of the sea – the LORD on high is mighty' [39].

'Lord,' I wondered, 'why are you reminding me about this?'

Although by then extremely wealthy, my brother Thomas and my dear husband, Anthony, were not the cut of men who would let mammon rule their heads and blacken their hearts. For they had learned not to trust in such uncertain riches, but instead to place their trust only in the risen and living Lord, who gives all good things to be enjoyed. So they were mindful to employ their good fortune to the glory of God and for the good of His Church. This included funding, sheltering and helping such outstanding Christians as Bishop Hooper, Mister John Foxe, Mister John Knox, and many others of Christ's godly preachers who, if they were still living in our world today, would not forget the brotherly and courageous support they received from Anthony and Thomas.

When Queen Mary came triumphantly to the Crown, she was determined to straight away unpick this seam of heretic Protestantism that was by now

---

39   Psalm 93:4;

sewn into the very fabric of England. However, she was stalled at the start by the scattered debris of Queen Jayne's aborted rule.

Queen Jayne and her husband, Guildford Dudley, were brought to trial in November and found guilty of high treason. Both were duly sentenced to death; Dudley by beheading, but Jayne, in accordance with the prescribed punishment for a woman found guilty of treason, was sentenced to being burned alive in public on Tower Hill. At first, we in London had been given to believe that in Her Majesty's infinite mercy, Queen Mary had realised full well that this young couple had been used but as mere pawns by Northumberland, and so was thereby moved to spare their lives. Thus the captives were confined over winter at Her Majesty's pleasure in the Tower of London, where Mary set about persuading them embrace the Catholic faith. Lady Jayne was in many ways still but a child having only just reached sixteen years of age. Yet child or no, she refused to be pressured by her tormentors into renouncing her Protestant faith.

However, Queen Mary's stance was soon to make shift. January saw a popular rebellion break out, precipitated by Queen Mary's imminent marriage to Catholic Prince Philip of Spain. Many in England were abhorred by the prospect of a foreign marriage – whereby we proud English might become but a province of Habsburg Spain once Prince Philip ascended that throne. And others, even conservatives, had little desire to be once more dominated in religion by the Pope and Rome. Therefore many joined in with this uprising, calling for Jayne's release and the restoration of the English throne to a Protestant monarch.

As a token of great gratitude for his release from such long imprisonment in the Tower, the Duke of Norfolk volunteered to lead the forces sent to put this rebellion down. This he succeeded in doing, but only to die very shortly thereafter.

Although Lady Jayne herself had played no part in these disturbances, Philip pressed Queen Mary to have her beheaded, so that it might serve as an end to her being used as a focus for any possible future unrest. Mary readily complied, though it was quite within her power to deny her Spanish groom. However, when likewise pressured to act against her half-sister Elizabeth, Mary agreed only to her being sent to the Tower instead.

From her rooms in Partridge House at the Tower, Lady Jayne would have witnessed earlier that same morning, the headless body of her young husband being driven back past her window from his public execution on Tower Hill. A little while later she too was brought to slaughter on the scaffold, only she met her death in the relative seclusion of Tower Green. After execution, her slender and lifeless corpse was left where it had fallen by the block, in a pool of congealing blood, for several hours before her cousin the Queen granted permission for its removal. The death of this young woman was to my mind, the most awful of travesties and clear evidence of the ruthlessness of the new regime to come.

With February passed and Queen Jayne and her supporters now excised, it was time for Queen Mary to return her attentions to the task of rounding up the leaders of the recent Reformation. And better still, to attempt to return them to the old religion.

In March injunctions were issued ordering all clergy to choose between their position in the renewed Catholic Church in England or their wives, in order to bring them into line with the Roman Church whose clergy were forbidden to marry by the Pope.

At Saint Mary the Virgin in Merton, our own priest was so harried for refusing to forsake his God-given wife in favour of this now enforced state of celibacy that he resigned. He was duly replaced by a zealous Papist, who then threw out and burnt the simple wooden table that my brother had arranged in the centre of the church for our purified Protestant communion. In its place the papist priest re-erected an elaborate alter in the chancel, surmounted with a great crucifix and surrounded by a communion rail to keep

Christ's common people at a distance.

Cranmer's Prayer Book was removed and the Latin Mass was brought back along with every other vestige of Popery so hated by us. Then the cruel Papists set earnestly upon persecuting all those good Christians who, in line with their good conscience, had refused to submit to Queen Mary's commands. Up and down the country, our leading Protestant preachers were rounded up like runaway dogs, choked by chains and soundly brought to heel. Like an old hag set upon a woodpile, stick after stick Queen Mary picked out and 'examined'; and those that could not be made to conform, she tossed upon her fire to burn.

To hope and to strive for something that one never achieves is painful enough. Yet it is far less painful than achieving one's goal, only to then see it snatched away and destroyed. That is how we pioneering Protestants felt. We had come so very far with this struggle for our faith, and then in the halt of one heartbeat, it was gone.

*   *   *

At the coming of Queen Mary, Anthony and I had already taken to our house at Cheapside. On a Sabbath we would bide there as quiet as mice ever hopeful that no over watchful Papist would realise that we were absenting ourselves from Church and so report us. There, we also sheltered many displaced Protestants, to shield them from wicked persecution. To those we could not help get out of harm's way, like the many already rounded up and thrown into prison, Anthony and my brother openly sent money to help ease their confinement.

We knew what we were doing by aiding and abetting these people. For disobeying the will of Queen Mary, we could be deemed guilty of treason and, if caught, as such could expect traitors' deaths. And for disobedience to the Catholic Church we could expect a far worse punishment. But regardless of the danger, my brother and Anthony and I continued in this, because our duty lay first in loving our Lord Jesus Christ.

So we carried on with our Protestant faith by gathering with our trusted friends to take table together[40], locked inside our private chamber with one eye following the Scriptures while keeping the other trained firmly upon the door, ever fearful of the knock that might at anytime come. Thus we continued to take strength from reading the Gospels together in defiance of the harsh new regime that would deny us even this simple communion with our Lord. But then came the most damning proclamation of all, stating that from henceforth each and every one of Queen Mary's subjects was to come into the churches to be registered and there to receive the Popish sacraments.

After this, Anthony said that hiding good Christians away in our home was no longer enough. Instead, my husband thought that God's will might better be done by us now helping as many as those who wished to escape the country for good to do so. Without a permission to pass port, it was impossible for any dissident to leave the country by normal means. But Anthony was a mercer and he had the means at his disposal to spirit these people overseas. He was backed up by his vast personal fortune as he financed these refugees, helping them to start new lives and then sustaining them once they had reached safety. Thus we set about removing many of the very same men as wanted by Queen Mary from out of her reach and across the sea.

Among those we helped to flee was our family friend, John Foxe, along with his pregnant wife, whom Anthony arranged passage for by way of Ipswich. Though our good Christian Archbishop Cranmer had already been sentenced to death and was awaiting that outcome at Bocardo Prison in Oxford, Anthony had managed to help smuggle out his family from England, along with Mister John Knox, too.

No matter how careful Anthony and Thomas were in handling this clandestine new cargo, somehow rumours of it got back to the authorities. Armed

---

40   Communion..

men suddenly appeared at our house one day and ransacked it thoroughly, looking for papers or any other incriminating evidence that might be had against my family. Both Anthony and Thomas were dragged out into the street by men with halberds[41] for all to see. Helpless, I stood with my young children clutched at my side as, like criminals, the two men were taken away to be brought immediately before the Queen's commissioners. There they were charged on suspicion of having 'conveyanced away the Queen's enemies' and also for not conforming themselves to Popery, contrary to Queen Mary's express command[42]. In short, if the first charge was proven, Anthony and Thomas would be deemed guilty of treason.

Traitors are tied to a horse drawn hurdle and then drawn down the cobbled streets to their place of public execution. There, they are hung by the neck until almost dead, before being cut down and while still alive laid out upon a butchers trestle. Then their bowels are drawn out of their still breathing bodies and burnt before their own still seeing eyes. After that, so as to deny traitors any last dignity, the privies are sliced off and held aloft for all to see. Then at last, the suffering is ended – by severing the head with an axe. Yet for the family left behind, the horror continues... because the already butchered corpse is then hacked further, into four pieces, and the severed head is paraded away on the end of a spike to make a show of it at Traitors' Gate[43].

If found guilty of the second charge of denouncing the Catholic faith, then my husband and brother might have forgone that previously described pleasure and instead be burnt alive as 'heretics'.

The two would neither admit nor refuted the charges set against them, saying instead that they would stand guilty or no by any evidence that the Commissioners could produce. As a result, while Mary's agents gathered their case, Anthony and Thomas were

---

41   A weapon comprising of an axe-like blade and a steel spike mounted on the end of a wooden shaft.

42   By this time Thomas had already been forced to attend Mass by order of the Council – British Library, Harley MS 353   fol. 141v.

43   Traitor's Gate is at the Tower of London.

hauled away and thrown into the prison at Fleet. And what became of me? I at first was to have been seized, too, only to be very quickly set free upon the discovery that I was with child. I believe the commissioners thought such action might serve as a useful tool with which they might better break my husband. He could therefore be incarcerated bearing the increased pressure and heartache of not knowing how I and his unborn child would fare without his protection.

How I grieved for my beloved Anthony and Thomas! I was alone with three young children and a babe in arms, and pregnant, not knowing if I would ever see my husband alive again. My only real comfort came from Christ, with the knowledge that my loved ones were being made to suffer not for any ill doing on their part but only for good. As I sat trembling and alone in a quite chamber reading my Bible by the light of a solitary candle, I found my faith strengthened as I revisited this passage[44] "For the eyes of the Lord are on the righteous and His ears are attentive to their prayer, but the face of the Lord is against those who do evil." Who is going to harm you if you do good? But even if you should suffer for what is right, you are blessed. "Do not fear their threats; do not be frightened." But in your hearts set apart Christ as Lord. Always be prepared to give an answer to everyone who asks you to give the reason for the hope you have. But do so with gentleness and respect... It is better, if it is God's will to suffer for doing good than for doing evil.'

My dear grandchildren, let me tell you who are innocent of the this world and in the quietude of Lincolnshire, so far removed from the taint of London, what the Fleet Prison is like. It is a stinking, sodden, putrid pile on the east bank of the River Fleet, long notorious for the cruelties inflicted upon its prisoners. Yet for its governor it is as lucrative an establishment as The Lock was for my Father. For each and every slight comfort to be had there, as with all common prisons, there is a monetary price to pay. For the deeper the misery, then the higher is the inclination to escape from

---

44   1 Peter 3:12-17,

it. And by reason of the misery to be had there, the Fleet commands the highest fees in all the country.

Each turn of a key, each release of a shackle commands a handsome fee. On top of this, each inmate is compelled to pay for his daily board and lodging, and those who cannot pay suffer upon stale bread and water. And what a wicked concoction that is! For it is a diet not designed to sustain the body from starvation but more to block up the bowels and intestines so that the ensuing spasms of gross constipation might depart just a little more suffering upon the unfortunate inmate.

Little wonder that those walking by outside it are assailed by the begging cries of those trapped inside – cries for money to help ease their plight. The sight of a sea of desperate hands in waves reaching out from barred windows or grills, pleading for a penny to buy them some comfort, is indeed the most pitiful sight I have ever seen. Nevertheless, day after day, I went to The Fleet in the forlorn hope that I might be able to gain an audience with either my husband or my brother. Or even to catch a momentary sight of them would have been enough ease.

Every time I went there, I took with me a purse full of coins and tried to reach the grasp of as many of these miserable inmates as I was able. For every soul reaching out to me for help was my beloved Christ, as it is revealed to us in the Gospels[45] and I could not deny Him succour. And although each time I went away again, empty handed and denied the sight of my loved ones, my heart none the less was filled with the knowledge that I had at least that day eased the suffering of some of those others who shared that dreadful place with my loved ones.

During the entirety of their imprisonment there, Anthony and Thomas were held in separate cells and unable to communicate with each other. Thus from day to day, and week to week, both were deaf and blind to the fate of the other, and only receiving such snatches of words of news as their wretched captors would allow them.

---

45   Matthew 25:31 to 40,

Severally each was regularly examined[46], during the course of which, Anthony and Thomas would each in turn be goaded by their tormentors.

'Your brother hath already confessed! Why not do likewise and make things easier upon yourself for we already have the names and places of your accomplices? Why make for yourself so much unnecessary pain when all you need to do is write down your confession?'

My husband later told me how he would confound his gaolers by replying, 'Sirs, as my brother hath already confessed all, then I can see little more that I am able to tell you that you do not already know.'

Neither man would break and thus foolishly condemn himself and his brother prisoner from out of his own mouth. And so their ordeals at the Fleet continued.

All the while, Anthony later told me, more good Christians were being rounded up and exhibited to my husband and brother in an effort to break their will and to show how lost, then, was the Protestant cause. Amongst those now imprisoned were many older merchants and contemporaries of my own late father. How it grieved Thomas to think that, had he lived, then even he might have suffered a similar indignity. And yet it also gave him comfort to know that Father was in heaven with our Lord.

Then, just at the point when their spirits were ebbing low, my two men somehow discovered that the entire jury who had sat upon the case of Sir Nicholas Throckmorton were also in the same prison.[47]

Throckmorton had been arraigned upon a charge of High Treason. Yet the jury men, in return for discharging their sworn duty by acting upon their good consciences to acquit the said fellow, instead of acting to please the Queen Mary's Commissioners by finding him guilty, found themselves consigned to The Fleet. They were prisoners and yet not in the same close sense as Anthony and Thomas.

Not every prisoner is treated equally, and some are detained by the Crown and yet not confined to the

46   Examined = tortured.
47   The trial of Sir Nicholas Throckmorton took place on April 17th 1544.

107

Fleet Prison building itself. Providing that they had the means and the will to compensate their turnkeys for the loss of 'earnings' some, if allowed to, could instead take up more comfortable lodgings in a particular area just outside of the prison wall, aptly named the 'Liberty of Fleet'.

As it happened, many of these jury men were also London mercers and brothers in guild with my dear Anthony and Thomas, and therefore most certainly must have had knowledge of their own particular plight. So it was that these good Christian fellows were then able to strengthen my men's hearts and resolve. For these jurors were able to locate the whereabouts of those upper cells in which Anthony and Thomas were being held. Thus they actively contrived to deliberately congregate beneath those windows and talk to one another in a very loud fashion about anything and everything that they might have heard touching upon the matters that Anthony and Thomas might next be facing 'examination' about. By these means, my husband and brother learnt the real truth and situation about many things before their captives had further chance to interrogate them. The pair soon came to realise how little solid evidence the authorities had against them and so could play their hand accordingly. With luck, they might even soon be released.

Meanwhile, by that time others had been released from The Fleet. And as many of these were also fellow mercers, they began to bring pressure to bear upon the authorities for their comrades to be removed from that stinking prison at least and then instead to be put under house arrest at the grand home of the Marquis of Winchester.

Many of our fellow Protestant reformers had the Marquis of Winchester marked down for a Papist. Yet this Winchester was a chequered beast indeed, who could change his dots for stripes in a heart beat. Even John Knox had denounced the Marquis as the crafty fox Shebna during his last service before the late King Edward.

When Edward had died, and Lady Jayne Grey was pronounced Queen, it was Winchester who had delivered the Crown Jewels to her. Then, when Queen Jayne fell, it was Winchester who rose to be among the first to proclaim Lady Mary as Queen. Later, Winchester had been so firmly against Queen Mary's proposed Spanish marriage that even after it had been approved, he had been heard swearing that if Philip dared to set foot in England, then he personally would set upon him. And yet it had been Winchester who had so lavishly entertained the couple at his home at Basing on the day after their wedding. Then, as my men folk were being cast into his care, the Marquis was savouring his position as Queen Mary's Lord Treasurer.

Although Anthony and Thomas were now in much more comfortable surroundings, the Commissioners' orders still stood: that on no account should the two prisoners be allowed to meet and so they were to be kept closely confined to separate rooms at opposite ends of the house.

However, by stealth and some judicious bribery of their gentleman attendants, Anthony and Thomas were able to come together on numerous occasions when the Marquis was either at dinner or abroad from the house and about his business.

Also at about this time the Catholic Lord Bergen of Zoom came to court, bemoaning to the Lord Treasurer about the absence of two of England's premier merchants at a time when there was an unprecedented demand in his country for their now missing merchandise. Thus, partly influenced by this and abetted by the Marquis himself, whose favour we were able to 'secure' with a gift of fine velvet and chests of sugar valued at more than two-hundred-pounds, at last Anthony and Thomas' 'liberty' was restored.

However, both realised that all they had really bought was a little more time. For with so many uncertain individuals involved in executing the escapes from England, Anthony and Thomas knew that should just one be found and made to talk, then Queen Mary could have them both seized and imprisoned again in an instant. No. It was far too dangerous for either man to linger much longer in England when they could so quickly be out of both sight and mind somewhere – in Antwerp, for instance.

'Then it is settled,' my husband said, and my brother readily concurred. 'I have two fair houses in Antwerp, so we must hurry and gather up our families and go there!'

However, neither I nor my sister-in-law Mary would agree to the plan.

Oh, in my heart I so badly wanted to go to Antwerp with the others and to go without delay! But the mere thought of going to sea seized me with dread. I knew full well how bad a traveller I was upon the water, so dare not risk a rough sea journey where my heave might pitch me too early into labour and forfeit the life of my unborn child. No, I was determined to stay in England to see our precious baby safely delivered. Then, and only then, would I agree to follow on to join Anthony in Antwerp. I must have argued my case exceptionally well, because in the end my husband reluctantly agreed that this course of action was for the best for all. But what about my brother Thomas? Well, that was an entirely different matter. His wife Mary would not hear a word about Thomas and her leaving all they had and enjoyed in England.

I knew Thomas better than any other person alive – even better than his wife knew him. And so I saw through the mask of bravado that he was wearing to calm her fears. I had also seen the wicked red marks fresh upon his neck and upon his body that he had carefully kept hidden. These were marks left over from his cruel 'examinations' in The Fleet at the hands of the commissioner's torturers. And I saw too that hollow look deep within his eyes, the countenance of a man so nearly broken. So I went straight away to Mary at Merton with a mind to rebuke her sternly for her selfish nature.

Mary had an angelic looking face for a full grown

woman, yet if only the poor box at Merton gained a penny for every occasion that I had heard her berate my brother then there should never be a hungry mouth in the parish again. So many of our family friends and acquaintances had agreed that poor Thomas hath a crow to pull with that one.[48]

'Sister,' I pleaded with her, 'you are staying here out of covertness and the love you hold dear for my brother's lands and belongings. But hear me well. For I fear that if you do not let him go, then the Lord's hand shall be upon you!'

I now regret those words deeply. Not that they were too harsh, but because they were not harsh enough to make the stubborn woman change her mind. For the consequences of her refusal would live on to haunt both her and me forever.

---

48   She was an argumentative woman and this was said about her. A later quote from The Shyp of Folys 1570 states –'A wrathful woman. He that her weddeth hath a crow to pull'.

Chapter Twelve

Anthony had soon fled abroad with our precious children. My youngest sister, Elizabeth, and her husband had already gone ahead of them. As already decided, I remained behind and was fast approaching the last few months of my pregnancy. Yet how was I was to remain free from Papist interference before and after the birth of my child?

I was lucky. As providence would have it a good Christian gentleman friend of Anthony's offered me the use of his country lodge, Chilswell, set upon the Hinksey Hills just south of Oxford.

The house was set in a high and lonely place at the end of a rough and muddy blind track. When I arrived in spring, the meadows still lay water-logged and filled with gently nodding snake's head fritillaries, just like the ones in the meadow down Watery Lane at Merton, when I was a child. And hares. I saw hares as big as a rat-catcher's cat, darting madly away on hearing my approach. How lonely I felt then, deprived of the company of my children.

The view from the windows of my lofty nest was one I grew to love as I awaited patiently for the child now roughly stirring inside me to make its entrance upon the world. Every morning and sunset filed me with awe and wonder at the beauty of this, God's unspoiled creation. To the west lay the green crowned Cumnor Hurst, and to the south, Boar's Hill. How I loved to watch dark shadows of cloud chase across the sunlit hills! And how the light played upon the landscape picking out the criss-cross tracks meandering between tiny scattered clusters of houses! To the east, was the royal hunting forest of Bagley Wood; a mysterious place filled with ancient gnarled trees and the scent of wood smoke from vagabond camps.

Tracing the line of several deep valleys leading to and from Chilswell, beyond the flood plains to the north, I could clearly pick out the singularly high spires of Oxford, where I knew that so many good Christian friends were now being held for our Lord's sake. Often I would raise up mine eyes in that direction and pray for their deliverance from this time of evil persecution.

When I did venture out from my cosy refuge to take the air for the good of my health, my company consisted mainly of wild-eyed ewes grazing upon the rough pasture all about. Occasionally they would be accompanied by a leather-faced shepherd who passed me by with a nod but barely a word of greeting before going upon his way.

As spring passed warmly into summer, fritillaries gave way to clouds of butterflies and swarms of bees and hoverflies busy about the drifts of wild summer flowers. Just the once, a brock[49] lumbered across my path before disappearing into the deep undergrowth of bracken. And then, when I lay uncomfortable at night, I would listen out to the lonesome owl cry somewhere off in the moonlit woods. And I would think of my children, snuggled asleep in their beds in Antwerp and wondered if they remembered me, their mother.

Yet, more important to me than the peaceful seclusion, was that Chilswell stood far away from the nearest town and, more importantly to me, away from a church which I would otherwise be compelled to attend. Besides, in my late condition, I could neither be expected to walk some great distance to comply nor made to ride. For the time being, my unborn child and I were safe.

While awaiting the birth at Chilswell, I was able to confer with our dear imprisoned Archbishop Cranmer and his bishops, and to ask their advice on whether I should allow my child to be baptised in the Popish fashion and what the consequences would be upon my Protestant standing. Lovingly, these goodly men did all in their might to set my poor mind at ease, to which end they kindly confirmed that in their learned opinion, of all the Papist sacraments, this baptismal one was the least corrupted and that I might suffer it to be done. Yet they also were at pains to add that to be certain, perhaps it would be best if I left the country

---

49   A country name for a badger.

immediately after the birth in the hope of a Protestant baptism perhaps being conducted elsewhere.

I saw through their thin veil of polite ambiguity. By and by, I came to think that they had told me this knowing full well my potential for defiance, and also the grave consequence should I be discovered with an unbaptised child by the Papists, and then subsequently refuse to let them carry out their vile Popery upon it. Then I would be deemed by the State to be both guilty of treason and heresy, and then in the absence of my husband, who had already escaped their charges, revenge might be exacted upon me in his stead. On both counts I could expect to be burnt at the stake and most likely my heretic child would be consigned to the flames with me.

My child was born shortly afterwards, and before I could get away, news of it leaked abroad. I suspect by some jailor's interception of my letters or mayhap by some loose-tongued serving girl. Before even the decency of my lying in was done, a priest had been alerted, and then two burley men were summoned to escort me to a nearby church where my baby would duly be baptized into the Roman faith. But in defiance and still not convinced upon the sanctity of such a ceremony, I set about to thwart it in the only way I might, other than by outright rejection. I used my guile.

For this ceremony I was expected to supply, at mine own cost, salt, which I was to obediently carry to the church and then hand over to the priest. Meekly, I appeared to conform. Yet when I went to the kitchen, instead of the requisite salt, it was sugar that I scooped up and tied into my prettily embroidered handkerchief to hand to the Papist priest. Praise be to God that he was made none the wiser! For he took it and used it, so that my daughter was baptised with sugar and so this Popish act was rendered void by mine own hand.

Afterwards, and satisfied that I was now compliant with my Papist Queen's wishes, I was left unimpeded as I hastily made my preparations to join the rest of my family in Antwerp. Although we had enjoyed the luxury of two extensively furnished houses in England, our London home and the other in the country, in Essex, I decided most willingly to forsake such comforts for my new child and me in return for the greater luxury of being free. I saw to it that all my furniture and household possessions were scattered about to my good friends' houses, so that none might be left for the Queen's carrion crows to pick over once I had departed. All I kept back were a few clothes and a large feather bed. Such a small price to pay, I thought, to be able once more to follow mine own conscience and to worship our Lord in the Protestant manner.

I laid the feather mattress in the bottom of the ageing hulk, in which I had bribed a brave master to sail me across to the Low Country. When I say that this was an old hulk, I jest not, for even the master had good reason to declare: 'May God speed us, good lady, safely to Antwerp... and if He does, then this ship shall never set to sea again!'

For five tempestuous days and nights, my tiny baby and I were tossed and rolled upon the unrelenting waves. I clasped her tightly as she screamed, and I spewed out earnest prayers for our deliverance from that watery hell. During the first terrible night, at a moment when I thought the ship was doomed, that verse from Psalm ninety-three that the Lord had given me months previously, suddenly flashed through my mind once more. 'Mightier than the thunder of the great waters, mightier than the breakers of the sea – the LORD on high is mighty.' I clung to this comfort as tightly as I clung to my baby. And so we were delivered and soon reunited into the tender loving keeping of my dear husband. My joy in being with Anthony once more and being able, at last, to introduce him to his new-born daughter was quite overwhelming! For me, that was one of the happiest moments of my life, and of course also those of being able to kiss my other little ones once more.

*　　*　　*

As I have said before, my brother Thomas and my husband were in partnership together as mercer-merchant adventurers. During the late reign of King Henry and his son, King Edward, Anthony and Thomas, along with other English merchants were already trading with the Canary Islands and maintained factors[50] there. The islands were a Spanish dominion but opened to the English some fifty years before via a commercial treaty with King Henry's late father. But with the deplorable state of English trade in general caused by a slump late in Henry's reign, it was time to broaden our merchants' horizons.

In fifteen-hundred-and-fifty-two, my menfolk became part of the syndicate that funded and sent out three ships and one-hundred-and-twenty men to go to Santa Cruz in Morocco, in search of a vastly lucrative cargo of sugar, dates, almonds and molasses. This they obtained in return for traded English goods that included cloth, firearms and copies of the Old Testament for the many Jews of that country who controlled much of its commerce. The Portuguese, who monopolized this trade for so long, were outraged and lodged a bitter complaint about our propagation of heresy and our arming of the 'infidels'.

After the successes with Morocco, all eyes then fell on a far more distant and yet infinitely more lucrative prize – the tropical coast of Africa. A year later, and armed with Portuguese maps and charts obtained under the most dubious of circumstances, and with the aid of a Portuguese seaman of some great repute, Antonio Pinteado, our ships then headed for the most jealously guarded Portuguese trading territory of all – the fabled Gold Coast of Africa.

Yet this quest to open the gold Coast would prove the most difficult challenge the trading English had so far faced. Getting to the coast posed few problems, but the notorious Guinea current, coupled with prevailing winds made getting away from it again almost impossible. They only true and tested way to do so, was to try to slip off southwards out of the flow of

50   Factor – one who acts for somebody else, especially in the business of buying or selling. An agent.

the current, but by doing that, it would then leave our ships at the mercy of the notorious equatorial calms and good luck before somehow a ship could sail westward into the open Atlantic.

A ship might find herself becalmed for months at a time, and all the while with her crew in danger of sickness and disease. Once widely broken out and left unchecked, sickness could carry most of a crew off to their maker. Yet this is an accepted part of life's lot for both merchant adventurers and mariners alike. None are blind to the huge risks involved, or to the vast fortunes that could be made off the back of just one successful venture.

After avoiding the Portuguese fort at Elmina, and obtaining as much gold as they could, this first expedition of ours then tried hopefully to make its way back towards England. But, unfortunately, the mariners had picked up some dreadful illness upon the way. It was so bad that one out of the three ships in the party had to be abandoned altogether for want of enough well and able-bodied hands to sail her. Pinteado was but one casualty amongst the dreadful ensuing death toll.

Out of the one-hundred-and-forty men who had set out, only forty stricken survivors reached England alive. Amongst those wretched few still clinging to life was a young Yorkshire lad named Martin Frobisher. He came to be upon the voyage as he was a ward of Sir John York, one of the other backers in this enterprise. Most likely upon realising that his flimsily educated and barely literate ward, Frobisher, was of no use for any of the city employments considered suitable for a young gentleman, Sir John had decided to cut his loses by sending the swab to sea.

Martin Frobisher? Why is it that whenever I hear that name I think of the argument of old between my nurse-maid and the rat-catcher in the kitchen of our London house when I was a child? The rat had been cornered and the rat-catcher hit him – with four, five, six thwacks with his club.

'Have a care Sir!' Maggie had all but jumped

upon the man as she cried out. 'Surely there is no need to smash the beast to a pulp?'

To this, the rat man immediately stopped. Then, catching Maggie in his wooden stare, he proceeded to lean down and gently prod the lifeless rodent with the tip of his blooded club. Squeaking, the rat had suddenly sprung back into life and tried to make off under the kitchen table. Thwack! Thwack! At last the rat man finally dispatched it.

'There Mistress,' he said grinning broadly, 'vermin takes a lot of killing'.

Vermin. That is what Frobisher turned out to be. Vermin!

Although the loss in human terms on that first expedition was horrific, the profit made on that one trip was nothing short of spectacular. Yet our city merchants' jubilation would not prove long-lived.

Shortly before their arrest, in the summer of fifty-four, Anthony and Thomas had been amongst those backing the dispatch of another expedition to the Gold Coast. They had no patent to do so or official permissions from Queen Mary, but instead acted upon those previously given by Edward and Northumberland for the first. This time, however, command of it was entrusted to my most excellent sea-faring brother, John Locke. John had taken a recovered Frobisher with him as being 'useful', but the wretch was captured by Africans and handed over to the Portuguese at Elmina.

Otherwise, the voyage was a great success and returned to England the following year with a rich cargo, including four-hundred pounds of gold[51] which in turn meant an enormous and much needed profit.

However, this enterprise was soon to be challenged. The Portuguese must have caught wind of our company's activities, for a full two weeks before my brother had even set foot back on English soil, and an ambassador from them was already at court lodging a complaint before Queen Mary and her new Spanish husband, Philip. The ambassador clearly asserted that by Papal Donation and by the title of prior discovery,

---

51   Gold was a much scarcer commodity then and therefore worth many times fold its comparative worth now in monetary terms.

the whole of that Guinea coast belonged to Portugal and therefore we English had no right to trespass upon it. Furthermore, he demanded the return of all of the gold that we English merchants had landed and the prohibition of any further expeditions into Portuguese Crown Territories.

Anthony was by now in Antwerp but kept closely informed of developments back home when the remaining merchant adventurers were ordered to appear before the Privy Council to answer the Portuguese charges. They of course denied any wrong doing against the Crown of Portugal because they had not traded in any of their possessions and not met with any soldiers or agents of their king. In fact, the local African chiefs of those places where the English had traded had assured our people that they were independent, sovereign princes and therefore not subjects of the King of Portugal.

Further more the merchant adventurers insisted that their business dealings in Africa had been conducted along exactly the same lines as they already used unhindered in Europe and Asia – trade with independent peoples who were friendly towards England. Our merchants flatly denied that Portugal had any jurisdiction in any of the places they had traded, adding that 'we merchants who, by common usage of the world, do use traffique in all places of the world, as well Asia and Africa and Europa, and have never been restrained from resort to any places.'

What the merchants had said was true in substance. The stretch of coast that the Portuguese were claiming as their territory stretched for over two thousand miles and was 'policed' by one fort at Elmina and with a scattering of priests and factors along the rest. The merchants insisted that common international understanding of 'occupation' of a territory lain in the fact that such occupation was both visible and effective – and as the merchants had neither made contact with any Portuguese, or indeed been challenged by anyone as they went about their trade, how then could it constitute a possession?

Though the Privy Council argued in the merchants favour, a decision was made by King Philip to prohibit the trade, and Queen Mary had no choice but to obey her husband in this matter. His reasoning must have been that if he allowed Englishmen to trade in Portuguese Africa then what was there to stop the English from then entering the Spanish New World? However, he did not order the return of the gold.

Yet how does one set about making hungry beggars of men who still know how and where to go to find meat? King Philip's judgment amounted to mere words, and so some expeditions to Africa carried on regardless.

Chapter Thirteen

I have heard from the cruel mouths of some reformists-cum-lately that had my family and I been as zealous in our Protestant faith as we claimed, then perhaps we should have chosen to spend our exile in that most pure Church of Geneva or gone into some Protestant German enclave, instead of retreating to the source of our wealth and comfortable house in Antwerp. To those people I say, why should I have needlessly put my young children's lives at risk from the exertion of just such an arduous journey and to a country where my husband would be unable to provide for our needs or those of others fleeing?

Was it not better that I could take my new baby and young children to a ready home? Was it not better to take them to a place Anthony knew and where he could offer a safe house for other exiles en route to elsewhere to use? Being so close to his business and ships meant that my husband could continue to use these to aid the persecuted to escape from England and then to finance their needs as he then sent them safely on their way. Although our self imposed exile in Antwerp was to last for just a few years, we had no way of knowing that at the time. Queen Mary might have lived on for decades, and so the need of support like ours for our English Protestant faith may have then proved all the greater.

The reason that we chose to go Antwerp was not because it was easier for us to keep up with our Protestant faith and sharing our Gospel. For it certainly was not, unlike the most perfect Geneva.

We chose Antwerp because it is the greatest city north of the Alps; the very epicentre of the entire international economy and, better still, it was heaving full with merchants of every tongue and hue imaginable. It was so much the better for dissenters, like Anthony and me, to get lost in that city, and to help the steady stream of English exiles to our door to also disappear.

Hundreds of ships passed in and out of this port every day and over two-thousand carts clattered through its cobbled streets every week. We could be far across the sea from our homeland and yet Anthony could still conduct his business and remain in the company of many of our own English merchants. Therefore we could pass on news from home and smuggle letters from the scattered English Protestant in Europe back to England.

Yet more inviting than this commercial aspect to Antwerp was the way in which Anthony knew that there was no tiny parish church to which we would be held accountable. Instead, we would be expected to worship at the towering Onze-Lieve-Vrouwekathedraal – Cathedral of Our Lady – in the Popish manner alongside a great mass of other people. Of course, we never did attend mass there, and the Cathedral being so large and the crush so great, that no one could vouch for certain as to who had attended a service or not. Coupled with this, my husband and I had a large townhouse with doorways that opened out onto two different streets, so if a neighbour should comment that they had not seen Anthony and me pass out that way on a Sunday to attend church, then I could simply suggest that maybe we had gone out from the house by the other door.

Unfortunately, there was something that Anthony had not anticipated. There was also a chapel especially set aside for English merchants to attend, at which they were expected to do so on feast days and holidays, and to attend upon their Mercer Governor there. Anthony had attended there in the past, but that was when the Governor at that time was a fellow Protestant and the services shaped accordingly. Now, however, the new Governor was not, and this attendance with him was something that my poor husband Anthony could not eschew.

Therefore, on the night before his first attendance, Anthony became so upset that he made himself quite ill through worry. Such a great sickening feeling welled up from the pit of his stomach that it laid him grievous low in despair – at the thought of playing his a part in any such act Popery. Yet what else could he do without drawing the Papists' attention to his family?

This Governor knew exactly what we Lockes and Hickmans were. Yet as the Lord would have it, although Governor Hussey was a Papist himself, he was no cruel persecutor like those from whom we had escaped in England. We felt assured about this when Hussey said to Anthony quietly: 'Though I have the power to bark, I do not bite.' And he added that he was personally contented to bear with Anthony upon this matter of conscience for as far as he might, but without actually being seen to do so. Therefore my husband was able to discreetly absent himself through some acceptable excuse or another.

To live in Antwerp was to ever reside in constant reminder of the struggles thus far we Protestants had made for our love of Christ and His teachings. For it was here in Antwerp, when I was still a girl, that Master Tyndale was so cruelly taken from one of our own mercer houses. It was he, who had so wonderfully translated the Bible from ancient Greek and Hebrew texts. And then had them printed in English so that men, like my own father, could smuggle them into London. For more than five-hundred days, Tyndale had suffered a dreadful imprisonment in the Castle of Vilvoorden before being dragged out into its shabby yard, tied to a stake, strangled, and burnt.

I myself found Antwerp such a dark place in spirit; a place I could never have grown to like even had it been Protestant. According to folklore, the town had got its name from a most sinister legend which in many ways seemed enshrined in its darkness. Legend told of a giant called Antigoon who had supposedly lived beside the river Scheldt. He controlled the river crossing and exacted a charge from any wishing to pass over it. For those who dared refuse the giant his payment, he cut off one of their hands and threw it into the Scheldt. Eventually the giant was defeated by a youthful hero named Brabo, who cut off the giant's own hand and threw that in the river. Therefore the town became known as Antwerpen, a corruption from the old Dutch words for 'hand' and 'to throw'.

Within a very short time of my arrival in Antwerp, I proved with child once more. Now in that place, where a woman was lying in after the birth of a child it was the custom to hang out a little piece of lawn[52] beside the street door where they lived. I knew that I could not hope to conceal the birth of this latest child for long and so, again to cause confusion in my neighbours' minds, I hung out some lawn beside both of my doors. Likewise, as for mass, when the question of my child having been taken from the house to be baptized arose, the confusion of the doors could once more be brought into play.

Avoiding a Popish baptism in Antwerp was one of the most dangerous courses of action I have ever undertaken. For in that place there was such seething hatred amongst the local inhabitants for Anabaptists[53] that the Magistrate, accompanied by a band of armed monsters, used to go out at night and enter, at will, any house where he thought that there might be un-baptised children being kept. If any were found, then he would have them dragged screaming from their beds and tied up into grain sacks along with rocks. Then he would gloat as he ordered their helpless parents to watch as the sacks were then thrown into the Scheldt and the children drowned like unwanted puppies.

I wanted my children baptized in the sight of God, in obedience to faith in our Lord Jesus Christ. And I wanted them baptized as Protestants. But now I hear you, my beloved grandchildren, ask: 'Why did you undertake such an awesome risk?' In my defence let me say that a fuller understanding of the Bible, as it is so with all learning, is gained through the passage of passing years. And at that time I did not understand biblical baptism. This was only explained to me many years later by our dear friend and pastor, John Smyth, when we resided in Gainsborough. John had pointed out to me that our Protestant Church in England, itself in infancy, and still finding its way forward, had missed the true significance of baptism and still retained the

---

52 A type of cloth.
53 Those who refused infant baptism for their children.

Papist notion that it is a sacrament of the Church rather than an ordinance that symbolises spiritual reality. If baptism is termed a sacrament, then it may be wrongly viewed as something that, combined with faith and good works, provides a special means of grace. But the Bible makes it very clear that God's eternal salvation is received by grace through faith alone: 'For it is by grace you have been saved, through faith – and this not from yourselves, it is the gift of God – not by works, so that no one can boast. For we are God's workmanship, created in Christ Jesus to do good works, which God prepared in advance for us to do.' [54]

According to what the apostle Paul wrote in chapter six of his letter to the Romans, baptism is a person's public identification with Christ. This is undertaken by someone who accepts what the Lord Jesus Christ accomplished on his or her behalf when He was crucified as God's sacrifice for sin, and that he or she has placed his or her trust in Christ alone for eternal spiritual salvation. When a man or woman receives the Lord Jesus as his or her Saviour, he or she dies to the authority or ownership of sin. In Christ, believers have died to sin, and this in New Testament times was signified by baptism. As new believers in Christ went down into the waters of baptism – often a river or some other expanse of water – they were testifying that through their union with Him they had been buried with Him in His death. And so, having died to sin, they were no longer under its condemnation and bondage. Then these people arising from the water signified that their union with the risen Lord had also effected their resurrection from death with Him. This indicated that they had entered new life. In short, baptism is a believer's public identification with Christ, and it is undertaken as a willing step of obedience to Him.

And so, today, how my mind rages and my blood boils when, as I walk through a church yard, I see the graves of un-baptised babies allotted with those of criminals – whose spirits were branded by self-righteous

---

54 Ephesians 2:8 and 9.

hypocrites as unredeemable! What deep and painful wounds must fester in their parents' hearts! As I pause at these grave sites, I wonder how even the most stupid of men dare enforce their assumptions about the final judgement that belongs only to Him who commanded: 'Let the little children come to me, and do not hinder them, for the kingdom of God belongs to such as these' [55]. And yet, as I consider the folly of others, I do well not to forget that day of baptism at Chilswell – when I used sugar as a substitute for salt and thought it really mattered!

In Antwerp there was a secret Calvinist congregation close by. I considered it providential and managed to make contact with some of the godly women of that persuasion, though at first they were extremely suspicious of me – because I could have turned out to be a Catholic spy. But I was able to prove that my earnest desire was also sincere by showing them that I was willing to entrust my baby's life into their hands. I agreed to give them my newborn son so that they might take him in secret to be baptised. In bargain, I was not allowed to attend or even have a hint of who or where their Protestant minister might be. Such was the great danger to him!

I tell you now, the awful feelings of foreboding that I felt handing my beautiful newborn baby over to those veiled strangers was almost overpowering. At the very last moment I felt my trembling hands move to snatch him back, but then the thought of my Lord steadied my hand and heart. That faith was duly rewarded, though I was never able to thank in person those fearless Godparents who had stood up in the sight of God to vouch for this strangers' child.

*　*　*

When William was just around five or six years old, I had seen him to bed in the evening in as fine a state of health as his boisterous younger brother, Henry. Yet I was awoken in the night by the pitiful

---

55   Matthew 19:14.

sound of his groaning. I ran to his bedside and laid my hand upon his head to check for fever. It was then that I saw how contorted his small face was and how unnaturally tightly his tiny jaws were clenched. I called out to Anthony in such a panic that he in turn came running half naked to see what the matter could be.

'What ails him?' he kept asking in fear as he too felt our son's body.

'I don't know,' I cried, 'I don't know!' I had never encountered such a condition before, but even so sensed that my son's life was in danger.

It was then that William suddenly started convulsing. Anthony shouted out for our servants to come and help and then to fetch a draft of Rosa Solis to help bring William out of his fit. One scurried back with it almost immediately, and then the other assisted Anthony as he tried desperately to pour some of the liquid down William's throat. But he could not get the cup past the boy's locked teeth. It then took the two serving men to hold William still enough for his father to get the restorative into him. And then, in the process, Anthony knocked out two of William's milk teeth, though this at least opened a gap through which to pour the medicine and thereby get it into the stomach where it could hopefully set about its work.

But William grew paler and paler, and so some of our friends and neighbours hurried to our house to pray with us. By then Anthony and I had already consigned ourselves to believing that our eldest son had only but a short time to live.

Eventually, our boy lay so still that we could barely tell if he was dead or alive. His breathing was so shallow that his little sunken chest barely rose and fell with the effort at all. In order that we might know for certain, and also to spare his little brother the sight of William's poor face at the moment of his death, Anthony placed a fine linen napkin over Williams face – so we might much better see when our son breathed no more.

With lighted candles now set at each point of my son's death bed, we sat with our remaining children and neighbours and prayed. Then, just as dawn's light was creeping across the windowsill, William suddenly began to stir. Yet we did not dare to hope – but instead thought it the final rally that so oft precedes death in its last throw.

But William stirred the more, and so Anthony drew off the napkin. And then, to our amazement, our son opened his eyes, but made no sound at all. Then Anthony lifted William's head gently and gave him another draft of Rosa Solis, after which William fell asleep once more, this time breathing more soundly. When he awoke again some time later, William was all but recovered – as if he had never been ill at all!

We could only imagine that the meat he had eaten for supper the evening before had not agreed with him, and because he had not been able to vomit it up, it had afterwards caused this terrible reaction. Yet whatever had ailed our beloved child, we knew that it was God in His infinite mercy who had delivered him back to us.

*   *   *

From time to time, other Protestant exiles from England made their way to our house to seek my husband's help, which of course, he never refused. For a time, we were even joined once more by Mister John Foxe and his family, who lifted our spirits greatly. My husband helped Mr Foxe with much needed finance so that he might travel on to Frankfurt, where he proposed to preach at the English church and to minister to our refugees in that city.

Uplifting testaments of our fellow Protestant came our way, but then so did tragic ones that strengthened our resolve never to give up our rightful cause and also heightened our utter revulsion with regard to our Catholic persecutors.

One such account I recall in particular came to us by way of a young gentleman named Michael Reniger. He told us about a woman he had known who had been martyred at Litchfield for the Protestant cause. Her name was Joyce Lewes and she was but an ordinary gentlewoman in most respects but one. She had proved herself as an extraordinarily steadfast and true follower of Christ and as such paid the ultimate price for being so.

In her younger days, Joyce did not appear to be made of the stuff of martyrs. Indeed, she was then a vain woman, more concerned about her good looks and her clothes than about her spirit. When Queen Mary's proclamation came, at first Joyce obediently attended the masses. But then something happened after she heard of the cruel martyrdom of a young Protestant man she knew. All of a piece, it turned her against the Papists.

When her husband subsequently man-handled her into church – to try to make her conform, she defiantly turned her back as the priest cast the holy water. And so she was fined, tortured and imprisoned for more than a year – but still she refused to recant from her 'wicked Protestant heresy'.

Then the writ eventually came from London demanding her execution. On the eve of her death she was being held at the Sheriff's house when two priests arrived 'to hear her last confession'. But instead of praying with her as expected, they instead set trying to torture her into submission once more. They failed.

Master Reniger told us that, come the next day when the bill [56]men paraded the lady through the streets to her place of public execution, he and many of her friends gathered to walk beside her as a sign of their solidarity and support. Joyce was by then in body as weak as a new-born lamb, but still as strong in spirit as a lioness.

She had stumbled and shuffled along the way causing much anguish amongst those looking on. Some there in authority were even reviled at her fate, yet too fearful to try to stop the proceedings lest they should find themselves next condemned to the flames.

When Joyce fell for the final time and was

---

56   Bill = a written statement charging someone with a crime. A bill is also a long-handled weapon with a hooked blade. Armed men would have led the prisoner to the place of execution where the indictment would read out prior to the punishment being carried out.

unable to get to her feet unaided, her friends demanded that she be rested for at least a moment or two and be given a little strong drink to bolster her before her coming and most terrible ordeal. A mercy went out for some wine to be quickly fetched from the Sheriff's own kitchen and given to her. Yet, even as Joyce lifted that one last cup of comfort to her lips, she smiled defiantly and announced loudly that she was drinking a toast to 'all those who love the Gospel and desire to see the overthrow of these wicked Papists'.

With that the bill men wrestled the cup from out of her hands and dragged her on towards the waiting stake.

Yet her suffering was mercifully quick, Master Reniger informed us, for the under sheriff was much moved by this brave woman's plight – and so allowed gunpowder to be spread amongst the faggots of wood. It burnt so hot and furiously that once lit, Joyce barely had time to cry out before she was gone on her away to Heaven.

My husband gave that young man five pounds in gold to help him on his way, a sum being so far beyond the young fellow's means that Anthony never expected it to be repaid, just as he never expected any monetary return on any of the vast sums of money that he gave to countless others in this way. Yet this man Reniger went to Leuven to study and graduate as a Doctor of Divinity. When he eventually came back to England and to the Close at Lincoln[57] , he sought us out to repay the money and ever after acknowledged the help that my husband had given him. He only died a few years ago, after a long and good life in the service of Christ.

Indeed, there were numerous others whom, had they still been in life today, I am certain would have readily testified likewise to the generosity of my good husband. Anthony, of course, did not give to and assist people for the praise of men but only out of his great love for and duty unto his God.

And so we lived this double life in Antwerp – until that most joyful day of all days, when wonderful

---

57   Remiger was later a sub-dean at Lincoln.

news reached us from the lips of the master of one of Anthony's own ships. 'Bloody' Queen Mary was dead, and her half-sister Elizabeth had just come to the Crown of England. Suddenly England was a Protestant kingdom once more and we could go home, at last, to what remained of our friends and family.

Yet our joy was tinged with great sadness – brought about by the loss of the life that we had known before and which could never be the same again. So many of those whom we had loved and known had not been as fortunate as we had. For Queen Mary burned to death more than three-hundred good Protestant souls and tortured and broken countless more. Amongst those burnt were well loved shepherds like, Thomas Cranmer[58], Bishop Hooper, Hugh Latimer and Nicholas Ridley and so many more. And amongst the broken beyond restoration was my own dear brother, Thomas.

After we had fled to Antwerp, as time went by, Thomas had became so consumed by fear of further imprisonment in The Fleet and of more of the horror and torture already meted out there, that he had outwardly feigned conformation to the Popish religion. He did this as much to keep his family out of harm's way as for himself. However, the pretence and the strain of it all must have grieved his conscience beyond what his deep and active mind could bear. For he was dead within months of gaining his false liberty. And then, quickly following on after him, into their graves went seven of his and Mary's young children. Mary deeply regretted not coming away with us when she had been begged to do so, but we have no doubt that she eventually forgave herself. She spent the rest of her life being a lay preacher and took up the Christian work that her late husband had undertaken.

I never did despise so much another living being as I had that wretched Queen Mary! There was never another human I was to encounter whom I considered so evil. Never. No woman with such blood-stained hands can be counted as a Christian Queen of England. She was a murderess and a heretic – though

---

58   An eye-witness account of Cranmer's death is included at the end of this book.

it was the word 'heretics' she used when hunting and slaughtering Protestants, people who desired nothing more than to follow the teachings of the Bible, and whose uncomplicated faith in Christ compelled them to stand against a rule of terror.

So many Christians we had known were now gone. Many of these good brethren had refused to flee in the face of cruel persecution and, instead, like Joyce Lewes, had chosen to defy Bloody Mary for the sake of their beliefs. Therefore I add that our joy at returning home was tinged with guilt – because we had not made such a stand as they had made. And yet now I no longer feel that way. We were meant to live as and where we had lived: 'For we are God's workmanship, created in Christ Jesus to do good works, which God prepared in advance for us to do' [59]And there was so much more for us still to do...

---

59   Ephesians 2:10.

Chapter Fourteen

What can I say about my sister-in-law Anne regarding her relationship with our mutual and dear friend, Mister John Knox? That she had an adulterous, lust-filled and unholy affair with this preacher? For this is how many wicked tongues would have it told, and to that I would counter, 'Look to the source'. For evil people should not judge the saintly by their own grubby morals.

So how do I set this down without sounding as if casting great aspersions upon her fidelity? 'Tis a subject I have avoided broaching in the past for just that very reason. Yet now I have come to an age to realise that I need not fear, for I can write down only what I know to be true and then leave the interpretation of such to others.

I was never especially a friend to Anne as she was growing up. Not out of any dislike, you must understand, on either of our parts, but merely by reason that she was so much younger than I. Anne was much nearer in age to my little sister Elizabeth and so it was that those two birds bonded as fledglings. My particular involvement with Anne would come much later.

Anne was the oldest daughter of Mister Stephen Vaughan, a neighbour of ours at Cheapside. He was of a mercer family; younger than my own father but not nearly as wealthy. He was not, however, always as a committed Protestant as my good father but nonetheless professed a great admiration for William Tyndale who was also in the Low Countries.

Mister Vaughan was also a member of the Merchant Adventurers Company, and at one time Governor of their factory at Antwerp, and so had many dealings with my family in business as well as in pleasure. Though, and I say this with no boasting, our family was rather more cultivated than theirs and we had better taste in literature and a wider range.

When I was just two or three years of age, Mister Vaughan had been seized and brought before the

Bishop of London on the most grave charge of heresy, and thereafter sent to defend himself against the most dutiful of persecutors of heretics, Thomas Moore.

We did not know on what terms Stephen Vaughan was able to clear himself of such charge, suffice to say that he may have been pressured into certain actions out of fear for not only his own life but those of his family, too. For it was Mister Vaughan who was commissioned to find Tyndale in Antwerp and to invite him to the English House. This he did, and it was from that house that Tyndale was arrested.

Vaughan had married a silk woman at court and together they had three children; Anne, Jayne and Stephen – who like me and my siblings were all educated together. The Vaughans had a wonderful tutor named Mister Cobb. A teacher of his calibre would normally only be available to families much beyond the means of the Vaughans' purse, but he was not beyond that of George Brooke, the son of the sixth Earl of Cobham, who lived with them also whilst his father served abroad.

Anne's mother died in the same year as my brother Edmund, and then her father remarried to Margery Brinklow, the widow of another mercer. This woman was of an unshakable Protestant outlook and who undoubtedly served to fortify Anne's enthusiastic religious beliefs, before and after the death of Stephen Vaughan, which came just three or four years later.

It was not surprising therefore, that after being in such close proximately to another like-minded young person, that my brother Henry should fall in love with spirited, red-headed Anne and she with him. Indeed, the two married in fifty-two, and it was during that first winter of married life together that Henry and Ann acquired an unexpected house guest – one of the great mainstays of England's hope for Protestant reform – the Scottish preacher John Knox.

Knox was a powerful Protestant preacher and destined to become the chief reformer of the Scottish Church, yet earlier he had almost died at the hands of the French. Before this time, and in his native Scotland, in the wake of the murder of Catholic Cardinal Beaton, Knox had been captured by French soldiers, acting on behalf of the regent of the Scots' young Queen Mary Stuart. As a result, he was imprisoned as a galley slave and then viciously tormented by his captures for the sake of his heretic beliefs.

Though broken in health but not in spirit, somehow Knox eventually gained his freedom and took up refuge in England, where in forty-nine he obtained a licence to preach in the Church of England at Berwick. Obliged as he was to use the new Book of Prayer, Knox however modified it along his more radical Protestant lines, and his powerful preaching soon drew him a strong congregation.

In the very same year that Knox had been appointed as one of King Edwards's six royal chaplains, the Duke of Northumberland overthrew Seymour to become the new regent. John Knox publicly condemned the coup d'état during a sermon. Nonetheless, Knox was such a powerful preacher that Northumberland recognised his usefulness and so invited him to London the following year to preach at court. There, by chance, he was introduced to my brother Henry and Anne.

Almost at once, from their very first conversation, something seem to spark off a great understanding between Anne and the preacher. Soon the two were often to be found sitting together in some quiet nook of the house or pacing of the garden, discussing some point of faith or such, for hours upon end and often far into the night, and forsaking food for their bodies in favour of feasting their spirits.

However, all did not go smoothly with Knox in his public life. During his very first sermon before the King, Knox spoke out about the need for a revised edition of the Book of Prayer which he and a number of other chaplains still considered to be full of unnecessary Popery. This ignited greatly heated debate between Knox and its writer, Archbishop Cranmer.

Meanwhile, seeing Knox as potentially very useful politically, Northumberland offered to make him a bishop. But Knox declined and returned to the north. Nonetheless, he was invited back to London several times more to preach before the King and so naturally stayed each time with his dear friends, Ann and Henry.

Knox happened to be in London when young King Edward died and the aftermath involving Queen Jayne. By January, after Mary had come to the crown and started rounding up and imprisoning such good Protestants as Archbishop Cranmer and many of his bishops, it became far too dangerous for Knox to stay in England. It was then that my husband Anthony and my brother Thomas arranged for his passage upon one of their ships across the sea to the Low Countries. They also gave him a great deal of money to see him on his way.

Knox was sad to leave, for he told us on the eve of his leaving that he had never thought that he would have become as fond of any other country as he was of his native homeland; and yet he now found more sorrow for England's present state, and his fears for her future even exceeded those he held for Scotland.

One might have expected the controversial friendship between John Knox in exile and my sister-in-law in London to have ended then, or to at least to have waned, but it remained firm. Perhaps this was because, whatever the gossipmongers circulated, their friendship was strictly platonic. Indeed, at the time when Knox departed from London, Anne was happily married and already a mother of one child and expecting another, while Knox himself was by then newly espoused.

Throughout his time across the sea, Knox continued to write to Anne and their special friendship began to grow even stronger despite their living so distantly from each other. Then, in his regular letters, John Knox began beseeching Anne to come to join him in Geneva with his growing flock of English Protestants waiting in readiness for the day when they would bring the Protestant Gospel back to England once more and carry on with the 'good work' started in King Edward's time.

To this day, I do not know if Henry knew or gave his consent or nay to what was to happen next. For by then, Anthony and I were deep in troubles of our own or no longer in London to give Henry our counsel or support. But in the spring of fifteen-fifty-seven, Anne bent to Knox's insistent will. And so, taking her and Henry's two young children with her, she headed off to join the preacher in Geneva.

I realised from his letters to me at the time, just how miserable Henry was made by Anne's going, but not in one line did he reproach her for doing so. Not even after he had learned that their little daughter, Annie, had died only days after his wife's arrival in Geneva. Though he anguished in his words at her loss, he never blamed Anne for her death.

At home in London, when news of this strange liaison got abroad, Henry had to field the taunts of 'cuckold' and the cruel rumors put about that his wife had been taken in by this lecherous man Knox, who appeared to preach against women in one breath, while honouring them with his body the next.

However deeply wounded by these remarks, Henry refused to rise to the bait. In hindsight, his response may have served him well. For besides her work in translating John Calvin's sermons into English so that they might be smuggled in to England and to the faithful still caught in Mary's realm, Anne started to write her own pieces. It was when these items of literature began to filter through from across the sea that Henry's perceived personal position, as a hapless deserted husband, may have saved him from the strong possibility of Queen Mary's Catholic commissioners' backlash – of 'examination' over his estranged wife's inflammatory Protestant writing.

Yet far more dangerous than Anne's writings, was Knox's own pamphlet entitled *"The First blast of the Trumpet Against the Monstrous Regiment of Women"*, the purpose of which was to demonstrate how monstrous or unnatural it was to have a female monarch upon the English throne. In it he said that the *'the rule of a wicked woman, yea, of a traitoress and a bastard'* was an abomination in the sight of God – Knox clearly having in mind Catholic Queens Mary Tudor and Mary Stuart, the latter ruler of his own home of Scotland. It was a dangerous and highly seditious piece if writing, upon which at first even he dare not sign his own name! In England it was swiftly condemned by royal proclamation.

With the death of Queen Mary, Anne returned home, just as Anthony and I and hoards of other Protestant exiles forced to flee the country had. Unfortunately, John Knox's journey home to his native Scotland was to be somewhat hindered by the fact that the newly enthroned Queen Elizabeth vehemently refused him leave to set so much as one foot upon English soil. Even as a Protestant and a former prisoner of her half-sister Mary, she too had been deeply offended by Knox's pamphlet and particularly by his use of the word 'bastard'. Once spited, Elizabeth never forgave him for his words, or indeed his followers.

My sister Anne appeared outwardly, at least, to settle back into married life with Henry and to carry on their lives together. However, she never once relinquished an ounce of the newfound independence that her close involvement with Knox had opened to her. Over the coming years, she steadfastly continued to campaign for English Church reform and to act as an intermediary for her beloved friend's moves for reformation. This she did through her translations and spreading of the news coming in from Geneva and from Knox himself, who was by then back in Scotland.

When my brother Henry later passed away, he bequeathed to Anne all of his worldly goods and made her the sole executor of his will. For me, this, along with the strong and unique sense of being 'family' that is often evident in communities of committed Christians, bears testimony to his faith in Anne and her fidelity.

Chapter Fifteen

In Queen Mary's reign, Rome had recovered its position of power within the English Church, much to the distaste of the majority of the nation's subjects. It was true that only a minority of Mary's subjects had been Protestant, but nonetheless it is equally true to point out that the majority, although liking the old forms of worship, had not wanted their Church resubmitted to Roman control either. In many respects, the attitude of Mary's father, King Henry, had mirrored their own, whereas Mary's had not.

England was also still reeling from the trauma of the burning of so many hundreds of fellow countrymen and women. Before, such widespread and severe persecution had only swept in on the wind of rumour from abroad and not as a reality at home. The general revulsion over these many killings had only served to steel us English against such further acts of monstrous tyranny. And thus, if anything, this served to ease the way for Protestant Queen Elizabeth to come to the Crown.

Like Anthony and me, almost a thousand religious exiles flooded back into England from the Low Countries, and from stronghold cities such as Geneva and Frankfurt. We were brimming with excitement and anticipation. Again, the way was now cleared for the Church in England to be reformed according to Calvinist ideals. But, again, we were to be roundly disappointed.

*   *   *

Though controversy might rage as to whether Queen Elizabeth might be considered a bastard according to the law, one had only to spend but a short while in her company to be convinced that she was truly the offspring of King Henry and Anne Boleyn. Her Majesty was indeed a fiery mix of her mother's volatility and tantrums stirred in with a large dose of her tyrannical father's black rages. And if any good Protestant thought that for one moment Elizabeth would pick up and continue upon her dead half-brother's path of Church reform, then they were to be very sadly mistaken.

Under Elizabeth, England's aim would be the struggle for her liberty, prosperity and above all, her religion; that is Elizabeth's religion. For although were once more a Protestant country and free from the Papist control of Rome, it was to be Protestantism a la King Henry mode, with all the pomp and ceremony to which he had so faithlessly clung. Elizabeth was fanatical in upholding her father's standards; for by doing so was the clearest and strongest way she had of reinforcing her somewhat tenuous claim to the throne itself. If she roared at her subjects like the cub of her father the lion, who would then dare to question her place at the head of the pride?

Elizabeth's Church would conform to those Protestant doctrines laid down in the Thirty-Nine Articles of Religion and the system of public worship as laid down in the Anglican Book of Prayer. Above all, it was to be about subordination to the established hierarchy of bishops and, ultimately, to the Queen herself on matters of religion. Even where previously such matters as to what caps and robes the clergy should wear had been considered less important requirements, or even 'optional' in some cases, Elizabeth insisted upon her own exacting demands. Dissenting clergy or 'non-conformists' as they became known, were open to experience her full wrath. And yet I can see that this was also the time when ordinary English citizens began to seize liberty from clerical domination and start to form a new attitude towards the clergy; that they become the servants of our communities and not the masters.

My sister-in-law Anne shared with us a letter sent from Mister Knox, while he was still awaiting a homeward passage from Dieppe, in which he sent salutations in the postscript to my husband. This letter outlined his judgment upon this bastard English religion now promoted by Elizabeth, declaring that 'we ought not to justify with our presence such a mingle-mangle as was now commanded in our churches'; for it was not the leaving off of the surplice, or the removing of external monuments of idolatry that purges a Church from superstition. Performing services for appointed Saints' Days, collects in remembrance of this or that Saint, not used by the Prophets or commanded by Christ, nor found in the prayers of the Apostles, nor received in any well reformed church, are all in Mister Knox's conscience, no small portion of Papist superstitions. In his opinion, nothing ought to be used in Church services that the Lord hath not sanctified, either by percept or by practice. Furthermore, that Knox could not prescribe to Anne how far to expose herself to dangers for these imperfections in religion which she cannot remedy; but herein she will be instructed by God's Holy Spirit. They were words that we all took to our hearts.

My fourth son, Anthony, was born in the November of fifteen-hundred-and-sixty and we again chose to have our child baptized at Saint Olave's Church. The minister who had been so of our liking in Edward's time was now dead, but the incumbent was sympathetic to our primitive Church ideals. He, we, and many other such zealous Protestants, would not give up our fight so easily. So in the fullness of time, my friends and family would find themselves at odds with the State once more...

*   *   *

After his return from Antwerp, Anthony fell out of touch with several of his factors. For a long time he had neither heard from his trusted man, Thomas Nicholas, in Tenerife, nor had he received a long overdue and expected shipment of goods. If there had been any sort of general trouble in the Canaries, then neither my husband nor his new partner had heard of it. That was, until a letter arrived for the attention of the Queen's minister. From that correspondence we learnt that our man in the Canaries had fallen foul of the attentions of the dreaded Inquisition.

Mister Nicholas had been seized almost twenty months before word of it had eventually come to us. After he had justly refused local overtures for protection money, all of Anthony's goods in Nicholas' safekeeping had been embargoed. Then our factor had been clapped in chains and thrown into a darkened hut of less than two paces in length and deprived of seeing daylight at all.

At first Nicholas had no idea why he had been detained, but then charges were brought at his subsequent arraignment, claiming that he had been reportedly heard by several bystanders, two common prostitutes and two thieves, saying that the English Mass was as good as, if not better than the Catholic one. He was also accused of refusing to take part in the Catholic Mass on the islands, which were of course, a Catholic dominion. It was also said that Nicholas had bragged that he would rather give all of his money away to the poor than to waste it upon buying bulls of Rome.

In his defence, Mister Nicholas denied saying any such things at all and even called upon a host of reliable witnesses to bear this out, and to their credit they did so. All the same, Nicholas was tortured and cast back into his dark prison once more while those in local authority tried to gather new charges against him.

But after his persecutors failed in that, Mister Nicholas was then brought back before the Inquisition and told that Queen Elizabeth was an enemy to the faith and that she had been widely preached against as being an anti-Christ. They even produced several Flemish witnesses to confirm this, using people who claimed to have been in London and who also swore that Elizabeth was maintaining Jewish laws and allowing circumcision; and that there was outrage amongst her own clergy against her rule.

Rightfully, Nicholas exclaimed that these were but wicked lies and that he was outraged at this slander against his Queen and so stood in her defence. Then, publicly, he also disputed the authority of his judge,

Francisco de Coronado, to try him of these 'offences', because the judge himself was a self-confessed Jew and therefore by the Papists' own laws, was not allowed to be an officer of the Inquisition. However, the judge refused to hand on the case to another, which again was an act contrary to their own law, and there was no recourse open to our factor or a higher authority at hand to whom he could appeal.

Then Nicholas shouted out that surly God had already shown His judgement upon two of the false witnesses against him; for one woman had been strangled in her bed after childbirth and one of the men hanged for it. Yet his well argued defence seemed to be of no avail, because he was subsequently incarcerated once more in his tiny prison cell.

However, not all was lost. Nicholas had earned the sympathy of several Spaniards looking on at the proceedings. They, having heard Nicholas demanding the right to be tried before Christ instead of this judge, thought it their Christian duty to then help him by getting some letters off the island so that others might know of his plight.

In his letters, Mister Nicholas begged Queen Elizabeth's Mister Chamberlain to inform the King of Spain of his plight and of the way in which the Queen of England was being portrayed. He also requested that the Inquisitor General of Spain to be asked to look at the evidence of the case and the circumstances in which my husband Anthony had been deprived of almost six thousand French crowns worth of goods. Nicholas also added that the loss could have been even higher because, prior to his arrest, his accusers had also tried to seize another ship of Anthony's which was loaded with sugar. But acting on a warning, the vessel had broken out of the port and escaped, though Nicholas had also been briefly detained over that incident as well.

Meanwhile, Mister Nicholas had been joined in his prison by another of Anthony's men in the Canaries, Mister Kingsmill. Kingsmill had also fallen victim to trumped-up charges, after refusing to pay his own accusers with 'protection' money; evidence indeed that innocent Englishmen were falling prey to systematic and unchecked corruption abroad.

Kingsmill's own troubles had begun at the end of Queen Mary's reign. Three English ships and a pinnace had arrived in port and, after landing a part of the cargo with Kingsmill, then proceeded on towards Guinea. It was at about that same time a ship from Flanders was reported missing.

On Grand Canary, the malicious official in charge was hopeful of obtaining a large bribe – by falsely accusing the English of having stolen the cargo of the lost Flanders vessel and of then sinking her. He also sequested all of the items that Kingsmill had landed. But when Kingsmill was asked to pay up for the release the goods, he refused to do so.

Later, when news came through that the missing ship had in fact been wrecked on the coast of Bretagne, Kingsmill went to the official and requested the immediate release of the confiscated goods. But the official refused to allow this and instead claimed that the seized goods were prohibited items. And then, even after Kingsmill spent over one-hundred doubles proving legally that they were not, the goods still remained impounded.

Meanwhile, Kingsmill's house had been subjected to a raid by an officer demanding to inspect his books of account. Clearly against all expectation, Kingsmill immediately obliged the man – even producing a Spanish translation. But the officer, not content with that, then had all of the chests in the house broken open, amid a flurry of protest by the enraged Englishman. Inside one was found a duplicate set of Kingsmill's accounts, only this time kept in English for Anthony's benefit. This was seized. In another chest, there came to light almost four yards of velvet and a piece of silk which was also confiscated on the grounds that it was forfeited. In all, over fourteen thousand ducats worth of my husband's goods was taken.

Kingsmill was informed that he was guilty of breaking a law passed back in the reign of King Henry. That was at a time when so much money was being taken out of Spanish dominions by dubious means that two laws were brought in compelling all foreigners residing within Spanish territory to keep their records of account in Spanish – so that the Spanish-speaking officers there could understand what was written down. Henceforth factors broke this regulation on pain of paying a hefty fine – of one-thousand ducats! It was this law that some of the Spanish authorities were now exploiting.

Kingsmill, like the majority of other foreign merchants had obediently complied, but after consulting lawyers upon this matter, had also kept a duplicate record of their transactions, tallying in every detail with the Spanish account, but this time in their own English language for the benefit of their masters back home. As these laws were primarily aimed at bankers, of which there were none on the Islands, the English thought that they had not transgressed it in any way and had indeed been at pains to comply with Spanish legislation.

When this officer had seized the duplicate English account book he demanded a fine. Kingsmill refused to pay. In response, this officer had a friend make a further complaint against Kingsmill, which of course he then adjudicated to his own advantage. My husband believed that all these hardships had been maliciously brought about, fuelled by the practice of officers being involved in such cases subsequently being rewarded with one third of any goods confiscated by way of fines.

After four years' imprisonment on the Canary Islands, Mister Kingsmill was eventually taken to the Castle of Seville in Spain, where the Inquisition had him hung in chains for seven months. When at last he was released, the priests told him that he would never be allowed to leave either Seville or Spain again. And when Mister Kingsmill – dutiful servant to the end – asked again for Anthony's goods to be released, still they refused.

By the month of May in fifteen-hundred-and-sixty-four, both Mister Nicholas and Mister Kingsmill were still pleading by letter for Queen Elizabeth's Minister to seek justice on their behalf. But justice in Elizabeth's court proved slow and elusive, unless of course Elizabeth turned out to be either the accuser or the plaintiff.

Both men eventually escaped the Spanish territories, but the stories of their wretched experiences, and those of many others so badly treated across the seas, only fuelled a growing hatred amongst English merchants and sailors for these Spanish oppressors. And such embers of discontent may so easily be fanned into the flames of war...

*   *   *

I enjoyed being a mother. And so I tried to devote as much time to my children as my dear mother had to my siblings and me. Yet by the time William had grown older and more adventurous, I had three other young sons and a daughter who needed my attention, along with another child on the way. In consequence, William was sometimes left to his own devices. And so it happened one day that, not long after our return to England from exile, William suffered a terrible accident that was witnessed by his less adventurous younger brother, Henry.

William was out and about with fellow students from St Paul's when he and some others climbed onto the roof of a house. Later, William could give no sound reason for doing so other than acting out of sheer daring.

Once atop the roof, William lost his footing and started to slip down the wet thatch. Henry screamed out in terror as William tried, desperately flaying his arms about, to find some hand-hold that would save him. But there was nothing to grab. So William fell to the ground like a stone and landed heavily upon the cobbled street below with a sickening crack.

My son lay upon the ground, motionless, as a crowd quickly gathered around him to see this unfortunate child – who had obviously broken his neck. But, suddenly, William stirred, jumped up like a startled hare, and then ran off, leaving nothing behind him other than the remnants of a broken school slate. According to all reason, such an accident should have killed him, yet miraculously he had survived, unscathed by the fall. God had preserved his life because there was still much in store for William. For indeed, 'we are God's workmanship, created in Christ Jesus to do good works, which God prepared in advance for us to do'.

'It is time,' Anthony told me, 'for us to send William away and into the hands of our fellow brother mercers to learn the family trade...'

Chapter Sixteen

As with the proposal of marriage from the King of Spain, in trade Queen Elizabeth was loathe to show her true hand. In the days of both her father and grandfather, alliance with Spain had been valuable, for it had been made on equal terms by which England stood to gain as much as she gave.

Elizabeth rightfully feared that now an alliance between England and Spain, be it in bed or by treaties of trade, would be no such thing. For she had seen how ill used England and the English could be when she observed King Philip II's previous marriage to her half-sister Mary. Then, Philip had become King of England in both name and deed, and he had subsequently turned this realm into nothing more than a pawn in the hands of the Habsburgs. And he used England in war with France for his own gain, while England reaped nothing but loss.

But with Queen Mary dead, and Calais lost, the words Spain and Rome could now be spat out in the same curse. The merchants of London blamed both Rome and Spain for the depth of depression English trade was now suffering. No, Elizabeth would have no match with Spain, and yet Spain would prove slow to realise that. And neither would Her Majesty be dictated to by the King of Portugal over English trade with Guinea.

In fifteen-sixty-one, Elizabeth's Minister, Cecil, was instructed to tell the Spanish Ambassador that, 'The Pope had no right to partition the world and to give and take kingdoms to whomever he pleased.' And in the spring of that same year, the King of Portugal sent an ambassador to Queen Elizabeth, too, with the renewed demand that English expeditions to the Gold Coast be stopped.

Anthony used to say that Queen Elizabeth received ambassadors from both countries like an innocent maiden entertaining her first romantic advance from behind a fan, to cover her blushes and thus make it impossible to catch the true expression of her words. The eyes might look bright and so full of promise, while the lips yet hidden from view firmly mouthed the word 'no'.

Elizabeth gave the Portuguese Ambassador her assurance that she would command her subjects not to trade with any part of Africa under Portugal's dominion. As ever, it was a reply from the Queen that could read two ways.

Queen Elizabeth and Cecil tended to favour the same view as previously put forward by the English merchant in the reign of Queen Mary; that the Guinea coast was not in fact governed by Portugal, but was instead self governed by mostly independent African princes. Therefore, by her command, she was only prohibiting the English from visiting Elmina, which of course no English merchant wanted to visit anyway. In fact, Elizabeth encouraged trade with the African chiefdoms on either side of Elmina, or at any other place where the Portuguese were not seen to be in actual occupation.

Secondly, any English merchants thinking about sending ships to Guinea were commanded that they must first make their intentions known to the Lord Admiral. On doing so they were then simply advised about the Queen's promise to the Portuguese Ambassador and asked to observe it. After that, they were allowed to proceed.

Thus, under the rule of Elizabeth, voyages to the Gold Coast continued, with even the Queen entering the gold trade as a kind of adventurer herself. After all, she was responsible for the good use of her tax payers' money, much of which went on maintaining the navy. What better way then of making certain that idle ships in peacetime did not become a drain on the treasury than to send them out upon some enterprise that might help them earn their keep? Anthony remarked that it made sound business sense to him and the other English merchants.

Thus four royal ships were committed to this

endeavour, with Her Majesty finding all the equipment and paying over five-hundred pounds towards the provisioning of the vessels. The crews' wages were paid by the merchants, who also provided the trade cargo for the outward journey and kept up the ships' repairs. In return, a predetermined share of any profits went straight back into the Treasury, with the State bearing the risk should any ship be totally lost.

My brother John, recognised as an exceptionally good commander, took charge of the first expedition of that year – fifteen-sixty-one. They encountered terrible weather, but nonetheless managed to make over three-thousand pounds in profit. With subsequent expeditions there were always heavy casualties, mostly lost to disease and sickness, although John took every possible step to minimise the loss of his men. And so they respected him very highly. Other sailors were much less fortunate and life for them was often short and miserable, and yet many were willing to gamble against such dreadful odds in the hope of surviving to reap enormous riches for themselves.

Despite such loss of life, which sometimes included the loss of ships as well, almost every expedition ended with a spectacular profit. In fact, the cargoes of gold and ivory and other luxuries proved so lucrative that an expedition could afford to lose two out of every three ships sent and still make a huge profit.

And so, again, the King of Portugal dispatched an ambassador to protest against the English trade. This time it was on the grounds that his county's monopoly of the Gold Coast trade was lawful due to Portugal's conquest and effective occupation of those lands. But as luck would have it, Cecil was able to call an English witness to testify to the contrary, and confirming that Elmina and another fort at Cape Tres Puntas were the only Portuguese possessions along that entire stretch of the African coast. His name was Martin Frobisher and he had been held captive in Guinea for a number of months before his release and repatriation to England.

Now exasperated, the Portuguese Ambassador

went on to argue that the conquest of the neighbouring African chiefdoms had been undertaken peacefully – through their conversion to Christianity. But not to be outflanked, Queen Elizabeth replied that if that were indeed true, then the Ambassador had best advise his king to command that these recently acquired Portuguese subjects desist from trading with us English. Furthermore, Her Majesty would not order her subjects to stop trading at any place where they were already warmly received.

The Portuguese Ambassador, in response, probably expressed the official outrage that was expected of him, but both Elizabeth and Cecil knew full well that he was but an empty vessel, a mere messenger given the task of posturing. Quite simply, Portugal could not afford to go to war upon such a matter. The bulk of her most lucrative trade came into Portugal via Antwerp, and so passed through the Channel at the mercy of the English Navy. Thus under Queen Elizabeth and her Lord Cecil's guidance, my family and England's merchant adventurers steered a brave course unto ever new trading horizons...

Chapter Seventeen

My son must surely remember much of the following story well. However, he was still a youth and it was long ago, and so he may not know the detail in which it was related to me by Mister Randall after what had come to pass. So I will recall it anyway, that he might remember it with fondness and may be enticed to add a little more with his own re-telling.

It is all about Russia; that vast barbaric land as far north as good Englishmen dare travel, and where up until my son's own lifetime no English man had dared set foot.

In the winter of fifteen-fifty-two, an ambitious undertaking was beginning to form amongst our merchant adventurers, by way of a quest to find a North East Passage to Asia. There had been a terrible slump in our English cloth trade and our merchants were desperate to find new markets for their trade. Cathay and the Moluccas bore too hot a climate to want our heavy English wool, but reason prevailed that if only we could find passage to the cooler, northern climes of Asia, then a ready market might ensue.

And so these merchants, including of course members of my family, organised a stock company and styled themselves as 'The Merchant Adventurers of England for the Discovery of Lands, Territories, Isles, Dominions and Seignories[60] – though it soon became more simply known as the Muscovy Company. Thus armed with a patent from King Edward, The Muscovy Company had been granted the monopoly of making such discoveries of hitherto unknown trade opportunities in any regions lying to the north-east, north or north-west of our realm.

Not long before King Edward's death, this enterprise's first expedition of three ships set off in the May of fifteen-fifty-three with one Hugh Willoughby as its commander and Richard Chancellor as his second. However, whilst lying off the coast of Norway, a great storm blew up and separated Willoughby and a second

---

60   Lands held under a feudal Lord.

ship from Chancellor and his.

Thinking Chancellor and his ship the Edward Bonaventure lost, an undaunted Willoughby carried on to round the North Cape and continued on eastwards until he discovered the coast of Nova Zembla. By this time it was August and the season for exploration almost over, because soon after this month the harsh Artic winter begins to set in.

Being amply supplied with provisions and with himself and his men in good spirits and robust health, Willoughby decided to head back to the coast of Lapland, where he decided to anchor for the winter before resuming exploration the following spring. It was to prove a fatal mistake. Willoughby and his men had grossly underestimated the severity of the cold that they would encounter. For, the following summer, Russian fishermen would come upon the still anchored ships to find them full of rotting corpses. Every man aboard had frozen to death.

Meanwhile, Chancellor and the men of Edward Bonaventure made their way to Vardo, a pre-agreed rendezvous point. After Willoughby failed to show, and now believing the other two ships lost, Chancellor and his men proceeded on the mission alone. When he came to the mouth of a great gulf we now know as the White Sea, he explored it, hoping to find new markets for the English. At its southern point he found the Russian village of Archangel and so wintered his men there until spring.

During his stay, Chancellor found out that this county's only trading contact was mostly overland and through the agency of the Hanseatic League, and that the League abused its monopoly by charging the Russians extortionate prices for European goods and actively took steps to keep other would-be European traders away.

Armed with this knowledge, Chancellor immediately seized the opportunity to journey to Moscow so that he could present his credentials from King Edward to the Russian Emperor. After a long interview, at which he was warmly received, Chancellor managed to obtain leave for the English merchants to seek terms to trade in Russia, and on very favourable terms. Having reached his goal, he returned to England in the summer of the following year.

Returning from a subsequent voyage of negotiation two years later, the Edward Bonaventure was wrecked on the east coast of Scotland during a storm. Chancellor was drowned, but an ambassador from Russia, travelling for the first time on board a ship bound for England, survived and soon became the first representative of a Russian Emperor to be received at court in London.

By now, Queen Mary had come to the throne and King Philip of Spain installed as the King-consort of England. To the relief of the Muscovy Company, Mary issued a new charter for the company to trade in Russia. Phillip, meanwhile, also lent his own authority to the enterprise. This set a precedent for much later, because it implied that he did not consider English voyages to the north-west as an infringement of Spain's monopoly as granted by the Pope. It was a precedent that the incoming Queen Elizabeth would seize some years later. While she continued to be seen to refuse the sanction of letters of patent to areas south of the Azores, she would however willingly grant patents freely for this and other northern projects.

Therefore, in the December of fifteen-sixty-six, the Bill for The Merchant Adventurers Corporation, for discovery of Russia, and new trades, was read for the third time and passed by Parliament. The Muscovy Company could now turn its full attention towards building a trading partnership with Russia, which was both a promising prospect and one that seemed beyond the interference of Spain and Portugal.

*   *   *

About eighteen months later, in April, Mister Thomas Randall came to visit Anthony at our country home in Essex. Not only was Randall a long-standing and dear friend of my husband, but he was also an ambassador in the service of Her Majesty Queen Elizabeth.

Randall explained that Queen Elizabeth was now proposing to send him to visit the Emperor of Russia, and our friend in turn was offering to take my son William with him on this exciting expedition 'to see something of the fashion of the Muscovy', as he termed it.

When I first heard Mister Randall's suggestion, my heart was set firmly against this prospect for my son. William was on the cusp of manhood and only just returned to us after so long abroad as a part of his mercer apprenticeship, so I had hoped to spend a little more time with him before we lost him to trade once more.

William, on the other hand, was extremely excited by this prospect and adamant that he should be allowed to go.

'I do not want him to go,' I said. 'He is not yet eighteen and I have heard it told that Russia is a barbaric place. Besides, Husband,' I argued fervently, 'how often have I heard you tell of the great number of men you have lost at sea on this expedition or that?'

'To the tropics? Then yes,' Anthony countered, 'that is perfectly true, Rose. But it is the hot, sultry climate and the sickness to be had in those wretched lands that carry off our men. Russia is different... and this trip is different! In going northwards at this time of year, sickness is not a concern,' Anthony added reassuringly. 'And I agree with Thomas here, that it is a golden opportunity for our boy to see something of the world for himself. I went on my first long sea expedition before I was William's age. And look at your own brothers, John and Michael, how many times they have gone away? And each time, praise God, have they not returned home again safe and sound? And we both know that William is more Locke than he is Hickman.' He laughed at the last point he'd just made.

Anthony was right. Our second son, Henry, had also turned out to be very much like me – a studious lover of his books. Both William and Henry had attended St Paul's school, where their father was once Surveyor, but it was Henry who went on to be promoted by the Company of Mercers and continued on to Cambridge University. William was a dutiful scholar but had not the passion for devoted study that would envelope his other brothers.

When still young, Henry was ever the trouble-free son who ne'er gave a worry to his caring parents, whereas William had always been very much like his Uncle John. Both were born slight in frame and of such pale and gentle countenance and manner that it belied the courageous lions housed within. Both were incurable adventurers. And both have caused me as much anxiety about their wellbeing as any other family would have to endure through the course of a dozen lifetimes.

'My dearest Lady Rose,' Mister Randall added in support of what my husband was saying, 'by all accounts, Russia is a harsh and strange land, and yet Christian too, I am assured. And not the Popish form either! So is it not our Christian duty to set them our example of how a good society should conduct itself? What better an opportunity could there be to temper your son for seeking out new trade opportunities beyond the sea? That is if he intends to take up his father and grandfather's business in earnest.'

'I do!' William exclaimed emphatically.

And thus my husband and Mister Randall eventually edged me gently into giving my blessing to the proposition. After all, what else could I do? How could I argue against such truths? Even so, I was a devoted mother and still harboured deep uneasiness about letting my dear son go. Then I thought of my mother, and then of my father, and of all of the sons that they had let go. So I felt a little ashamed of my initial response.

We bade farewell to William at the start of May

because, until that time of year, the great sea to the north and beyond is often ice-bound, as it is all about the coasts of that vast land. My son looked so young and slight against the muscular frames of his seasoned companions. I watched him on the deck as he took off his cap and waved it heartily as his ship and its party slipped away from the quay and on towards the mouth of the River Thames. As I turned, with tears running down my cheek, towards Anthony, he held me close and assured me that all would end well for our boy. I tried with all my heart to believe him, yet still this mother's loving concern for her child would not let me be.

Four months later, Mister Randall had returned to our home and was sitting by our fireside. Over a goblet of wine he began recounting the events of that journey. As he did so, I knew that my anxieties prior to the expedition had not been unfounded.

By all accounts the crossing went well, and after about a month or so their ships were already in the White Sea and lying off shore near their final destination. Mister Randall, thinking it good for both the body and soul of all aboard, allowed the party to break their journey by putting in a little way down the mouth of a river. There, the gentlemen were given a little respite before making for Archangel and the tough journey ahead – over land to Moscow.

Apparently my William leaped at the chance to be able to take a pleasant walk upon the land after being aboard the ship for so long and so eagerly disembarked with the others. It was a pleasant morning, even amongst the bleak and lonely landscape. They hauled their small boats ashore at a lightly wooded spot, and decided to take a relaxing stroll and a meal there before heading back to the ship and concluding their passage.

It was on the short way back to their ship that Mister Randall had a mind to ask for William. When he did, he was told that Mister Hickman had boarded one of the other shallops and so thought no more of his absence from the party.

As the ships journeyed on, now hugging

the coastline as they made their way down towards Archangel, the terrain ashore quickly became more desolate by the mile, and it became criss-crossed by countless muddy inlets where small rivulets and streams tipped out into the vast bay. It was a place barren of human life or settlement and looked uninviting in the extreme. It was an unfriendly a landscape as one might wish never to encounter.

Then, only much later as it was nearing the strange twilight that passes for night in the brief Russian summertime, Mister Randall suddenly thought to check up on William, to make certain that all was well with him, especially as the Ambassador had promised Anthony faithfully to take every possible care of his dear friends' son.

William was not in his place. And when the other ship was then scoured from bow to stern in search of him, still William could not be found. Mister Randall was horrified and could only conclude that our young lad must have somehow been accidentally left behind on the shore.

Chapter Eighteen

Immediately Mister Randall commanded the ships to drop anchor and ordered his men ashore once more. Then they sounded trumpets as wood was hastily gathered and set afire to make a great fiery beacon. If William was out there somewhere, trying to catch up with them in the gathering darkness, he might then see it and listen better for their frantic signals and somehow find his way to them.

Then Randall, as he later freely admitted to my husband, threw himself upon his knees with all the others and prayed for William's safe return, he also silently and secretly commended William's soul to the Lord. For, in truth, he did not expect to see him again.

While all this was happening, my son had meanwhile managed to pick his way back out of the river mouth and onto the seashore in an effort to catch up with the ships. In all that time he did not come across a house or settlement, and he met only one other person, a strange-looking and wizened old man, who of course could not understand a word of English or any of the other languages William spoke. Nonetheless, somehow the two managed to communicate by using both signs and stick drawings in the sand, and this was enough for the stranger to be able give my son some directions that would help guide him over several difficult to traverse creeks and obstacles that he would soon encounter.

With fervent prayers for his own deliverance, William set off again and made for where he had hoped Mister Randall and the ships had gone.

For more than fifteen miles he then trudged through a veritable wasteland. With the onshore wind buffeting and numbing his ears, there was no way in which he could have heard the trumpet signals from his rescue party. Nor could he have seen the firelight for the many high banks that lay betwixt him and any hope of rescue. And yet, as God would have it, just as he and the rest of the expedition were fast giving up all hope, William sighted his comrades. At first he could barely believe his eyes, but then he shouted out to them and every face in the group looked towards him.

It was only when he was safely aboard ship again and heard the ship's pilot talking with Mister Randall that William began to realise the full potential for great danger in which he had been. For this local man explained that, had William been forced to lay up somewhere to sleep, being alone and unarmed as he was, in all likelihood he might have been overcome and devoured by the multitude of wild beasts that inhabited those parts – especially deadly bears and hungry wolves.

Drawing towards Moscow, the principle city of Muscovia and the seat of the Emperor of Russia, the waterway played out, and so the party was forced to hire the local unshod trotting mares.

'These beasts are nothing like our fine English horses,' Mister Randall explained. 'They are massive, robust creatures renowned for their sure-footedness and strength and ability to endure the dreadfully rugged terrain of that country.'

The passage onwards with these beasts of burden was very arduous. So much so that many of their English riders, having been shaken about so much and for so long, found that some had nosebleeds while others even bled from their ears. And yet, Mister Randall was amazed to discover that William was the only man amongst the party left unscathed or unaffected by this gruelling hardship.

And so Mister Randall later exclaimed to Anthony with raucous laughter, 'Mister Hickman, you have in William a son that you may send to whatever corner of the world you may! For I am certain that he could endure any hardness ever sent his way!'

I remember the great look of delight on my husband's face as his friend continued to recount in minute detail the rest of his sojourn to Moscow. For Anthony would have dearly liked to have travelled to Russia also, but by then his great travelling days were already behind him. Yet he felt that hearing about this epic journey first hand from his friend was almost as good as having travelled through that amazing land himself.

Mister Randall said that he had found the people not ill-natured towards us English, but were cruder in their manners. That which might pass for ill-breeding, or even offensive amongst our own fellows passed without adverse comment amongst the Russians.

He said that the Russian people's greatest passion in life was to drink. Thus it was that they often drank until even the man who was considered the most sober amongst his peers needed to be led to bed by his wife. And while being entertained, Russian guests do not seem to worry if the host's table is scant, or if the meat is of poor quality, as long as the drink he serves is good. Then all other shortcomings, no matter how great, are forgiven.

Mister Randall added that it is not unusual to be offered at one time as many as a dozen different kinds of drink of varying fortified strengths – from spirits and liqueurs to other stranger brews. One particular favourite of the Russians is clear like water and yet its taste is tart enough to take the breath away, while yet another is similar to mead and made with flower honey so thick that it clings to the lips like ship's tar, albeit in a quite pleasing way.

From his account, the appearance of the Russian people can apparently be quite deceiving. Everyone seems able to afford buckskin and many wear it for want of good cloth. And even those dressed in greasy or ragged clothing that, in London one might pass in the street and easily take for some poor wretch, can bring misconception. Because in Russia such people own the horses they ride!

'Women proudly sit astride their trotting ponies and ride them like men do, Randall exclaimed, 'and no one looking on bats an eyelid!'

He also described how these women all have at least one ear pieced and adorned with gold and silver rings, and how both men and women alike walk with a purposeful gait, and though their weather-worn faces look wise, there is also a world-weary sadness set about them too.

'These ordinary Russian folk are, on many counts, not a very godly people,' Mister Randall noted with a raise of his eyebrow, 'although they profess fervently to be Christians. Though not Papists, they crouch themselves low with their foreheads touching the ground, in deep homage, when coming upon one of their holy crosses set out of doors by the roadside. However, once they are inside their own homes they seem steeped in sin. They seem to find no great shame in defiling another man's bed and his wife, and indeed often make little effort to hide such transgression. And their women cover their tawny faces with some sort of thin plaster that they then set about gaudily painting in their lips and their eyebrows so that when done, some look like harlots. However, others have become so skilful at this art that the finished article might deceive any poor young unwary man into thinking that they are far more beautiful than be true!'

Anthony laughed and replenished Mister Randall's vessel.

'And what of the land?' I asked trying to change from this indelicate subject. 'Is it as good as in Surrey?'

Mister Randall obliged.

'No, it is not at all like Surrey,' Randall laughed. 'The soil is sandy and not very fertile at all. There is more waste and scrubby ground than areas fit for growing grain. And yet, pristine woods and forests they have in abundance. Trees stretch as far as a man can ride in a week and beyond; everywhere teaming with wolves and bears and so many other dangerous creatures that one never dare travel alone or unarmed, and never by night!'

Mister Randall explained that the Russians did manage to grow corn, even though the ground was not thawed enough for ploughing or planting until much before May. This meant that as soon as the corn was ripe it was cut and dried as quickly as possible before the cold frost closed in once more and spoiled it.

Then Mister Randall told us how the winters there are so long and severe that they last for seven months and with so much snow that there is no grass or pasture to be seen. So all the precious cattle and sheep and such are brought indoors with many a Russian happily sharing his home with his skinny livestock.

Evidently, the Russians' houses were not huge, but always carefully positioned on the highest ground to keep them raised as much above the snowline as possible and therefore all the drier come the thaw. The walls are made of great tree trunks with the gaps in between being in filled with moss to keep in the warmth and keep out the drafts. The pitched roofs are made of rafters which are then covered with thick shingles of bark, which Mister Randall noted were very efficient at running off the rain. In each room there is a stove to help stave off the bitter winter cold, yet no one worries for lack of fuel as there is always so much at hand; much more than they can expect to burn in one season. But of course to run out of supplies would bring disaster.

'They sleep on beds made of bearskin, with fur for blankets, and they use their saddles for pillows,' Randall continued, adding that he found it rather odd considering there was so much wildfowl everywhere in that country and that there could be no shortage of feathers or down for either stuffing pillows or mattresses.

'Unless,' Anthony surmised, 'the Russians go without such comfort on purpose, so that their bodies do not softened and weakened against the harshness of that country.'

Mister Randall agreed that this was possibly so.

'And as for the dead that die in winter,' Mister Randall marveled, 'they cannot be buried immediately because the ground turns as hard as iron for half the year. So they are left in their coffins until the soil can be broken into to at sewing time. And yet the wonder of it all is that apparently these bodies do not decompose...'

I immediately thought of my mother and Merton and then tried to shake that thought from my head.

'Instead,' Mister Randall explained, 'the cold

turns the corpses as hard as stone, and so even many months later they look just as they did on the day they died. And thus I have seen the Russians storing meat carcasses hung frozen from the rafters in their outbuildings so that they may it eat it as fresh throughout the winter.'

Mister Randall also explained how each man in Russia, no matter how lowly his station, lives in the sound knowledge that upon his death he shall have a wood coffin; for wood is so plentiful there as to have almost no value at all.

'But what of Moscow? And the Emperor?' Anthony asked. 'You have said nothing of him yet?'

Randall did not straight away answer. Instead he drank down his wine and then, reaching over to the jug on the table, refilled his empty goblet set beside him. Then, having gathered up his thoughts and primed himself with a huge gulp of his drink, Mister Randall continued to answer my husband.

'How to describe Moscow?' Randall sighed deeply. 'It is quite unlike any other city I have seen. The architecture is so different, yet in its own way elegant, while the streets are very rough and in utter chaos! Of a morning one might meet with seven or eight hundred sledges, coming and going and loaded with fish, and wheat, and all manner of wares, and all impeded by such disorderly conduct. The Emperor's palace is built of brick and yet is more like a fortress to keep his Majesty's subjects out. Though once inside, everything cries out of incredible wealth. When we dined, there must have been above two hundred guests at the table, and all were served in golden vessels! And as for the Emperor?' Mister Randall's tone darkened. 'He drinks too much and laughs too loudly. And he loves and hates with equal ferocity. He is extremely intelligent and apparently never forgets a thing. In their language, the Russian people call him 'Grozny'...'

'Grozny?' I asked.

'Yes, Grozny,' Mister Randall replied. 'I asked our translator what it meant and he explained that the Great White Sea, when it is frozen in the depths of winter is grozny, or snow storms that white-out everything from view and blind a man's eyes are grozny. The crashing of thunder or sheets of lightening, or to find yourself alone and unarmed in the forest with a great bear charging towards you with its front limbs raised and its teeth snarling, all of these are grozny he told me. All are awesome – as is the Emperor!'

Randall quickly quaffed some more of his wine before concluding.

'In a short time we quickly learned much more about him. The Russian Emperor can be witty and charming one moment and unimaginably cruel and ruthless the next. It is freely said that when he was just thirteen years old, the Emperor ordered a rival prince to be thrown to a pack of starved hunting dogs. Then he looked on as they tore the poor wretch to pieces. He is sexually and morally depraved – and yet is even contemplating asking Queen Elizabeth to marry him! Once, that is, he has rid himself of his current wife! Yes, he is a tyrant beyond imagining, and now, by Royal consent, he is a close trading partner to our country. His people may call him 'Ivan Grozny' but already those in our company call him Ivan the Terrible...'

Anthony could appreciate at once the dilemma. Trading with Russia offered wonderful opportunities that would give the English the capacity to make incredible profits. And yet it would make our sovereign Queen Elizabeth an ally of undoubtedly the cruelest tyrant alive. My husband and his friend went on to discuss the implications at length before, happily for me, moving on to other future opportunities like the New World that was suddenly opening on the horizon. It was an horizon with great possibilities that Anthony looked forward to sharing in with our son.

In the year of our Lord, fifteen-hundred-and-sixty-nine, Ivan Vasilivich, self-styled 'Great Lord Emperor of all Russia, Volodemer, Moscouria, Emperor of Cazan, Tuersky, Vgorsky, Permisky, Vadasky, Bulgaria, and many others; Lord and great Duke of the

Low Countries of Nourogrod, Chernigosky, Resansky, Polotsky, Rastow, Veralaue, Bealosera, Owdorsky, Condinsky and all Siberland, Great Commander of all the North Parts, Lord of Leifland and many other Northward, Southward and Westward' granted to his 'Sister Elizabeth, by the grace of God, Queen of England, France and Ireland, Defender of the Faith', and the right worshipful fellowship of English merchants, the privileges of trading freely within his vast Empire.

*   *   *

At about the time of William's voyage, my brother Henry died. His widow Anne then married a man five years her junior. His name was Edward Dering and he was an extreme Protestant preacher, one of the most notable of his day, whose enthusiasm for his calling was only superseded by his lack of tact.

In fifteen-hundred-and-seventy-three, Dering had been lecturing on an Epistle at Saint Paul's after which he was suddenly seized and hauled before the Star Chamber[61]. In the December, his preaching was prohibited on the personal orders of the Queen herself. The slow road to our renewed persecution had begun.

This was also the same year in which my beloved husband Anthony suddenly died. So swift was his passing that he had not even time to make out his will.

---

61   The Court of the Star Chamber's purpose was to hear cases of political libel and treason.

Chapter Nineteen

Throckmorton. Whatever possessed me to marry Simon Throckmorton? Had my father been alive he would surely have smelt the rat out. I did marry him though. My dearest Anthony had died leaving me utterly bereft but I was still considered to be of a marriageable age, and a good prospect for another man to take as his wife. Especially so if he were a widower like Simon Throckmorton with a motherless brood to yet raise up. Fate and families contrive to bind such loose ends together with undignified haste; it is an English way of survival.

It should have been a good match. The Throckmorton family were generally highly regarded. At least they had been so under the late King Edward, and Sir Nicholas Throckmorton who had been a fellow prisoner with Anthony at The Fleet was particularly admired and respected by Lord Burghley. Some Throckmortons had positively thrived under Queen Mary and then also gone forward to find favour with Queen Elizabeth. But a few, in Her Majesty's royal opinion, were cast so shadowy to have no true colour that could be determined.

I learned from my brother that there was some ridiculous cloud of doubt and malicious gossip strung about the question of Simon Throckmorton's religious standing.

'Some ill-doer has put it about that Simon is a closet Catholic. The rumour is quite outrageous, for I know the fellow to be nothing of the sort,' my brother assured me. 'Once he is seen to be married to a good upstanding Protestant, then the wind will be taken out of that particular sail for good!'

So I was the good upstanding Protestant chosen to marry Simon Throckmorton. As a Christian duty I obliged, thinking that my role would be one of a benevolent matron to his motherless children and as an honourable companion to him as we stood on the cusp of old age together.

I was so wrong! His children hated me, and Simon's affection towards me barely bubbled above lukewarm. Perhaps the only good thing I could say about my life in Huntingdonshire was that at least it was not too far away from my sons, Anthony and Henry, when they were at university in Cambridge.

Simon Throckmorton always bemoaned the fact that he was born a third son. A third son, as he would so emphatically state, is so often overlooked and under-provided for, because the heir and the 'spare' usually take the lion's share of the family fortune, leaving little left but scavenge for any unfortunate enough to be born after them.

Simon was also deeply jealous of his brothers, who had forged ahead with successful lives while he whined and malingered in the rural backwaters of Brampton. Yet, as I once pointed out to Simon, my late husband Anthony had also been a third son. But that had not stopped him from carving out a good position in life for himself and for my family. Simon though, lacked Anthony's ethics in both matters of commerce and honour.

Instead, early on in adulthood, Simon had decided to attach himself like a leech to one of his father's friends, Sir Robert Tyrwhitt, hoping that success by association would bring him good fortune. Indeed, my husband was elected to Parliament twice under Tyrwhitt's patronage but ultimately his association with the man would prove to be his downfall.

I remember Anthony and my brother Thomas talking about the affair involving the late dowager Queen Katherine and this Tyrwhitt's part in its investigation. Under King Henry, Tyrwhitt's star had risen strongly and seemed set to burn brightly, especially so when the old King married Robert's cousin by marriage – Katherine Parr, as she was then.
It was at about this time that Tyrwhitt was knighted and became Queen Katherine's Master of the Horse.

Katherine had been a good woman, by all accounts, who deserved much better than that which love had meted out to her. Four times she was married and three times she was widowed.

She was only fifteen when her family married her off to Lord Edward Burgh, the second Baron of Gainsborough. For good or for ill, the coupling was short, for her first husband died after they had been together for only four years. No doubt, having done her duty by her family for a second time – having again been widowed – her hopes may have risen to consider the possibility of remarrying for a third time, at last out of her own feelings and with her childhood sweetheart, Thomas Seymour.

But this was not to be. King Henry, having handed over his fifth wife, Katherine Howard, to the axe man shortly after visiting the Burgh's manor house at Gainsborough, had apparently taken a liking to the serial widow and made her his last Queen.

After the King's death, Sir Robert Tyrwhitt and his wife remained in attendance on the dowager Queen Katherine and her teen-aged step daughter, Lady Elizabeth. And then, at last, Katherine married Thomas Seymour.

Seymour had once suggested that the Lady Jayne Grey join Katherine's household, in the chance that perhaps he might be able to broker a marriage between her and his nephew, King Edward, but much to her parents' disappointment that had never happened. Perhaps his attention was drawn too much in another direction, perhaps towards Katherine's young step-daughter, the Lady Elizabeth?

It appears that Lady Tyrwhitt was much disturbed by Thomas' neglect of his wife Katherine during the final year of her life, and especially when she was pregnant with their first child.

Lady Tyrwhitt was especially outraged after she claimed to have repeatedly witnessed, during that pregnancy, Thomas' blatant attempts to woo the young Elizabeth with the apparent complicity of two of the lady's personal servants – Catherine Ashley and Thomas Parry.

At the time, Elizabeth could have easily still hoped to have succeeded to the throne should both her half-siblings have died without an heir, a point not to wasted upon the much older Seymour. If Seymour in the meantime were to lose his poor, aging wife in childbirth, then he might easily persuade a young and infatuated Elizabeth to marry him? He could in turn have become her co-regent and, as such, become the most powerful man in the realm. All was possible.

It was after Katherine had indeed died after childbirth that Lady Tyrwhitt and her husband informed Kind Edward's Privy Council of this matter, and it was then that the seeds of both the Tyrwhitt's and my husband Simon's downfall were truly sewn.

Alarmed by this rumour, the Privy Council then sent the Tyrwhitts to personally oversee the day-to-day care of Lady Elizabeth at Hatfield, while at the same time quickly removing both Ashley and Parry. Together Tyrwhitt and his wife were carefully instructed to try to glean as much damming evidence from Lady Elizabeth as they could, so that it could then be used in a trial against her and Thomas Seymour.

This should have been simple for a man of Tyrwhitt's intelligence and one already so well versed in the cross-examination of others. And so flattery, threats, stories of Seymour having already confessed all were tried in vain. Lady Elizabeth should have been an easy nut to crack, and yet although she was only fifteen at the time, she proved more than a match for Tyrwhitt.

Lady Elizabeth would admit to nothing. Instead, she broke down into floods of tears to put him off his guard and then sulked, or else attacked the integrity and motives of any who dared accuse her of a sexual liaison with Seymour. She used every weapon at her disposal as she wriggled, like an adder with its head caught in a cleft stick, this way and that, to free herself. And then she even brought counter charges against Tyrwhitt.

Although Tyrwhitt was convinced that there was some sort of secret pact between Elizabeth and her two servants, Master Parry and Mistress Ashley, to withhold the truth, they too proved equally unshakeable in the face of interrogation. 'They all sing one song,' Tyrwhitt complained, 'and she hath set the note for them.'

The two servants were afterwards richly rewarded for their steadfast loyalty when Elizabeth did indeed eventually come to the crown. Parry was immediately knighted and made treasurer of the household, while Mistress Ashley received enormous consideration thereafter.

Elizabeth was one to e'er hold a grudge. If you crossed her and succeeded in keeping your head, you can be certain that she never forgot or ever truly forgave. Although Tyrwhitt and his wife had treated Elizabeth gently, she never forgave them for their part in her so near a downfall.

After Elizabeth succeeded to the throne, both Sir Robert Tyrwhitt and Simon Throckmorton's fates were firmly sealed. In the Queen's eyes Tyrwhitt was no more than a dirty dog and my husband no more than a fellow dog that had lain down with him and risen up infested by the same vile fleas. And no matter that Tyrwhitt died a full year before my Anthony; or that Throckmorton had taken me as his wife, a woman well known for her strong Protestant views, in Queen Elizabeth's eyes Simon would remain stigmatised by association until his dying day.

Chapter Twenty

The New World. This is where my younger brother, Michael, had always insisted that Englishmen's hopes and dreams of fortune lay waiting to be turned into reality. He had always been a bright boy, keen on education and bookish like I was. And yet unlike me, it was not the weightier issues of Christian faith that occupied his mind. No, Michael was obsessed with the New World and finding a passage beyond it. The world is round, and so therefore if only we could find a sea route around this new landfall, then logically we must be able to reach Asia and Cathay. Then we would have new and direct trade routes that would bypass those already monopolised by others or terrorised by Barbary pirates, who attacked our ships, intercepted our cargoes, and enslaved our sailors.

My late father had kept my little brother Michael in grammar schools at home in England until he was about thirteen years old. To follow on in his older mercer brothers' steps, Michael too was then sent across the sea, away to Flanders and France to learn the languages there and then to see the world.

When I next saw him, he was almost a full-grown man, rugged of body and with a seafarer's swarthy skin. He spent fifteen years in perpetual travel, during which time he passed through almost every Christian country in the world. He went to Portugal and Spain, where he saw first-hand the value of their trade with the Americas. After that, he went to Venice and Greece and to conduct trade with the Levant.[62] All the while, this New World vision of bright new trading prospects burned on in his mind like a guiding beacon.

Then, in fifteen-hundred-and-seventy-six, it looked as though Michael's dream was about to come true when he became one of the main financial backers in an expedition sent in search of the fabled North West Passage to Cathay. How I wish that my dear husband Anthony was not by then dead, for I know that Michael would have listened to him. If he had, then he could

---

62   The Levant – the countries boarding on the eastern Mediterranean.

have saved himself from so much grief and the villainy of that wretch, Martin Frobisher.

My brother had come home to London to take up a position in mercer management as a worshipful agent of the Muscovy Company. Although previously the Company had firmly declined any suggestions in relation to trying more exploration to the North West, Michael was hopeful that changing circumstances in trade might soften this attitude.

My brother was long experienced with trading in the Levant. Yet like others, he had become disillusioned by the huge losses they were suffering through the veracious piracy that plagued those waters. A better trade route to Asia was needed desperately.

While Michael had still been on his travels, for years he had made a thorough study of this possibility, which had occupied his quieter moments. He reasoned that since there is a great land mass in the southern hemisphere, nature must surely then balance that out with another to the north. And since there is Magellan's sea passage to the south, likewise it must have an opposite? Consequently, Michael built up a wealth of written notes upon the matter, the credit for which that barely literate Frobisher would later lay claim to as his own.

It was written into the Muscovy Company Charter that it should finance just such areas of exploration. So, believing that the time had come for trying just such a daring venture, Michael desperately needed an outsider to independently approach the Company anew with the suggestion. This someone, backed up by the patronage of the Earl of Warwick, turned out to be Martin Frobisher.

Frobisher was a hardened seafarer by then who would undertake anything just for as long as it promised to bring him wealth.

When he came to the Company to request that he be permitted to make an attempt to find this elusive passage, Michael was a member of the committee which examined Frobisher's proposal. However, when the other Company members rejected it, Michael resigned to become Frobisher's chief ally.

Michael used our family connections to get close to Lord Burghley, who then obtained a command from Queen Elizabeth herself – that the Muscovy Company must give way and honour its charter. This it reluctantly did. But although Michael now had Government patronage for the enterprise, it did not have financial aid from the State. Instead, Michael would have to obtain support for the project from amongst the wealthy mercers and nobles of the City.

However, Frobisher's unscrupulous dealings at sea in the past made potential financiers very wary of his involvement, but by year end Michael had secured the necessary backing, including a huge investment of his own.

Frobisher took command of three vessels, the twenty-five ton Gabriel and the slightly smaller Michael, along with a ten-ton pinnace[63] and a total of thirty-five men. And after a farewell audience with Queen Elizabeth, weighed anchor at Blackwall on the seventh of June, fifteen hundred-and-seventy-six.

In a storm the pinnace was lost and the Michael abandoned, but Frobisher continued on in the Gabriel until he sighted a coast, which he passed on the south until he found an inlet, which he did not hesitate to name Frobisher's Strait, in honour of himself.

As expected, he could see the New World to port and Asia to starboard. Then, when he sighted Asian people, at once he struck shore upon an island. However, these people turned out to be hostile and captured five of his best men, leaving him and the others to barely escape alive back to the safety of their ship. With such a loss of crucial manpower, it made further exploration impossible.

Even so, with his surviving crew of thirteen and a captured Asian, who was later presented to the Queen, Frobisher swaggered triumphantly back to London in October with the great news that he had indeed discovered the North West Passage to Cathay.

---

63   Pinnace – a small sailing boat formerly used as a tender for merchant or war vessels.

However, apart from the Asian, Frobisher had brought back little else of value to justify the great expense of this expedition. That is apart from a rumour that spread quickly – that Frobisher had claimed to have found a small lump of ore believed to contain something 'valuable'. Scant evidence indeed one might say with hindsight, but it was enough to fire the imagination and fool any would-be doubters into believing that he had found success.

My brother received that very stone in front of several highly placed independent witnesses whilst Frobisher was still aboard ship. Michael broke it up and gave some part of it to the assay master of the Tower of London and another to two other gold refiners. But they found nothing of value in it. Then, shortly afterwards, Michael gave a piece to one John Baptista Agnello. This Agnello produced a grain of gold which my brother, in turn, then immediately delivered to the Queen.

On the advice of Agnello, Michael was to have Frobisher dine with him but to mention nothing of gold. Instead, over the table, Michael told him that three or four assayers had found nothing in the stone but that a fourth had found a little silver – enough to have the discovery deemed worthwhile and to satisfy Frobisher's curiosity. However, Michael did set down a true account about all of this in writing for the Queen.

Secretary of State Francis Walsingham then interviewed Michael and told him that, in his opinion, Agnello was a fraud and therefore demanded three or four pieces of the same stone to give to men of his own choosing to make proofs. This they did and found a little silver, which then dampened Walsingham's disapproval for further ventures to be made.

Agnello, meanwhile, said that he was eager to have a friend supply a ship of his own to join with the next trip into Cathay, and said he would pay Michael twenty pounds per hundred tons of ore and teach him the art of extracting gold from it.

Walsingham then came back to Michael saying that he would move Queen Elizabeth forward in issuing a licence for my brother's venture to be allowed to collect more ore on the receipt of the thousand pounds he had previously offered for it. Then Walsingham asked if Frobisher knew of this matter. Michael assured Walsingham that he did not, adding that no one else did either – that is apart from the Queen, Agnello, and Walsingham himself. He smiled, which Michael later said seemed a strange thing for Secretary Walsingham to do, for he was not a man especially renowned for smiling.

Within two days, Walsingham instructed my brother to then tell Martin Frobisher everything and to give the Secretary another piece of the ore. Michael readily complied on both counts.

On the twenty-eighth day of March, Michael was summoned by Sir William Wynter to his house to talk with him on a matter of great importance. He went and, with others commissioned by Her Majesty, was asked 'to consider upon all matters requisite for the furnishing and dispatch of Mister Frobisher for Cathay'. Wynter told Michael that this ore was a far greater treasure than first thought. He added that tests upon Walsingham's piece had been carried out and that, before Wynter's own eyes, the specimen had produced gold. According to the assayers estimation, it should likewise be possible to extract more than four ounces of gold from every hundredweight of ore.

On the strength of this report, my brother was certain that Her Majesty had been fully informed about every aspect of the matter and in that rested assured that he could proceed in good faith from thence forward. For in whose hands can one better entrust one's affairs than those of Her Majesty and her most honourable Secretary?

And so it was, with the blessings of just such eminent backers, proposed that a new company – the Company of Cathay – should be formed with Michael as its Governor. The only problem being with that was that, although he repeatedly petitioned the Queen for articles of association, and in reply they were promised, they never actually materialised. In much the same way as the subscriptions to this new company were promised, by the nobility, merchants and even Queen Elizabeth herself, yet only a few at the outset paid what was due, and so compelling Michael to put up even more of his own money. Frobisher was duly appointed Admiral of the mission and both he and my brother were to have a hundredth part of any future cargo brought home.

As a member of the Cathay Company, Queen Elizabeth lent the expedition one of her ships from the Navy and gave one thousand pounds against the costs. The two-hundred-ton Aid came from the Queen, with the strict proviso that it only be used to take on a cargo of more gold ore from whence the first sample had come, after which it was to return home immediately. On no account was it to pass any further into the Frobisher Straights.

Aid was to be accompanied by the Gabriel and the Michael, which had made its way home after its failure to complete the first expedition, plus a couple of de-constructed pinnaces. With these vessels Frobisher was expected to undertake further exploration along the straight until he came into the South Sea.

As it turned out, Frobisher as usual chose to do exactly as he saw fit. Disregarding Queen Elizabeth's request to find Cathay, he instead loaded a total of two-hundred tons of ore, from a new location, distributed this cargo among all three ships, and then came home.

But on hearing that Frobisher had claimed this new territory on behalf of the Queen, Her Majesty, instead of pouring out her wrath on him for disobeying orders, gave him a heavy gold chain to wear as a mark of her pleasure. She named her new lands, Meta Incognita, and a third expedition was then quickly arranged for the following May.

In the interim, a panel of experts oversaw the attempted assaying of the ore and studied Frobisher's reports, but time seemed to be too short for any firm conclusions to be made. However, the panel did inform the Queen that all looked promising and that in their opinion the next expedition, comprising fifteen ships, should go ahead. My brother, meanwhile, was finding it extremely difficult to raise such a large sum of money to finance the expenses of this largest-ever undertaking of its kind, so again was forced to pledge his own credit and that of the Company's to cover it.

The intention of this third expedition was to simply gather more ore and to plant one hundred colonists upon Elizabeth's new territory. Bad weather and ill luck soon put paid to that. Unable to properly fix his latitude, Frobisher went astray from his previous destination and found himself in an entirely different strait. After two hundred miles, he eventually admitted to his crew that he was lost.

Threatened by deadly fields of drifting ice and gathering storms, Frobisher was forced to summons all the ships and return to the Frobisher Straights. All about there, his men dug up ore from whichever unrecorded placed they saw fit and loaded it into the ships in a disorderly manner. All the while, the weather was much harsher than it had been during the previous expedition, causing the ships to need frequent freeing from ice. And the disaster intensified when a ship carrying the would-be colonists' supplies sank, resulting in that part of the plan having to be abandoned completely. Thus, as soon as possible, the entire company set course for England.

Meanwhile, back in London, my brother had been completely undone. Panic had set in amongst the other members of the Company. Their confidence had been rocked by rumours of the latest ore consignment being worthless, even though at that point testing upon the second shipment of ore had not yet been completed.

Those members who had not yet paid their subscriptions, now ratted on their pledges, and in consequence the 'Company' was unable to discharge its debts. And its debtors now saw the 'Company' as being one and the same as Michael Locke. So these creditors turned upon my brother like a pack of baying wolves.

On his return, even Frobisher turned upon my brother, and with such unwarranted venom. He stormed in to Michael's house one night with forty men and terrified his wife and young children. Frobisher accused Michael of swindling one of the backers out of more than a thousand pounds and of keeping false accounts. Yet when later inspected, these accounts proved that my brother had done nothing of the kind. To the contrary, he had exercised scrupulous integrity in all his business dealings.

Meanwhile, Frobisher had paid his own men, at Company expense, more money than was due to them. He had also taken a large some of money for his own wage, and yet went about telling everyone that he had received nothing. There was a unicorn's horn found on one of the islands and estimated to be worth a thousand pounds or more, and yet this was given to the Queen by Frobisher as if it were his own personal gift and not on behalf of the Company, to whom it belonged legally.

There was also a ruby, one suitable for a prince and more than an inch square, that was supposed to be presented to the Queen. But this 'vanished' along with many other rubies, diamonds, sapphires and other precious jewels from the second journey, which Frobisher allegedly sold off privately.

As for his accounts, the scoundrel kept none for any of the three voyages, and he refused to answer any questions upon any of his doings. Through his boasting to the Queen after the second voyage, he was given hundreds of pounds to distribute among his men. They never received any of it. In Michael's estimation, Frobisher wasted and pilfered in excess of ten thousand pounds of Company profits. And these my brother was then expected to make good, along with all other loses.

And so, in consequence to the desertion of all who had been a party to the ventures, my brother was left ruined. Oh, he pleaded for certain to Francis Walsingham and others at court, but to no avail. For even the Privy Council now argued that the so-called Cathay Company did not exist. Since the Queen had not granted any articles, there was, legally speaking, no such company!

Out of the thousands of pounds of his own money invested, at the end of the venture Michael personally owed very little. But it was the crushing cost of the charter of the freight ships, for which he had signed on behalf of all of the other investors, for which he was being pursued.

Over the following years, Michael found himself imprisoned for debt eight times. He was held in The Fleet and served time in almost every other London prison too, save for Newgate. Each time he was incarcerated resulted in him being unable to carry on any business that would have enabled him to earn money to either pay off his creditors or to help him support his large family of fifteen children.

Thus, for years, my brother pleaded for justice whilst his plight swung betwixt hopeless and intolerable, no matter how much the rest of my remaining Locke family tried to ease his burden. As for me, I was remarried and bound by my husband's financial goodwill, even though I brought mine own goodly inheritance into that marriage.

Eventually, Michael was freed of his debt. But he has never been able to regain his previous good standing that Frobisher destroyed. And yet how did this Martin Frobisher fare? How did he who in his career had thrice escaped the hangman's noose after being charged on three separate accounts of piracy? While Michael was languishing in goal, Queen Elizabeth, no doubt still bedazzled by Frobisher's golden charm, appointed him captain of one of her ships ordered to prevent the Spanish from encouraging Irish insurgency. Later, he served as Sir Francis Drake's vice-admiral in an expedition to the West Indies. And later still, for his services to the realm, including those in the war that was still to come, he would be named as one of four 'men of the greatest experience that this realm hath' and deemed the stuff of heroes. And so he was knighted.

Such was the natural justice of this most unnatural Tudor realm. A good and honest man might be made to suffer while the rogue is rewarded and prospers. When my brother was ruined, I from that time forth saw Queen Elizabeth in a darker light than most.

Chapter Twenty-One

Once in a lifetime, or indeed once in the span of several lifetimes, something may happen of terrible magnitude about which there can be no explanation. This may be something so cataclysmic that it serves to remind us mortals about the importance of living humbly and doing what is right in the sight of our Creator. My sons and I bear witness to just such an event, and so I feel it right that I make some mention of it now – because we may not see the like of it again for a very long time.

It struck during the Easter week on the sixth day of April in fifteen-eighty. It had been such a fair, crisp and bright day, but as the gloom of evening fell I firmly felt the chill air begin to bite. And so at about six of the clock I had decided to retreat to our great chamber to sit snug beside the fire, where I read my book as I waited for dinner to be served. Then, all of a sudden the whole house began to shake – sending a large log falling from the fire and out across the hearth and onto the floor, where it lay smouldering. I sprung to my feet and cried out for help as all about me rattled and shook, but no one came to my aid. Then above the clattering clamour, I heard the maidservants screaming out in terror.

Quickly, I took up the iron fire tongs and, stumbling, managed somehow to grab a hold of the log and put it back into the fireplace, just as the mad shift all about me abruptly ceased. Then I ran out into the hallway to find calamity all about me. One of the maids was upon her knees trying to pick up a tray full of food that had been dropped as she was fetching it to the dining room.

Meanwhile, another girl just lay cowering on the floor in the corner, with her head in her hands, sobbing hysterically. Much of the slipware from the dining room table had toppled and shattered – when furniture had danced across the floor. And there was not one of the family portraits upon the walls that was not shifted askew and made to hang crooked.

My husband Simon had gone outside, thinking that with so much rumbling that the roof of our house must have collapsed. And yet, thankfully, he returned to report that he had found but a roof tile or two shaken off and lying upon the grass below. Praise be to the Lord that, for us at our house in Huntingdon, these were the least of our worries, even though around four of five of the clock the following morning the house again shook, but not for as long as it had the day before or nearly as severely.

At nearby Ely Cathedral, the bells had rung out wildly all on their own as ancient stonework plummeted to the earth below, and at Stratford part of the castle had collapsed. Later, my son William told me that in London a pinnacle on Westminster Abbey had fallen along with countless chimney stacks. Two children had also been crushed to death by stones falling from the roof of Christ's Church Hospital. Surely, this was yet more work of the devil being visited upon us!

Yet the greatest toll on English lives was exacted around the south-east coast and at sea. Our city merchants reported over one hundred ships lost in the Channel, while eye witnesses, who had survived the crossing, reported waves as high as houses hurtling their vessels to and fro and up and down – as if these were toys in the hands of a malevolent child.

At Dover, a great noise was heard over the Channel just before the land slipped away to open a new and glistening white stretch of chalk cliff face. And in the two great sea swells that followed, more than a hundred people were drowned. In the second quaking, as the people there lay sleeping in the wake of such sorrow, a number of houses completely collapsed killing still more.

Why something so terrible should strike us we do not know, and yet one can only stand in awe and fear of the power behind it. Perhaps it served as the forerunner of other awesome events to follow that year. These in turn would lead to even more shifts to our world. For later that summer King Philip would invade Portugal and, on defeating its army, make it yet another part of the ever ravenous and devouring Spanish Empire. And then in the fall, Drake would return to Plymouth in glory – having circumnavigated the globe! Just those two events would soon shape the course of our island's history...

*　　*　　*

I came to my husband Simon Throckmorton's deathbed feeling like an intruder. He lay propped up upon his pillows, flanked by my stepsons and their friend whose steely eyes fixed upon me so intently that I felt obliged to quickly make my farewells and leave. My husband tried to mouth something to me as I took up his hand in mine and kissed it, but his mumbled words were inaudible to me.

I had walked but a little way along the long gallery towards my chamber when I had a sudden compulsion to turn about and go back to confront my stepsons' companion as to who he was and over my inferred expulsion.

As I reached the door and opened it but slightly, I was met by the most damning sight. For I am almost certain that this so-called 'friend' amongst my step-sons was none other than a Catholic priest administering to Simon the Papist last rites.

Silently I closed the door once more, turned and hurriedly walked away. How could this husband of mine have deceived my trust for so long? How could they have all done so?

As soon as I could, I made my leave. Packing all my belongings, I returned to London and my eldest son, William, and did my best to distance myself from this by now rapidly tarnishing name of Throckmorton.[64]

*　　*　　*

The uncompromising and spirited nature of Queen Elizabeth, combined with our country's

---

[64] Simon Throckmorton died on 27th March 1585

defiant stance on Protestantism, swiftly became the dual focal point for renewed English patriotism in the face of growing foreign power. The predominantly Catholic Continent did not acquiesce, but instead set about launching a Counter Reformation – to return now Calvinist enclaves in its midst back to the power of Rome and the Pope, and of course also to rid the English throne of its heretic bastard queen.

Relations between Queen Elizabeth and King Philip of Spain had begun amicably enough. In fact, it had been widely reported that the Spaniard had been quite taken with the young Elizabeth and was even eager to ask for her hand in marriage. However, over the following years his patience with her had worn leaf thin, and as both their political and religious agendas clashed increasingly, the monarchs drifted apart. They became irreconcilable.

In his younger days, King Philip's actions had often proved as secular in nature as Queen Elizabeth's. Although the Spanish monarch had often criticised the Pope in the past, as King Philip aged, he became more and more pious, and then almost fanatical in his Catholic faith. In consequence, his personal religious beliefs began to play an ever greater part when it came to making decisions. Soon Philip had come to regard himself as the temporal leader of this Counter Reformation, and it was an attitude that in itself would soon begin to pose a real threat to Protestant England.

In the past our merchants' exploits in the Canaries, Africa and beyond had mainly served to annoy the Portuguese and had little real effect on Spain. But by now, apart from Portuguese irritation having become Spanish, it was the wanton action of 'privateers', and not us merchants going about our lawful trade, that angered the Spanish King. For wily Queen Elizabeth and her advisers had come to realise that England, unless she stood steadfast, was in danger of losing her hard-earned independence of Rome. Therefore, by capturing Portuguese and Spanish treasure ships, Her Majesty could not only increase her own wealth in order to maintain England's defences, but could at the same time financially damage those who might steal her liberty. Thus these adventurers saw whatever mayhem they caused our enemies as a righteous act. Of course Philip considered such action as an outright overture to war.

And so, with King Philip's absorption of Portugal, his stance towards ending the Protestant 'problem' of England and the Netherlands hardened. One of the first signs of the ending of King Philip's previous restraint came in fifteen-eighty-two, when he made a public offer of a handsome reward to any person who would murder the Prince of Orange – William the Silent. In consequence an attempt upon his life followed soon afterwards. He was shot and gravely injured but, miraculously, he had survived. And then still more attempts upon his life followed swiftly, but these also failed.

In the following year, some eighteen months or thereabouts before my husband Simon's death, there came the most shameful of Catholic plots. It was widely believed that King Philip was also behind these. The main leader of the English Catholic conspirators was an Ambassador for Spain. His name was Sir Francis Throckmorton, a distant kinsman of Simon.

The plot had been to assassinate Queen Elizabeth. Then the French Henri Duc de Guise would have invaded England with his troops and placed the imprisoned Catholic Mary Stuart, exiled Queen of Scotland, on the English throne in Elizabeth's place. Throckmorton was arrested and, after Sir Francis Walsingham had him tortured, gave a full confession. The traitor was duly hung at Tyburn.

Then in fifteen-eighty-four, Antwerp fell to King Philip's General Parma. This was no great impediment to our English trade because most of our mercers had already left. Those heady days of Antwerp being at the centre of commerce, as they were when Anthony and I had lived there, were long since over. The city had already been occupied before by the Spanish, in the fifteen-seventies. Then they had ransacked the

English House and so wrecked our trade that, when it was eventually considered safe for us to return, and its people all but begged us to do so, it was already too late to rekindle the embers of Antwerp's past trading importance to us. Instead, we had in the meantime negotiated extremely generous privileges to trade at Walcheren and so deserted the beleaguered city of Antwerp forever.

However, once Antwerp had fallen to the most recent Spanish assault, it left the way clear for a similar Catholic advance on the Dutch and Calvinist north. This was also the year when the enemies of Prince William of Orange finally succeeded with their plans to assassinate him.

By early fifteen-eighty-five, the Guises and the Catholic League in France declared themselves as allies to King Philip, with the intention of fighting the Huguenots[65] to the death, in an attempt to prevent the imminent succession of Protestant Henry of Navarre to the French throne. This was at the same time of Queen Elizabeth negotiating terms with the Dutch by which she would become their ally and protector. By doing so Elizabeth must have known that she was courting war with Spain, but by then she had little choice in the matter because England's own survival depended upon standing beside the Protestant Dutch against an impending Spanish-led Catholic onslaught.

At home Elizabeth survived two more assassination plots, again centred in the idea of putting Scottish Queen Mary on the English throne. As a result, an association of patriots formed which numbered in the thousands. The members of this association pledged themselves to pursue to the death any who tried to make further attempt upon their beloved Queen's life.

Meanwhile, abroad, our merchants suffered the seizure of all of our English trading ships in Spanish ports. In August, Queen Elizabeth made her treaty with the Dutch, pledging military aid yet stopped short of naming King Philip as their principle aggressor.

In London, all was hot with talk and fear of

---

65   French Protestants.

our imminent invasion by Spain, and hatred seethed against every Catholic in the land. Catholics were viewed suspiciously as Queen-killers or as traitors. Then there followed reprisals and counter reprisals between our Protestant alliance and the Catholic forces, and yet still neither King Philip nor Queen Elizabeth moved to declare war directly. That is, not until Queen Elizabeth then had her cousin, the exiled Mary Stuart of Scotland, executed. This was after yet one more Catholic plot against our sovereign had been discovered.

With Queen Mary dead, King Philip could then make a claim to the English throne himself, and so it was that he finally ordered the invasion of our country. A huge fleet of impressive-looking but, in effect, lumbering Spanish galleons – the Armada – was sent up the English Channel. The Armada was despatched to destroy Elizabeth's fleet as it made its way on to Holland. There, waiting Spanish forces would be taken aboard to make the short trip across the Channel to invade the English mainland.

But as God's providence would have it, our much smaller but faster ships – equipped with larger canons – and the fickle English weather would thwart King Philip's ambition. After a battle raged in the Channel, the Spanish fleet was defeated off the coast of Holland. The stately galleons were no match for our better equipped little English ships, with their officers and crew better experienced in seamanship and combat. Perhaps the ponderous Spanish giants, proudly streaming every banner and flag, and captained by elegant grandees bearing many ancient and noble titles, had presumed too much on their sheer size and Spain's formidable but seldom challenged might. Whatever their mistakes, our fleet, led by Admiral Sir Francis Drake, made surprisingly short work of the Spaniards. Assisted by the quirky winds that our sailors had long before learned to harness for advantage, Drake set some of his own ships on fire and then sent them drifting into the tightly massed Armada. The destruction was enormous. And then, as what seemed to be a miracle, the weather joined forces with us against our enemies. A storm of incredible ferocity scattered the Spanish fleet – those vessels that had somehow survived the devastating combination of fire and cannonading – sending most of the ships to the bottom of the sea, or dashing them against the rocky coastline. Many a Spaniard in that doomed fleet ne'er set eyes on his sweetheart again.

Amongst those valiant English ships was our Mary Rose. In preparation for the widely anticipated Spanish conflict, she had been converted into an armed merchantman with heavy ordinance installed amidships. She served us most nobly at the Armada's defeat whilst under the reliable command of Captain Fenton. Courageously, he brought the Mary Rose to Frobisher's aid when he was attacked by the Spaniard's flagship, the San Martin. After that Mary Rose pounded a broadside through an enemy galleon. Thomas and Anthony would have been so proud of her!

But they would have been outraged by the manner in which our victorious English sailors were treated upon their return to port. These men were not permitted to leave their ships and go home to their families until they had been paid – and so they spent many long weeks in the cramped and sickness-ridden little ships while money was being raised to secure their discharge. Consequently, many of the brave men who had survived in one of our nation's greatest battles died shortly afterwards, in appalling conditions on their own ships. They succumbed to illnesses that could easily have been avoided by simply being allowed to return home.

Chapter Twenty-Two

Meanwhile my own dear son, Anthony, was fighting a battle of his own. Anthony, my fourth son, was so very long and thin when he was born, and with such finely slender fingers that old Maggie had exclaimed on first seeing them that they 'look like skate fish bones to me, my Lady!' Yet to me, his mother, he was always to be my beautiful boy. A mother never should have a favourite amongst her children, and in truth, I never have. Yet with Anthony, I had something special; a kind of empathy I should say. He was gentle, studious and kindly natured, and of all my children, the most like his mother when it came to a passion for learning and books. And although all of my children have been raised as the Lord's faithful servants, Anthony excelled in his love of Christ and his zeal in proclaiming the Gospel. If only the church had been reformed then, I am certain that he would have devoted his life to full-time ministry.

When his father died, Anthony was not yet thirteen years of age; no longer a child and on the threshold of manhood. Of all of my children, I believe that it was Anthony who was most affected by my beloved husband's sudden death. William, eleven years his brother's senior, was already a mercer and away at his father's business across the sea. Walter was settled in London and twenty-two-year-old Henry was at Cambridge and already a Master of Arts. My daughter Mary was married, and our two other sons, Eleazer and Matthew, were still young. Then, when I remarried, Simon Throckmorton had Anthony sent away to University at Cambridge.

In the April of fifteen-hundred-and-eighty-three, Anthony moved from Peterhouse, where there had been much trouble of late over the extreme preaching of one Robert 'Troublechurch' Browne. Browne was the practitioner of a movement that urged all true Christians to separate from Elizabeth's English Church and to instead worship according to the customs of the early Church, as recorded in the New Testament of the

Bible. As a result, Browne was expelled.

Meanwhile, with the help of a high placed friend at court, Anthony had obtained a mandate bearing the signature of Queen Elizabeth herself, for him to succeed in obtaining a Fellowship at Corpus Christi, with a special dispensation to override any existing college statutes that he must first go into Orders before taking up that position of Fellow.

Apparently, Queen Elizabeth scanned each and every word of that document as it was set before her, as indeed it was her custom to do with all official papers. By all accounts there was often a certain amount of negotiation before she signed anything that she herself had not commissioned.

'And why exactly am I to consider granting this young man a dispensation?' Elizabeth had asked of Sir Francis Walsingham.

'His family have served you well in the past, Your Majesty,' Mister Secretary prompted.

At this the Queen had frowned, half gritted her blackened teeth and narrowed her eyes, before snapping her reply: 'A Puritan merchant and a complaining adventurer. That was all his father was! And, I might add, conducting his business at our command.' And with that she had pushed the paper back towards Walsingham in disdain.

But Mister Secretary was not so easily deterred. 'He was also a great favourite of Your Majesty's late father, yet I was thinking more of this young fellow's grandfather, Sir William Locke. I am certain that Your Majesty must recall the great loyalty and service that Sir William showed towards your late father, the King.... and especially of course to your dear mother, his wife, the Queen Anne.'

Walsingham had chosen his words well, for Queen Elizabeth's eyes had all but sparked at this unexpected remembrance of a great kindness done to her much maligned mother, Anne Boleyn.

'Locke? Locke... yes of course!' she concurred. 'He was indeed most dutiful towards my mother concerning my father King Henry's Great Matter...'

Elizabeth's countenance lightened, and then she quickly reached forward, grasped the document once more, and snatched up her great quill. Pausing only to ink its tip, she quickly scratched out her grand and suitably regal signature.

'A dispensation to forgo the taking of orders?' She had smiled knowingly and tightly at Walsingham as she made one final flourish of her pen. 'God's teeth, 'tis but little enough to ensure that we have one less Puritan amongst our clergy to contend with!'

After being duly elected, Anthony was admitted to his room at Corpus Christi a few days later. For three happy and prosperous years he remained there – at peace and unhindered under the headship of the Master at that time, the kindly Doctor Norgate.

However, not all men at the college were pleased with the situation or of our evangelical persuasion. I can think of two in particular; Henry Rewse and John Brome, who had become Fellows not long after Anthony and had taken orders as stipulated. They began to goad my son by claiming seniority over him, and they drew Anthony into heated disputes with themselves and so caused him great distress.

When Doctor Norgate died, in the November of fifteen-hundred-and-eighty-seven, a new Master was elected, and it was then that my son's great troubles really started. The new Master was John Copcot, a Doctor of Divinity, and he was widely known to bear a hatred of zealous Protestants such as we were. Worse than this, Copcot was a close associate of Archbishop Whitgift, who would soon become the scourge of all good Protestants in our land.

Copcot immediately made his intense dislike of us known to Anthony, who at first did not take it to heart. Why should he have? After all, he had come up against opposition to our family's spiritual stance for as long as he could remember, for he was no recent convert to our way of life. Anthony was a truly born again Christian. Yet this opposition from Master Copcot was different, Anthony later told me. It was as if this Master was set on nothing less than bringing my son low in the eyes of his peers – to utterly humiliate him and destroy his reputation as a young man of good character. My well worn body with its unsteady hands is full of years as I write these words, but it enables me to testify to having met two kinds of Church people: those like Copcot and others like Anthony. The Copcots of this world are religious, while people like Anthony are spiritual. The spiritual differ in that they seek, find and enjoy a personal and loving relationship with the true and living God.

Knowing that Anthony had migrated from Peterhouse and suspecting that my son might be of the Brownist[66] persuasion, Copcot began pressuring him – by getting others of Whitgift's Anglicans to agree that it was only right and proper that, if Anthony was to continue to enjoy his position at Corpus Christi, he be made to become Deacon and submit himself to take Orders. But Anthony would not be turned by their threats and bullying, and he refused to be drawn upon his personal reasons for declining Orders. Instead, he referred Doctor Copcot once more to the special dispensation he had received from the Queen. A heated argument ensued, in which Rewse and Brome backed the Master like two yapping lick-boots. It ended with Copcot revoking my son's Fellowship and giving him notice to leave his room.

Of course, much aggrieved by this unwarranted action against him, Anthony immediately appealed to the Vice-Chancellor of the College, who in turn ordered Master Copcot to proceed no further. And so with that Anthony assumed the matter to be at an end.

However, just three days later and without any notice, Doctor Copcot gathered about him a quorum of Fellows to hold a snap election and then ordered them to make the decision that Anthony should be ejected from his chamber by force and turned out of the college permanently. At the same time, Copcot also made them pass an order suspending any Fellow subsequently

---

66 Brownist – a follower of Robert Troublechurch Browne, a Separatist.

in dispute with the college from profiting from their Fellowship, and also prohibiting them from seeking public funds in any case then brought in the recovery of a Fellowship revoked. In short, the Master hoped to not only eject Anthony from Corpus Christi but also to cut off his means of seeking any redress.

But my son had become too good a student of the Law to be thwarted by the scoundrel, and so had the matter put again before the Vice-Chancellor who, as before, again ruled in Anthony's favour. And this time he also forwarded the matter on to Secretary Walsingham. Although Walsingham personally saw no case for Anthony to answer, he then passed the matter on to Archbishop Whitgift for his learned consideration. I feel here compelled to explain that Doctor Copcot was, at that time, also the Archbishop's chaplain.

'Hickman has been dealt with no differently than he would have been done had I been in Doctor Copcot's place myself,' the Archbishop declared. 'Moreover, the lawyers that I have consulted with are of the opinion that Hickman's dismissal was legal.' My son's only recourse after that was to appeal to the Chancellor of the University himself – William Cecil, Lord Burghley.

Willow-wand Burghley was always much happier persecuting Catholics than he was of Protestants and 'twas also widely known that he held no love for ecclesiastical jurisdiction or for interfering bishops either. So, he immediately sent word to Archbishop Whitgift to ask what had been done in relation to this matter.

However, Burghley in the meantime was persuaded by his Vice Chancellor and others at Corpus Christi not to proceed to a full hearing and the impropriety of allowing University matters to be decided by any outside authority. In view of this feeling, Burghley then happily allowed the matter to be referred back 'in house' to be dealt with.

As a result, after much ado, in fifteen-ninety-one it was certified that the proceedings against Anthony had been unjust and contrary to the customs and statutes of the College, and that Anthony's ejection and deprivation of his Fellowship were illegal. And so my son was duly reinstated – again.

Although we, his close family, knew how deeply distressed and humiliated Anthony had been throughout this unprovoked hounding by Whitgift's cronies, we had no idea of exactly how great a toll this was all taking upon my dear son's health.

Yet even after this wickedness by Doctor Copcot, Archbishop Whitgift's cohorts' persecution of Anthony was by no means over. [67]During the long vacation of ninety-two, while Anthony was away from Cambridge and visiting with me and his brothers in London, yet another plot against him was put into action. This was the same year in which Lord Burghley was taken so gravely ill with an attack of palsy, but although greatly weakened, had survived.

The then Master of Corpus Christi College was one Doctor John Jegon. In Anthony's absence, this Jegon had taken it upon himself to call a very irregular meeting amongst whatever number of fellows that could be mustered up from those scant few still in residence at that time. This miserable man then induced them to vote his own brother, Thomas, in as Proctor[68] of the college for the coming year. But since Anthony was then senior Fellow, by rights he should have been considered the most suited man for the position.

After Anthony returned to Cambridge and resumed his studies, at a subsequent meeting his peers duly voted him into the same position of Proctor – the position into which Jegon had already moved his brother Thomas – and presented him to the Vice-Chancellor as such. Upon hearing about the majority decision, Doctor Jegon naturally refused his consent and Anthony found himself yet again suspended.

After much fruitless disputing the matter at the college, in the August of fifteen-ninety-three, Anthony, supported by six of his Fellows, wrote to Lord Burghley to request that he instruct the Vice-Chancellor to abide

---

67   The following information can be found in Athenae Cantarigienses – p222
68   In certain universities, a proctor is an official responsible for discipline and for invigilating at examinations.

by the opinion of the University. For whatever reason, Lord Burghley unexpectedly declined. Yet Anthony knew full well it was because of his personal religious stance against the current Church settlement to which, in all good conscience, he could never be made to adhere.

Anthony's position at Corpus Christi had been made now all but untenable. And since he was by then a Doctor of the Civil Law, he left Cambridge and moved to London to act as an advocate in association with his brother, Henry.

*   *   *

How they came to scorn us committed Protestants at Queen Elizabeth's court! They caused us discouragement and spoke of us as 'Puritans', as if that word being in their mouths was as coarse grit. Though I can see no shame in that word, for we are true Christians, who have fought long and hard to reform this tainted Church into one that is akin to that pure and primitive Church of the Gospels. And as we do so we wish to drive out Papist idolatry and un-biblical tradition, and thus purify the Popish services still forced upon us in their Anglican guise. I am not surprised that the recently celebrated Master Shakespeare hath observed that a rose by any other name is still but a rose, therefore to be called a Puritan is no less a title than that of true Protestant.

By fifteen-ninety-three, those advisors at court whose kindly disposition towards us Puritans might have kept cruel censure against us at bay had by then either lost their positions of power or had died away. Even our staunchest ally at court, Sir Francis Walsingham, was dead.

Thus, that year saw in a new Act of Government inspired by Archbishop Whitgift which quickly sparked our fears of renewed persecution. The passing of this Act Against Puritans henceforth made it illegal for any man; woman or child to absent themselves, without good cause, from Queen Elizabeth's proscribed church service for a period of more than one month on pain of punishment. Not only that, it made a criminal out of anyone who encouraged others to stay away from church also, be that in either word or in deed.

Private conventicles, such as those we and other Bible-believing Christians had become used to holding in our homes, were now forbidden. In short, we were compelled to come forward on Sundays to present ourselves in Her Majesty's church and submit ourselves to the still Popish services and religiosity that was against all that we held dear as the Lord's express bidding. If we did not submit, then we refused on pain of imprisonment, without bail, until yielding to the Queen's wishes and dutifully conforming ourselves to her liking. If we should not do so, then after three months' imprisonment we faced banishment from England or even death. And simply offering shelter to such transgressors would be a punishable offence. The passing of this Act felt like the coming of Bloody Queen Mary all over again.

Many of our own godly ministers conceded that, for the time being at least, the wind was against them and that they would do best to bide until a time of better prospect. And that, considering the Queen's great age, must surely come soon, when it would please God to impress His will clearly upon those then in power to make changes. Better to flavour this stew by being amongst its ingredients within the pot, they concluded, than to be left upon the side to spoil.

But other Puritan clergymen could not abide the strict imposition of the Church upon their own conscience, and so they continued to preach in their own fashion until found out and deprived of their livings. Even so, many intended to return to the Church and their former position when further reform came. Queen Elizabeth was old and it was she who was holding back the waves like a failing low-land dyke. The consensus amongst most of these Puritans was that Her Majesty would either eventually crack under their ever growing pressure or be swept away altogether by death. Time was not on her side, and so they and we inclined ourselves to believe that therefore it must be on ours. Meanwhile, the one dark cloud looming great on the horizon that might still change everything was the question of succession. Who would reign over England when the childless Queen Elizabeth died?

Yet at this same time, there were others now in the country not only thinking the unthinkable but also speaking the unspeakable: that we Bible-believing Christians, if not finding it possible to be a part of Queen Elizabeth's Church of England, should then set ourselves apart from it entirely and form ourselves into independent New Testament-styled congregations with our own appointed leaders.

To the State, this was sedition. Because to deny the authority of bishops was to deny the authority of the Queen, which was treason. Anthony had privately spoken to us of such matters; matters that he had heard spoken of by the like-minded Robert Browne.

'If,' Anthony argued, 'after the passage of so much time, the Church will not accept the need for reform, then maybe the time is come for us true Protestants to set ourselves apart from it to save ourselves from the taint of its impurity?'

'But Queen Elizabeth would never allow that,' his brother Henry had countered coolly.

'No, she certainly will not. She rejects Luther, Calvin and Knox, and yet calls herself a Protestant. Queen Elizabeth rejects Rome because Rome rejected her and denounced her to the world as a bastard and a heretic, and so she acts as any other woman scorned. And yet there are many of a mind to think that, secretly, the Queen longs for reconciliation with Rome before she dies. For that reason, she treats the Anglican Church like her pet. She will not allow it to wander off too far along a pathway from which she may not be able to call it back to heel.'

Then, just after the passing of this Act, Henry Barrow and John Greenwood, known to Anthony to have been members of 'Bretheren of the Separation' congregation in London, just south of the river at Southwark, were executed by Queen Elizabeth for upholding those same beliefs as Robert Browne had once preached but later recanted. Anthony had known Greenwood from his time at Corpus Christi.

Henry Barrow had been held in The Clink prison in London and then in The Fleet for almost six years for recusancy. On one occasion, in the November of fifteen-hundred-and-eighty-six, John Greenwood had gone to visit him and was seized by the goaler and brought before Archbishop Whitgift. Although he argued against the legality of his arrest, he too found himself committed to prison.

Under an act originally directed against Roman Catholics, both men were ordered to pay a heavy bail or remain in prison until the sum was forthcoming. Throughout this time Barrow vigorously maintained the principle of separatism and denounced Elizabeth's Church as 'false worship' and her bishops as persecutors and oppressors.

While imprisoned, the pair collaborated on composing tracts in support of their Separatist views, writings which were then smuggled out by their friends to be printed and distributed amongst others. Therefore, by fifteen-hundred-and-ninety, Archbishop Whitgift and his bishops were pressed to find another means of either making these dissidents recant or to silence them forever.

John Greenwood was eventually released and, in the autumn of fifteen-hundred-and-ninety-two, duly elected to the position of 'teacher' of the Separatist Church. However, that December he was arrested at a house in Ludgate and imprisoned. Barrow and Greenwood were then tried together on the capital charge of 'devising and circulating seditious books' – a charge by which the Archbishop was certain he would easily secure a conviction. Even so, Whitgift and his cronies were still seeking to pass a more stringent measure through the Lower House[69] against 'Brownists'

---

69   House of Commons.

and the followers of Barrow, with the clear intent of the utter destruction of both.

My son, Anthony, was already in London as the final trials of Barrow and Greenwood played out. And although he and others late of Cambridge brought forth every legal argument in their friends' defence, all could see that the balance of justice had been e'er so cunningly tipped against them from the outset. (Even the sending of a simple letter from the defendants held in prison inexplicably took up to five days to reach the court and its attention, whereas those in return often arrived with obscene swiftness).

On the twenty-third of March, fifteen-hundred-and-ninety-three, Greenwood and Barrow were found guilty of all charges against them and sentenced to death. Yet even then Anthony and his legal friends would not abandon the fight. Somehow, they managed to get word to Queen Elizabeth, pleading for mercy on behalf of the accused but knew not for certain if, or how, she would respond.

Early on the day after sentence was passed, the pair were duly brought forth from their cells and their irons struck off. As they were about to be tied to the cart that would take them to their place of execution, the Queen's messenger hurriedly came with a reprieve, and so they were returned to prison.

Then on the thirty-first day of March, the two men were again brought out of prison very early and quietly taken to the gallows, where the nooses were slipped about their necks. But yet again, they were reprieved and carried back to prison. Anthony later heard that behind the scenes Lord Burghley himself, although frail in health, had on both occasions succeeded at the last moment to intervene against Whitgift and to stay the pair's execution.

Then, on the fifth day of April, although it had been received with such dislike to have almost had it entirely cast out, the new measures in law so urgently sought by Archbishop Whitgift against such religious 'dissenters' as these two good Christians was allowed to pass by the Lower House. This being despite Lord Burghley's angry turn upon Archbishop Whitgift to warn him 'against shedding the blood of men who held the faith[70] professed in England.'

As if out of spite, the Archbishop and his men then contrived to hasten the executions. So, early on the morning of April the sixth and amid great secrecy, in the company of two elderly widows carrying their winding sheets, Greenwood and Barrow were taken to Tyburn and hanged.

It was rumoured afterwards that Queen Elizabeth had asked the Earl of Cumberland 'what end' the two men had made. He is said to have replied, 'A very godly end,' and that Barrow and Greenwood had 'prayed for Her Majesty and the State.'

When I heard of their deaths, my blood ran cold. Fine young men, good mothers' sons, were being slaughtered once more in the name of religion by a Queen of England. It was too much to bear, to think that again true Christians were poised to face yet another bloody tide of martyrdom. Had we gained nothing in the past sixty years?

---

70   Protestant.

Chapter Twenty-Three

And so again, many committed Christians chose to flee the country – to Calvinist strongholds on the continent. In the past, King Philip had tried to repress Calvinism in his Netherlands territory, and so in the space of just one year during previous unrest, the Spanish had slaughtered eighteen-thousand Dutch Protestants. Nonetheless, amid an uneasy truce, there were now reformed churches there and many Separatists had already secretly left England to settle in Amsterdam, where they might enjoy some degree of freedom of religion.

My heart will never relent, nor will my spirit ever give up the good cause, but I knew even then, at almost seventy years of age, that I was far too old to survive such a journey across the seas. And what if I had tried to do so? What would I have gained? The right to be able to die as Puritan exiled on foreign soil? No, my beloved Anthony and I had not fled under Mary simply to die in the comfort of our faith elsewhere. We had removed ourselves then only as a temporary measure, until the time was right to continue the fight for our cause once more at home – in our England.

I must mention here, that in some lonelier moments of deep despair in Antwerp, when in exile during the bloody reign of Queen Mary, I had often prayed earnestly to God to take either her or me forth from this world. But now I wanted to stay to fight on against this latest outrage.

Even though the Church to which I was now expected to subscribe, though imperfect, was not Papist, I had not lived through and endured so much for the sake of upholding the true path of my most blessed Lord only to be dictated to once more by yet another Tudor tyrant. The Queen was making demands as to what I must believe and how I must worship when conducting myself in matters of faith. I might be old, and I knew even then that my life must almost be spent, and yet I was determined never to submit my relationship with my Lord and Saviour, Jesus Christ, to the unrighteous dominion of another. 'Come,' I said to myself, 'let them burn me! That is if God does not choose to take me first.'

And yet this new great danger for us Puritans was not only from within. For yet, even then, the Queen's captains were keeping a wary watch upon the Spanish.

'I am of an age,' I told my sons, 'when I have already far outlived many I have long known, as has our Most Sovereign Lady. Queen Elizabeth is like an old barren ewe near ready to die. As soon as she lies herself down in the field, then the Catholic crows from across the sea will be flocking to come pick at her eyes. And if they invade us, and may Our Lord forbid, they defeat us, then any persecution we faithful Protestants have suffered up until now from our own crown will be as flea bitings in comparison with what may be to come. All the more reason for us to be prepared. And that, I feel, we can no longer do here.'

My newly married son, William, was also clearly decided. Outwardly we should in the meantime conform ourselves by attending church services as ordered. Yet we would do so only at the churches that Anthony himself would seek out for us, where the parishioners and clergy were known to be amongst those still unwilling to wholly submit themselves unto this new Act. It would take time even for Queen Elizabeth to seek them all out.

Inwardly, we decided that we would make shift elsewhere. As soon and as far away from the confines of London and the spies at court as we might. And there, in our new refuge, we would prepare ourselves for the struggle that must surely lie ahead. Yet, where could we go without William having to give up our trade. And where would we have ready access to ships if not in London?

* * *

A growing number of Puritan dissenters were

no longer willing to sit meekly by and let the ways of Elizabeth's Church go unchallenged. Many of these, like us, saw it as a huge mass of old stinking works; a pack of Popery and a puddle of corruption. Yet unlike us, they were not opposed to violent action to make their point.

There had been an attack on Queen Eleanor's Cross at Cheapside[71] before. During a violent protest against the Papists, on Midsummer's Night in fifteen-eighty-one, many of its lower images were smashed and mutilated. The ever serene statue of the Virgin Mary had its arms broken off and the infant Jesus snatched away. Not only that, but her entire body had been haled by ropes and made almost fit to fall before the perpetrators were discovered and compelled to flee. Queen Elizabeth was so incensed over this bold act of vandalism that she offered up a goodly reward to any who come forward to name the perpetrators. But the offenders were never found.

In the year of fifteen-ninety-five, the statue of the Virgin Mary was once more repaired with a new, naked and rather misshapen infant replaced in her motherly arms. Yet soon again another attempt was made to pull it down. This time the crucifix was replaced by a pyramid, and the Virgin Mary replaced by an almost nude Goddess Diana complete with water running down from her naked breasts.

Outraged at these fanatical doings, Queen Elizabeth had the Virgin Mary yet again restored, and was of the mind that a plain cross, the symbol of her kingdom's faith, should be acceptable to even to the most ardent Puritan. And so she ordered a gilt one to be placed at the summit of the ancient monument.

Twelve nights later, the monument was attacked once more. This time, in the process of having her crown hacked off, the Virgin Mary was almost decapitated. Her breasts were stabbed, and again her naked child was stolen away. Despite the Queen's best efforts, such was the underlying hatred still remaining among the vestiges of public Popery.

---

71 A contemporary depiction of the Cheapside Cross appears towards the end of this book.

'Oh, this cross is one of the jewels of the harlot of Rome,' a brave and forward clergy man said, 'and is kept here as a love token, and gives them hope that they shall enjoy us again.'

Chapter Twenty-Four

Despite the defeat of the Spanish Armada, the threat of Catholic forces coming to enjoy us again remained very real. By that time Drake was dead, but our brave sailors still continued to fight at sea to maintain our slender freedoms, even occasionally resorting to daring raids of hit and run. During one such skirmish our English hero Sir Martin Frobisher engaged with a squadron at the siege of Brest. Near Fort Crozen, Frobisher took a gunshot wound in his side from the Spanish and yet still managed to crawl back to his hole to die at Plymouth a few days later. His hollowed-out carcass was buried at Cripplegate, outside the walls of the City of London, in the Church of Saint Giles.[72] Thus this grandiose rogue was finally laid to rest in a church dedicated to the Papist saint of beggars and cripples instead of being laid to rest, as one might have expected, near his estate in Yorkshire and his illustrious Wentworth in-laws. Ironically, close by in that same place lies our late dear friend and the most humble of men, Mister John Foxe.

In fifteen-ninety-six, the Lord Admiral, along with Essex and Raleigh, fell upon Cales[73], burnt the shipping and sacked the town. For this cause Queen Elizabeth took the Mary Rose, the ship that my late husband Anthony and my brother Thomas had built.

For me the loss of that vessel marked out the end of an era – the end of that of Sir William Locke's sons. Only my brother Michael now remains alive. And of my own children, my son William is the only merchant. The Lock in Cheapside is picked clean and gone and the golden age of our Mercery all but sold away.

About this same time, a childhood neighbour from Cheapside brought to William's attention that Lord Thomas Burgh, for some long time away in Queen Elizabeth's service against the Spanish, had fallen into desperate financial straits. The affairs of his estate in Lincolnshire, having been left so long to

---

72   Frobisher's soft organs were buried in St Andrew's Church, Plymouth, Devon.
73   Cales was the English name for Cadiz in Spain.

their own devices, had now brought him to the brink of bankruptcy. No longer a well man either, Burgh had begged the Queen to allow him to come home to recover and settle his affairs. But, angrily, Elizabeth had refused. She might as well have handed him the nails to drive into his own coffin. Now, as the Burgh family found itself left with no other option than to sell off its long held seat of the Manor of Gainsborough, my son William had a mind to purchase it.

Gainsborough Hall has proved a godsend. It is a large Hall House with manorial rights over the small and unincorporated town of Gainsborough. And although this is situated well inland, is also a sea-going port of the River Trent and so within easy passage to the Low Countries. It seemed ideally suited to our needs. And so, William sold up most of our interests in London and I moved with him to Lincolnshire.

Before leaving London – which had been so much a part of my life – forever, William commissioned a painter to make likenesses of my sons to serve as keepsakes. Lincolnshire was a long, long distance away, and either by ship or by carriage it would be a difficult journey for someone of my great age to make. So at least, if I might never be fit again to travel that great distance south to see my sons, at least through their portraits I would still have my family about me. To William's own painting he chose to have the inscription 'DEVS MI' [74]added; a sentiment I thought most befitting.

Gainsborough Hall was not, however, to my new daughter-in-law Agnes' liking. She pined for her previous house in London, where she had lived in comparative luxury with her late husband and our family's dear friend, Sir Wolstan Dixie.

For William and Agnes, their marriage had been one made out of mutual respect and friendship, and with the sincere hope for shared companionship in their old age. For although Agnes was still of childbearing years, she and Wolstan had no children in all of their marriage, thus none were expected of this one either. And so, in time, Agnes' inherited wealth would go to her

---

74   Most probably abbreviated for 'DEVS MIHI' meaning 'God be with me'.

nephew and my son William's to his.

'It is so old fashioned!' Agnes groaned on first sighting the Hall. 'Come winter I'll wager it's as cold and draughty as an old barn!'

'Now there,' William soothed her with his silky tone, 'I have already commissioned some fine oak panelling for all of our family apartments. Come, let me show you the inside and tell you of all the wonderful modernisations I intend to carry out. Just for you, my dear!'

As they walked off, arm in arm, through the cobbled courtyard and inside the huge, yawning oak doorway, I tarried a little outside – taking in every contour of this wonderful building.

I liked Gainsborough Hall immensely. It is just like the large, timber-framed houses of my grandfather's era that have stood, cheek by jowl, all along Cheapside for all of my memories. When I first saw it, it reminded me of how all houses used to be when I was a child and at a time when brick was hugely expensive, even for families as wealthy as ours.

For over one-hundred-and-forty-years, this manor house had stood still whilst both time and fashion had moved on swiftly, and yet I could envisage the great potential in this house to be a beautiful and comfortable home once more. Even more attractive than this prospect was the fact that the Hall came with a licence for its own private chapel. This meant that we need never attend the parish church close by, unless we wished to do so. Instead, we could engage a preacher of our liking to minister to our needs.

The Great Hall, stripped bare of all furniture or ornament, was at that time like an empty heart of the centre of this once vibrant house. Looking up at its great arch-beamed roof, I always felt as if it was like stepping into a church – a white-washed walled church, plain and simple in a most aesthetic way. When Agnes stepped into it she could not see a use for all the rustic space. Yet when William then stood beside her he glanced at me and smiled, and then I smiled back. For our minds were of one accord.

'Do not fret, Agnes,' I said. 'This place was once fit for purpose and I am certain that, given time, it shall find fit purpose again.'

Beneath the main body of the house, William's man, Goode, found several cellars and interconnecting passageways – including one that led down to the Burgh's private but now disused wharf by the River Trent. These my son soon set quietly about improving while the restyling and bricking of the East range of the house was shortly in hand.

The kitchens proved extremely good, and the family accommodation was more than adequate for our simple needs and our modest Hickman household. And, despite Agnes' initial reservations, there was one part of the Hall that turned out to be particularly to her liking. This was the brick-built tower suite of bedrooms that Lord Burgh's great grandfather had built and which housed a fine set of chambers, each with its own ensuite guard de robe[75].

It was in one of these chambers, or so one of Burgh's former servants told us, that King Henry's fifth wife, Queen Catherine Howard, had stayed – during her last and most fateful visit away from London with her husband. It is such a pretty suite, with a fine view overlooking the gardens beyond, and yet I wonder if Queen Catherine found it in her heart to enjoy it when she was here. For as my father had told me long ago, even as this Queen had rested here, on her way back from York, ill-wishers were already plotting against her and her Catholic sympathies.

While Their Majesties, Catherine and Henry, were still here in Lincolnshire, some person amongst their courtiers submitted certain information to Archbishop Cranmer by which he accused the Queen of having engaged in extramarital affairs. Following on from this, Cranmer – unshakably loyal to the King and acting in good faith – then slipped a similar message into Henry's hand during mass on All Saints Day. Henry was so enraged by the note that His Majesty's

---

75   A primitive form of lavatory.

gentlemen were hard pressed to stop him from taking up his sword and seeking out his wife at once, so as to lop off her head himself!

Surely, even as Catherine stood in the still and quiet of this Gainsborough room, she must have had an inkling of how the sands of her time as Queen were fast pouring away, and that men were even then fitting her neck for the block. Most likely she had. And, for certain, she was not the only person to harbour such suspicion. For when William's men were fashioning a new chamber at the far section of the East Range, they stumbled upon something most chilling. As they worked upon the adjoining closet wall to repair a crack betwixt two beams, they came across a curious message scratched into the plaster of the wall. 'Trust truth only'[76] it read and was signed with the name of P Tyrwhitt, a nephew of a past Lady Burgh and a minor member of King Henry's entourage. What gossip and plot, I pondered, as I ran my fingertips over the writing, had this sensitive and essentially good young man overheard? It had obviously troubled his conscience so deeply that he then dared to commit his mind to the wall.

---

76 This is still legible on a wall at Gainsborough Old Hall today.

Chapter Twenty-Five

Early one morning, barely a week before Christmas, a messenger galloped in across our frozen courtyard. I could see immediately from his livery that he had come from my son, Henry, in London.

From the Solar landing window I watched him as he quickly slid from his saddle. He let drop the reigns without a care, leaving his panting horse steaming in the chill cold air. Then he hurried towards the house. His haste unnerved me.

As I backed away from the window and left the Solar landing to make my way down the wide and winding staircase, William was already on his way up to me with an opened letter in his hand. As he neared, I saw the sorrow in his eyes. He reached out his hands, at first to steady me, and then to gently hold me as I crumpled into his arms. It was then that I felt it... like fragile ice beneath horses hooves, my heart shattered into a thousand shards at the bitter news upon that most bitter winter's day. At just thirty-seven-years of age, my beloved son, Anthony, had dropped dead the previous day. My beautiful boy was no more.

*　　*　　*

When William discovered the true plight of the poor of Gainsborough, he knew that it was his God-given duty to act. For he was now the Lord of this Manor, and as such saw himself as the protector of these people, Gainsborough's weakest citizens. He could see with his own eyes that it was not poverty itself that held these poor wretches so low, but the excess profit that others made upon the back of their suffering.

The price of bread and almost every other commodity was far higher than even that to be had in London! And yet raw materials were lying all about and in plentiful supply. It was clear to William that local traders had for far too long, with the knowledge of the Burghs and others, been able to set inflated prices for almost every basic commodity. They kept away other suppliers – who could offer competition – and thus maintained a monopoly that enriched themselves but impoverished the community.

William was born a mercer, and so was schooled from the cradle upon trade's effects of supply and demand. So long as the demand for goods was high and the supply limited, then the price would remain unfairly inflated. But once the supply of goods was increased, then the price that could be charged for them would naturally fall to find its own level. If the price of goods fell, then the advantage would be for the poor and against the interests of the existing monopoly of rich traders, and potentially lower profits for William himself.

And so, against the goodwill of the local gentlemen, and regardless of objections voiced by those old and noble Lincolnshire families, my son increased the number of yearly markets and openly encouraged traders from near and far to flock into the town. The result was an immediate drop in prices – as goods flooded in and the demand for such items eased. Prices were slashed almost overnight! As a result, the burden upon the poor was much eased, but the wealthy town traders who had previously fed upon that poverty were now angry at my son. How they raged at him! Yet he would not suffer their indignations to move himself from his just course.

William was also appalled by the overcrowded housing provided for the poor and the high rents they were charged. And so he enclosed the common field and encouraged the poor to build their own homes upon it and then charged them a realistic rent. Again, this brought forth a vent of anger from the local gentry. They complained bitterly about the money they were losing from the so-called Poor Rents, and from then forward took every opportunity to bring law suits against William. But he countered these with those of his own, and so he succeeded in preventing unscrupulous men from undoing the good changes he had effected.

These same wealthy townspeople then expected William, as the new Lord of the Manor, to build again their long-crumbling and dilapidated Parish church, and so to restore it to its former Popish glory. Of course Willliam refused to do so. He argued: why should they demand him to now make good all that which past years of Burgh neglect had caused? And why should these wealthy nobles demand this huge expense to be made out of his purse, when they knew full well that it was also against his own religious beliefs?

My son's most public response was, 'Why should I build up this church that for so long your previous Lord had allowed to decay? Am I at once responsible for so much neglect before my time?'

But privately, and to like-minded Puritans, he would say, 'Why should I build up this church that refuses to allow itself to be reformed? Besides, God's true Church is not to be found in a building. Instead it should live and breathe wherever true Christians have chosen to follow Him in true worship. Therefore, if these nobles are indeed good Christians, then let them make do in a barn or in the churchyard – if they will not contribute to the cost of repairs themselves!'

Later, when the local gentlemen of Gainsborough fell upon my son, like a pack of hunting dogs, snarling for action to be taken when part of this church was then deemed unsound and in danger of collapse, he responded to their demands for safety's sake. At his own expense he made secure the still sound parts by way of props and by demolishing those parts that were not.

And so over the ensuing years, these same noble gentlemen of Gainsborough engage my family in court – time after time, charge after charge – of one sway or another, trying to make William bow to their will. He in response continues to launch counter claims, aided of course by our own able family of Hickman lawyers.

'They squeal for justice, so let them have justice,' my lawyer son Henry, advised.

Justice? Strangely, I am suddenly put in mind

of something that Thomas Cromwell once said; 'Oh, justice is what you are threatened with.'

I know full well also that these same disdainful local nobles refer to me as 'the crow', and to my beloved son as 'that threadbare fellow'. How they love to hate him and to slander our good Hickman name! I tell you now, I am so proud that William steadfastly refuses to be intimidated by them. Remembering his dear brother Anthony's words, William says: 'Yet speaking out doth not still such slanderous tongues. Instead let time and God be the judge of us'.

Fools! They can not comprehend that their disdain and hatred of us Hickmans is as nothing to us, and it is that which we will gladly endure in following our Lord's example. And are we not exhorted in His written word to do as much? 'Consider it pure joy, my brothers, whenever you face trials of many kinds, because you know that the testing of your faith develops perseverance. Perseverance must finish its work so that you may be mature and complete, not lacking anything.'[77]

---

77   James 1:2-4.

Chapter Twenty-Six

That chill February night, William made shift along the corridor like a madman shouting at the top of his voice. I managed to rouse myself in the blackness to meet the commotion as he reached the bright moonlit Solar landing beside my chamber door.

'Help! Somebody help!' he pleaded. And as I reached out to touch him, I could feel that his hands were all of a tremble and saw how his eyes were strangely wild. Quickly, I lifted my arms about him. Sobbing, he collapsed into them with his head in my breast, like my little boy of old.

Within an minute or too, a swathe of light flickered up the staircase as William's good man, George Holmes, came running up the steps and onto the landing. My housekeeper, Mistress Goode, panting heavily, followed closely on his heels.

'What is it, Maister?' George asked, but could not get any sense from his master. Instead, all that William was now capable of was gesturing towards the direction of his chamber. So George hurried off to see for himself.

Then, still holding him close, and by the light of Mistress Goode's candle, I led William into my chamber and set him down on the bed next to me.

'Rosa Solis, Goode!' I blurted, urging her towards my night cupboard. She hurriedly took up the bottle within and poured some of the precious liquid out.

'William, William!' I called, trying to coax him to drink it. And after a moment he did so, and all of one gulp.

'Tell me what has happened, William?'
The shock of the remedy loosened his tongue.

'It's Agnes...' he blurted out. 'I think she is dead!'

'Dead? No. Surely not! Maybe she is just sleeping...' I could not believe her sudden and unexpected death possible.

'I awoke,' he gasped, 'and turned over and she was there... with her eyes wide open looking back at me. I asked, 'Can you not sleep either, my dear?' And when she did not answer I touched her face and she did not move...'

George came back and into my chamber just as William had finished speaking. He looked at me and, with a tear now in his eye too, shook his head mournfully to confirm the awful truth. Agnes was indeed lying dead in the bed.

We never knew what had caused Agnes' death, though at the time William feared that perhaps she had been poisoned. A year before, at the height of heated arguments between William and the local gentry, one of our servants was slain in the town. It was a warning, my son believed.

However, our physician, who came in the morning, said that he could find nothing suspicious about Agnes' death or to indicate either poisoning or any other kind of foul play. He also said that the fact that William had not heard his wife cry out, or to make a sound in any way, meant therefore he had no reason to reproach himself. In all probability death had come upon her so swiftly that she had no time to make any noise. To the contrary, though rare, the physician said that he had seen such deaths in the past – whereby patients had died in just such a manner. They met their death wide-eyed and suddenly, as if the life forces had just been sucked out of them all of a piece. It had been God's will to take Agnes when he had, and that was an end to it.

Agnes was interred in the crypt at the parish church, amidst great chattering from our enemies – directed upon how we hypocrite Hickmans deemed the church not worthy of our money but good enough to house our rotting corpses. Yet I tell you now, were there but six feet of swampland, yet consecrated holy by our own zealous Puritan Church, then we should all be happily buried there. But for now there is not, though does not the Bible declare that the whole earth and everything in it belongs to God? Anyway, at this time even we Hickmans seem to have no choice other than to have our earthly bodies laid to rest there within that building.

*　　*　　*

Within a month, my son was introduced to Elizabeth Willoughby, a suitable and young prospective wife of a good and noble Puritan family. And so they were married.[78]

It was at about this same time that a clergyman dismissed by the Bishop of Lincoln from Elizabeth's Church for preaching forward Puritan views, came to settle in Gainsborough. If only my sister Elizabeth's last husband had still been alive! For he was a godly man and the Bishop of Lincoln afore this new man had come to the post, and so might surely have treated the Reverend John Smyth better.

Smyth had been born locally at Sturton-le-Steeple, just across our River Trent, in Nottinghamshire. He had been a Fellow of Christ's College, Cambridge, and he had been a student of the redoubtable Separatist, Francis Johnson. Because of his dismissal at Lincoln from Elizabeth's Church, he came to our town as an independent Preacher and Lecturer.

The vicar of the Parish of Gainsborough at the time, John Jackson, was a clergyman of dubious ability. It was his failings in his own ministry that led Jackson into paying John Smyth to preach in his stead.

Smyth, with his powerful spiritual presence, quickly drew to himself the friendship and respect of many devoted Christians amongst the parishioners. And yet he also attracted a great deal of ill favour from the less enlightened quarters of local townspeople. Complaints were quickly brought before William in his capacity as Lord of the Manor and Justice of the Peace. In response to these charges, my son quickly engaged Smyth to come privately to us and preach at the Hall on the very next Sunday. And he, in response, obligingly did so.

To our delight, we found Smyth to be amongst

---

78   In Tudor times re-marriage so soon after the death of a spouse was considered appropriate and necessary.

the most committed of Christians it had been our privilege to meet in many a long while. So we welcomed Smyth to preach to us in our home as often as he might, and thus began our close association with both him and his followers.

*   *   *

In the October of sixteen-hundred-and-one, William's first child was born at Gainsborough Hall. She was a sweet little daughter, baptized as Anne. But it pleased the Lord to take her back to Himself the following autumn.

Then, just a month or so after the death of this child, Elizabeth gave birth to a second baby girl – my beautiful granddaughter Frances. I was at once completely and utterly enchanted by this new Hickman babe.

I so love my grandchildren! For, indeed, at one point in my life, I had resigned myself to never living to see any grandchildren. It seemed that none of my sons would ever proudly continue the Hickman family name. Then, in the year when I became sixty, my son Walter married and soon had three sons and a daughter. Dixie (named in honour of my late husband Anthony's, kinsman – Wolstan), a sister, Elizabeth, and her brothers, William and Walter, all of whom I have barely got to know well enough, especially after William and I moved to Gainsborough. In truth, I soon became too frail to suffer a carriage ride to Lincoln, let alone one for a visit some two-hundred miles south to London.

My son, Anthony, although he had steadfastly refused to take orders upon taking up his Fellowship at Cambridge, nevertheless lived his life as if he had, and declined any thought that might have led him towards marriage. Meanwhile, his older brother, Henry, had taken up a fellowship and spent the greater part of his adult life at Cambridge, too. Then, shortly after William's dear Agnes died, Henry married as well and soon had children. But yet again I do not know them.

And so, to at last to be under the same roof as

new Hickman life is one of the greatest blessings in all the bounty of God that the Lord hath bestowed upon me. Yet still, I hoped that, God willing, I might live to see my son William have a son of his own and so carry on his father's name.

Chapter Twenty-Seven

Queen Elizabeth was dead. She and I had been contemporaries but I was already older than she was at her date of death. Therefore, from that point onwards, I began to look ever more closely towards my own demise – that now must surely also be very near at hand. When the Queen died I felt that there was still so much more that I desired to help William achieve, yet I had begun to resign myself to the likelihood that maybe I had already fulfilled all those plans that our Lord had purposed for me to realise.

Above all else, the one thing that I had most privately wished for was to be able to redeem any lingering doubt that the name of Hickman was in any way inferior to that of Locke. By rights, my late husband Anthony should have been knighted for his services under both Henry and Edward. And then, Queen Elizabeth, while making good use of him, despised his zealous Protestantism and so never bestowed upon him the honour that he very justly deserved.

Thus, I had longed for some means by which William might receive a title other than the one that accompanied the purchase of Gainsborough Hall – that of 'lord' of the manor. A knighthood is what I had hoped for my husband's eldest son, but then I had to concede that I would not now see that happen.

We zealous Protestants had planned for Queen Elizabeth's death and had already prepared a petition to take to the new monarch. In it we asked for his consideration towards the reforms we so earnestly desired for the Church in England. So, when word came that King James VI of Scotland – soon to ascend his aunt's throne as James I of England – was already upon the road south to London, a band of representatives made move to meet him on his journey so that they might present it to him unannounced.

When the King and his bodyguards came riding into sight, our band of Christians dismounted and prepared to serve His Majesty with their paper.

'Sire,' our appointed spokesman explained on presenting the document to the King, 'we represent more than a thousand of Your Majesty's subjects and ministers, all groaning under one great burden of human rites and ceremonies. We are not factious men wishing to cause division in the Church, nor are we schismatics wanting the dissolution of the State ecclesiastical. We are merely faithful servants of Christ and your loyal subjects, who desire the redress of certain abuses of the Church. In our obedience of God and in the service of Your Majesty, we could do no less than to acquaint you with our grievances, Sire.'

What our signatories to that document were asking for was sympathetic consideration of matters that had always affronted us true Protestants in England the most. Many of these had already been amended in the State Church in Scotland. Some of our points were foundational to essential Bible-based Christian doctrine while others were less so. An example of the latter was the signing of the cross over babies brought forward for baptism. And there were also other superfluous rituals – like the habit of bowing at the mention of Jesus' name, or the use of a ring in the marriage service. But we believed that these, as trifling as they may have seemed to some people, also needed elimination. Because indeed we were and still are striving to re-build a purified Church; that is a Church held accountable to the teachings of the Bible rather than the corruption of centuries of human tradition and error. Just one such practice was the pressure that Elizabeth had so recently exerted upon ministers: to wear the hated cap and surplus, which then set our 'shepherds' apart from the flock, which runs contrary to the teaching of New Testament Scripture. We wanted a sermon to be said whenever communion was administered, for we believed that preaching was at the bedrock of our ministry, and so we pressed for non-preaching ministers to be ejected from their pulpits and replaced with those who did preach the word of God. We asked that, in churches, only the Old Testament and New Testament be read, and not the highly questionable Apocryphal books, many of which were still being used and smacked of the Papists. And, of course, we asked for the Sabbath to be kept holy.

For a fleeting moment King James Stuart took the document into his hand, before swiftly handing it on to one of his entourage for 'safe keeping'. Despite his promise to give our concerns his soonest attention, we were to hear no more from the King upon our own great matter for more than a year.

As for my son William, he had also set off upon the Great North Road to meet James Stuart on his journey southwards. On meeting with the King, William fell to his knees and pledged his loyalty to our new sovereign, truly thinking and saying that he believed His Majesty to be 'the best hope now for England'. Later, when William returned home to me at Gainsborough Hall, his face was as bright as the moon hung in a cloudless sky. King James had knighted my son at Belvoir Castle. Thirty years after my husband Anthony's death, his first born son was now Sir William Hickman!

*   *   *

Plague had stalked London for most of that first summer and autumn of King James' reign. In consequence, the conference arranged for that November to air our Puritan grievances was postponed until the threat from this vile pestilence had died with the first hard snow of the London winter.

When we eventually heard that conference was at last to be held at Hampton Court, it was as if a bright glimmer of light had suddenly brightened up the dull January horizon. Yet our hopes were to be wickedly dashed – like a tempestuous sea shattering a ship of dreams against a rocky shore.

Our good men did not yet know King James. Nor did they know that our new sovereign had not been able to cast out of his mind the great humiliation he had already suffered at the hands of the reformed Scottish

Church, especially that so bluntly meted out to His Majesty by Andrew Melville, the greatest Presbyterian preacher since our friend Mister John Knox.

'God's silly vassal,' Melville hissed, as he grabbed the King by his arm and publicly scolded him aloud. 'There are two kings and two kingdoms in Scotland. There is Christ Jesus the King and His Kingdom the Kirk, whose subject King James VI is, and of whose kingdom he is not a king, nor a lord, nor a head, but a member!'

However deep the festering bitterness was within His Majesty's heart, or the depth of the personal slight felt at those stinging words, surely King James must have realised that this statement, in essence, was true?

Therefore, our Puritan delegation set foot into that conference to face their sovereign without an inkling that King James was already determined not to allow such a humiliation to be dealt to him again. Certainly not in his new kingdom. Not in England!

Two of the four good Protestant summoned to represent us, were known to my family; John Reynolds, the Dean of Lincoln Cathedral and President of my late son's college of Corpus Christi, and also John Knewstub, a Fellow of my son Henry's St John's College, both of Cambridge. With despairing hearts, they later let us know how this meeting had passed.

Although invited to present their case, none of these four had been allowed to speak during the first of the three-day session. Instead, they were forced to sit silent while Archbishop Whitgift, ably abetted by his man Bancroft, held centre-stage. There he was allowed to use his influence to both scrutinise and unfairly prejudice – without challenge – our Puritan pleas for reform. His and the King's own disdain for us Puritans was so painfully plain for all to see, and to our good representatives' eyes and ears it made wicked mockery of the whole proceedings.

When at last our men could take no more, and spoke out in defence of our beliefs, Bancroft moved to silence them by way of a statute that stated schismatics were not to be given leave to speak. They challenged this by saying that they were not, nor had ever been, 'schismatic', and that they held no desire to rent themselves away from the Church of England. They sought only certain reforms.

And so the King relented, and let them have some say. But he cut short any suggestion made by our fellows, no matter how meekly or mildly put forth, upon the subject of reforming the hierarchical structure of the clergy. Then he slowly repeated aloud but one single phrase: 'No bishop – no King'. And since he was clearly not prepared to be drawn upon that subject, our clergy were forced to move on.

Some acceptance on the part of the Archbishop's side was reached upon the need for minor changes to the wording of the Book of Prayer. And when Dean Reynolds suggested that a new translation of the Bible should be undertaken, that was agreed also.

However, when our good clergy put forward our proposals for reform, for which we Hickmans had long ago heard Mister John Knox reasoning, which were now accepted in the Scottish Presbyterian Church, King James suddenly boiled angry.

'If these be the greatest matters you be grieved with,' he had shouted as he banged his fist upon the arm of his great chair, 'I need not have been troubled with such importunities and complaints!'

As for hearing pleas for the Church in England to be reformed along the same lines as his native country's Kirk, he coldly added: 'Presbyterianism agrees with a monarchy as much as God is likely to agree with the devil'.

Many of our fellow Puritans felt sick with dismay upon hearing of the disappointing outcome of that meeting. Yet more worrying was the report of the angry mutterings of the King that had clearly been heard as he stormed off from the proceedings.

'If this be all they have to say, I shall make them conform themselves, or I will harry them out of the land, or do worse!'

It was shortly after this, that Archbishop Whitgift imposed a whole new raft of rules and regulations upon the entire clergy of the English Church. From henceforth, they would be compelled to submit themselves unto the very letter of one-hundred-and-forty-one canon laws on how they were to conduct themselves and the services of the Church. Those who refused to sign their names to these laws would be removed from their livings and deprived of their licence to preach.

'Whitgift thinks that if he can cut off the head, then the body will die!' Smyth said to my son, William, making triumph out of news of such adversity. 'Just as our dear Lord's enemies thought His followers would fall away if He were crucified. Strange irony then, that the testaments of the Gospels should so clearly be wasted upon such as this Archbishop!'

'Yet what of the King?' I asked.

'The King?' Smyth did not see my tack.

'Why, if the King's own Scotland has a reformed Church, is he so set against the reformation of our English one?'

It was a question upon which Smyth said he dare not ponder. All he would say was that if this question were to be followed to its ultimate conclusion, then the answer might be one unthinkable for every true Protestant in the land.

Many good clergy at first refused to be bound by the Archbishop Whitgift's new commandments. But then, after heavy pressure was brought to bear upon them, the greater part relented and submitted themselves to his rule.

However, a heart-core of our most zealous Protestant shepherds refused. Amongst them were many already known to, or even members of, the growing underground congregation that John had gathered to meet for services in our own Great Hall at Gainsborough. If the Church of England was no longer willing to accept them, then they now had no other choice left open to them, than to reject that Church in return. And so they would have to separate themselves from it.

In the wake of the Hampton Court Conference, and the ousting of many good local clergy from their churches, John Smyth's congregation went from strength to strength. From far and near they came, from Lincolnshire and from across the Trent in Nottinghamshire and Yorkshire. Some even spoke of having known Anthony from his days at Cambridge. I cannot tell you what a comfort it was for me to hear my late son's name so warmly met upon their lips.

But increasingly inclement winter weather and the whittling down of good travelling hours of daylight, hampered the long trek on the Lord's Day undertaken by those having to journey the furthest in the shires across the Trent. As a result, a part of John Smyth's congregation decided it prudent to split from our group and form a second one, to be based at Mister William Brewster's home of Scrooby Manor. There they could be ministered to by the eminently capable Reverend Richard Clyfton[79]. It was a move brought on by necessity and a bold and dangerous choice of location for William Brewster, because Scrooby Manor belonged to the Archbishop of York and Mister Brewster, as Bailiff of his estate, was in his direct employ. Not only that, Brewster was also engaged in the King's service, because he held the office of Post Master at Scrooby, where he managed the provision of fresh horses and accommodation for His Majesty's messengers.

Whilst our own Bishop of Lincoln was perhaps a little less zealous in enforcing his powers upon us, bishops from elsewhere were more vigorous in theirs. Toby Matthew, the incoming Archbishop of York was one man who seemed set upon breaking up the Separatist cluster that was so active in his diocese. He particularly targeted his efforts upon absentee church members in Scrooby. Many of those people who were subsequently threatened, fined, or subjected to spells in prison, had worshipped with us as members of our congregation in Gainsborough. As a result of being fined, harried, spied upon and sometimes even imprisoned, many were now

---

79   Deposed vicar of Babworth Church.

finding the struggle to maintain their commitment to faith almost at breaking point.

If these true Christians were now to be persecuted by Whitgift's minions, as was my own dear son, Anthony, then William and I would move heaven and earth to help them endure. For we were decided. Their cause was now ours.

*   *   *

In the June of this same year, praise be to God, my good daughter-in-law Elizabeth was safely delivered of baby boy. They baptised him Willoughby. My prayers in this respect had been answered. William now had a son of his own to help carry on my dear first husband's line.

Chapter Twenty-Eight

     If our hopes for religious tolerance had been dashed upon the rock of despair with the incoming monarch, then so had it been for the Papists'. Their own hopes had ridden high upon the back of King James' late executed mother, Mary Queen of Scots, having died a 'martyr' to the Catholic cause.

     Yet, as we had witnessed, His Majesty seemed indifferent to pleas to make shift in any direction in matters of religious reform – other than to clamp down hard upon any who threatened to unbalance the status quo and the shaky stability of his new realm.

     News arriving from London in the November of sixteen-hundred-and-five was as shocking and worrying as it was unexpected. A monstrous attempt had been made by a Catholic group to blow up King James and His Majesty's Government as Parliament was in session. Now fear ran rife that there might be more attacks of terror or assassination attempts to follow. Many of the 'gun powder plotters', as they had become known, came from our part of the Midlands, the area in which we now lived, and from across the nearby River Trent, where Catholic dissent seethed most abundantly. As a result, there came about an even stronger crackdown upon any who dared show dissent.

*   *   *

     There was a youth amongst Mister Smyth's congregation whose presence and bearing commanded my attention as soon as I set eyes upon him. Judging by the closeness of the bond between this young man and Mister Brewster from Scrooby, I at first I took the younger man to be Mister Brewster's son. For all the world they seemed like father and son; Brewster administering the firm but loving hand of fatherly guidance to young Will, who received that loving lead like the most dutiful son. I soon learned that in flesh they were not kin, but through faith in Christ they had become true family. I could see that. Everyone could see that.

Will Bradford, as I was to learn, was of no relation to Mister Brewster at all. Young Bradford was an orphan, though not some poor wretch plucked from the gutter of life's byway. Rather, he was a young man with prospects and a goodly inheritance in the offing – once he had come of age. The problem was that he had not yet come of age. And his remaining family had all but washed their hands of him since he had proclaimed his desire to join with these other Separatist fellows. 'Twas not an unexpected situation, for zealous Protestants are often most hotly put down by those of conservative Anglican persuasion. As I subsequently grew to know of the young man's situation, the more I came to admire this youth for the courage of his conviction.

Young Bradford's family were of Austerfield, a small village close to the town of Bawtry, where the county border of Yorkshire blurs into that of neighbouring Nottinghamshire. His family were yeoman[80] farmers, with his grandfather coming into land at Austerfield through marriage into an ancient, and once prominent, family of the district – the Mortons of Bawtry. Will Bradford's grandmother was Alice Morton, who died while Will's own late father was still young. Will had never met this grandmother, but Alice's brothers and half-brothers were very well known figures in the district.

In the year of thirteen-hundred-and-ninety, a Robert Morton and his wife, Joan, had founded a hospital and chapel on the uttermost edge of Nottinghamshire's parish of Harworth, adjoining Bawtry. It was dedicated to Saint Mary Magdalene.

The Morton's also made a most generous gift to the Prior of nearby Saint Oswald's, in return for supporting a chaplain at Saint Mary Magdalene, so that mass might be regularly conducted and prayers said in perpetuity for the departed souls of Robert and Joan and other deceased Mortons. Thus, for more than three-hundred years the Mortons had chosen to inter

---

80   Yeoman farmers were land owners.

their departed family members beneath the chapel, with masses and prayers being said for these dead – until the crown had made the Catholic Mass illegal.

In effect, the chapel of Saint Mary Magdalene was a chantry. Indeed most parish churches were once endowed with chantries, maintaining a stipendiary priest to say mass for the souls of their donors. When the monasteries had been dissolved under King Henry, chantries had survived mainly intact, only to then be dissolved under King Edward's Chantries Act in fifteen-hundred-and-forty-seven. With that Act passed, all these chantries' former properties were appropriated by the Crown.

Amongst its illustrious fore-bearers, the Morton family could even boast of a Secretary to a King and a Sheriff of Nottingham, amongst other eminent kinsmen. Yet in much closer times, as I have lived through, they could also lay claim to a troublesome Catholic or two. For with the King's split from Rome, the Morton family had since also rent, with half the family being loyal to the Protestant Tudors while the other half remained defiantly Catholic.

In the reign of Queen Mary, cruel Papist persecutors rounded up many of our friends and burnt them to death in the name God. And then later, when Queen Elizabeth came to the throne, she in turn had Catholics burnt in the name of the State. Yet I ask this: how can any true follower of Christ be a heretic? And how can a person who burns to death another call him or herself a Christian? Surely, Christ looks on and weeps with sorrow at it all?

I see now that my past hatred for the Papists is a sin. For in the book of Hebrews it is written: 'See to it that no one misses the grace of God and that no bitter root grows up to cause trouble and defile many'[81] .Bitterness kills souls. Because slowly but surely it eats a person away like the plague, while at the same time spreading unto the destruction of others! As I have followed the life paths of Queen Mary and Queen Elizabeth, I have found that they shared more than the flesh and blood

---

81   Hebrews 12:15.

of their father. They have shared and then reacted to the greatest bitterness. Bitterness rooted deeply in their childhood. May I not be so ensnared!

And hath not Christ instructed me through the Lord's Prayer that I should love mine enemies, and to forgive them for their trespasses against me? I understand now that in the past I have not truly understood the intention behind my Lord's command, and only now do I begin to see it more clearly. Our Lord Jesus, immediately after His teaching on how to pray in the Gospel of Matthew, then adds: 'For if you forgive men when they sin against you, your heavenly Father will also forgive you. But if you do not forgive men their sins, your Father will not forgive your sins' [82]

For so long I have been so bedazzled by my own zealous Protestant cause that I had become blinkered to the suffering of those of others. I mean, of course the Papists. Tolerance of the ordainary Papist is something that I now desire with all my heart. May there yet be some way in which we true Protestants might be able to show our Papist counterparts the tolerance we so desire for ourselves. But this is not easy when there are those who persecute us.

I know of many ordinary English Catholic subjects who abhorred the burnings and persecution of our martyred Protestants as much as we did. This is true of Christ-honouring souls like, for example, the Governor at Antwerp. He afforded to my husband, who differed greatly from his own religious ideals, that most precious gift of all – tolerance. Yet I fear that a general tolerance such as this in the matter of religion can never be whilst their Pope and his hierarchy of cardinals and bishops contrive for the utter destruction of Protestants.

I believe with all my heart that the manner in which my fellow puritans and I have chosen to worship our Lord is the way that He hath commended to us by means of the Gospels. And I also believe that in many parts the Papist's way is corrupted. Yet who am I to oppress them in their own belief that their way is true?

---

82   Matthew 6:14 and 15.

This is not a harvest for man to reap. Nor is it for him to separate the sound grains of wheat from the chaff. That is for God alone to do. Therefore, is it not better that we – all who claim to be followers of Christ – should agree to disagree until we stand before our God in heaven and submit ourselves at last to His judgement?

For if we can cast off our perceived hatred for someone, if only for a moment, and try instead to find some area of common ground upon which to build, to find some seed of compassion towards them that we might cultivate, then might we not better come to know and understand them and they us?

Unless we can learn to show compassion to those opposed to us, then how can we expect to receive any such compassion in return? It is with those enemies that we know and understand, that better and longer lasting treaties may be formed. And then maybe these better than even with those who claim to be of similar ilk to ourselves.

I know what it is like to subject to unyielding Catholic ecclesiastics as in days gone by in England. Yet now I see all about me so-called Protestants who are out to do us 'Puritans' as equal an ill as any Papist persecutor of the past. Both we zealous Protestants and Catholics are now treated alike by this King as we were under Elizabeth's subjugation. And no longer do we find ourselves as merely undesirable, but now also as enemies of the State! In truth, the only enemy to all is this stubborn intolerance of one another. Yet all it would take is one godly prince amongst the many to stand and condemn the wicked old ways and then with a brave heart embrace pluralism.

*   *   *

There was a Protestant man of my late son Anthony's age, but with a wife and a brood of small children to support. In the tavern in the small town where he conducted his business, the man met a childhood friend long absent from those parts. The man extended his warmest welcome to the friend, who looked tired and dusty from his travels and down at heel in both his boots and his fortune. And so out of that past friendship and good Christian charity the man paid for his poor friend's supper.

After the friend finished his meal, he got up from the table and made to go upon his way.

'Where shall you bide the night?' the man asked.

'I shall find a barn or some shelter to suit my simple needs,' the poor friend replied.

'Nay,' the man said, 'you shall be my guest in my own home.'

Although the man insisted, his poor friend could not be dissuaded from making his own arrangements. And so, reluctantly, the man made his goodnight and went home to his family.

The following day, the poor friend was arrested at a house not far from the town. Unknown to the man, it transpired that the poor friend was a long time away before because he had gone to Rome and had taken orders as a Catholic priest.

Meanwhile, Francis Walsingham's spies had been following this priest closely, and so later came to the other man's house and sized him also.

Shortly afterwards, both men were cruelly executed. The one for being a priest against the Crown's forbidding, and the other for buying him supper. Yet where was the worse crime and who was the greater criminal?

In just such a manner, death also came to a member of the Morton family from Bawtry. Robert Morton was the younger half-brother of Will Bradford's late grandmother. Like his two brothers, he had chosen to go to Rome where he took Holy Orders.

After barely a year in the Catholic priesthood, Robert then chose to risk great danger in order to return to his home and to minister as a simple priest to those in need of spiritual comfort from one of their own.

Robert Morton was caught close to the town of Bawtry, performing a Papist mass in secret. Someone nearby had informed upon him, and so the priest was arrested and brought to London. On the bright summer's day of June the twenty-eighth, fifteen-hundred-and-eighty-eight, Robert Morton was taken to Lincoln's Inn Field in London to face the vilest of public executions for the sake of his faith.

And so when young Will Bradford then grew to an age to understand God's true word, and subsequently expressed his desire to become a zealous Protestant, his uncles who had charge of him might well have harboured strong objections. For if that remaining family still held fast the old religion hidden deep inside their souls, then they might well have felt a great hurt at the things past inflicted upon their dead family and chapel.

However, if that were indeed so, then I was soon to learn that there was even more hurt than this to turn them against Will Bradford's association, and against William Brewster in particular.

The mother of Alice Morton, Will Bradford's great-grandmother, had died when she was young. Her father, Robert, then remarried, and so Alice soon had three half-brothers who, when grown up, all later went to Rome. Alice also had a full brother, Anthony Morton, who unlike his sister lived unto a great age.

Although England split from Rome, Anthony had steadfastly remained overtly Catholic. Having refused to give up his faith in the old religion, he was subsequently stripped of much of his land by way of fine for his defiance of Queen Elizabeth. This Anthony Morton was, I believe, still alive at the very same time as young Will Bradford was attending the Separatist conventicles at our Hall.

For the entire length of young Will's life up until that point, Anthony had been involved in a long running legal dispute over the Morton family chapel at Bawtry. Although for all intents and purposes this Chapel of Saint Mary Magdalene should have been dissolved, it had not. And no one seemed to know for certain why that should have been, other than it had perhaps been on account of simply being overlooked, especially as a member of clergy was still in receipt of payment to act as Master there, and to conduct twice-weekly services at the chapel, whether anyone attended or not.

Then, in fifteen-hundred-and-eighty-four, a new man was granted the mastership of that chapel. In truth, the long ride there from this incumbent's other churches coupled with the small stipend offered by the position, probably made the position of Master there seem more trouble than its worth. Apart from that, there was also the ambiguity surrounding the chapel's continued existence to be considered.

This period was also a time of heightened patriotism, when the now Catholic minority found itself caught up in a frenzied backlash of hatred, especially in the wake of the recent assassination attempts against Queen Elizabeth. And so feelings were running hot – with all Catholics being deemed capable of treason and plot, and the Mortons in particular.

Alice Morton's half-brother, Nicholas, was not only Catholic but had been a Papal Emissary. And it was he who had delivered the despised Papal Bull of excommunication against Queen Elizabeth. He was also one of the emissaries who had acted as go-between for Queen Mary Stuart of Scotland and her 'friends across the sea'.

And when Philip, Earl of Arundel, was indicted for high treason, it was stated in evidence that it had been Nicholas Morton, with others, who had plotted to kill the Queen and then rally an army to overthrow the Government and reclaim the Church. Therefore, to God-fearing English Protestants, the Morton's were like the antichrist's disciples, while to the God-fearing local Catholics still fighting to hold on to their own religion, the Mortons were looked upon as their champions.

Any Protestant clergyman venturing into Bawtry at that time must have surely been aware of both the past and recent Morton interments made within the chapel of Saint Mary Magdalene. And they must have been equally aware of the bare earth burials mounds within its grounds, all of which had been made instead of the normal burials at the nearby Parish Church. And so one might have guessed at this tiny chapel's significance to those die-hard Papists still within hearing range of its single bell.

So, whether by accident or, as some claimed, by deliberate conspiracy, the new Master then entered into an arrangement with one Thomas Robinson and two others, to sell off this redundant chapel and its benefits and lands. This is how the estates of Saint Mary Magdalene Chapel came to be divided up and sold off in part as a free farm. The beautiful and well ordered chapel was then systematically stripped of its furnishings and decorations – to instead be used to house cattle and horses that defecated upon the tombs of those buried within.

For Anthony Morton and his family, this was of course distressing in the extreme. As a result of this vile desecration, he then entered into a long running court case against the men involved. So, in the very same year as young Will Bradford was born, a warrant was issued by the High Commissioners for Lands Ecclesiastical at York against the master and the others for 'the profanation and ruination of the house and chapel of the Hospital'. This claim was subsequently backed by the Archbishop himself, who then pressed hard for its repossession. Yet even he was denied it, and so the wrangling went on for many years.

In defiance of these orders, one of the transgressors, of whom all were Protestant, had then been heard to rail in public that he and his associates would 'shortly pull down the chapel to utterly destroy it for good and all...'

It would be of no small wonder then, if young Will Bradford's family had then taken so strongly against this youth's association with us zealous Protestants as to wash their hands of him. That would go a long way to explain why such a young lad had been left to his own devices instead of being gathered in the bosom of his remaining family at home. And especially so when one considers that the Master at Saint Mary Magdalene, who had caused the Morton family so much angst, was none other than one James Brewster - William Brewster's brother.

Chapter Twenty-Nine

'How much does he want to borrow?' The amount was incredulous to William. He could not quite comprehend how much money my brother Michael was asking for. 'Surely he cannot be in so much debt as this again?'

Michael was always in debt. In debt and living in near penury despite the huge inheritance he had received from our late father's will. All of it, and a great deal more, had been lost in his terrible dealings with Martin Frobisher.

For more than thirty years now, Michael had often to borrow money simply to live. He was even much in debt to his own poorly placed sons, and yet the dream of fortunes waiting to be made in the New World still taunted and occupied his mind.

'It is not for debt,' I replied, as I held Michael's letter still clasped in my hand. 'It is for investment. It is venture capital that he requires – for an expedition to plant a colony in Virginia.

'Virginia?' William sighed. But it was not a sigh of outright dismissal or dismay at my brother's boldness in asking. It was simply that our entire family was aware of Michael's lifelong dreams of America, and exactly how much he had ventured before, and lost.

Michael was still living in London and of course could not have avoided hearing about the leading merchants' newly formed Virginia Company and its daring plan to send three ships in that coming December, with over one-hundred colonists to the late Queen Elizabeth's virgin territory in the New World.

No, I think William sighed because for one fleeting moment he too was tempted to invest in this new venture. Yet he resisted. Such ventures were for men of far less years than my son's fifty-seven years, let alone for a man as old as my brother!

'America! I have no doubt that it is an opportunity but waiting to open. But such uncertain fortunes are neither for us, Mother, nor for Uncle Michael. Not now.

But for others at some time in the future... yes! I can see many advantages to settling a new land well beyond mere profit.'

So it was that I reluctantly wrote to my brother telling him that we could not help. I hated being the person to end this dream for him, yet I think that our refusal was, in a way, a kindness. Sometimes in life we set our hearts upon that which the Lord had already decreed we may not have. Such things may be destined in His great plan for some people, but not for all of us. And yet it does not make the longing any the less painful to bear.

* * *

John Smyth had been cited, once more, for preaching at Gainsborough without a licence. And although my son had written several times to the Bishop of Lincoln in the past to make excuse for this, patience in Lincoln had worn thin like the silver plate upon the noses of the late King Henry's debased coinage.

I find Mister John Smyth to be a born leader, and as charismatic a man as he is handsome. With his somewhat wayward countenance, deep and soulful voice, and his outstanding preaching, he attracted followers to Gainsborough as easily as the overripe pears in our orchard attract hungry wasps at the end of a summer played out. They swarmed to his side to hear him preach, because they had been won over by his honest voice delivering honest words. Yet, for these 'sins', he was fast becoming a wanted man.

At that last summer's end, when he was with us still at Gainsborough, he met once more with Mister Brewster and the outstanding preacher Clyfton, who had since the previous winter split away in the bad weather to form an independent congregation across the River Trent at Scrooby.

On that memorable day, amongst the delights of the fading summer flowers, I recall observing Mister Smyth from a distance. He had stood, talking intensely with several others, after having taken our conventicle under God's great blue canopied openness. From the looks upon their faces and the language of Mister Brewster's ever animated hands, I could surmise the nature of their conversation.

Leaving! They were talking about leaving, and I certainly could not blame them for wishing to do so. For when the cold wind blows it will turn any head around. These Separatists had fought their good fight here long and hard, and yet they had been unable to gain the ground from the King so desperately needed for the foundation of their newly formed Church. Not only that, but friends at The Close in Lincoln had written a letter of warning that Archbishop Toby Matthews, spurred ever onwards by Archbishop Whitgift, had approached the Bishop of Lincoln to join with them and Southwell to take decisive action against all Separatist elements within the adjoining three counties. And whilst Lincoln yet stalled, it must surely be only a matter of time before he was made not only to relent but also to act.

Like the leaden clouds that had gathered in about us at the end of that sultry afternoon, the forces for these Separatists' final persecution were drawing ever closer. For since the conference at Hampton Court, dissenters of the Church could now be conveniently described as dissenters of the King, the Head of the Church. In short, this was tantamount to treason. And the certain remedy for treason was death.

Now there seemed only one sensible path for Mister Smyth to take, and he needed to take it quickly. That day in my gardens was a coming together to mark a parting of the ways – for the two congregations to bid farewell to one another.

As a chill began to set in and the dark clouds, already threatening, piled in on the horizon, the bowels of the Hall were even then being emptied of the belongings of John Smyth and his followers. For the past week or so, items of household furniture and personal effects – lives crammed into wooden chests and baskets – had been quietly received into our house, lost amongst the general comings and goings to be hidden below. My son's most trusted men were secretly loading up the cart to take yet one more load through the vast brick-line underground passageway – down to our private wharf and onto one of our waiting ships. They took every care to be especially vigilant as they did so, and to take every advantage presented to cover over the tracks of our departing friends, so that none might know for certain exactly how their escape had been effected. Within the hour the tide would begin to turn and our precious human cargo would be on its way to freedom.

Meanwhile, John Smyth and William Brewster braved the blackening skies above to tarry, just little longer, to make brief farewells and speak warmly of future reunion. How this put me in mind of just such heartfelt farewells during my late husband Anthony's and my time of persecution, and of those that we had helped then to vanish away! I realised then that our move to Gainsborough had been to fulfil this very purpose.

William and I knew full well that once Mister Smyth and the others had indeed been found to have gone missing, then the hue and cry for this Gainsborough congregation would cast its suspicious eye in our direction. When this happened, my son, I am proud to say, acted as had my husband Anthony in the time of Queen Mary, when he had been brought before her commission. Anthony never did lie about his involvement in smuggling good Protestants abroad, for he was too pure a man to break the Lord's commandment with a lie. Instead, if quizzed and pressed, and even asked directly, he could say firmly and without perjuring himself: 'If this indeed be so then you may have me guilty as charged, as soon as you bring me your evidence!'

William and I knew the risk we were running. And we knew that our enemies would make short shift of informing the authorities of their suspicions about our involvement. When they did, praise God, it was without evidence, and so there was nothing to be done against us.

But later that fall, when William Brewster then came asking for help of the same, we dared not again aid passage from the Hall or from our private wharf. For by then we knew ourselves to be under a watch. Instead, William helped Mister Brewster in contriving to make an escape attempt far to the south of the county, near Boston.

'For who would expect you to leave from Boston?' my son William reasoned with good logic. 'For certain, the moment your party is missed, the searchers will hurry either here to Gainsborough or to Hull. But not to the farthermost end of the county!'

William was of course right. Attempting to gain a passage from Boston would mean making a journey of more than sixty miles across land. It would be difficult and extremely hard on the women and small children in the party. For six difficult days, at least, they would have to travel along the lesser known byways – gradually making their way to the port of Boston, where they would bribe a ship's master to take them across to Holland and freedom.

They dare not stop to make shelter near a town or to ask for anything upon their way for fear of arousing suspicion. And they dare not make great fires at night, for these would attract attention from the curious. There would also be no cooking or fireside warmth. With the nights turning chill, it would be most difficult indeed, and yet nonetheless this escape route was highly possible.

And thus, with September all but spent, the Scrooby congregation left their homes, all of a piece. They took with them only those very few precious things they could carry, after quietly and gradually selling what they could not. Mister Brewster had written his letter of resignation to the Archbishop of York, relinquishing his position of Bailiff and Post Master, just before he went upon his way with his family.

And with them, and with my blessing, went my own young maidservant, Dorothy.

Then the Archbishop's men came. From across the Trent they swarmed upon Gainsborough – like a cloud of black flies – and rudely entered the Hall unannounced to challenge my son.

William sat upon his large, carved oak chair in the Great Chamber. He appeared unmoved as they crowded in upon him, before he then raised his voice and rebuked them sharply. He began by reminding them that he was the lord of this manor and not the Archbishop of York. And as such, he was not answerable to their master on matters temporal. And yet still the Archbishop's men persisted.

Then their chief man asked William outright as to whether or not he had helped Mister Brewster and his 'most wicked gaggle of dissenters' escape upon one of our ships in Gainsborough.

In response, William calmly called for his man, Goode, to fetch our family's Bible. This Mister Goode did quickly. And then, after William received it into his own hands, in front of his accusers, he placed his left palm upon it and proceeded to make a solemn oath that he had not helped these aforementioned people to board any of his ships in Gainsborough.

After William had done this, the Archbishop's man had no good reason to press him further. And so the disgruntled gang, with some muttering, turned and went on its way.

From thence forth, with each day that passed without further harassment or news, we knew that the chances of Mister Brewster and his band of friends escaping to safely across the sea were improving. And as the cold weather began to bite, as arranged, we waited for word that all was well with them to come on our ship from Amsterdam. But to our deepening consternation, none came. And so we began to worry about the congregation's safety...

Chapter Thirty

How could my son and I look upon them and not feel the deepest compassion for their dire circumstances? I remember the sight of them vividly. They stood in the yard by our kitchen door – women with exhausted children clutched in their failing arms, or clinging mournfully at their mothers' bedraggled skirts. Beside the women stood the weary menfolk, with the look of defeat set deeply in their eyes and etched upon their faces. William Brewster and his congregation had been betrayed in Boston. They had been betrayed by the very men they had paid to carry them across the sea to freedom.

At first everything seemed to have gone well. Mister Brewster and his lead men had managed to find an English captain who, with the persuasion of an enormous bribe, agreed to pick the party up from the seaward side of Boston and then take them across the sea to Holland.

After the group braved the wicked elements for a night and a day of hiding at the appointed rendezvous, a desolate spot known as Scotia Creek, the ship had indeed arrived to take the party aboard. Once on ship though, the women's tears of gratitude soon gave way to bitter wails of disbelief and despair – as they realised the treachery unfolding before them. Not only did these wretched mariners then hand them over to the authorities, but before doing so they robbed the congregation of everything of value.

For the women there had been the deep humiliation of being grappled with by the rough seamen, who searched the women beneath their dresses for hidden jewellery and money. Then, after their menfolk were seized and thrown into goal in Boston, they found themselves cast penniless upon the city's streets, where they were expected to fend for themselves and their hungry children.

For the men there followed an uncertain period of imprisonment – before the party was eventually sent on its way with orders from the magistrates – to return from whence the group had come and there to turn themselves over to the authorities, no doubt for further punishment. But instead Mister Brewster's congregation made their way to Gainsborough, where they turned to us for help. They did so reluctantly, for they justifiably feared that they might be bringing us into new danger.

'It is not for me that I ask,' Mister Brewster explained to my son. 'For it is me that the Archbishop wants to silence more than any other man here. But the others... they trusted me to take them to safety and I have failed them. And so if you can help them you shall forever have my undying gratitude.'

'Undying gratitude,' I remember my father quoting the words of a conversation he once had with Thomas Cromwell, 'now there is a commodity that cannot be cheaply bought. And yet once it has, then it is a commodity of no practical use to the buyer whatsoever!'

And so Mister Brewster and his congregation huddled around a hastily lit fire in the Great Hall, gratefully eating whatever food our kitchen could provide at short notice. Meanwhile, William and I had retired to the privacy of the Solar above – to discuss with Elizabeth what we might best do to help our returned Separatists.

'If they are not returned to homes and the bailiffs then come for them, the Archbishop will send out his searchers. Will they come searching here, William?'

I recall well that this was Elizabeth's greatest and most natural concern. That these brutes would enter the Hall once more and thus find incriminating evidence against her husband. For she is a most dutiful wife and loving mother to my grandchildren.

'They would not dare trouble us again after the last time,' my son had replied. 'For that would be harassment. Matthews knows that he overstepped his authority then and I do not believe he will want to be seen doing that once more. Not to a man so recently knighted by our reigning King.'

'True, William,' I agreed, 'but they set a watch amongst our ships after that most recent incident.'

'And they may do so again,' William had interjected, 'so our friends below shall have to sit it out until they tire of it and go home to their wives.'

Dear William had joked about in an effort to try ease dear Elizabeth's fears, but I remember her continuing to frown – with her brow furrowed like that of her agitated little brown dog that lay cringing upon her lap.

'What if they do come?' she continued, still rightfully afraid for her children 'What if they come and they find these people hiding in our house? What then?'

'These people who seek refuge are our family in Christ,' William reminded her. 'Would you have your good husband turn them away?'

Elizabeth had sighed gently, lowered her gaze, and then nodded in agreement that she would not. With that, William smiled and then, taking up Elizabeth's hand, kissed it gently before saying, 'Then we shall put our trust in God. Just as my mother and father put their trust in God in the past. He protected them then and likewise He shall protect us now. Of that I am certain.'

With those words spoken, for a moment I no longer saw my son William standing before me. Instead it was as if my dear husband Anthony had come back to me to guide us through this time of trial.

Winter was a bad time for travelling anywhere, let alone across the sea in tempestuous storms. So it made best sense for the Separatists to wait until spring, when the roads would be just thawing and the sea would be much calmer for crossing, before making their move. And so that is what was planned. Come spring, my son would get them away in one of his ships.

Meanwhile, we quickly made plans to help hide Mister Brewster and those others most at risk, deciding that they should stay with us at the Hall. But when we put this to them they refused. Instead they responded by saying that they would not put our family in such danger for their sake. So, instead, William gave them money and horses and whatever else they needed for getting distant of this place. To others amongst the congregation – who were still able to find refuge amongst family and friends but were in great need of funds – we also supplied with money to see them through the coming months.

Thus we all waited through winter quietly, though worrying about reports arising from our own men... of some strangers in the town who were regularly to been seen setting fresh watches near William's vessels at tie. Searchers must have been in Gainsborough all along, just waiting for Mister Brewster and the others to try again at making good an escape. If the Scrooby congregation were to get away to Holland, we realised that it could not be done safely from Gainsborough.

So William got word to Mister Brewster and arranged a secret rendezvous to take place at some safe house far away, where they might sit at table together to consider afresh the scant options now left open for their removal over seas.

The port of Hull, closest to the Archbishop's see, was bound to be tightly watched by his men. Thus a ship leaving from Hull for the Continent could expect to be closely scrutinised and searched. 'Yet what of a ship leaving from Hull to travel along the Humber towards Gainsborough or Goole?' William surmised. What if such a vessel was then brought about short of her supposed destination, returning to bypass the port of Hull and then to head on out to the open sea unchallenged?'

The banks of the tidal River Humber covered a vast expanse of land. It was too vast to have patrolled all of the time, and so that is where we found our advantage. For there was a lonesome, ill populated stretch upon the Lincolnshire side over which a close family tie of ours had authority and perhaps the will to look away at any set time. So it was that my son and Mister Brewster's lead men fell upon making their way out from the Humber.

The roads were yet too rutted and muddy from the past winter snows for carts to get through them or for women and children to walk along them, and the weather was still far too damp and chill for camping. So it was decided for the women and children to be conveyed, with what few chattels they had left, along the river by way of barge, down the Trent and then along the Humber.

Meanwhile the sight of the remaining men, making their way in stages to a meeting spot close to Hull, would do little to raise any suspicion. Mister Brewster himself, a competent Dutch speaker, could easily pass in and out of the port in the guise of a Dutchman as he searched out a sympathetic fellow 'countryman' willing to convey the party away to Holland.

Again, everything seemed to work out according to plan, except that the women being conveyed by barge reached the pick-up spot a day before they had expected to. There the wind upon the Humber blew up to make rough waves, which sorely set the barge in an unnatural motion. It was enough for the mothers to then beg the crewmen to put into the calmer waters of a creek mouth, so as to ease the seasickness of their crying and vomiting children.

It calmed the sickness for certain, but it also meant that for so long as the tide was out in the Humber, their cumbersome little craft was fixed firm and marooned upon a bank of mud and so unable to make shift away.

The Dutch ship duly arrived the next morning, as did the remainder of the men. There they made pace upon the shore in an anxious state, because they were unable to spy their womenfolk's vessel hidden by dense reeds and banks of long grass. Nevertheless, with much persuasion the Dutch master had the men start with their embarkation, which they eventually made under Mister Brewster's advice.

But, suddenly, with one boat full of men aboard and with the row boat about to return for the second group, the ship's captain spotted a great company of armed men, on both horse and on foot, making haste along the shoreline to intercept them. Naturally, there was immediate and great consternation all about as the captain then weighed anchor, acting on the fear of having his ship boarded and impounded. Those of Mister Brewster's men already on board could do nothing – for fear of jumping into the freezing water and drowning. And so their ship turned about mid-river and made off towards the sea – while the men watched helplessly as their women and children were captured and taken away.

Meanwhile, Mister Brewster and those men still ashore hid amongst the scrub in fear of their lives, yet also in the knowledge that no real harm would befall their now taken families. The women might then have been wailing in sorrow and their children crying in terror, yet from past experience all knew that they were not in any real danger. For what use were a straggle of women and children to the authorities?

Events bore this out. The women and children soon found themselves hurried from one magistrate to another, with none knowing what to do with them or wanting the worry of incarcerating the party. For they feared not only the cost of doing so but also further inciting local sympathies towards the women and children's plight. In the end, they had no real choice other than to let them go free.

And so it was that the remaining menfolk, who had all along been able to shadow their women, were able with our help to get their women and children soon across to Amsterdam also, where the reunited congregations rejoiced.

From time to time, we receive letters from Mister Brewster, who for a year or more now has been settled with his congregation in Leiden. They have, sadly, parted company from Reverend Smyth and Reverend Clifton, who remain in Amsterdam.

However, Mister Brewster assures us that they are more than ably served spiritually by Reverend John

Robinson, originally from the nearby village of Sturton-le-Steeple, a little way on the other side of the Trent. We have also begun to smuggle in literature written by both him and Reverend Robinson in support of Separatism and encouraging those like-minded Christians still remaining in England. By and by, Mister Brewster says that he will covertly return to the North and bring us the monies once lent to his people, and for the outstanding fines set against his good person, which after his departure William learnt had been anonymously paid out to the courts.

So this good bread is now cast upon the waters on a current to foreign climes. Here, as both Church and State remain resolute in being set against dissenters, William continues to both receive and help those wanting to join our good Protestants abroad. Most of our finest reformists now languish in exile in Holland, as does our hope for a Church renewed. This is hope for better days, when the Church is properly reformed and these exiles might at last return to their homeland.

As for me? My father lived and died waiting for the reform he thought had come. Now I am resigned to the fact that I too must die without seeing that hope of both our generations come to fruition. And yet I still have hope. Hope that my sons may yet live to see change come about, or that my children's children will see it. Hope and faith are the most enduring of gifts, and the only heritage of real value that I have now to pass on to you who come after me. Above all else I hold faith most precious. For without faith there cannot be hope.

Of my father William Locke's twenty children, only my poor brother Michael and I now live in this world. Like me, my brother knows well the pain of seeing children die whilst brimming with youth and promise. He, having been so recently bereft with the loss of his sons, Zachary, Eleazer, and Benjamin, is like our own father in that he has not seen the greater part of his own vast progeny growing to reach adulthood. They were like fresh lush fruit snatched from the vine while we who are shrivelled and spent cling on. It all seems somehow so unfair, and yet we know that we should not dwell upon our loss – because nothing is truly lost when loss on earth amounts to gain in heaven.

Our parents, our siblings and our friends are already gone, as is the way of life we once knew. Michael and I are amongst the last of the beacons of our age that once blazed so bright. We are like hour glasses in the time of clocks and pocket pieces, or like the last weary tolls of the old watch bell. I can write no more, for there is nothing now left in me to be written. Pray God, someone else may yet pick up my pen... and complete the tale.

Lady Rose Hickman died on 21st November 1613 aged 87 years; just one week short of the seventieth anniversary of her marriage to Anthony Hickman.

The End

Author's Notes

When I was only newly arrived in Lincolnshire, my new and ever helpful neighbour suggested that I might like to visit the Old Hall which was only just up the road. But when I replied, 'Oh, what is it like?' I was astounded to hear him say that he did not know, because he had never been there himself. 'But I've heard that it's very nice,' he added apologetically. So out of curiosity I went...

From the moment I first walked into a hushed Gainsborough Hall I immediately felt a strange connection with it, though I did not know why. Not only had I never heard of this building before my move, I had never seen pictures of it.

The Great Hall was breathtakingly beautiful and far beyond my expectations, as were the magnificent kitchens. Yet I was puzzled as to why such a wonderful building was so devoid of visitors. So, half expecting to see more people upstairs, I ascended the newel staircase. At the top, to my renewed amazement, I found this upper floor was completely empty of tourists, too. I was the only visitor there!

I found the landing and the Solar with its great red-curtained bed and squint [83]quite charming! I could just imagine myself there in days gone, sitting beside the leaded lights and looking out across the townscape and the tall masts of sea-going ships moored on the River Trent just beyond the Hall.

Then, despite my seriously arthritic knees, I climbed the winding tower staircase and admired the view – imagining what it must have been like before the mass of surrounding buildings had encroached so closely upon the Hall. And I thought the tower suite of bed chambers, with their en suit garde de robes, quite fascinating.

Then, I paced purposely down the long corridor and entered into what to my mind seemed the most unpromising part of my self-guided tour so far – the

---

83   A small window-like opening allowing those in the Solar bedchamber to able to 'see and hear' those in the Great Hall below.

Great Chamber. However, as I neared the dark and grimy-looking portraits hung on the far wall, my heart inexplicably began to thump, and I felt the hair on the back of my neck stand up. And then I saw her! My eyes had fixed upon the rather stern-looking countenance of this elderly Tudor woman. I was immediately fascinated by her and yet I did not know why.

According to an inscription painted directly on the portrait canvass, Lady Rose Hickman had already reached what in those days was the ripe old age of seventy years when this likeness was painted. It was also conveniently dated 1596.

Not once, but twice, as if in an attempt to make certain that there could be no mistake about these facts at all, the portrait was also inscribed 'Rose, Daughter of Sir William Locke, Knight. Married to Anthony Hickman'. She is dressed all in black, bare-handed and clutching a glove in her right hand, which according to a book I read on early portraiture was to show that she was a widow. Her gown is plain and unadorned apart from a buckle at her waist, there's a fine gold trim to the cuffs, and of course there is a Tudor ruff at her neck. Her hair is completely hidden beneath a rather scholarly looking black cap. Her face is long and pale, as is her nose, set above thin pink lips that barely hint even a smile, and her cheek bones are well defined with a natural-looking blush. In her youth, I can see that she might have easily been considered quite striking.

It is her eyes that caught me in their gaze though; large, dark, all-seeing eyes beneath thin arched eyebrows. And once those eyes had me trapped, I found it hard to then draw myself away. This, I thought, was a lady to be reckoned with. Though she might well have been considered to be in her dotage by the time this picture was executed, she looked like a woman still possessed of a razor-sharp mind, and not afraid to use it! And yet, there was something else about Rose that I found engaging, and even almost vulnerable. I know it sounds crazy, but at the time I felt as if there was something this lady needed to tell me. And so I must have stood looking up at Rose for the good part of half an hour before I managed to tear myself away to complete the rest of my tour of the building.

In the gift shop down stairs, I browsed among the books and souvenirs and picked out two postcards; one of Rose's portrait and its companion piece and one of her son, Sir William Hickman, dating from the same time.

William did not look at all the threadbare fellow, a description of him that I would read later. Like his mother, Rose, he was dressed all in black. His doublet was fastened down the front with a neat row of nine pearl buttons, ending just beneath what appears to be an intricately woven pointed linen collar that's edged in a fine gold-coloured lace. The cuffs of his sleeves are also edged with a fine gold-coloured trim, and his clasped hands wear fine brown leather gloves. Either that or his hands are cast in very deep shadow. He also appears to be wearing a plain black cloak.

William's face is also long and thin, with striking facial similarities to his mother's. His hair is brown and short and with a definite wave and slight greying at the temples. And he has a moustache and a long thin beard that's typical of other portraits of men I have seen of that time. In fact, with his tall black hat, he put me rather in mind of a well-dressed Guy Fawkes.

Like his mother's portrait, William's is also inscribed in pale lettering – telling again that this likeness was painted in 1596 and that William was then aged forty-seven. At the top left-hand corner, picked out in shades of blue and white, is the Hickman coat of arms. And some way below are the words, Sir William Hickman, Knight – wording repeated towards the bottom left of the painting. After my first visit, something niggled at me about that painting, but I just could not put my finger on what it could be.

Since the gift shop was so quiet, I asked the lady behind the counter if she could tell me anything about Rose Hickman's life. She replied that she could not, but handed me a little booklet for sale that she said contained all that was known about Lady Rose and had been written by a former Keeper there. So I purchased one, which I later read at home with some disappointment. Although it was very informative about the Old Hall's history, its fascinating connection to the Mayflower Pilgrims, and is beautifully set out, it seemed to have so little real information about Lady Rose's long life. Except, that is, that she was supposed to have written an autobiography before she died, and that while living in London her husband Anthony had helped to smuggle hunted Protestants abroad during the reign of Catholic Queen Mary.

Later, Rose and William had allowed Christian Separatists – including some of those men who would eventually become known as the Pilgrim Fathers of America – to meet at the Old Hall. When I later asked at Gainsborough about Rose Hickman's memoirs, I was told by the then Keeper that these were 'presumed lost', and so I gave up hope of finding out any more. Yet I could not stop thinking about Rose. It was as if she would not let me rest.

When I wrote The Mayflower Maid, I had not intended to dwell on Lady Rose's character in the book, apart from relating the story of how she had avoided a compulsory Catholic baptism for her first child and of her subsequent flight to the Low Countries. But then, during the drafting process, I found myself dreaming about Rose and even hearing her speaking – all of which I put down to an over active imagination. Nonetheless, I let Rose's character begin to develop in that book, and as a result received innumerable requests from readers asking me tell them more about her. I could not, but still allowed Rose to 'come and go' in the sequel books, Jamestown Woman and Restoration Lady, in which she is fondly remembered by her maidservant Dorothy/ Bessie.

It was while I was writing the closing chapters of Restoration Lady that I had the irresistible urge to move the storyline from Lincolnshire down to south London, where I had grown up rather unhappily. I had no idea why I wanted to revisit Merton in particular other than perhaps just being away from it for almost forty years. Anyway, I somehow suddenly felt a strange sort of nostalgia for it. And then, when I consulted my co-author and husband, Roger, about this planned change of location for the plot, he suggested that, if it felt right, then I should go ahead. So ahead I went...

Just before Restoration Lady was published, I wrote an email to the Parish Office of St Mary the Virgin Church in Merton, to say that not only had I included a scene from my novel in their church, but that in my 'Author's Notes' at the back of that book, I had also explained to my readers why, on a personal note, this particular church was so special to me.

When I was an unhappy girl of eleven, during times of great personal distress, I used to run off to this church to find sanctuary there, a quiet haven for prayer and reflection. My teen-aged brother, Geoffrey, had died recently. And I had a far from easy relationship with my mother who, unlike me, was a committed atheist. I believed that my 'quiet times' of reflection then – in that lovely parish church – nurtured my life-long love for old buildings and helped to strengthen my spiritual wellbeing.

In response to my letter, I received an emailed reply from the Parish office congratulating me on the new book. They then kindly suggested I contact Doris Dean, a lovely lady who wrote for the Parish Magazine. I did so, and we enjoyed a wonderful telephone conversation during which I told her about my vivid memory of being inside St Mary's and what a comfort that building had been to me. Then, just a few days after Restoration Lady was launched, I unexpectedly received something from her in the post that would rock my world and leave me utterly dumbfounded!

When I opened the brown envelope, a copy of the parish guide book to St Mary the Virgin slid out[84]. Minutes later, as I stood in my cosy country cottage kitchen waiting for the electric kettle to boil, I quickly thumbed through the booklet and admired the beautiful

---

[84] 'St Mary the Virgin – A guide and History' by Lionel Green.

photographs, which suddenly brought many mixed childhood memories flooding back to me, though I had not been back to that church in person for over forty years. So I made myself a nice cup of tea and settled down at the kitchen table with the guide book and started reading the text. It spoke at length about patrons of the Benefice. In the past, every church had one who held the advowson with a right to present an incumbent of his choice upon the church. This later reverted to the crown until the 14th of March in 1553, when Edward VI sold the Rectory and advowson at Merton to a certain Thomas and Mary Lok.

The text went on to tell how this Thomas' father had been Sir William Lok, a Sheriff of London who was knighted by King Henry VIII. It also spoke of how, when plague had struck London, he had moved his family out of the City and to the safety of Merton. His wife later died in childbirth there and was buried somewhere in St Mary's Church.

The guide sated that, among that family's young, grieving, motherless children, there was an eleven-year-old Rose Lok, who had lived until 1613 and left a written record of her childhood reminiscences at Merton. And that was all the information it had about her.

It was then, as I finished reading those words, that I began to feel as if I had entered the 'twilight zone'. I simply could not believe that what I had just been reading was true! I knew for a fact that Lady Rose Hickman had died in 1613 and had written an account of her life. Furthermore, I knew that clearly visible beneath the dark and cracked varnish of her portrait were the words 'Daughter of Sir William Locke'.

So I immediately went to my computer and logged onto a genealogy site that I had frequently used for my own family research and began to trawl through all of the posted family trees – including that of Rose Locke and its variant spellings. Sure enough, there she was! She was listed as having lived in Merton with her father and later marrying an Anthony Hickman.

This was the same Rose. This was my Rose! She had spent much of her childhood in Merton, just as I had. And she had undoubtedly sat in St Mary's Church as young girl, grieving for her dead mother (and as I later discovered, a dead younger sister, too) much in the same way as I had sat grieving for my dead brother. Then, quite unknowingly, forty years later, I had followed Rose to her last home in Lincolnshire and then written her into my novels. I could not have made up a more curious coincidence if I had tried. That is if I were the type of person who believed in coincidence in the first place. At last, I was beginning to understand why I had felt that connection with Rose's portrait during my first visit to Gainsborough Hall.

The back page of the parish guide contained a list of footnotes, and among them I found a manuscript reference number relating to Rose Locke's memoirs. But there was no mention as to where it was being held. So I took a wild guess and telephoned the British Library. The number I quoted matched their pattern of indexing, and so I ordered a copy and expected a typed transcript to arrive. Instead, I received a computer disk.

I hurriedly loaded it onto my laptop – to find that it contained photographs of twenty pages of scant writings from what appeared to be a very old and grubby-looking notebook made of rough handmade paper. As I began to read, I cried tears of joy! It was Rose Hickman's original biography and written in her own hand. At last she was truly speaking to me!

But her memoirs were not the great and long literary masterpiece for which I might have naively hoped. Instead I found much fewer, but nevertheless heartfelt, words about a collection of incidents that she must have felt most important in her life, and so worthy of passing on to her children. Yet most importantly above all else, woven among these accounts was a testament to Rose's own unshakable faith in God, and a strong reminder to her children that they should never lose sight of Him and of their own faith.

For this reason, I declare that this simply written

and slim little volume is the most uplifting piece of Christian writing I have read for a very long time. This is the account of a real woman living through extremely volatile times of religious turmoil and persecution. And all the while she steadfastly holds on to the belief that each and every step along her difficult life's journey had been predestined, and that God had personally delivered her and her loved ones from harm.

I do not believe, however, that Rose's account as it stands is complete. For it covers a period only up until the early 1570s and only makes mention of her life with her first husband, Anthony Hickman. It also ends very abruptly with her son, William's, return from Russia and the court of Ivan the Terrible before Anthony's death. What about the subsequent forty years leading up to 1610, when this account of Rose's was actually being written?

Also, during my research I found the memoirs (written between 1670 and 1699) of a later gentleman, Sir John Bramston, the great, great, great-grandson of Sir William Locke. He was the son of Sir John Bramston of Boreham, Knight and Lord Chief Justice of the King's Bench. Sir John's grandmother was Bridget, the daughter of Mary Hill, who in turn was the daughter of Rose's youngest sister, Elizabeth. He writes of finding pages of this same account inside a family Bible that once belonged to Rose.

'I find it in wast paper in her bible, which hath binn carefully preserved by the females in the familie according to order and is now in the hands of my sister, Lady Palmer, being given to her by the aforementioned Mary[85], her and my grandmother.'

Sir John then goes on to say that, when he came to write his own memoires, he no longer [86]had it (Rose's memoirs) at hand to refer to, and so 'must ask again if my sister still hath it'. If the papers were being handed around so much, almost eighty years after they were first written and on 'waste paper', then perhaps parts of it were already lost through neglect?

Perhaps Rose never had time to complete her

---

85   He is referring to Mary Hill, daughter of Rose's younger sister Elizabeth.
86   The Autobiography of Sir John Brampton

autobiography. That of course could be true, but in the opening pages she states that she is writing in 1610 and that she is above eighty-four years of age – which ties in exactly with the dating on her portrait – three years before she died. So there was plenty of time in which to have completed it.

Of course, the one event that I was hoping to discover Rose writing about in her memoires was the sheltering of the Separatist congregation at the Old Hall, and of her involvement in their subsequent escape from England. I did not, and in reflection that is not in the least surprising – considering the danger in which such a confession might have placed the remaining family.

So I admit quite freely that some passages in this 'fiction' version of her autobiography relating to those events are speculative on my part. However, having researched the rest of Rose's family history, I would be very surprised if she had not stepped in to help these persecuted folk in a similar manner to that which I have put forward.

Whenever forced into writing in 'missing threads' in this life story, I have tried extremely hard not to be led astray too far from the probability of how events might have played out. Instead I have opted in favour of probability over anything too far fetched or fanciful, which other novelists might be tempted to include just to sell more of their books. Over the course of my research (spanning some three years) while writing both this story and my New World trilogy of novels, to which this book is the natural prequel, I feel that I have grown extremely close to Rose. And so I could not bring myself to write anything of which she might have objected or which I would know to be extremely unlikely to have happened.

Whether Rose's scant account is complete or not, through it she has given me a firm foundation for seeking many other avenues to explore in finding out more about her and her family. I now have more than enough to start researching her life in earnest and, in particular, understanding how it came about that she and her family would have risked so much. I know why Rose would allow Separatists to meet in her home at Gainsborough, and how deeply she might have allowed the family to become involved in helping both this group and the Scrooby congregation to escape to Holland when faced with intensified persecution.

The first thing I did was try to draw out a time line for Rose and her family, so that I could get a clear sequence of events. I found the date of her marriage to Anthony and so began to wonder why it was that the she did not seem to have her first child until so much later in life. According to information gathered at Gainsborough Old Hall, William was her oldest child and he was not born until just before her escape from England. He was the child whose Catholic baptism Rose had so cleverly foiled, or so claims the only available book I had so far been able to find about her.

During the age in which Rose lived, people would almost certainly not have been using birth control, and so it seemed odd that she should have married in her late teens and yet not conceived a child before she had almost turned thirty. I was also curious to know why Rose had not mentioned the name of this 'first' child, nor that of a subsequent child she writes about being born in Antwerp. Then again, if her account was primarily for family members, it would go without saying that they already knew.

Then I suddenly thought of William's portrait hanging in the Great Chamber and what had been niggling away at me earlier. Since Rose's age proves correct on her portrait when it is tallied against her known age at writing this account in 1610, then one must assume that the age for William on his portrait was almost certainly correct too. If so, then William must have been born at least five or six years before the family's exile to Antwerp and not as stated in the Old Hall's literature.

So I thought that there was a slim chance that perhaps a record for his baptism might still exist somewhere. But where to look? I concluded that it would have to be somewhere close to where I knew the Hickmans had lived at the time. Rose told me through her biography that she and Anthony had two houses; one in London and another in Romford in Essex. Anthony is also found described as 'Gentleman of Woodford Hall, Essex'.

I drew a blank in Essex, but was thrilled to discover a baptismal record for a William Hickman, son of Anthony, dated June of 1549 at St Olave Church, Old Jewry, which had stood close to Cheapside before it was destroyed in the Great Fire of London. Amongst the same church records, I also found a baptismal entry for a Henrye (also son of Anthony Hickman) in the December of 1550 and for an Anthonye (son of Anthony Hickman) in the November of 1560. As research progressed, I later found him described as '4th son of Anthony Hickman of Woodford Hall' against his listing in the alumni of Corpus Christi.

Clearly none of the above could be Rose's 'first child' as previously described and originally thought to have been born just prior to her escape to Antwerp. Nor were they the subsequent second Hickman infant known to have been born there. However, I am now almost certain that I can prove where exactly this 'first' child was born. Again, I have the account of Rose's relative writing later to thank for that.

Rose mentions that her husband Anthony and her brother Thomas were already languishing in the Fleet Prison for helping others escape England illegally when they were joined by the jury in the treason trial against Sir Nicholas Throckmorton. They were sent to the Liberty of Fleet after Queen Mary became angry at their failing to bring in a guilty verdict against Sir Nicholas. That date of that trial is on record as having taken place on April 17th, 1554 so Rose must have already been pregnant at that time. We also know that Latimer, Ridley and Archbishop Cranmer were ordered to be transferred to Bocardo prison in Oxford by the Privy Council on March 8th 1554. Rose writes about asking these imprisoned men for advice upon the validity of the Catholic baptismal ceremony. Therefore both these dates indicate to Rose's child being born sometime in the second half of 1554 or else very early in 1555.

Rose simply states in her account that she was given the use of a lodge by a gentleman as she awaited the birth of that child; that it was called Chilswell, and that it stood far from any town or church – both very necessary if the birth of her child was to avoid detection and the consequence of an enforced Catholic baptism. In this relative's memoires, he says that he thinks that Rose was referring to place known as Chilswell Farm in Cumnor, Berkshire – within sight of Oxford. When I checked it out I found that there is a very old Grade II listed building there known as Chilswell Farm, dating back to at least the early C17 but possibly earlier. Its location exactly fits that which might be expected of Rose's Chilswell, which remains to this day a quite and isolated spot.

We also know from Rose's account that this child was subsequently taken to a church for baptism, presumably somewhere in that area. But as yet I have not found the baptismal entry for him/her – if one still exists. Rose also says that the child born in Antwerp was baptised secretly into the Protestant faith, so of course we could not expect to find an official record of that.

However, I then had a breakthrough. By chance I found an entry in a very old Baronetage of England backed up by another from Collins Peerage of England, that listed Rose and Anthony Hickman's sons in birth order as William (1), Henry (2), Walter (3), Anthony (4), Eleazer (5), Matthew (6), and, in addition, a daughter named Mary.

After this, yet another source explained that the custom of the hanging out of a piece of cloth after the birth of a child in Antwerp[87] was only done in the case of the baby being a male. Therefore, if this listing is correct and Walter, the third son, was born in 1552 and baptized at St Olave's in London, and Anthony,

---

87   The Travel Journal of Antonio de Beatis-Edited by Hale and Lindon (The Hakluyt Society 1979)

the fourth son, recorded as being baptized at the same church in London in 1560, the male child born at Antwerp must have died young and his name remains unknown. Again, if this list is correct, then Rose's other known sons, Eleazer and Matthew, were presumably born after the Hickmans' return from exile. Curiously, to date, I have found no baptismal entries for either of these sons. The identity of the child born at Chilswell, as I stated earlier, is at present still unconfirmed. All I can say for certain is that the Chilswell birth is not that of Mary, William, Henrye, Walter or Anthony.

The choice of the name of Eleazer is interesting because John Knox's so named son, Eleazar, was born while Knox was in 'exile' in Geneva. 'Eleazar' or 'Eleazer' is a biblical name meaning 'God's help'.

I have not found any more records of Matthew up to the time of writing, but a third version of Rose's memoirs [88], gives 'the offspring of this Old Gentlewoman this present year 1637' and notes Matthew as having had three children: Frances, Mary, and Rose. Independently, I did however come across two slim entries for an Eleazer Hickman in a London assessment of the late fifteen-nineties. There is also an entry in the parish and probate records – 'Administrations in the Prerogative Court of Canterbury, 1609-1610 p.10' – for Eleazer Hickman of St Martin's Fields, Middlesex, mentioning 'Dixius (sic.) and Wm. H., nephews' which most definitely must relate to Rose's son.

Rose's only known daughter, and eldest recorded child, was named Mary. Marye Hickman was baptized on the 6th of January 1547 at St. Olave Old Jewry. She reached adulthood and in most known genealogical family trees is listed as being is thought to have married a man named Ansham of Ealing, (although the third version of Rose's manuscript states her first marriage as being to a ' - Agmonsham alias Ansham Esq.') before subsequently marrying a Richard Philips of Middlesex. During my own research, I have found a marriage entry for Marye Hickman dated 13th April 1567 at Saint Olave Old Jewry in London to one John 'Amondesham'.(

---

88   B.L.Add.M.S. 45027 fol.8.

'Amondesham is an earlier form of the name 'Aunsham' and so it is not surprising to see an established family of that name listed among the Mercers of that time.) To the date of writing, I have found no further information as to any issue from this marriage, nor any records of Mary's second marriage or her death. However, there was also at that time an established Philips family amongst the Mercery.

Walter Hickman married Elizabeth Steynes or Staines of Essex and was the ancestor of the Earl of Plymouth through his son Dixie Hickman's marriage in 1616 to Elizabeth Windsor, daughter of Henry, 5th Lord Windsor. His name appears in official records as having been a Justice of the Peace in Middlesex. And like his brother Henry, Walter became a Member of Parliament. (A more detailed biography of Walter and his siblings can be found in my non-fiction companion book 'Lady Rose Hickman – her life and family'). At the time of writing there is a rather splendid portrait of Walter hanging at the Hall in Gainsborough.

I can also be certain that William, Henry and Anthony are indeed Rose's and Anthony's sons, if I go by the records already mentioned, and also from a reference in an excellent book about the history of London Mercers[89] which mentions both Henry and Anthony, sons of Anthony and Rose Hickman, being promoted by the Company of Mercers as 'gifted' students during the 1560s – by which time William would already be busy learning the family trade in readiness to take over when his father later died. Also, the Alumni listing of Cambridge of that time bears out this family tie because it also cites the better known Henry Hickman (listed as a son of Anthony Hickman of Woodford Hall) as being also the brother of one Anthony Hickman of Corpus Christi.

It is the rediscovery of Rose's hitherto little-known son, Anthony, that I have found the most exciting of all my research for this book. Interestingly,

89   'The Mercery of London: by Trade, Goods & People,1130-1578 by Ann F. Sutton.

Rose makes no mention of this son in her narrative, or of his troubles at Corpus Christi, which again makes me suspect that maybe the copy of the existing biography of Rose is not complete. In fact, the only one of her nine known children mentioned by name or in any depth is her oldest son, William, and an inclusion of family tree, of sorts, only appears in the much later third BL manuscript of 1637.

The entry according to Alumni Cantabrigienses (Venn, J & Venn, JA , Cambridge 1924) reads: 'Anthony Hickman matriculated, pensioner[90] from St. John's Michaelmas 1575, migrated to Peterhouse, B.A., 1579-80; M.A. 1583 ; L.L.D. Fellow of Corpus Christi, 1583-8, where he had a long dispute with the College. Adm., advocate, June 16th, 1583.'

I found original transcripts of portions of the correspondence relating to this matter amongst the Portland Papers held at Longleat House, including one written by Archbishop Whitgift, and another in Anthony's own hand, in which he competently states the legal case against his dismissal from the university. At this point I would very much like to acknowledge the generosity and kindness of a good friend, Dr Jeremy Bangs, Director of the American Pilgrim Museum in Leiden, for transcribing these from their original (difficult for me to decipher) Tudor script and into meaningful English that I could.

This 'long dispute' at Cambridge arose after there was an objection raised by a new Master, Doctor Copcot, coming into Corpus Christi. This related to Anthony Hickman's dispensation, signed by Queen Elizabeth, which had 'excused' him from taking orders, a normal requirement of one taking up a Fellowship.

I immediately wondered why Anthony had wanted to avoid taking orders. Was it because he was a Puritan? I asked Jeremy Bangs, a scholar of the Mayflower Pilgrims (as he is extremely knowledgeable about the Separatists of that time) if this might be the case. Jeremy replied that 'Puritans had no objection to becoming ordained in the Church of England... some

---

90   'Pensioner' means that his father could afford to pay for his food or commons and defray other expenses.

later broke away to become Separatists.'

Therefore this then led me to pose the question, to Dr Elizabeth Leedham-Green of Corpus Christi, as to whether it was possible that Anthony Hickman's refusal to take orders could mean that he was a Separatist? She responded by saying that 'it is certainly possible that Hickman should have resisted ordination on the grounds of disapproval of the Elizabethan Church settlement as the Presbyterians did.'

Perhaps we may never be able to say categorically that Anthony Hickman was indeed a Separatist, but it would explain why his mother Rose and brother William should have risked so much to help the Separatist congregation at Gainsborough.

Interestingly, William Brewster matriculated December 3rd, 1580 at Peterhouse (before entering the service of William Davidson in 1583). Robert 'Troublechurch' Browne was also resident at Cambridge at the same time as both Brewster and Hickman.

Hickman suddenly left Corpus Christi some time after June 1591 (I have found a list of legal expenses regarding the Landbeach suit at London submitted by him at that time) at about the same time as active steps were being taken to curb Puritan influences from within the college. The History of Corpus Christi College states that 'his (Hickman's) being again suspended by a major part of the Fellows in Dr John Jegon's Mastership (Dr Copcot having gone), within two years of his having been restored – this censure however was taken off upon his submission, and he left the College soon after.'

It is worthwhile to note that at this time there was a concerted effort being undertaken by Archbishop Whitgift to destroy illegal 'dissident' congregations in and around London, with such Separatist notables as Barrow, Greenwood, among many others being held in prison under questionable legal circumstances. A trained lawyer, unafraid to be seen challenging the Archbishop, would no doubt have been useful to the cause at that time.

Anthony Hickman, a Doctor of the Civil Law,

died unmarried in London on December 13th in 1597. He was buried in the Church of St Bennet, Paul's Wharf, which was destroyed in the Great Fire of London in 1666. (Incidentally, the John Jegon who had been the bane of Anthony's final years at Cambridge later became the Bishop of Norwich and in turn deprived John Robinson of his living. Robinson was pastor to and a leading figure of the Separatists' Congregation in Leiden).

Both Henry and Anthony were Fellows at Cambridge, which might explain Henry's rather late foray into marriage, and why Anthony died single. There is, however, still a slight query about Anthony which I would like to try to address here. In my research I came across a curious entry for one Ann Hickman, mentioned in 'England, Scotland, Ireland: Musgrave's Obituaries Prior to 1800, Parts 1 & 2', compiled by Sir William Musgrave, 6th Bart., of Hayton Castle, Co. Cumberland. It was entitled very long-windily by him as 'A General Nomenclator and Obituary, with Reference to the Books Where the Persons are Mentioned, and Where some Account of their Character is to be found'. Here Ann Hickman is listed as 'daughter of Anthony Hickman, LL.D., wife of Rev. Ric. Dukeson' and having died in September 1670 aged 66. This is very odd considering that the records of Fellows at Corpus Christi categorically states where and when Rose's son Anthony died and that he was unmarried. A simple error, probably, by Musgrave as Ann Hickman (1604-1670) in most genealogical sources is recorded as being the daughter of Anthony's brother, Henry.

The waters are further muddied by a portrait of one Anthony Hickman, held in a private collection. The sitter bears a striking family resemblance to that of Rose, Walter and William Hickman, and the costume and style appears to be contemporary. The inscription states that the sitter is in his 36th year and is dated 1605 and with addition of November 3rd. (Incidentally, a similar inscription on Rose Hickman's portrait reads in Latin 'XBRIS.27' - December 27th – could this be her true birth date, although most genealogists have it recorded on their trees as the 26th). A further inscription 'Anthony Hickman' picked out in gold matches the lettering of both Rose's and William's portraits at Gainsborough.

According to church records, Rose's son Anthony was baptised on November 17th 1560, which means that if the customary fourteen days' lying in period had been observed beforehand, then his birth could have occurred on the third.

Many of the Hickman paintings, including Rose's and William's, were 'inscribed' or re-inscribed in a similar way some time after their original execution. Other portraits still in the family collection are also known to have been re-inscribed at some point and with errors. I tend to think that this portrait is indeed of Anthony, Rose's son, based on his close family resemblance and on the fact that I can find no other Anthony Hickman in the extended Hickman family of this age in 1605 that this can possibly be anyone other than him.

Also, there may be a clue in the subject of the painting itself to bear out that this is indeed Rose's son. The gentleman in this portrait is sporting an extremely long beard, much longer than his brothers'. Previous zealous Protestants, when breaking away from the 'Old Church', had grown long beards as an outward symbol of their having done so. Most famously Archbishop Cranmer had done so after the death of King Henry VIII and on leaving behind of the old unreformed English Church for the reforming one under Edward VI. Bearing in mind that Anthony may possibly have been a Separatist himself, perhaps he too had grown his beard to signify this.

On the question of children, there is the subject of Rose's second marriage to Simon Throckmorton. On various genealogy sites and family trees, I find a number of children attributed to Simon by Rose, yet this seems rather odd. For one, Rose was by the time of her marriage to Throckmorton in her late forties –

too old I suggest to have produced the eight or more children I have at times seen attributed to her in the decade or so after she remarried. Also, I have to refer back to Rose's own autobiography. On writing about her and Anthony's trials, Rose clearly states that this is intended as a record for her children and refers to Anthony as 'their father', which surly she would not have done if some of her these children were nothing to do with Anthony.

In a second copy of part of Rose's biography (in a completely different hand and probably copied as a writing exercise and inscribed at the bottom of the page with the words Elizabeth Hickman), which I had received from the British Library as a companion to the first, the opening page has the addition next to Rose's description of her first husband being Anthony Hickman, the words 'by whom I had all my children'. I therefore have no trouble in believing that this distinction was made deliberately by Elizabeth to perhaps distance the Hickmans further from the Throckmortons and to clarify family ties for future generations.

Simon Throckmorton's father, Richard, had been a brother to Sir George Throckmorton of Coughton Court, Warwickshire. Sir George had been a knight in Henry VIII's court but strongly opposed to the break with Rome. Although the vast majority of his nineteen children and over one-hundred grandchildren were ardent Catholics, there were some, however, who were strongly Protestant. For example, his grandson, Sir Nicholas Throckmorton, who had been in the Fleet Prison with Rose's husband, was one.

Many of the Catholic members of this Throckmorton family became involved in plots against the Protestant throne of England. Two of Sir George's granddaughters were the mothers of men involved in the Gunpowder Plot of 1605 against King James. A third granddaughter was the wife of Edward Arden, executed in 1583 for his part in a failed assassination attempt against Queen Elizabeth. Another family member, Francis Throckmorton, was executed in 1584 for acting as a go-between for Mary Queen of Scots and the Spanish Ambassador in yet another plot.

As a devout Bible-believing Christian, and therefore not someone likely to be swayed by mass hysteria or superstition, Rose might also have chosen to distance herself from the Throckmortons of Huntingdonshire for yet another reason – the Warboys Witch Trials.

Warboys was a village very close to Brampton. In the fall of 1589, ten-year-old Jane Throckmorton, the daughter of Simon's nephew, Robert, accused a female neighbour of being a witch. Her actions set in motion a four-year-long drama which culminated with the hanging of three of local people. Within weeks, their accusers issued a much publicised version of events by way of a pamphlet entitled 'The Most Strange and admirable discoverie of three Witches of Warboys, arraigned, convicted, and executed at the last Assizes at Huntingdon, for the bewitching of the five daughters of Robert Throckmorton Esquire, and divers other persons with sundrie Divellish and grevious torments: And also for the bewitching to death of the Lady Crumwell, the like hath not been heard of in this age.'[91]

Although Robert Throckmorton 'won' his case, he appears to have done so at great cost. Shortly after the executions he left Warboys: the village in which he and his mother had lived and he and his children had been baptized. He lived out the remainder of his life removed from the county.

For the other events in Rose's life, I have been able to find much invaluable information by sifting through the Calendar of State Papers for the entire reigns of King Henry VII, Edward VI, Mary Tudor and Queen Elizabeth-all of which are available on line, though many only by subscription. Richard Hakluyt's works, mentioned by Rose herself, are still available and an interesting source of background information. With the help of these I have been able to piece together much of Rose's family exploits in trade as well as Anthony Hickman's and thus bring an extra dimension

91   Copies survive in the British Library, the Bodleian Library, and the Norris Museum Library in St. Ives, Hunts.

to Rose's own brief account of these.

The thing that has most struck me though, on reading Rose's account of her family's lives and beliefs, is the feeling that perhaps for too long William Hickman has been given an undeserving appraisal by both current local information guides and Gainsborough based websites that repeat some very negatively slanted material without questioning its source.

In the book that I previously mentioned buying at Gainsborough Hall, William Hickman is described as 'nouveau riche' and 'living in London at the time when Lord Burgh was negotiating with money lenders for loans, William was already in an ideal position to acquire his own country house and estate like so many of his fellows.'

'Nouveau riche' certainly did not describe the Hickmans. Like the Lockes, they were a well established wealthy Company of Mercers family long before even the Burgh's came to Gainsborough Hall and their title. The Hickman and Lockes were amongst the premier London families of the times and widely considered as evangelical backbones of the Reformation of the English Church.

The Hickmans already enjoyed numerous houses in London, in the Low Countries and country estates too. (William as first born most likely inherited all of Anthony's estate in Essex so did not need a manor and estate at Gainsborough to keep up with the noble Lincolnshire Joneses).

In addition, Rose Hickman's own direct ancestors, Leofric Earl of Mercia and Lady Godiva, were responsible for repairing and beautifying the Minster at Stow, the original seat of the Burgh family, more than four hundred years before the land at Gainsborough passed into the first Lord Thomas Burgh's hands and the Hall was even built.

William may have been considered as a meddlesome incomer who upset the existing status quo. I tend to surmise that perhaps the dust, that for too long had been allowed to clog up the natural channels of good business practise in Gainsborough, was just kicking up against the new broom that had come to sweep it out.

I see William as a good Christian man coming into the town and then breaking the local monopoly that undoubtedly had the power to fix artificially high prices for its own produce by restricting outside trade. As such, I am not surprised that these locals would have made a fuss and want to try to get back at William Hickman through the legal system.

I also find charges against William – that he 'abused his authority as Justice of the Peace by bringing dubious law suites and counter law suites against his opponents' are a matter for conjecture, and they are certainly out of character for what my research evidences as a devoutly Christian family. Might not this version of events again have been coloured by Hickman's 'opponents' and their frustration at coming up against a man who was neither constantly absent from his manor and his manorial duties, and who was more than a match for them when it came to legal matters having 'on call' several close members of his family more than adequately versed in the Law.

We shall never know how the ordinary folk of Gainsborough felt in the response to more goods coming and inevitable lowering of prices for them. Their views were not directly recorded for prosperity, and where there is scant mention of any complaint it is always via one of the Hickman's detractors.

I hope that now, by way of this novel, many of these negative connotations attached to the Hickmans can be seen as probably undeserving. Yes, I fully accept that William Hickman upset a good many 'local people', but all I am asking is for my readers to consider the source of those complaints.

Shortly after King Henry VIII's marriage to Jayne Seymour, he faced a potentially dangerous uprising centred upon noble Lincolnshire families – many of whom were against the break with Rome and Protestantism. Many of these same families prospered under Queen Mary and became in Queen Elizabeth's reign closeted Catholics. Therefore these families, many of whom lived around Gainsborough, could not have been expected to welcome the overtly Puritan Hickmans with open arms, especially when they then tried to address the previous mismanagement of both the town and their estate.

I sincerely hope, therefore, that today's local people will now look at the 'values' that Rose Hickman has set down in her memoirs and that her family had lived by and compare that with the negative accusations raised against them at the time, and then maybe agree with me that there seems to be serious discrepancy between the two.

As for being described as a threadbare fellow by a very disdainful Sir John Thorold, whose ancestors 'were ruling Lincolnshire before the Norman Conquest in 1066', (and also reputedly descended from Lady Godiva), surely this speaks volumes about William's attitude to ostentatious shows of wealth. He undoubtedly owned at least one fine suit of clothes for best, as is illustrated by his portrait. He could certainly afford to dress richly every day, but obviously chose not to for this observation to be made by his enemy.

Yet look at Rose Hickman's family attitude towards giving unto others. In particular note the recorded remarks of her father, Sir William Locke, who incidentally was fabulously wealthy- when he asked for the mourners at his own funeral not to buy new mourning clothes on his account, as he considered it money wasted that might be better spent on the poor – a sentiment carried on in all of Rose's Lock sibling wills. Giving to the poor, and not by a mere token amount, was deeply rooted as a Christian duty by these early zealous Protestants.

Both the Lockes and the Hickman's are also known to have given away huge amounts of their personal wealth to aid other Protestants in need. Not to loan but to give – just as the Scriptures would have taught then to do. And that is an important difference between the

Hickman's at Gainsborough and many of the other local wealthy people of the day. The Hickmans did not pay lip service to the New Testament commandments of Christ but instead tried to emulate them by their deeds.

An often over looked inscription on Sir William's portrait reads 'DEVS MI' – most probably abbreviated for 'DEVS MIHI' meaning 'God be with me' – hardly befitting a man accused by his opponents of being guilty of un-Christian and uncharitable acts.

There are so many questions surrounding the persecution of the Separatists that remain unanswered. Why did William Brewster's Scrooby congregation choose to travel over sixty miles across Lincolnshire to attempt their escape at Boston, when Gainsborough or the Humber would have proved a much nearer and more logical point of departure? Could it have been that these were already being watched? And when the Scrooby congregation was betrayed at Boston and stripped of all items of value, where did the members obtain the huge amount of money needed to finance their second escape attempt the following spring? Why not from the Hickmans?

I had hoped to find more answers to these later questions in Rose's writings. Maybe she chose consciously not to finish her account or include sections about hiding Separatists in her home at the Old Hall. By allowing John Smyth's Separatist congregation to meet inside The Hall, the Hickmans were risking imprisonment, the seizure of their lands, and ultimately banishment from England. Aiding dissenters was still illegal and it could still have been dangerous for the family had these facts come to light or fallen into the hands of William Hickman's enemies. Although William Brewster and company were by then safely in Leiden, he was still helping to produce pro-Separatist writings to be printed and sent back to England, acts that the State would have considered sedition. But having travelled with Rose through over six months of solid daily research into her life, I do not believe that Rose would have balked about setting these events down.

Maybe Rose did finish her account in full and that part of it was later deliberately removed or destroyed for that same reason. Or perhaps it might have been removed to distance the family from the later political Puritans of the English Civil War. We shall probably never now know.

I would like to propose that maybe now it is time for us, and the people of Gainsborough in particular, to revisit this period in history and perhaps even allow it to be rewritten a little – to show the Hickman family in a more deserving light and to proudly reclaim them as local worthies of note – for all the right reasons – instead of as the unpopular, money grubbing, meddling incomers as they are portrayed at present, a stance no doubt taken by their rich opponents at the time.

The religious reforms that Lady Rose and her family had fought for would not begin to materialise until after England had suffered a bloody civil war. One of Rose's direct descendants would follow on in her spiritual footsteps – by later becoming patron to the founder of the Methodist Church, John Wesley, who would in turn preach one of his first sermons in the church-like Great Hall at Gainsborough.

I shall be eternally grateful for that day when I first walked into the Great Chamber at Gainsborough Old Hall and gazed up into the face of Lady Rose and pondered. For since that day my life has changed in so many ways for the better. Through Rose I came to know about the Separatists she sheltered, and through her writings I have learnt why they were persecuted and had to flee England, ultimately to found the colony of Plymouth in New England and so become the Pilgrim Fathers of a great new nation.

Through Rose I came into writing historical novels at a time in my life when I thought any such creative opportunities had long passed me by. Following on from writing my first novel, The Mayflower Maid, I met Russell Hocking of Pilgrim Tours (www pilgrimtours.co.uk) and soon became his Senior Guide. This work enables me to revel in the delights of sharing all that I have learnt about the Mayflower Pilgrims, as visitors explore the Mayflower Trail with us. We have a lot of fun as we retrace the Separatists' historical footsteps around the very countryside and sites they knew so well.

Only now, when I stand before that portrait of Rose Hickman, I am almost certain that I can see a smile beginning to creep across her face.

Rose Hickman and her family tree.

Here follows several simplified extracts from both the Hickman and Locke family trees.

Offspring of **Walter Hickman**, of Woodford Hall

1. Walter b about 1480-1540
m. Alice Jephson or Jepherson of Froyle

1. William
2. Dorothea
3. Anthony
    m. Rose Locke.
4. Clement.

Family Tree Of Sir William Locke Showing Rose Hickman's Line.

Sir William Locke,
Knight and Alderman of London. d.1550 and
buried at Mercers' Chapel, London.

m1. **Alice Spence** of London b 1490? d.1522
(buried at Mercer's Chapel, London)

1. **William Locke** b.1511 - d.1517
2. **Philip Locke** d.1524
3. **Jayne Locke** b. Aug 29th, 1512
    m. Robert Meredith of London, mercer

4. **Peter Locke** d.1517
5. **William Locke** b.1517 - d.1519
6. **Richard Locke** d.1516
7. **Edmund Locke** b.? d.1545
    for the love of Sir Brian Tuck's daughter.
8. **Thomas Locke** b. Feb 8th, 1514 – d 30th October, 1556
    merchant, (Buried Mercers Chapel)
    m. Mary Louge or Long b.1518 - d 1578.
    (Buried Mercers Chapel).
    Married at St. Peter's Church, Cheapside,
    London 19th January 1544

9. **Matthew Locke** b.1521- d.1552   merchant
    m. Elizabeth Baker (d.1551)

m2. **Katherine Cook**
    (dau. of Sir Thomas Cook of Wiltshire, Knight)
    d. Oct 14th, 1537, buried at Merton

1. **Dorothy Locke** b. -
    m1. Otwell Hill of London, mercer
    m2. John Cosworth of London, merchant.

2. **Katherine Locke** b.-
    m1. Thomas Stacey of London, mercer.
    m2. William Matthew of Braden, Northamptonshire.

3. **Rose Locke** b.1526 - d.1613
    m. Anthony Hickman (d.1573)
    28th Nov 1543 St. Mary-Le Bow, London
    Anthony was a Mercer of London and son
    of Walter of Woodford.

    1. Mary b. Jan 6th 1547
            m1. John Ansham or Amondesham of
            Ealing 1567.
            m2. Richard Philips of Middlesex

    2. William b. June16th1549- d.1625.
            m1. Agnes Draper d. Feb 22nd 1600.
            m2. Elizabeth Willoughby b. - d.1622
            a. Anne b. Oct 4th, 1601 - d. Sept.1602
            b. Frances b. 31st, Oct 1602 - d.c1674
                    (m. William Rokeby 1624)
            c. Willoughby b. 25th, May 1604 - d. 1649
            d. William b. 18th, May 1606 –
                                    d 3rd Sept. 1607
            e. Thomas b. 21st , Feb 1607-
                                    d after 1625 Lawyer.
            f. Mildred b. 11th, Oct 1610 -
                                    19th June 1628

    3. Henry b. Dec 7 b 1550- d.1618
        buried at Gainsborough.
                m. Anne Wallop – widow of – Eccleston,
                (08.04.1601)

           a. Anthony b-d.1647
           b. Elizabeth
                   m. Sir Henry Fynes or Clinton
                   (son of Henry, Earl of Lincoln)
           c. Anne Hickman b.1604-d.1670
                   m. Richard Dukeson,
                   Rector of St. Clement Danes.
4. Walter b. 26th Aug. 1552 -d. Dec 29th, 1617
           m. Elizabeth Staines of Essex, Nov 21st,1586.
           a. Dixie b.-d. Oct.10th 1631
                   m. Elizabeth Windsor, dau. of
                   Sir William Windsor, 5th Lord,
                   b.- d Nov.2nd 1631
           b. Elizabeth m. George Alington of Swinhope
                   at Gainsborough, 1617.
           c. William d. unmarried.
           d. Walter d. unmarried.
           e. Anne Hickman-
                   buried 19th Sept.1598 at
                   St. Mary Magdalene,
                   Richmond, Surrey.

5. Unknown child born at 'Chilswell'
   Nr. Oxford c.1554/55

6. Unknown child born in Antwerp c.1557/58

7. Anthony b.Nov.17th, 1560- d. Dec 13th, 1597

8. Eleazer born before 1573-d. 1618.

9. Matthew born before 1573-d before 1637.
           m. unknown
           a. Frances
           b. Mary
           c. Rose

   m2 Simon Throckmorton of
   Brampton after 1573. No issue.

4. **John Locke**, went to Jerusalem in 1553,
   and Guinea in 1554 – d. in France

5. **Alice Locke**   b.1528 d.1537

6. **Thomasin Locke** b. - d.1530

7. **Henry Locke**   b.1536 d.1570-71
   m. Anne Vaughan b.-d.-

8. **Michael Locke** b - d 1616? , of London, merchant;
   m1. Jayne Wilkinson.
   m2. Margery Peryn, Wid. of Caesar Dalmarias,
       (father of Sir Julius Caesar, Knight).

9. **Elizabeth Locke** b. Aug 3,1535.
      m1. Richard Hill, Mercer of London (d.1568),
          had 13 children
      m2. Nicholas Bullingham, Bishop of Worcester.

10. **John Locke** b. Oct 13 1537-d. Oct 14th 1537).

The Locke DNA Project.

The Locke DNA project was started in 2005. This project was started to try to connect the many Lock / Locke lineages of England and the USA. By comparing the male Y chromosome, we can tell which Locke branches are related, and which aren't.

Knowing which branches share the same Y chromosome, the family researchers can then focus their research specifically on the branches that are a DNA match to each other, in hopes of being able to connect the branches using the paper records.

The DNA project is in dire need of more Lock/Locke men from England to get involved in this project. With the help of our British Cousins, our trees may grow in a way that we could have never imagined. This project will be a benefit for both British and American Lock (e)'s alike.

For more details visit www.lockeroots.home.comcast. net/~lockeroots/DNA1.html or contact Donald Locke, email address: lockeroots@comcast.net

American readers may be interested in the theory that Rose Hickman's great, great, great nephew, William Locke, settled in Woburn, Massachusetts, having sailed to America as a young boy. While in some quarters yet another of her descendants is purported to be John Locke the famous philosopher.

Below is the genealogy put forward by John Goodwin Locke in 'The Book Of Lockes' published in 1853 demonstrating that John Locke the Philosopher and William Locke of Woburn were first cousins.

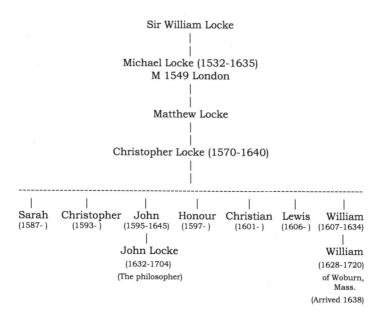

Sir William Locke
|
|
Michael Locke (1532-1635)
M 1549 London
|
|
Matthew Locke
|
|
Christopher Locke (1570-1640)
|
|

Sarah	Christopher	John	Honour	Christian	Lewis	William
(1587-)	(1593-)	(1595-1645)	(1597-)	(1601-)	(1606-)	(1607-1634)

John Locke
(1632-1704)
(The philosopher)

William
(1628-1720)
of Woburn,
Mass.
(Arrived 1638)

However, errors have been found elsewhere in this volume and, as at the time of writing, John Goodwin Locke's assumption cannot not be fully proved and substantiated by existing paper records. Hence widespread DNA testing amongst fully documented and partially proven lines may prove of immense value to family researchers.

Monuments and Memorials

There are very few surviving monuments to members of the Locke and Hickman families of this era. Rose's husband, Anthony, along with many members of the Locke family are known to have been interred in the Mercers Chapel in London. Sadly all traces of their burials were destroyed during the Great Fire of London Likewise many London church records were also lost at that time.

The crumbling Gainsborough parish church of Lord Burgh's time is now gone, apart from its medieval tower. When the main body of the church was replaced by the beautiful present Georgian building, any older memorials that might have been in the floor were lost. However, the crypt below remained accessible right up until the 1950s when it was bricked up to dissuade the attempts of vandals then who had tried to get into it. Last eye witness reports, from some within the clergy, claim to have seen the burials of both Burghs and Hickmans still evident below and possibly some also of the Knights Templar, who it is believed had an earlier church upon the same site before the medieval structure was built.

During my extensive research in writing this novel, I found the following epitaph written for Rose by members of her own family in 1637 which I personally think may be fitting to have on display inside the parish church in recognition of her support of many of our early Protestant Anglican clergy.

> *'God gave unto this matron in her dayes,*
> *As pledges firm of his afflictions [sic] deare*
> *Such happy blessings as the psalmist sayes*
> *They shall receive as serves the Lord in feare.*
> *Her self in wedlock as fruitful as the vine*
> *Her children like the olive plants to be.*
> *And of her issue in descendant line*
> *She did her childrens', childrens' children see.*
> *And freed of the Babilonish awe*
> *Peace permanent on Israel saw.*

Now having fought a good and Christian fight
Against the spiritual common enemy
And excercis'd her self both day and night,
In oracles divine continually.
And kept the sacred faith with constancy
Even in the midst of persecutions rage
Express'd by worthy works of piety
From time to time as well in youth as age.
She finished her course and doth possess
In heavenly bliss the crown of righteousness.'

Most of Rose's male Locke family members were mercers, with the exception of her brother John Locke. Many of these left wills, which survive today, stating their express wishes to buried within the Mercers' Chapel in the City of London, which we have no reason to believe were not carried out. At that time, will-making was very much a part of the dying process, and so the probability is that once ill enough to contemplate drawing up a will and decided upon a place to be buried, one usually did not then travel far from it.

Sir William Locke, contrary to some Locke genealogy websites was buried in the Mercers Chapel and a contemporary account of his funeral also survives. Many female members of Mercer families were also buried in this chapel, including Sir William's first wife, and also Mary (Long) Locke – Rose's sister in law. Unfortunately the original chapel was lost in the Great Fire of London.

Rose tells us that her family were at Merton in 1537 in order to avoid the plague still raging in the City. In 1499, it is known that a John Lok and his wife Jayne obtained the lease of an estate opposite the church which in later times was known as Church House. Lockes would continue to reside there in Merton for at least one hundred and forty years after. (I recall visiting Church House, in my childhood when it was in a much dilapidated state. It was probably a later building but upon that very same site as John Lok's residence).

Today no memorials survive inside St Mary's Church in Merton dedicated to the Lockes. Much of the interior of the church was laid to tiles, probably in the Victorian era, and so any slabs that may have existed are probably lost beneath those.

However, I am eternally grateful to fellow Locke enthusiast, Lionel Green, for the following information. According to John Aubrey, who recorded all of the memorials in St. Mary's in 1673,[92] Sir William Locke arranged for a brass plaque to be inset within a marble gravestone which bore the following words:

> *Pray for the Soule of Kateryn Lok,*
> *sumtyme the Wife of William Lok,*
> *Mercer of London, who decessed the*
> *xiii of October, Anno xv xxxvij. On*
> *Whose Soule Jhesu have Mercy. Amen.*

Parish records from before 1559, the end of the Marian era, no longer survive. However, below are a few of the earliest Locke burials recorded after that date. These may be of interest to genealogists.

1608 October 18th
    .... A man son of Thomas Lock Esquire.
1613 Sept 23
    Lock, Edmund sonne of Thomas Lock Esquire.
1619 April
    Lock, Mrs Elizabeth gentm.
1621 November 30th
    Locke ffrancis, gent.
1633 December 26th
    Lock Thomas, sonne of Thomas Lock Esquire.
1647 February 6th
    Locke, Mr. Thomas Esquire.

On the north wall of the parish church of St Mary Magdalene, Richmond, Surrey is a very colourful memorial to Walter Hickman of Kew who died in 1617. Walter was one of the original Vestrymen of Richmond

---

92   J.Aubrey 'The Natural History and Antiquities of the County of Surrey 1718/19 Vol.1 p.224'.

in 1614, and took an active part in local affairs. One of his sons, Dixie, married the eldest daughter of Henry, Lord Windsor, and through her were descended the Earls of Plymouth. The inscription reads;

Memoriæ Sacrum
Here under resteth ye bodie of Walter Hickman of Kewe
in this Pish. Esq. who had,
By his wife Elizabeth, the daughter of Nicholas Stanes
of ye County of Essex 3 Sonnes viz.
Dixie, Married unto Elizabeth Windsor Eldest Daughter
unto the Right Hon. Henry Lord
Windsor; William & Walter Unmarried; & one Daughter
named Elizabeth married unto George Alington ye
younger of Swinhop in ye county of Lincoln Esq. He
lived ---- yeares and on the xxix day of December 1617
he exchanged this mortal life for a better expectinge a
joyfull Ressurection.
Dixius Hickman, Armiger ejus primogenitus Et filius
mæstissmus, hoc Monumentum posuit.

The part of the inscription clearly intended to give Walter's age at death in 1617 is left empty.

Inside the redundant Holy Trinity Old Church, Wentworth, South Yorkshire, above the door is a large monument effusively praising Sir William Rokeby of Skiers, and his wife, Frances Hickman. Frances was the granddaughter of Lady Rose Hickman, and featured heavily in my first novel, The Mayflower Maid. According to the monument, she was married to William Rokeby for fifty years, and so obviously inherited Rose's longevity (a marriage entry for Frances 'of Bawtry' and William 'of Hotham' appears in the Yorkshire registry for 1624). There are many other Rokeby monuments to be found at Kirk Sandall, near Doncaster, another redundant church which like Wentworth is in the care of the Churches Conservation Trust.

An account of the death of Archbishop Cranmer by an anonymous bystander.

I have included this eye witness account of the death of Archbishop Cranmer because I believe my readers will find it edifying. As with the execution of Thomas Cranmer, I have not done so out of any love of such cruel and gory detail but in order to show the true extent of how the courage and faith of these and other early Protestants was put to the ultimate test. Many of the freedoms of conscience, especially in that most personal of all – our religion – we enjoy today as the result of the heavy cost to just such men and women. One does not have to share in a martyred man's beliefs to admire his courage in giving up his life for them.

But that I know for our great friendships, and long continued love, you look even of duty that I should signify to you of the truth of such things as here chanceth among us; I would not at this time have written to you the unfortunate end, and doubtful tragedy, of Thomas Cranmer late bishop of Canterbury: because I little pleasure take in beholding of such heavy sights. And, when they are once overpassed, I like not to rehearse them again; being but a renewing of my woe, and doubling my grief. For although his former, and wretched end, deserves a greater misery, (if any greater might have chanced than chanced unto him), yet, setting aside his offences to God and his country, and beholding the man without his faults, I think there was none that pitied not his case, and bewailed not his fortune, and feared not his own chance, to see so noble a prelate, so grave a counsellor, of so long continued honour, after so many dignities, in his old years to be deprived of his estate, adjudged to die, and in so painful a death to end his life. I have no delight to increase it. Alas, it is too much of itself, that ever so heavy a case should betide to man, and man to deserve it.

But to come to the matter: on Saturday last, being 21 of March, was his day appointed to die. And because the morning was much rainy, the sermon appointed by

Mr Dr Cole to be made at the stake, was made in St Mary's church: whither Dr Cranmer was brought by the mayor and aldermen, and my lord Williams: with whom came divers gentlemen of the shire, sir T A Bridges, sir John Browne, and others. Where was prepared, over against the pulpit, a high place for him, that all the people might see him. And, when he had ascended it, he kneeled him down and prayed, weeping tenderly: which moved a great number to tears, that had conceived an assured hope of his conversion and repentance...

When praying was done, he stood up, and, having leave to speak, said, 'Good people, I had intended indeed to desire you to pray for me; which because Mr Doctor hath desired, and you have done already, I thank you most heartily for it. And now will I pray for myself, as I could best devise for mine own comfort, and say the prayer, word for word, as I have here written it.' And he read it standing: and after kneeled down, and said the Lord's Prayer; and all the people on their knees devoutly praying with him...

And then rising, he said, 'Every man desireth, good people, at the time of their deaths, to give some good exhortation, that other may remember after their deaths, and be the better thereby. So I beseech God grant me grace, that I may speak something, at this my departing, whereby God may be glorified, and you edified...

And now I come to the great thing that troubleth my conscience more than nay other thing that ever I said or did in my life: and that is, the setting abroad of writings contrary to the truth. Which here now I renounce and refuse, as things written with my hand, contrary to the truth which I thought in my heart, and written for fear of death, and to save my life, if it might be: and that is, all such bills, which I have written or signed with mine own hand since my degradation: wherein I have written many things untrue. And forasmuch as my hand offended in writing contrary to my heart, therefore my hand shall first be punished: for if I may come to the fire, it shall be first burned. And as for the Pope, I refuse him, as Christ's enemy and antichrist, with all his false doctrine.'

And here, being admonished of his recantation and dissembling, he said, 'Alas, my lord, I have been a man that all my life loved plainness, and never dissembled till now against the truth; which I am most sorry for it.' He added hereunto, that, for the sacrament, he believed as he had taught in his book against the bishop of Winchester. And here he was suffered to speak no more.... Then was he carried away; and a great number, that did run to see him go so wickedly to his death, ran after him, exhorting him, while time was, to remember himself. And one Friar John, a godly and well learned man, all the way travelled with him to reduce him. But it would not be. What they said in particular I cannot tell, but the effect appeared in the end: for at the stake he professed, that he died in all such opinions as he had taught, and oft repented him of his recantation.

Coming to the stake with a cheerful countenance and willing mind, he put off his garments with haste, and stood upright in his shirt: and bachelor of divinity, named Elye, of Brazen-nose college, laboured to convert him to his former recantation, with the two Spanish friars. And when the friars saw his constancy, they said in Latin to one another 'Let us go from him: we ought not to be nigh him: for the devil is with him.' But the bachelor of divinity was more earnest with him: unto whom he answered, that, as concerning his recantation, he repented it right sore, because he knew it was against the truth; with other words more. Whereby the Lord Williams cried, 'Make short, make short.' Then the bishop took certain of his friends by the hand. But the bachelor of divinity refused to take him by the hand, and blamed all the others that so did, and said, he was sorry that ever he came in his company. And yet again he required him to agree to his former recantation. And the bishop answered, (showing his hand), 'This was the hand that wrote it, and therefore shall it suffer first punishment.'

Fire being now put to him, he stretched out his

right hand, and thrust it into the flame, and held it there a good space, before the fire came to any other part of his body; where his hand was seen of every man sensibly burning, crying with a loud voice, 'This hand hath offended.' As soon as the fire got up, he was very soon dead, never stirring or crying all the while.

His patience in the torment, his courage in dying, if it had been taken either for the glory of God, the wealth of his country, or the testimony of truth, as it was for a pernicious error, and subversion of true religion, I could worthily have commended the example, and matched it with the fame of any father of ancient time: but, seeing that not the death, but cause and quarrel thereof, commendeth the sufferer, I cannot but much dispraise his obstinate stubbornness and sturdiness in dying, and specially in so evil a cause.

Surely his death much grieved every man; but not after one sort. Some pitied to see his body so tormented with the fire raging upon the silly carcass, that counted not of the folly. Other that passed not much of the body, lamented to see him spill his soul, wretchedly, without redemption, to be plagued for ever. His friends sorrowed for love; his enemies for pity; strangers for a common kind of humanity, whereby we are bound one to another. Thus I have enforced myself, for your sake, to discourse this heavy narration, contrary to my mind: and, being more than half weary, I make a short end, wishing you a quieter life, with less honour; and easier death, with more praise.

The strong hatred held by those zealous Protestants reformers against the Cheapside Cross that I mentioned in the novel continued. And yet there it still stood, in the middle of one of the City's busiest thoroughfares, in all its Popish glory long after Lady Rose Hickman's death, and even that of her children.

Then, in 1641, on the night of January 24th, the Cheapside Cross was again defaced, after which new attacks upon and defences of the Cross were waged in a battle of words by way of printed pamphlets and publications. Amongst these was 'A Dialogue between the Cross in Chepe and Charing Cross' – a part of which follows:

Anabaptist. O! idol now,
Down must thou!
Brother Ball,
Be sure it shall.
Brownist. Helpe! Wren,
Or we are undone men.
I shall not fall,
To ruin all.
Cheap Cross. I'm so crossed; I fear my utter destruction is at hand.
Charing Cross. Sister of Cheap, crosses are incident to us all, and our children. But what's the greatest cross that hath befallen you?
Cheap Cross. Nay, sister; if my cross were fallen, I should live at more heart's ease than I do.
Charing Cross. I believe it is the cross upon your head that hath brought you into this trouble, is it not?

With the City of London firmly in control of the predominantly Puritan Parliamentarians, the 'death warrant' for the Cheapside Cross was finally issued.

Aided by a rejoicing troop of horse and two companies of foot, Robert Harlow was duly deputised to carry out the task of its utter destruction. The official account of the time reads thus: -

'On the 2nd of May, 1643, the cross in Cheapside was

pulled down. At the fall of the top cross drums beat, trumpets blew, and multitudes of caps were thrown into the air, and a great shout of people with joy. The 2nd of May, the report continues, was the invention of the cross, and the same day at night were the leaden popes burnt (they were not popes, but eminent English prelates) in the place where it stood, with ringing of bells and great acclamation, and no hurt at all done in these actions.'

It is noteworthy to add that the Cheapside Crosse was pulled down on the same date as it was first erected.

The diarist, Evelyn, notes that he himself saw 'the furious and zealous people demolish that stately crosse in Cheapside'. Another commentator of the time writes; 'On Tuesday the crosse in Cheapside was taken down to cleanse that great street of superstition.' The letter writer, Howell, laments the demolition of such an ancient landmark and says that trumpets were blown all the while the crowbars and pickaxes were at work upon it. And in his journal, Archbishop Laud notes that on May 1st, a fanatical mob broke the stained-glass windows of his Lambeth Chapel and tore up the steps of his communion table.

'The Downfall of Dagon; or the Taking Down of Cheapside Crosse' is the title of a curious tract that was published on the very same day as the Cross' destruction. Here follows an extract from this pamphlet which reads as if the Cross is speaking as a living entity contemplating its death and making out its will:-

'I am called the 'Citie Idoll;' the Brownists spit at me, and throw stones at me; others hide their eyes with their fingers; the Anabaptists wish me knockt in pieces, as I am like to be this day; the sisters of the fraternity will not come near me, but go about by Watling Street, and come in again by Soaper Lane, to buy their provisions of the market folks. . . . I feele the pangs of death, and shall never see the end of the merry month of May; my breath stops; my life is gone; I feel myself a dying downwards.

Here are some of the Cross' bequests: - 'I give my iron-work to those people which make good swords, at Hounslow; for I am all Spanish iron and steele to the back... I give my body and stones to those masons that cannot telle how to frame the like againe, to keepe by them for a patterne; for in time there will be more crosses in London than ever there was yet...'

On the tenth of May, the 'Book of Sports', a collection of ordinances allowing games on the Sabbath, put forth by King James I, was burnt by the official hangman on the spot where the Cross had stood. At the height of the Civil War two years later in July 1645, a collection of crucifixes, Popish pictures and books were gathered up and burnt on the site of the Cheapside Cross.

Though the Cheapside Cross was no more, for many years after the image of it both standing and in ruin would remain in the collective memory of Reformists and conservative Anglicans alike, yet for very different reasons.

Index of reference material used in research

Contemporary eye witness accounts written by various individuals 1525-1603

Lord King's 'Life of Locke'

The Autobiography of Sir John Bramston

'Notes to the diary: 1550-51', The Diary of Henry Machyn: Citizen and Merchant-Taylor of London (1550-1563) (1848), pp. 313-323

'The Mercery of London: by Trade, Goods & People, 1130-1578 by Ann F Sutton

Calendar of State Papers from Henry VIII, Edward VI, Queen Mary and Queen Elizabeth

'The Age of Drake' – James A Williamson

Richard Hakluyt's various volumes of 'English Voyages of Discovery'

'Gainsborough Old Hall and the Mayflower Pilgrim Story' – Jennifer Vernon.

'Histoire De Belgique 3rd Edition' – H Pirenne

'The Baronetage of England' – Thomas Wotton, Edward Kimber, Richard Johnson

'The Travel Journal of Antonio de Beatis' – Edited by Hale and Lindon (The Hakluyt Society 1979)

'St Mary The Virgin – A guide and History' by Lionel Green

'Athenae Cantabrigienses' – Charles Henry Cooper, John Gray, Thompson Cooper

'The Book of Lockes' – John Goodwin Locke (published 1853)

'Henry VIII (King and Court) – A Weir 1988

'Lincolnshire Pedigrees'- Maddison, A R (Ed) 1902 Harleian Society

'Religion and Politics in mid-Tudor England through the eyes of an English Protestant Woman' by M Dowling and J Shakespeare, published in the 'Bulletin of the Institute of Historical Research, May 1982'

'Witchcraft and Conflicting Visions of the Ideal village Community, by Anne Reiber DeWindt

'Cheapside: The central area', Old and New London: Volume 1 (1878)

'Chronicles of England, Scotland& Ireland' R Holinshed 1587 edition,Vol. iii – p.936

History of Parliament Trust, London – unpublished article on Walter Hickman for 1604/29 section by Dr. Paul Hunneyball. I am grateful to the History of Parliament Trust for allowing me to see this article in draft.

My grateful thanks go to the following for their help and support in researching this book:

Roger Vorhauer, my co-researcher.

Russell Hocking, my friend and editor.

Dr Jeremy Bangs, my mentor and advisor on the Pilgrim Fathers.

Sir Nicholas Bacon, Bart.

Dr Elizabeth Leedham-Green of Corpus Christi

Gill Cannell of The Parker Library, Corpus Christi

Teresa Cross, Parish Office, St Mary Magdalene, Richmond

Graham & Valerie Boyes

David Agar of the Churches Conservation Trust (Wentworth Church)

Parish Office, St Mary the Virgin, Merton

Natasha de Croustchoff

Lionel Green

Beryl Bates

List of Historical Characters of Note

Boleyn Anne – second wife of Henry VIII

Cecil, **William**, later **Lord Burghley** – Statesman, and Queen Elizabeth's most important administrator and chief spokesman in the house of Commons

Cranmer, **Thomas** – Archbishop of Canterbury, Protestant reformer

Cromwell, **Thomas** – Advisor, lawyer and minister to Henry VIII. Staunch Protestant

Dudley, **John**, **Duke of Northumberland** – second Regent to King Edward

Fitzroy, **Henry** – Duke of Richmond- Henry VIII's illegitimate son

Howard Catherine – 4th wife of Henry VIII

Howard, **Henry** – **Duke of Norfolk**, uncle of Anne Boleyn

Katherine of Aragon – first wife of Henry VIII

Moore, **Sir Thomas** – Chancellor – executed after Henry VIII's divorce

Parr Katherine – sixth wife of Henry VIII

Philip, **King of Spain** – husband of Queen Mary Tudor

Seymour, **Jayne** – third wife of Henry VIII, mother of King Edward VI

Seymour, **Thomas** - brother of Queen Jayne, executed after 'liason' with Princess Elizabeth

Seymour, **Edward** – brother of Queen Jayne Seymour and Regent...

Walsingham, **Francis** – Statesman, Secretary and spymaster to Queen Elizabeth

Also by Sue Allan

The Mayflower Maid -

The first part of the New World Trilogy

400 years ago a group of like minded men and women fled England and religious persecution to start a new life on a new continent - America. One woman's story begins here....

In the infant colony of Plymouth in 1623 a woman lies consumed with fever. In her delirium she insists her name is not the one everyone has come to know and love her by.

The story of Dorothy's tragic journey amongst the Pilgrim Fathers is a vivid and moving account of a pivotal moment in history. The story of how she became the Mayflower Maid is an unforgettable tale of love and loss set amidst the strife and religious bigotry of Seventeenth Century England.

Jamestown Woman -

The second part of the New World Trilogy

Having weathered the perils of the Mayflower's voyage and the early days of the Plymouth colony; Dorothy neé Bessie and her husband Thomas are now cast adrift into even more stormy and dangerous waters. Seventeenth century politics are a violent and deadly business, as they are about to find out.

Sue Allan continues her spellbinding chronicles of the Mayflower Maid in 'Jamestown Woman', and once again fate casts her and Thomas into the paths of the great and not so good. The giant firgures of King James I, Captain John Smith and Oliver Cromwell cast their shadows over the lives of the Puritans as England is about to be engulfed by the horrors of The Civil war.

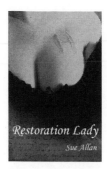

Restoration Lady -

The third and final part of New World Trilogy

The much anticipated finale to this wonderful story following events in post civil war England.

Stripped of her title and wealth Bessie faces revenge from past enemies, accusations of witchcraft and the catastrophes of the plague and Great Fire of London.

This concluding part of the New World Trilogy is gripping reading for all followers of Bessie - the Mayflower Maid.